What others are saying about

iR

iReckon is a one of a kind epic into the
behind man. A defining novel of our t
than the pursuit of freedom. It is not of
confines defined by man.

ng

Rola

Wrapped around the events that have hurt us all, the story takes the reader into the psyche of two characters both deeply involved. One was the orchestrator and the other badly damaged by the financial ruin inflicted upon him. Both have ambition to make the world a better place. The novel asks some very deep and demanding questions as to why any God would allow such events to occur. As the story comes to a close, answers are provided. They are not the answers that the reader would expect. They are however the answers to every question ever asked.

George McCall Researcher at the American University Jerusalem.

We all missed the obvious. This was the read of my life. I couldn't put it down. Heywood takes the universe, wraps it up with all the questions we have ever asked, throws in mankind for good measure and presents us with the greatest present of all time. I was humbled, exhilarated and joyous with this exciting, beautiful and truly unique view.

Dr Elizabeth Miller, Author, Mood Mapping

A cracking read from beginning to end. You will want everyone you know to read this book. You will implore them to do so. If you have ever wondered what the world will look like for our children and our children's children you must read this book. The greatest opportunity for all of us has been staring us right in the face all this time.

Mark Willis, MD, Von Essen Group

iReckon takes a helicopter view of mankind and then delves deep into who man really is. Nobody since Shakespeare has gone this far and nobody else will ever need to. This book was a spectacular read from the moment I opened it and, when I had finished it, the most enlightening experience I have ever had.

Matt Kenvyn, recording artist

Heywood delivers for us, a vision for mankind that has never been given before. In the height of a recession, in a notoriously difficult industry, I was so compelled by the messages given in this book that it convinced me to start a publishing arm to my media business. Orwell and the literary greats would be humbled by this book. Einstein, Leanardo Da Vinci et al would weep with joy.

Katrina Moultrie, Chairman and Editor, KMVF Media

Outstanding massage for the joy in all our hearts. I laughed and cried as the pages embroiled all of me in the intrigue. I have read it several times and I will read it again and again and again. I have never encountered such a beautiful experience. Heywood provides us with a completely new view of God and one, after all, that is more than all our dreams could wish for.

Liz Todd, director MOD

Riveting with twists and turns that explore the very nature and purpose of the human condition. Well written with every chapter telling an episode in a tale that goes beyond being just another very good read. Does he jump or does he not jump? That is the question that only the reader can answer.

Shane Walker Ph.D

iReckon is more than a beautiful story. It is a fast moving epic that transverse the history of time seeking answers to the fundamental question of purpose. Is there a God? Of course there is. However it is not the God that you and me might necessarily recognise. Your life really will be changed.

Ben Cohen Writer and public speaker.

The Bible provides us with one answer. Quotations from Chairman Mao provides us with another answer. iReckon provides us with the third answer. Six billion copies of the Bible and six and a half billion copies of the Quotations from Chairman Mao have been printed and read by people. Both books have changed the course of humanity. Greg Heywood in his novel creates a new direction and gives us all, a new meaning to life.

Lawrence Moore Poet

The perspectives explored in this novel, challenge everything we have come to believe. Heywood, in his life, has clearly encountered experiences and events that would definitely demand the very most from any man. The personal challenge he encountered in writing this book can only be seen as a credit to the integrity of all mankind. For me, at last, I felt that I really knew who I was and why all of us are here.

City Tribune, New York

iReckon provides an alternative view of mankind that rattles all the norms we ever believed could be true. I can't remember a moment in our history that could be this defining for humanity. No other moment ever will be again.

Professor J. St. B. Evans, Plymouth University

And finally God comes alive. He is real and exists. What is his purpose and why has he been so evasive? For ten thousand years man has grappled with these questions. Greg Heywood in this novel reveals all. It is a book of the millennium with nothing quite like it every written before, yet alone published.

James King Computer programmer

GREG HEYWOOD

I RECKON

THIS BOOK WILL CHANGE YOUR LIFE

KMVF

This book is a work of fiction with the names, characters, and incidents coming entirely from the author's imagination. Any reference or resemblance to an actual person living or dead, events or localities are purely coincidental.

Copyright © Greg Heywood 2010
All rights reserved
The moral right of the author have been reserved

Published by KMVF Media whose registered office is at 113A Monnow Street Monmouth Gwent United Kingdom NP25 3EG. The company is registered in England and Wales. The company number is 06598790.

Set in Times New Roman, Trajan Pro and Garamond
Type Setting by KMVF Media

Printed and bound in Wales by Europa printing

No part of this publication may be reproduced stored in a retrieval system, or transmitted, in any form or by any means, electronic, mechanical, photocopying, recording or otherwise, without the prior permission of the publishers.

This book is sold subject to the condition that it shall not, by way of trade or otherwise, be lent, resold, hired out or otherwise circulated without the publisher's prior consent in any form of binding or cover other than that in which it is published and without a similar condition including this condition being imposed on the subsequent purchaser.

www.ireckonbook.co.uk

KMVF Media:

www. kmvfmedia.com

Author:

www.gregheywood.net

PART ONE – IMMUNITY

PART TWO – SEVEN DAYS THAT MADE THE EARTH

PART THREE – THE FELLOWSHIP OF MAN,
THE MAKING OF THE SON AND THE ADVERSARY

Part Four – Love-The Emperor of Our DNA

Part Five – Visibility-Chairmen of the Empire

Part Six – Forsaken

Part Seven –Life, The Universe and Everything

For everyone I've ever known
'*I'm sorry*'

And for Chris
'*He always knew*'

IRECKON

THIS BOOK WILL CHANGE YOUR LIFE.

The truth has always been out there. Nestled beneath the lie, we all sense it.

A purpose *does* exist for mankind and it is colossal, bigger than eternity itself. A purpose that is so simple, so easy and so obvious but only one of the real greats of history – a man that has conquered his deepest and darkest fears – could tell us what has, all the while, been staring us right in the face.

Why is Helen, her beauty paralysing men, besotted with Wood? iReckon it is time to show you the most beautiful thing ever.

'But wonder on' till truth makes all things plain.' *William Shakespeare,*
A Midsummer Night's Dream, Act 5, scene 1.

FACT

All the commercial and government organisations in this novel exist.
So do their motives and their politics.

EVIDENCE

Ground breaking, scientific facts are given throughout the pages that
follow. The evidence presented is direct from the most influential
scientific minds of our time that live today.
This book tells you what will be found by the scientists in Cern,
Switzerland who have built the Large Hadron Collider. The 'Big Bang'
project is an attempt to replicate the moment following the beginning of
the universe.

TRUE

Every economic and social fact presented in this novel is true. The
cause of the financial tsunami that was coined *the credit crunch* has
been given many explanations. This is the truth. This is why it
happened. This is why these disasters continually happen.

This is who man really is.

PART ONE

IMMUNITY

CIBEUCE

2nd *January, 2421*

As I fall to my knees I don't have a choice. What I see is beyond belief and we had expected that I would experience complete overwhelm when I finally saw it. Tears, laughter, joy and fear engulf me. The contours of my face feel like they are rippling, my hands are shaking – my whole body is – and I can feel the warm soak of my semen on my clothing, seeping down my thigh. I don't see a woman or a man. What I see is beyond anything I had previously deemed as beautiful – far beyond. This is the reason for the human race.

My mind cannot comprehend this. Iconic imagery is crossed out all around me and I see a language that I don't recognise but one that I can read. My only thought is the repetition of my father's words that haunted me for many years, 'you can't shrink your way to greatness'. Nothing could have prepared me for this.

I had constantly known, silently, that I had run away from my dreams. But was I any different? Hadn't I been shackled by the parasitic groan that engulfed all our ears and had seemed to have done so for all our history, if not for an eternity? I too had given it all meaning by a set of labels which I had allowed to be taped across my mouth. All my hates, my loves and my desires had built for me a residue of guilt that had nestled into my life and made itself more comfortable as the years had gone by. And how warm the fire did glow when we had agreed our comfort amongst friends and engaged the pursuit in the wine fed party, hungry for the empires and the colonies that had built it all for us, angry with the men who had tried to ruin or dismantle it. Now all that guilt had evaporated, no longer hidden deep beneath an intolerable lie. The idea that it was 'deep' is so false, so inadequate and all my anger has gone, whisked away by the wind, lost in the faintest of a whisper.

I can't even wonder why. I know that I should fight the emotional torrent that is ravaging me but senselessly I don't. I feel immune. As I look at Dace I can clearly see his mastodonic vision and more consciously, I can feel it. His stage, Cibeuce is magnificent and it is no surprise. I know that I am the first man to see this, ever and you will all ask me to describe it. But how do I do that; it is not a physical thing and it is no longer a dream.

Now the mystery of my legends and of my myths has surfaced in a smile. This had never been about the man who could save me. Quite the contrary, this was always about my failure to see the man who could not. And my smile; how relentless it is.

On second thoughts, one persistent emotion remains for me. As I breathe the air and sense its beauty it is no longer preserved as a precious moment, fortuned by that second in which I am not distracted. Like me, this breath is not alone or borrowed or second-hand but instead it is as pure as the faith that makes me now feel free: I am forgiven.

I had been looking in the wrong direction. We all had. Whilst I had waited for the disguise to be unmasked and the new altar to rise before me I had sensed the burglary of my time by our news, by our debates and by the air of all the influence about me. Sometimes I had begged my world to give me more than I was hearing; refusing but beckoned by fate alone. Or simply, alone.

And whilst I had fostered these tears, all the actions of Wood had come and gone and I had missed them. It wasn't until it happened that I witnessed the hell that he had unleashed. Everybody did.

TANE WOOD

Above the clouded tomb the sun shone brightly. It always did. Wood was hanging out of a twelfth floor window smoking a cigarette whilst reading a note from the concierge that told him that on no account was smoking permitted in any of the apartments. As he looked down to the people on Manhattan's 86th Street he noticed that nobody looked up and saw him. Nobody ever did.

'I love you,' he muttered softly to himself, alone in his apartment. His phone rang as a fearful voice on the radio was calling for immediate population constraint now the total was nearing seven billion. 'No. There are far too few,' Wood retorted, engulfed with a momentary burst of anxiety.

Wood eyed his phone and even before he saw Stan's name on the screen, he knew that he would be fighting against the challenge presented to him by a man with lesser ambitions, constantly trying to downsize his. He felt that he had spent a lifetime doing this.

'Now, at least,' he thought, picking up his phone from the table in front of him, 'they've got good reason'. For a decade Wood had strived to have his voice heard, battling against a media tide that had always seemed to be shouting louder than him, screaming aimlessly in every direction in search of the truth – a rapidly expanding mushroom cloud emanating from an explosion that nobody wanted to claim responsibility for – the primary goal seemingly being to monopolise verbal space.

Tomorrow his column, *iReckon* would announce his feature length editorial for next Wednesday, on Christmas Day. Finally he would have his moment and what a moment; the critics were already asserting that the newspaper would be the most defining point in history – *the answer to life, the universe and everything* – and it was certainly the first time in the media that a newspaper was being circulated on Christmas Day dedicated solely to the assertions of one man. The principle of getting to print was demanding enough but Wood felt that he was holding everybody's hand through it and the anxiety was now beyond fever pitch. Careers, even livelihoods were at stake. 'All men die,' thought Wood. 'Not all men truly live.' He wondered who he was quoting from.

And then there was Stan, his editor, and any conversation with Stan demanded a whole lot more. 'Smoke and mirrors firing up my arse,' thought Wood, aware that the esoteric demand upon him was always greater in any sparring session he had with Stan. 'Let the lying begin,' Wood said as he pressed the green 'receive' button on his mobile phone.

'I've just seen your articles for Christmas Day,' Stan began. 'Everyone in the office is raving about it. Boy, it will knock the world for six. Tane you are pure fuckin' genius. *Yours is the Earth, my son and everything that's in it.* This is gonna be the biggest sale in editorial history; it'll be a world fuckin' record. The globe awaits you my friend. Get your ass into the office and come and have a look.'

'Jones still wants me to modify the texts, doesn't he?' said Wood, sceptically. He was aware that Stan's praise could be a disguise for a hidden agenda.

'No no no. Jones loves it. I've settled it with him. Done. Come on man, I can't fuckin' live without you. Get in. The office is buzzing about it – *they* can't live without you and...' Stan seemed to swallow on his own tongue. 'And, they've even mocked up an altar for you. Serious man. They are all praying to you. Everyone's walking round with holes in the knees of their jeans.'

'Is Jones there now?' said Wood impatiently.

'Tane, I've settled it. It's done. Come on. Trust me man? We love you. Look, you grab a coffee and I'll have Carlson pick you up. Say ten minutes. Yeah? Done. See you in a sec.' Stan hung up and Wood grabbed his jacket and scarf. He left his apartment and walked the five blocks to Central Park. He couldn't let Stan and Jones, his boss gain control of the agenda. The material that Wood had presented for the Christmas Day edition was highly controversial and Jones had consistently been reticent with it. Wood could not allow him to exercise his editorial fears at the last minute and cut key elements of the material.

Wood needed their courage and their commitment to see this through. He needed to be the demanding voice; the force and the challenge to those who would offer doubt, from those that Jones and Stan would seek approval.

Two hours later, he walked into Jones's offices downtown, on the East side. The employees at their desks had their heads down and, when they acknowledged Wood with their eyes, they were polite. Few muttered any words to greet him.

In Jones's office, Stan was sitting with his feet up on the table in a pose that Wood could only assimilate to a woman in labour. Jones was lounging back in his chair with one of his hands behind his head. His fingers on his other hand were idly flicking through a magazine. Jones Alwyn was the owner of the National Times and, alongside his other ventures, he had built the largest media conglomerate on the East coast of America. He had grown up in the U.K. and he had shown great promise as a teenage boy in the professional rugby leagues but an untimely, gruesome incident with a cat had left him with only one eye.

'Well?' said Wood, assertively, as he entered.

'Ah the king elect. I...'began Stan, getting to his feet. Jones sat forward.

'Stan. Do us both a favour,' interrupted Wood. 'Jan needs you in the press room.' Stan looked at Jones and Jones nodded his head. As Stan left he said to Wood. 'I can't wait for Wednesday's edition. This will be the greatest shot in history.'

Wood took a seat and said, 'Print it.'

'It's not as easy as that,' said Jones throwing his arms open.

'Yes it is,' Wood said adamantly and got up from his seat and walked towards the door.

'Tane, don't walk out. Listen to me. I need...' Wood left the room and Jones's words became too faint to hear. As he made his way to the lift, Stan saw him. Before Stan could hustle his way out of the press room and get to Wood, he had left.

'They'll lynch him if you print it,' said Stan to Jones as he returned to his office.

'Don't I fucking know it. The guy won't listen,' said Jones thumbing the front cover of *Money* which was lying on his desk. 'They'll lynch me too.'

'Do it,' said Stan. 'Life – who needs it.'

'This is not funny.'

'No. But I know you Jones. If you don't print this you'll lynch yourself. Who is the man who always says, 'the only life worth living is the life worth dying for.'

'Yes. OK,' said Jones. 'Thanks already.'

'Nice Girls Come Last – Beauty Topples Kings' said the slogan in front of Helen. She was shopping on Madison Avenue and bustling in and out of the zippy shops. Helen loved Manhattan. The crowded streets were filled with the most ingratiating heckle; people darting and thriving in the rush of life that they all helped to compose – friendly, laughing, loud and warm. She saw expressions of joy, sadness, arrogance, humility, anger and calm; everything on display and all of it forgiven by the island smile and the street decree. Here, Helen felt that she was living within an ingratiating charter of human charisma – in love and loved.

Adorning the majestic hub of New York, Helen sensed that her beauty would not oust or oppose her and she felt free. For a major city, she was pleasantly surprised by this, after her experiences with the other large conurbations where she had lived. In Manhattan, the simple acts were the norm; people smiled and said thank you. She sensed that the city had not been strangled by the pitiful regimes that had written the unwanted and uninvited memory of sad and angry faces she had formed and she now attributed to other cities in parts of Europe and the U.K.

But her freedom was beginning to find a new prisoner. When Helen and Wood, her boyfriend, had first arrived, Helen had hailed cabs to take her across the city. She had repeatedly sat in traffic jams, watching people walk on by and now she chose to go by foot wherever she went. The walking kept her fit and toned and she could decide her own pace and her route. But with the increasing public profile of Wood and her exposure with it, Helen needed to wear more and more items of clothing to maintain her outdoor preference. She was constantly compiling new disguises and her wardrobes were full of scarves and hats. She enjoyed the shopping and it was her excuse for the purchase she had just made for her seventh pair of shaded sun glasses. But this enjoyment was no substitute for the dogma that was beginning to hound her.

Wood rang her and asked her to meet him for a coffee at a cafe on 74th Street. Helen thought that she had more time than she did and she spent too long shopping in Macy's. Now, she was rushing to meet him, flying down 3rd Avenue, conscious that he would be sitting alone, getting impatient.

When she eventually arrived, the coffee Wood had bought for her was cold. Helen was pleasantly surprised with how calm Wood was with her delay and he hardly remarked when she apologised. His tone changed when she reminded him that they were due to meet with friends that evening in the Boat House restaurant. Amongst the party, were Maggie and David, her husband. They both liked Maggie but Wood had always found David, disagreeable. Helen asked Wood to be tolerant and Wood said, 'I am. He just can't tolerate me.' Helen and Wood flirted across this subject but it hadn't got better when Wood told Helen that Jones was likely to severely edit his articles at the last minute. They rushed back to get ready for their dinner recognising that they had lost track of time and as they feverishly paced back to their apartment, they began arguing. Helen said she could understand Jones's apprehension. 'His eyes are firmly on his wallet,' Wood retorted. 'And I'm the one filling it.'

'There is more to life than money,' said Helen

'Not to Jones there isn't. It's his only route to freedom.'

'You can be such an arse sometimes,' said Helen. 'I can't go anywhere in public at the moment unless I'm in disguise. I can feel the tension every time I walk down the street.'

When they got to their apartment, and their daughter, Pace had been put to bed, Wood kissed Helen's neck and apologised. 'Make me feel as though there is no tomorrow,' Helen had asserted and Wood had torn into her clothes as they made love. They got dressed in a hurry and raced down to the lobby when the concierge informed them that the taxi had arrived.

Helen looked stunning as she stepped out from the foyer into the street to enter through the door that the concierge was holding open. She smiled as she recognised his gesture and Wood saw a sensual, soft radiance as he captured her profile. He had always admired the way Helen held her shoulders back, highlighting her graceful neck. He had many moments, numerous ephemeral glances that impacted him every day when he looked at Helen and he was constantly astounded that he could never become complacent with her beauty. Helen was sensual in her love making and he had always been very attentive to her needs in the bedroom.

'How can you trust her?' Stan had once asked him after eyeing the length of her legs and commenting on them. 'Fuck me, simply magnificent. She should be on a catwalk,' continued Stan. 'I could spend a lifetime wrapped up in those.'

'Thanks for that Stan,' Wood had answered, sarcastically. 'Anyway, she is the dream,' Wood continued. 'If they ask her out and she says no, the dream dies so they don't ask her.'

'And that stops them?' laughed Stan.

'Yes. It allows the dream to stay alive.'

'So how come you asked her?'

'I didn't,' Wood answered. 'She got pissed and raped me. Fondest memory I have.'

The taxi driver was the first to ask for Wood's autograph that evening. 'Can you write *to Danny with love, from Jesus Christ.*' Wood had obliged with the cabbie's request and acknowledged the irony. 'I was asked to sign for John Lennon last night,' said Wood, smiling ingratiatingly.

They had eluded the paparazzi for once so Wood was thankful: the persistence of a body of press had become an unfathomable problem but he was relaxed with the steady stream of signatory requests, one line comments and approvals that accompanied him in public. He had come to know that if he left the party early or avoided those moments when he was deemed to be out of earshot, his public face remained unscarred.

Their friends were already sitting at the table waiting. David often told Maggie that he didn't know what all the fuss was about regarding Wood. Janet and her husband, Robert silently enjoyed the attention. Maggie had retorted to David that she thought Wood was the most influential man that had ever lived.

After dining David and Robert were in debate over whether it was Darwin or it was Freud who was right in their conclusions of *man*. Wood had found himself recalling the scenes from his window and he said 'they were both right'. He knew better than to debate humanitarian subjects with his friends so he had caught his audience for a moment when he had said this. Helen broke the silence when she had asked him, 'What do you mean? Go on then.' Simultaneously, David had said something but Helen's words drowned his voice into an incomprehensible mumble.

Wood chose to change the subject and excused himself to go to the cloakroom. But as he rose to leave his friends, Maggie beckoned him to continue so he told them that it was also more likely that both of the great philanthropists were wrong. David challenged Wood with this saying that Darwin had surely defined man. 'Not at all,' said Wood. 'Remember Nixon. Remember the day when he spoke to Neil Armstrong via telephone moments after he had taken the first steps on the moon. Nixon said, 'for one priceless moment in time, men and women from all nations are unified.' Everyone across the globe had been watching.'

'And?' said David, his facial expression contorted, suggesting he was confused.

'Well something immense was engaging us beyond mere survival.' Wood affirmed.

'Ok, but how does that define man?' said David.

'Big question. But then again what has sex and survival got to do with the humble telephone?' Wood answered, cryptically.

'Communication and resources my friend; nothing more,' said David loudly.

Wood left after hearing this and went to the cloakroom. David said, 'It is no surprise that America won the space race.'

Robert said, 'It was farcical that Russia was ever in it.'

Maggie turned to Helen. 'How has Tane been?' she asked, conscious that the media spotlight on her husband had intensified in the last week. Helen replied, 'It may seem wonderfully glamorous but it is not easy for him. His editor is very supportive.' Stan's manner had always confused Helen and she was not certain if she was correct in what she said.

Maggie said, 'Ignore them all. I think his work is brilliant.'

'On Wednesday it is done. Finally,' said Helen. 'The expectation is intolerable. I have never seen anything like it; all the hype. They have spent thousands announcing its release – or 'coming' as his editor calls it – and this is the second coming this week.'

Maggie turned to the table and spoke in Wood's absence. 'Maybe he had a point – about Freud and Darwin. You know, that they were both right.'

'I must hear this,' said Robert, smirking and searching the eyes around the table for approval.

'Well you must,' continued Maggie. 'The basis of Freud was that our key driving force is our sexual behaviour and our need to fuck. Darwin believed that we are driven by our survival instincts and the fittest will win. Maybe that is why the strongest always seem to be the biggest fuckers.'

'Or we just don't get it,' said Wood returning to his seat, concerned that they hadn't changed the subject and begun a new debate. He recognised that he had just made matters worse and resolved to remain silent. He knew that David would pursue this subject until he was satisfied that he had the last word.

Janet said, 'Whatever.'

David said, 'Darwin is definitely the man for me. They proved Freud was off his head. Complete nutter as you Brits would say.'

The evening wandered on and the debate seemed to have little sight of a conclusion. Wood often tried to change the subject but Robert and David were determined to air their views and they were locked in combat with this topic. The more intense the argument became, the louder their voices got. They talked over each other with increasing regularity until the conversation gained the intensity of two opponents shouting at each other, simultaneously rifling off verbal bullets. Wood thumbed his glass of still water and eyed their beer glasses. He had not drunk alcohol for over a year now – it was an agreement he had with Helen - but he kept thinking that it would be easier if he just joined them. They had certainly encouraged him. Wood decided to listen in to the conversation between Helen and Janet which sounded less of a combat mission but Helen leaned closer to Maggie and asked her if things had gotten better with their dog. Maggie rolled her eyes before she answered Helen. 'I can't bear it much longer. The damn thing's hiding all the time. Every time I open a door I clout the poor mutt.' Maggie leaned towards Helen. 'David insists that it needs a firm hand. That's what mastering is all about, teach them to be compliant and they love it, he keeps saying. But the damn thing's either locked in the utility room or being beaten.'

Later that evening when Helen and Wood were climbing into bed, Helen asked him if he was sure about the article on Wednesday going public. Wood seemed hesitant and then he told her why he hadn't slept last night. He said that he had woken with an awful start turning his stomach and filling his mouth and throat with acid.

'It wasn't a dream,' he began. 'I remembered when I was seven, on my birthday, when I lived in Kenilworth. I sat on my bike next to the gate by the fields at the end of our road. Being seven had suddenly seemed so old and then I had wondered what it would be like to be eleven years old and my mind had wandered to 22 and 33. I had tried to think of 44 and 55 but I had never believed or imagined that I could be that old; and here I am. I woke thinking that it had all come and gone. A bit like death; we know it is coming one day but it is too far off to imagine. I remember, as a child, we all scoffed all our chocolate on Christmas Day and never had anything left for Boxing Day. One year I had decided to put a Mars Bar in the fridge for New Year's Eve. I thought I was clever because I would have some chocolate and my two brothers would have eaten all theirs. New Year came and I ate the Mars Bar. Moments after I had realised that I now had no chocolate again. Suddenly, it had all seemed pointless.'

Wood left the bedroom and he flicked the switch on the kettle before he lit up. Wood smoked heavily and often at his kitchen window. Occasionally, he took the elevator to the 31st floor, entered through the door marked 'Private' and climbed over the board chalked with the phrase 'enter at your own risk' propped up against the broken fire exit door. This passage lead onto the roof terrace and when he had lit up, he would eye the colossal view he had gained of New York. From this height, as he paced around the terrace ducking the electricity cables, he would watch the stillness of Brooklyn and Queens, Harlem, New Jersey and squint past the Empire State Building in an always alluding attempt to spot any of the buildings in the financial district. He never tired of the fascination of the glory that stood before him although he preferred the view from his kitchen window and that was where he was now.

Here he could see for many blocks and all the crossroads they fabricated weaved in the linear pattern that conformed to the rules laid down by our ancestors who had designed and built them. But the crossroads seemed to be on the pavements and the roads themselves and invariably in the people who used them. He had watched countless people below; a thousand different walks at a hundred different speeds in every direction and he noticed how frequently people nearly or actually clashed by walking into each other. When they did he saw many different responses; most of the time an apology but sometimes worse. The apologies rarely seemed genuine – almost automated. In the evening, the tone changed and in the early hours Wood often witnessed scenes of aggression. Fights would break out and the bigger or fitter guy would win or, more often the mouthier girl. Cabbies got an awfully tough time, and sober police seemed intolerably forgiving with heavily intoxicated aggressors. He noticed how frequently the coppers had to bend down to retrieve their hat from the floor. Past 2am Wood had watched them fuck in public areas. Some more private than others but occasionally, the act was blatant, witnessed and caught. On one occasion, a woman who had stumbled upon two lovers had seemed to join in. 'Buy one get one free,' Wood had thought as every act imaginable seemed to unfold before his smoking eyes; everyone going in every direction doing everything and anything.

He opened the window in the kitchen and closed the lighter lid as the smoke began to feed from the end of his cigarette. As his eyes focused on the roads below a moment of disorientation made him grab a hand at the window frame and his sight turned to the red canopy directly below him on the street. Martello's restaurant was situated on the ground floor of their apartment block building and their canopy stretched the full length. Wood had eaten there occasionally and had often been intrigued with the difference in his view from the ground as opposed to the one he now saw. His curiosity was not so much with the alternative perspectives but from his desire to test its strength.

Each time he looked down on it he had wondered. He could not be sure that it would break his fall but his certainty that he did not want it to, was more defining for him. When he spoke to Helen about this she had asked him to stop and he could not understand why she had laughed.

Now, more than ever, he felt free to exercise his curiosity. He had told Helen that he wanted to find out. 'But that's at least a hundred foot drop. Anyone who jumps that will die,' she said to him.

'Not at all,' he had responded. 'They just don't get up.' But his controversy was less distinguished because he laughed too; only his tone had differed.

As he climbed out of the window and took a seat on the window ledge with his legs dangling towards the canopy eleven stories below him, he felt compelled to finish his cigarette first. The canopy looked further as he peered down on it now and he felt the full flood of his anxiety. Recently he had become frustrated with any inaction, especially his own. He had spent too long, too many moments and too much time pondering commitment.

It was midnight in Manhattan and the dust carts were filling their stomachs with the street debris. The men were making fun of their work by tossing the bags into the back of the truck from several yards. Their designs flipped from under arm, over arm, under their legs and over their heads sometimes facing the carts and at other times with their backs against them. Their skill compelled Wood to watch.

He heard their cheers with their successful throws and the scoffs with their failures but these sounds began to be stifled by noises that were getting louder from the apartment next door. A light went on in their kitchen and the darkness of the night faded a little as the glare penetrated the air from the window. Voices cried out with little rhythm or sense apart from a tone of anxiety. Even when the window was prised open the sounds made no sense until a young woman appeared from the opening, her upper body stretching out into the midnight air suggesting her hips were wedging her safe against the bottom of the window frame at her midriff. A cloth was tossed from the window and as it fell to the ground, barely distinguishable in the night sky, Wood vaguely sensed that it was her skirt. Other items followed, less recognisable apart from her stilettos.

She raised her head, arching her back and looked out to the stars. As she stretched her arms ahead of her she appeared to be reaching for the consternations that fixed her sight. A man's voice began to plead with her to scream. His request was accommodated by her vocal cry that Wood could clearly hear as her softly sung voice projected the phrase 'have me' repeatedly and in rhythm with the physical pulse of her body movement; a pulse that was not of her own making.

From nowhere Wood sensed that the girl – a *ballerina sparkle* in the Manhattan Skyline – had imposed upon him the status of voyeur and even though he had appeared innocently at his window, this gave him no excuse; a cigarette was no substitute for the act of being caught leering after a naked young woman being hammered from behind. But in a moment, his deemed guilt faded.

As her voice worked louder her fingertips reached further ahead of her. Several beats missed her screams but none more so than when she caught sight of Wood in her vision and turned towards him to gaze into his eyes. Wood was stunned by her look and he fixed upon her. She seemed resigned but committed and Wood was certainly less confused with the two words she mouthed to him, 'Help me.'

When the morning had come Helen had got out of bed early. She turned the calendar when she went into the kitchen to put the kettle on. 'Four days 'till Christmas,' she thought and she was uneasy with the realisation that she hadn't yet purchased a Christmas present for anybody; same as every year but, this year, she had no resolve to get the job done. She had a long list of actions to do and she was conscious that as it grew her anxiety with it did not. She added a little more coffee and a little more sugar to her cup before she poured the water on top. It was a habit she now had when she woke early and before she sat down she grabbed the National Times from the doorstep below the letter box. Her husband's name stood loud on the front page and nearly as loud as the title that accompanied it; *'Magnificent New Mankind. The Care Code.'*

Helen turned from the front page and the dialogue for her husband began. Page two and three shone with the imagery of Christ on the cross, the Vitruvian man, Mona Lisa and Einstein amongst a collage of influential icons. The gloss encircled the script across both pages and nestled within it, her husband's column heading *iReckon* was embedded above the title *'We Got God Wrong.'*

When Helen began to read Wood's words she reached for her cigarettes before she realised that she had given up before Pace was born many years ago. She tutted as her hand whisked away an imaginary act and then her eyes moved from the imagery to the text that was in print. As she read, she crossed one leg over the other and her arms knotted about her chest. Tears grew in her eyes and she hesitated. She closed the paper and tossed it towards the bin.

Today's edition by her husband did not have the impact of his Christmas Day articles but it was the latter that unsettled her now. She believed wholeheartedly in her husband's ambition. She never took for granted the strength of his conviction, the passion of his drive and the endurance he had faced. 'I reached that point of despair that most women must face,' Helen had once told Maggie. 'Maybe it was the age difference. I don't know. But I was fed up with talking to men who had little more to offer than a groin. You get to read all the signs. You know they will say anything to get a fuck. I really did start to think that nothing else was on offer. When I met Wood, I never looked back.'

'You really love him?' asked Maggie.

'Yes I do. He talks about living an eternity with me. I can't cope with being parted from him for more than a day.' Helen smiled.

'What is so different?'

'How do you put your finger on that? I've often wondered. All I do know is that he really does care. After all the seedy voices and the hyperactive loins, I found a guy who cares more than anybody I've ever known.'

'About you?' Maggie probed.

'He does and that's also the attraction. I desperately want it to be me.'

'He adores you. It's written all over him,' said Maggie wistfully.

'Yes I know. I do see that. And there's more – much more – more than I know.'

Increasingly, Helen was aware of the price that they had to pay as her husband's convictions had become more and more public. Lately, she had sensed a foreboding, a frightening reality that was beginning to dawn – a life threatening reality; a new fear, lurking as a shadow, getting closer every moment, ready now to step into the light and cheer as it picked the spotlight.

She reached for the paracetamol packet on the window ledge but did not take it. She got to her feet, went to the sink with her coffee and poured the contents down the drain. As the tears gently rolled down her cheeks she began to smile. She had read the Christmas Day article and wondered if her husband's words could be delivered by the skilful talent of his editor in the manner in which he had promised. Her tears stopped and her gaze wandered across the horizon seeing nothing. 'Maybe,' she thought, 'God could finally stop...'

But her thoughts were interrupted by a violent series of knocks at her door and a voice carrying loudly from the other side saying, 'Please open up. Are you there? This is an emergency. Please open up.'

Spontaneously Helen looked for Wood. The sudden interruption and its vociferous nature had momentarily confused her. But as she looked she could not see him. He had not been beside her in their bed when she had awoken and she had assumed, by habit that he would be at his desk in his study. As she entered the room it was empty and a further series of knocks rattled across the door 'Please open up. Is anyone there?' It only took a few seconds for Helen to realise that she was alone and it was her who should open the door. She hadn't been up for long and she hadn't checked her hair, her face or anything about her look. She knew that she would look a mess. Although, in the air of anxiety emanating from behind the door, her curiosity about her look pained no concern, her natural reaction caused her to hesitate again. She even, for a few seconds, searched the walls for a mirror until consciously she overrode her own confusion and commanded herself to answer the door. As she made to do so, she glanced through the kitchen and noticed that something was odd. She had sensed it when she had put the kettle on earlier but failed to follow her curiosity further, distracted by her husband's article.

Bemused, she stopped and took a second look and, instantly, she could not recognise anything out of the ordinary. It was several moments before the peculiarity did become apparent. As her eyes focused upon it, the cries from behind her front door took on a more obvious and disturbing relevance. When she'd gone to bed last night, the kitchen window had not been left wide open.

TREVOR HOARY

Davos, Switzerland, December 20th 2019

Reuters Blog
World Economic Forum
The Hoary Powerhouse of a New World Trade
Posted by: Oliver Edwards

Only last week, Reuters announced that Hoary was the best placed Chairman to lead the banking world out of our debt laden debris of the last decade. As the industry's mammothian herd descended upon this year's World Economic Forum in Davos, the alternative – at best – was incomprehensible whimpering. After the events yesterday, clearly he is the man who will do a whole lot more.

You would have thought that Roubini and Rogers - the seemingly prominent sources of foresight throughout the forever burdening financial meltdown – would have predicted his emergence as the powerhouse in world trade. However, breaking from their norm of insular indulgence, comments from both of the economic colossuses in the New York Post last week do now foretell his influence. Surely this must stand as the final judgement when we consider that both of these financial highrollers have wiped 5 percent off the greenback with comments made in a Bloomberg interview earlier this month.

The absence of many of the bankers who were normally expected to attend the World Economic Forum in Davos was just as interesting as those who were there. With the exception of the home team of Credit Suisse (which has maintained a relatively high profile) and UBS (which hasn't), the most senior bankers in town – at least the ones still putting on a show – were Hoary and... well, nobody else.

It is no surprise that the Hoary show has gone on. His ITCD International Bank has singularly emerged as the best placed survivor of the decade long saga that is the global financial system and positioned it as the industry front runner in a premier league of its own. Hoary's high profile attendance in Davos sends out a particularly stronger message than the – 'it's business as usual' – which he had stated at the same event a year earlier.

More than that, his presence tells the world not to lump him with the crowded Debt Beats and Davos Deserters who didn't dare show their faces for fear of how it would look on the front page of the New York Times or the Daily Mail.

Hoary could have been sat in the Queen's Carriage being the focus and the cheer of the procession. Having ravished the Davos agenda and shepherded in the B20 heads, the world's press has dissected his every word across the front pages of all global tabloids. His common theme is now undoubtedly prevalent in the executive sweat rooms across Tokyo, Shanghai, Frankfurt, London, Paris and New York; 'A cohesive agenda focused on sustainable, non-partisan, policy driven trade to promote open market confidence,' said Hoary and then concluded, 'An Era which will see us all redefine and reaffirm our commitment to contributing to social and economic development. A new forum for enterprise in which the B20 must now replace the redundant WEF.'

The response – almost a calling from a vibrant vocal panacea – more surprisingly, concludes towards a cohesive approval of his ideology. Some may argue that 'who'd have thought it' and it was undoubtedly timely following last week's regular denunciation of banking

by Lord Turner (formerly, Chairman of the UK
Financial Services Authority) as 'socially useless'. This
attack was not his first and, if the plaudits are to be
believed, it won't be his last.

Indeed, the tabulated accolade draws a singular
conclusion of Hoary's floret - a common heraldry has
been witnessed; they love him as a mother will love her
child, ready at all cost to protect him from a fall and
adorning of his pursuit and courage.

You be the judge – a sceptical Soros has called – but
it clearly now transpires, from the popular voice, that
Hoary has arisen as our finest offering. A man who –
faced with all roads open – has chosen the right one. As
his father, we can all be extremely proud of our boy; the
new hero of the crowd. And, from amidst the global
Muppets who now scamper and still claim the titles of
our political and commercial elite, we chant – arise
Hoary. The kings are dead, long live the king.

Hoary described his departure from Zurich Airport as a complete
palaver. The pilot told Hoary that the airport authorities had been overly
sensitive with private jets following their second fatal crash in ten years
which had happened earlier in the year.

'Both involved Cirrus SRs,' the pilot told Hoary.

'What are we flying in?' asked Hoary.

'A Cirrus SR.'

'Very comforting,' said Hoary, dryly.

'I wouldn't worry too much. The Cirrus used to be notorious,
dropped like rocks from the skies. Improved no end recently. Shame this
isn't a current model.'

The pilot continued to explain to Hoary that older planes had usually
flown for many hours and if they had never dropped out of the air, why
should they drop out of the sky today. Hoary resolved that he would let
providence determine the fate of his journey. 'At least,' he thought.
'This was not a Russian plane.' He recalled the 1950's when the
notoriously impoverished USSR government had purchased
malfunctioning second hand aircraft. They were aware that the demand
to engage world trade expansion – and get their people commuting –
was higher than the human tragedy that would result.

'Who are all these people?' asked Hoary.

'Airport personnel, Press and airport security holding the Press back from you. Oh and a load of guys from the Schultz & Rettung Zurich rescue services.'

'Rescue? We haven't taken off yet. What are they rescuing us from?' Hoary was trying to recall the last time he had encountered a flying trip that had demanded so much of his resilience.

'Precautionary, I think. I can't quite make out what the problem is. Seems that an oil spill has frozen on one of the wings but God knows how it got up there. The S & R rescue services are world renowned for their paranoia; seems that your presence has given it new heights. I'd get on board if I was you and wait it out. Make yourself comfortable.'

Hoary had declined a drink from the selection of alcoholic beverages that the air hostess had offered him after he had settled into his seat. He never drank alcohol and hadn't done so since he had joined the Anglican Church following graduation, when he was 22. He asked her if she had any peppermint tea. 'Yes sir. Sugar?' she asked and followed his instruction for one heap. When she returned with the warm brew, Hoary had finished trawling through his routine websites and logged onto his email. His phone rang and he was thankful to see the name on his mobile.

'Hoary?' said Michael, his CEO. Michael Houndsworthy was his closest confidant and the only man that Hoary held in great esteem. He was glad to have Michael by his side.

'Hello Michael.'

'Just a quickie. Brendan's on the hunt. Johnston needs an editorial on you and I guess he can't dig any dirt in all this good news.'

'Johnston?'

'Ah, you haven't heard. They've sacked Gordon. Johnston's the new editor and he hates bankers and world leaders. You don't stand a chance. He'll have great fun at your expense. I can't wait,' said Michael gleefully, tempting Hoary to take the bait, but he never did. Michael enjoyed his play with Hoary's complete lack of a sense of humour – typical, he thought, of highly driven men. Michael also enjoyed searching for Hoary's Achilles Heel but his endeavours had remained fruitless. More importantly to Michael, he felt obliged to keep Hoary aware of his political tripwires – the true sentiments of the men around him and their words and agendas that they hid from Hoary.

'What's the good news?' asked Hoary.

'Still searching for the bad. I can't find any, that's the good news. Your venture at the WEF has got the church bells ringing.'

'What's the form? Any themes?'

'Love and admiration by all account; universal so I hear,' Michael replied. 'Davos was just the ticket. Seems you beat me on the timing, unfortunately. I guess that I can't level the scores now.'

'Have you got the Sunday editorials?' asked Hoary. Michael knew that Hoary always wanted to read the news before anybody else.

'Not yet but they'll be on your email before you land. I also sent you an intriguing reply to your pitch for the concept of "fairest". I do wish you'd stop writing books on morality and banking, we've all got much less stressful trash to deal with. Anyway must rock n' roll. Well done on Davos, hail the new Messiah etc. Love you, bye.' Michael rang off.

Hoary put down his phone. He was wondering if the plane would make it onto the runway and the stewardess reassured him that it would. She told him that they should be in the air in ten minutes. Intrigued, he opened his email inbox and read Michael's message. It said;

'For God; fairest – fairgame – fairies. Could have gone to the dictionary but found this instead. Log on to Asylum.com and take your pick – let me know your choice? PS. Don't know why you're bothering, Johnston will have you anyway and if he doesn't, Brendan will. PPS. If those two fail, I won't. I will never let you forget that God is my dad not yours.'

Hoary logged onto Asylum.com and browsed the headline topics that flashed across his screen. He noted the statement directly below their logo, 'For All Mankind' and pondered the irony of the claim.

'Chore time doubled for women', 'Why being dumped can do wonders for you', 'Clever girls give longevity to husbands' and 'Real women reveal the worst advice.' Hoary scrolled the screen for more titles and wondered just how obscure Michael could be. He was distracted by a window advertisement for Holiday Inn proclaiming that, 'We're not changing the world overnight. Just the overnight world'. Their new 'Signature' faster & friendlier check in experience only necessitated a two second voice recognition signature process and, 'Your time is for you. Enjoy.'

A window next door advertised Compare.com insurance policies for £5 and Ryanair was promoting flights to Lamezia, Italy from £25. More flash screen headlines caught his eye and he searched through them. 'World's weirdest magazines', 'That'll do – stupidest fixes', 'Amazing

time-lapse beard video' and 'Ridiculous women's fashion trends'. Hoary
flitted across these statements and they failed to spark his interest. He
felt his search was in vain and found himself rubbing his hands together
with some endeavour. He called for a little more patience from himself
which was short lived as he found his link in the last rolling headline
which read, 'Who was the *fairest* of them all? - The sexiest women in
history'. He clicked the icon of a medieval al fresco portrait of a woman
and a script appeared;

Give up your tedious lists of the hottest popular
female celebs, 'high street hotties' or 'Page 3' models.
The twenty-twenties are coming and fortunately for you,
Asylum has higher standards. Or, if you prefer, we
delve into weirder depths of depravity – bring on the
new Era. We've scoured the history books for the hottest
women ever to have graced the Earth and our selections
epitomise everything that is great about the human gene
pool. They have seduced and corrupted, as well as loved
and honoured, some of history's great leaders. They
have libraries and galleries devoted to their beauty.
Undoubtedly, they were fair but who was the fairest of
them all?

1. **Eve** – The original – depending on which
account you adhere to. Before the Fall, she was
considered 'perfect' and God created woman in her
form, so she has justifiable bragging rights.

2. **Anne Boleyn** – Henry VIII found her so
irresistible he went against 1500 years of indoctrination
to marry her and took on the Catholic Church and the
Holy Roman Empire.

3. **Helen of Troy** – "The face that launched a
thousand ships"; she triggered the Trojan War. Helen
was a promise from Aphrodite to give Paris the most
beautiful woman in the world. Euripides claimed she
had left the mortal world, such beauty only possible in a
goddess.

4. **Marie Antoinette** – The lavish and extravagant queen of France was said to have indulged in all manner of deviancies, with all manner of people. The wife of Louis XVI, she prompted tales of sexual liberation far beyond her times.

5. **Cleopatra** – Cleopatra's looks were said to be matched only by her charm and deviousness – traits prevalent amongst attractive women of any time period. She used her 'assets' to entrance both Julius Caesar, and then his betrayer, Mark Antony.

6. **Lady Godiva** – Anyone with voyeuristic tendencies can thank Lady G for the term 'Peeping Tom', when a man named Tom was blinded after watching her ride through the streets of Coventry naked. Her novel approach to transport should have caught on.

7. **Venus** – An actual Goddess, Venus represented love, lust and beauty. Thus she was hot. 'Nuff said.

8. **Guinevere** – Hot totty to Knights. Guinevere and Lancelot were having an affair when she was married to King Arthur. While Arthur went to France to avenge his betrayal, in a war with Lancelot, Mordred moved in and married Guinevere himself. Unfortunately, she didn't make it all the way round the Table.

9. **Madame de Pompadour** – Paris' original fashionista worked her way through the ranks to become Louis XV's official mistress. She is remembered for her stunning porcelain face and voluptuous body.

10. **Marilyn Monroe** – The original 'blonde bombshell', she defined sex appeal. Her colourful career included an affair with an American President, posing for Playboy, marrying an American sporting hero, a very famous pink dress and diamond ensemble, and that scene over an air duct. The New York Subway hasn't been the same for opportunistic perverts since.

Hoary logged off and he peered through the porthole window. The Cirrus powered down the runway and climbed vigorously into the sky. He considered, for a moment, that it was very odd that men and women alive today would, one day, so easily be recalled from history. He was comforted by the knowledge that they were remembered for a whole variety of behaviours; certainly, the sexiest woman in history had been. 'The principle that life is fair,' thought Hoary, 'is indelibly smudged by the imposition of *fair game.*'

Hoary recalled a conversation he'd had with Michael last week. 'Whilst you have built a career that has consistently reached an agreeable acceptance from the world press,' Michael had begun. 'This is nothing compared to the reception you will get when your actions are finalised next week'. The Friday following Christmas Day would be his glorious arising and Hoary felt that he had being building all his life for this moment.

On Sunday, Hoary was alone in his morning room for most of the early hours of the afternoon. The sunshine would only drift past the southerly aspect after 3pm at this time of year. After his mid morning attendance at his local Anglican Church he preferred the solitude that he was afforded here and the view from his 16th century stone mullion leaded window across the grounds of his estate. This sight was made magnificent by the foreground presence of the largest horse chestnut tree on private grounds in England (as records had concluded in measurement of its eight metre girth). His Jacobean Mansion had once been the home of Henry VIII and the eastern wing remained reminiscent of this time. The 19th century Victorian additions, however, gave the house today, a size rarely conquerable in the English heritage but few knew of Hoary's private retreat. Most knew only of his apartment in Little Venice, London and this was especially true with the Press, exactly as Hoary wanted it to be.

Having studied, with no surprises, the last of the morning papers he discarded it to his Louis XIII tea table. He got up from his seat and went to find his wife and as he hailed her name, she responded, 'I was just coming to find you. Cup of tea?' Above the rim of his reading glasses, she could see the approval in his eyes. 'Won't be a moment. The kettle's on. Have you seen the papers? They love you today.'

'Yes, I have read them.' Hoary said. 'Not really the response I wanted. I don't need the whole world looking at me. Not at the moment.'

'Well, even the Express had something good to say. Maybe Gordon is turning face.'

'Gordon got the boot. Johnston's after me now. The article must have slipped in during the changeover.'

'That won't do. I heard that Gordon would side with you on the B20.' The kettle boiled and she lifted the pot from the Aga.

'Yes, but I can't have that. I need powerful attacks. Dismissal has significant survival value; wouldn't want the world to think that I am infallible. This faultless panacea concerns me, a little scary really. I mean, look what they did to the last guy. Thank God the modern world doesn't practice crucifixion.'

'Be careful darling. They still have their ways.'

It was some moments after his wife had poured the tea when the phone rang and Hoary had answered it. In the Orangery, Hoary took a seat and gazed across his formal gardens through the glass panelled doors.

'Brilliant coup Trevor. I sense that I should hail Caesar.'

'Hello Brendan.'

Brendan O'Sullivan was Hoary's CEO for ITCD North American Holdings, a man that Hoary did not admire. The two ornate fountains were jettisoning water from their spouts and filling the ornamental stone channel that stretched the length of the raised lawn parterre. The gulley separated the two fountains and classical box hedging weaved in symmetrical patterns either side of it. At the far end of the immaculate lawns, an iron railing fence stood proudly above the *ha-ha* and beyond the centralised gate, lay a wide acreage of parkland, flanked by Oak, Birch and Sycamore trees. The land dropped gently downhill to a large lake, around which, Hoary saw his wife walking their two Spaniels on her favourite route. He smiled as he watched.

'Michael was convinced you'd win this one,' Brendan said.

'Well, Michael needs to hold his call. It's still early days,' said Hoary, deliberately playing down his achievement. He did not like Brendan being aware of his manoeuvres and Hoary could not trust that he was; Brendan may be bluffing.

'Early? You surprise me.'

Hoary caught sight of a large, greyish white wing span at the fountain as a heron drifted in to land. He rose to his feet and grabbed his binoculars to watch the spectacle as he held the telephone to his ear.

'The B20 may be formed but it is not settled yet. There is still unrest in the camp. Exxon are trying to call the shots in North Africa and Xstrata won't have it.'

'Why? Too much oil?' asked Brendan.

'A bit more complicated. Xstrata want the ore that sits directly above it and BP are claiming researchers have discovered gold. The territory is awash with resources,' explained Hoary, hoping to distract Brendan's inquisition by playing down his ability to control the agenda of the B20 heads.

'You've had these episodes before. What's new?'

'No I agree but it all takes time and they do forget that it is African land.' Hoary watched a large flock of Canada geese – at least 40 in number – swarm onto the lake in fan like fashion and land. Their sheer numbers drove away a pair of swans who quickly scattered from the small island they inhabited and used as their nesting place in spring. Other wildfowl, mallards and moorhens joined the need to run for cover.

The B20 was a formation of the world's twenty largest corporations in the global commercial market place. Hoary had spent over ten years bringing these businesses into one forum under his supreme council and thus providing him with an unrivalled influential platform. The recent succession of his control, to position him as Chairman, was not yet public.

'Michael tells me that you have a Christmas present for the party. Any chance of a preview?' fished Brendan, testing the water with Hoary.

'Michael needs to...'

'Come on Trevor,' Brendan interrupted, sensing Hoary's reluctance. 'Stop excluding me from the kitchen cabinet. I came through for you in America despite Bernanke and Geitner, even Obama. Despite everyone and their horse if you think about it.'

'Yes Brendan, you did. I know you did. Be patient, nothing is certain yet. We'll speak soon.'

'Trevor?'

'We'll speak tomorrow. Goodbye.' Hoary clicked the red button on his Blackberry and watched the heron swallow another fish from the fountain pond. Hoary saw Brendan as no serious threat to his plans but he thought that he should check. He dialled out to Michael.

'Wondered when you'd call. Guess Brendan's been digging?' Michael said.

'Yes. You've aroused his Christmas spirit. Well done. Did you tell him?'

'No not yet. I'll give it a day,' said Michael. Hoary was instantly put at ease with this comment. He trusted Michael in the control and the timing of his endeavours.

'Johnston will be furious. He won't sleep knowing he may miss it.' Hoary said and watched another Heron land at the fountain and join in with the feast.

'He was almost complimentary of you in this morning's papers,' said Michael.

'Yes, my wife was saying. Not sure that was Johnston's work.'

'Whatever, we don't need that. Anyway, I haven't decided what to tell Brendan yet but rest assured. I'll get Johnston vying for you. We can't have him on side.'

'No we can't. I'm uneasy with all this positive air. It can only end up predatory and it will arouse my enemies.' Hoary knelt on the window ledge to gain a closer look at the two Herons, his binoculars still at his eyes.

'Enemies? Come now Trevor. You have competitors not enemies. The only enemy you need to watch is me. Anyway, the world loves you. No one will be able to touch you after Sunday. Today, you are merely the global Air Apparent but you'll get the mantle now.'

'It's dangerous to become too visible at the eleventh hour.'

By the time Hoary had finished his call with Michael, the two herons had flown off after gobbling a large feast of small fish. Hoary took his seat again and thought of his wife. His mind wandered from the pragmatic into the daydream and Anne Boleyn appeared. He noticed that he had been tapping his foot at some speed and stopped the action. He thought how confident Michael was of the delivery of their plan and he recalled Michael's final comments before they had finished their conversation.

'They haven't seen you coming and they won't. Ironic really; they will hail you as the New Saviour in the New Year. They love you. If only they really knew.'

PURPOSE

Cibeuce, Sunday 22nd December 2019

'**A**pples don't fall from trees and people don't die.' Dace eyed his graffiti and recalled that moment of frustration when he had written it. He had been pulling his hair out.

He is sitting on the floor in Cibeuce, in jeans and t-shirt with his legs crossed and his elbows nestled in his thighs. His hands cup his shaven chin and tears roll down reddened cheeks below his neatly cropped hair. All around him, painted on the floor, are pictures of a group of apes which he had individually named; Fight, Play, Feed, Offend, Argue, Comfort and Love. By his side is his seat. A thick plank of solid oak propped up on two breeze blocks and the wear in the wood suggests that he has used it often over the years.

He chokes back his sigh and grips his fingertips hard into the palms of his hands. He reads the phrase that he has etched into the bark of his seat: 'There is always at least one man who will stop you'. In a few seconds his tears stop falling and he jumps to his feet. As he talks, to himself, he calls for the 'Scar Wall' and trawls his gaze over the phrases he has written upon it.

All the walls in Cibeuce are covered in graffiti and the elaborate, meticulous, detailed, beauty alludes to the patience, artistry and, above all, the time given to their design. Thousands of years of endeavour were illustrated before his eyes and the deep channels of water erosion that fall from the ceiling of the colossal walls still fill the chamber with the calming sound of running water. The random spray of the waterfall had scarred much of the graffiti on this wall and Dace had chosen outrageous displays of colour and huge lettering to combat the erosion and retain eligibility to his writings. But still, even his most recent additions had been affected, wiping away the letter 'e' in 'Hitler had shaky knees'; the 'i' in 'Da Vinci was a fraud' and the 'l' in 'Jesus made love to women'. To a lesser extent, but still noticeable, the water had eroded the 'e' in 'Prince Charles is a farmer', the 'h' in 'Obama is not the anti-Christ' and the 't' in 'grounds men shouldn't kill moles'.

His tears return again. He knows that today is different and he feels no sadness. Quite the opposite. He can't laugh with his joy, he can only cry with it because now, the impact is more than ever. For an eternity he has watched so much happen but unlike before, he feels the exhaustion of all that time. At least his battle with it has become that much easier. For many, many years Dace had often wondered whether an act would come that would see him escape. In truth he knew it would. The grand master plan would eventually work – come what may – and he looked at his eternal message of hope; '*Survival – Find me*'. But *time* had always been able to taint his dream.

On the Scar Wall he looks at his latest edition which he had entitled 'Achilles Heel'. Under this, he had written, 'The arrow is removed, the wound is healed and the true hero is about to fly. Come on Hoary, come on Wood draw your bows'. Dace yawn but he is not tired, a little weary maybe, for he knows that the bow is about to be drawn and the final episode is starting. 'Come on boys, get on with it,' he screams in the caverns before him. 'Get me out of here'.

PART TWO

SEVEN DAYS THAT MADE THE EARTH

Monday – Lions

When Wood lost his $300 million he didn't blame anyone. He didn't even blame himself. In fact, everyone around him said that he was just his normal self, but he wasn't. He got hurt – it hurt like hell – and those closest to him wondered whether he could get through it. Wood had not underestimated this demand upon himself or even, the greater challenge – could he get it all back? However, he was about to learn that all this was nothing compared to what lay in store.

Mostly, those around him had always dismissed his success, claiming his empire was gifted to him by greedy men who had sucked Wood in and that he was the biggest sucker of them all. They said that he had been in the right place at the right time when it mattered most. If Wood had been anyone else, they would have been right but as soon as Wood had woken that morning he went straight to his fax machine. 'It had better be there,' thought Wood.

The morning had hardly settled in. True, the sun had broken above the horizon and the wild, plentiful, mosaic pitch of birdsong was engulfing the air. Even the sunlight was already grasping for pitch upon the grasslands as the clouds stunted its shots. It wasn't even 6am and Wood was out of bed although this wasn't unlike him. He usually, first thing, grappled in the kitchen amidst coffee jars, mugs, sugar, cigarettes and lighters but today, before his eyes had had the time to open, was different. He was hopping down the stairs, dressing in jeans and T shirt, brushing a hand through his hair, balancing on adrenalin.

His study held his fax machine and this was his destination. As he reached the bottom of the stairs, he skipped across the hall and swung the study door open. He saw the single sheet of paper, from Paul that had been received by fax, lying on the machine. 'I love you Paul,' he said out loud. A smile ripped across his face as he had lifted the flap that released the received page. Simultaneously, his eyes glanced at a bold note that he had pinned to a clipboard above it. The note read, *If all the world's a stage, make it yours.*

Paul Ryder had been assigned to Wood when he joined the National Times editorial team. Paul had been recognised in pressrooms throughout New York for his ability to trawl through layers of information and construct the disguised ideology of high profile personalities. The men and women in his profession knew that Paul had dug up the information that exposed the US motivation for the invasion of Iraq. Paul's diagnosis had sown seeds that were presented in the Oliver Stone film 'W'; in the scene in the presidential debating room where the 'drain the swamp' decision persuaded politicians to invade Iraq. Paul had concluded that the invasion was motivated by the need to control oil resources in the Middle East. Owning Iraq, allowed the U.S. to control the whole pipeline network stretching across three continents. Iraq was the central point. If Iraq was shut down, the whole swamp went dry. Paul had made these assertions to expose the real truth and defy the reasons given in all the moral propaganda that the American public were presented with regarding the horrific, tyrannical reign of Saddam Hussein.

Paul, his research assistant, should have sent the fax last night but it was here now and Wood quickly forgot his frustration with it being late. Paul had known that Wood was anxious to see his editorial for the National Times that was due for publication today. But Paul had been distracted with his eyes down in another novel; he had an obsession to grill the pages of every murder, mystery and suspense book he could find. Paul had simply lost track of time and this was not unusual for him.

He had originally tried to find a niche for himself as a critic of this literature and, having no luck, he decided instead to work his way up in the literary profession. He had taken a job as a researcher and that is where he had made his mark. Many of his colleagues had thought that Paul would achieve his own column but Stan had posted him instead to work for Wood. 'He's a great guy,' said Stan of Paul. 'But he can be a pisser.' Stan and Paul had never seen eye to eye. In one incident Paul had shouted '*Mrs* Angry to you!' retorting to Stan's claim that Paul was 'Mr Angry'. Most of the office employees on the floor had witnessed the altercation. 'Highly emotional,' Paul had continued, moving closer to

Stan and fixing his gaze upon him. 'Highly gay and highly charged. Highly paid will be your only option if you piss me off again.'

Jones had maintained that Paul and Stan acted like a married couple in public and probably were in private but Paul was very devoted to his childhood sweetheart, Peter. Others thought that Paul had missed out on his promotion owing to the tense relationship he had with Stan and Paul also held this view.

Wood lifted the fax and positioned the page in front of him so that he could read it. He continued to smile and knew that the words written for his column, *iReckon* were a bold prediction of the historical events that would unfold later today. By that time, his article would have been read by many people across the world. Wood was not concerned that his words would not come true; he knew that they would. He was highly driven to let people know how the shocking events that were about to unfold would do so and why. He knew that he was just beginning and that his article was only the precursor. The majority of people in the world did not know what was about to hit them.

National Times
Monday September 29th 2008
iReckon
Columnist *Tane Wood*

iReckon that the U.S. Congress will vote 'Nay' to the financial bailout plan. The Republicans will revolt and be accused of encamping in their territorial politics. They will fail to put their country and their people first.

The unmitigated backlash will see the major stock markets fall with the American equities being hit hardest – the Dow Jones Industrial index and the NASDAQ will drop by 7% and 9% respectively. World economies will begin to stagnate and decline. They will be gripped by fear, denial and confusion.

The cataclysmic hurt will escalate. The search for blame will transpose the corporate and political boundaries, crossing even the international frontiers.

President Bush will thump tables and drive the vote back to the House with success. Joe Public – as we now call our vociferous American voice – will accept nothing less. From west to east the ferocious winds will carry their screams to our ears.

'The greedy fat cats with their Lamborghinis and their bonuses must be hung. Nothing else will do.' They will cry.

'Where were the legislators?' They will ask.

'Why was this allowed to happen?' They will challenge.

'Who will be made to pay?' They will demand

Anger and concern from the pockets of Joe will also be voiced; 'Will Main Street pay the price?' They will inquire.

'Why should we bail out the bankers?' They will denounce.

'We will not be penalised through absolutely no fault of our own.' They will dismiss.

'Where was the contingency plan?' They will scream; even if there had been one that too would have been spent. I challenge that the next seven days will put the global financial meltdown on to all of our agendas and into all our living rooms.

But, it will take more than a week before anyone realises that this is not just another financial crisis. This is much more fundamental than that. When the plot unfolds, the aftermath will be recorded in the pages of history as a vast colossus. One that will surpass all that has gone before.

What is about to happen will define us forever and deliver universal change.

Wood knew that the collective opinion was that the vote would pass. People were in denial and they did not want to think about the consequences if it did not. Wood believed that this was not the time for faint hearts. The tsunami had landed and the time to run for survival had passed. Now, the painful truth was about to land. Mankind was just about to wake up to a vision of itself that would drown the life we knew.

Wood's mobile rang and it was Paul. He wondered why he hadn't rung Paul last night to chase up his article. 'The good thing about Paul,' thought Wood. 'He is always at the end of his phone.'

'Are you sure?' said Paul, cynically.

'What?' Wood enquired back.

'The article in The Times.'

'Yes. Certain. It's a given. Look, I need you to dig deeper into Trevor Hoary.' This was not the first time that Wood had asked Paul to research into Hoary and he was concerned that he had not received any material.

'Tane, give it up. You're pushing too hard. You'll lose everything.'

'Paul, I need the stuff on Hoary.' Wood demanded again, knowing that he was using the wrong approach with Paul but aware that he was committed now. Paul was always very enthusiastic about any subject as long as it was his idea in the first place but Wood had called this one from the start.

'This whole thing smacks of conspiracy.'

'Paul. Just get it researched. Give me what I need. Hoary has sussed out what I have. I'm sure of it. I can't let him do this, not his way.'

'But...'

'Paul, when this thing unfolds, the world may finally wake up. It's going to be that big. I can't let this corporate manipulator get one step ahead. His motives are...' Wood struggled for a word. 'I know this guy's more ruthless than Attila the Hun.'

'You'll lose your audience. You've already gone too far. I can't back you on this one,' said Paul, anxiously, concerned that Wood seemed to be obsessed with something that he felt didn't exist.

'By the end of this week, millions of people will be pushed too far. I need to land this one. Let them dismiss me now. They'll be desperate for views by the end of this week. I must be the voice they need. If the journos get their way, this thing will be nothing more than a crisis – a big one at that – but Hoary will be given his opportunity.'

'You're risking too much. Be reasonable to me. Your popularity is sky high. You have already established yourself as a good columnist. Don't throw it away,' pleaded Paul.

'I fear that I may not risk enough. I can't miss this opportunity,' insisted Wood aware that he really did need Paul's expertise to investigate Hoary. 'This happens once in a lifetime, maybe a millennium, even eternity.'

'What'll it achieve?' Paul challenged again, becoming more agitated.

'Paul. We would be daft if we just dismiss this one as the greed of the bankers. Are you really going to believe that both sides of the

Atlantic, they all decided, simultaneously that by lending boat loads of cash to subprime paupers they could all walk away with millions of dollars in bonuses?' Wood asserted.

'No. A reckless few exploited significantly relaxed industry regulations, lent too much, hid it in hedge funds and cleared off before the whole thing collapsed around their ears.'

'Well done Paul. Join the multitude that sits in judgement. Have you ever wondered why our history books are littered with the rise and fall of empires? So it happens to be hedge funds this time. And what do you think brought down Alexander, the Romans, the British and everyone else who ever built an empire.'

'Many different reasons, each with their own story.'

'Really? Or have we all missed the point? Just maybe, Paul, this is not about a credit crunch. Maybe, this is much bigger than that. This is about who we all really are. What human beings are all about? I need your help and you know that. Now, help me.'

'Oh yes, I'll help you. But how and with what? How are you going to discover the secrets to mankind? Why you? Don't you think that everyone has had a go? The greats in history have all had a shot and gone nowhere. We all do it, every day and why do you think you are going to succeed when others have so pitifully failed?'

'Yes but this time it is different. No one has ever asked the right question. I know I can.'

'You think you can? Come on,' said Paul, incredulously.

'Paul, the DNA of our greats does not die with them. It lives on in us today. It lives with us. Who are you or I to deny who has it or who does *not*?' said Wood, emphasising his final word.

'Bollocks,' said Paul, adamantly.

'Paul, I need the stuff on Hoary,' said Wood, frustrated.

'You're off your fucking head.'

'I am off my head,' Wood thought when he put the phone down. 'It's the only way anything ever gets solved,' he reminded himself, thinking that normal ideas only amount to everything that we already know. Paul had eventually agreed to research the work that Wood needed for his suspicions about Trevor Hoary and Paul had, as usual, requested a steer. Wood always provided him with this, in the form of a brief, consisting of a paragraph or a list of subjects for him to dig deeper into. Paul had been angry when he had come off the phone but he was usually angry and Wood knew this; it was his way. Wood walked into his hallway where he displayed the artefacts that he had collected in his life. They were there to remind him that it had more meaning than the addiction that a successful corporate career could inflict.

For thirteen years, after his graduation, he had embroiled himself totally within the brand culture of a major retailer. From the humbling beginnings as a management trainee he had risen to the regional board. At this point he had asked himself why he had spent seven days a week, twelve hours a day, locked up in a retail park shed constantly under threat; one slip of personal responsibility, one moment of political naivety or relapsed accountability would deem him unfit to deliver the mission – the sinful commitment of the crime. 'Off you go, now, we have already forgotten you,' would be the judgement and 'You are the enemy and we'll gladly destroy you,' they would announce, passing sentencing. The unforgiving politics of the senior culture had not bothered Wood and as the seniority intensified he too had engaged the playing field of tripping up his counterparts whilst dodging their tripwires. He had become disillusioned when he noticed that the outside world had seemed to pass him by. The realisation had set in and the first thing he had demanded from himself was to conquer the fear that this brought upon him by his deemed slavery to the salaried middle class life and the financial jewellery of suburbia. Now he had one life, it was his and he had to live it. No man had ever gone down in history following the conquests achieved whilst he had been locked up in a shed.

As he stood in his hallway before the small gold fleur-de-leys designed frame of one of his artefacts, he looked at the picture that it housed and into the eyes of Albert Einstein and then read the words printed below his portrait, 'If at first, the idea is not absurd, then there is no hope for it.' Below his name were the words 'German born American Physicist who developed the special and general theories of relativity and won the Nobel Prize for Physics in 1921.'

'What could the life of this man have been like,' thought Wood, realising that he was asking himself the same question that many people must have asked. He knew that Einstein must have asked a different question and strived towards a bigger goal. Whilst the genius of Einstein had been attributed to superior intellect, Wood wondered whether this was true. His own success and the excellence he had witnessed in others were born from commitment and sacrifice. Whilst many pondered an opportunity, few really took it. Fewer still were able to ride the obstacles and sacrifice the comforts that were invariably presented. On three occasions in his life, he had lived below the poverty line and faced the daily challenging ordeal of eating, sleeping, washing and clothing himself without any comfort.

As Wood reflected on his own audacious ambitions he wondered whether he would end up in his life facing the brutal unhappiness and bitterness that Einstein, Waugh, Churchill and many others had faced. He recognised that the loss of his excessive wealth had already given him deemed reason to submit to their paths, but he hadn't. He was firing on more cylinders today than he had originally been given.

'I'll win the Nobel prize for journalism when I explain the mystery of the Vitruvian Man,' Wood said to himself and looked at the graffiti style scribbling of his notes written all over the copy of Leonardo Da Vinci's work. Wood knew that he had surmised an explanation of Da Vinci's elusive configuration of the essence of man that was illustrated in this work. Wood's conclusion was highly unique and, he knew, infallible. The Vitruvian man hung next to Einstein's portrait. 'But not before Hoary has a go,' he thought. Wood needed a fag and he lit up. His anxiety demanded him to do so.

Wood grabbed a bowl of *easy recipe* porridge before he had finished his brief for Paul. His initial attempt had found its way into the bin and now it had become a list. When it was ready to send to Paul, he inserted it into the fax machine and a noise of thunder rattled about his room, seemingly from the streets outside. 'Too early for fireworks,' thought Wood, even though they had been firing over Central Park only last week. Wood decided to let his uncertainty with the noise pass and he pressed the send button. He was becoming increasingly irritated with the time his engineer was taking to fix his computer. He needed his email network more than ever this week. 'Sods Law,' was desperately insufficient.

> *Dismissal*
> *Absurdity*
> *Truth*
> *Opportunity*
> *Energy*
> *Tension*
> *Choice*

Wood ripped the page from the fax machine and thought again, 'not yet.' He swiped a pen line through it, crumpled the page and jettisoned this to the fate of his first attempt. The words on his list were hugely significant to the work he needed to produce but they were not yet applicable. He resolved that the ground work needed to be done first and so he started again and finally sent.

> *Disruptive technologies*
> *Aggressive Market share tactics*
> *Sub prime consumers default*
> *Banks Lending Ambitions*
> *Hedge funds*
> *Market Saturation*
> *Mission statements*
>
> *Emotional coping mechanisms*
> *Education mandates*
> *Kipling's 'If'*
> *Shakespeare's seven stages of man*
> *60s film: The Chase – Arthur Penn*

∞

Wood was watching Bloomberg news when the American Congress began the vote for the financial bailout plan. He finally finished his bowl of porridge after he had heated it for the second time. On the last spoonful he burnt his lip and reeled momentarily with his discomfort. It was short lived as he focused on the disbelieving presenters on the news channel momentarily silenced when the vote was defeated by 228 'nay' to 205 'yea'. Wood sensed their shock too, but this confused him. He knew that the vote would fail. Paul rang Wood.

'How the hell did you know? This is disastrous. People are shocked. They just can't believe it. The vote had to pass. It had to,' said Paul, becoming exasperated.

'It had to fail,' Wood began. He knew if he kept his cool, he could get Paul's commitment to help him. 'The Republicans know Obama will be the new President. They're already panicking about their office. Most of them know that they are on their way out and the last thing they need at the moment is to be dragged down deeper or implicated by this crisis.'

'Why?' Paul asked intrigued.

'They can't cope,' answered Wood assuredly.

'But what about us? They're the big boys. They're the ones looking after us,' said Paul worriedly.

'They're only Lions, nothing else.'

'Lions?' asked Paul puzzled.

'Confucius,' stated Wood.

'What?'

'Doesn't matter. Anyway get off the phone and get my work done,' Wood said with friendly irony. He wondered whether Paul would bite or whether he would react negatively.

'Already on it,' Paul began. Wood was relieved and he was not surprised by the speed of Paul's u-turn. 'You seem to be the only clown in town – not,' said Paul. 'Your column's popularity with the public is not that they love you, it's more. After this prediction, they absolutely need you.'

'Thanks Paul. Go away and finish the work,' said Wood, jokingly.

'I'll ring you,' said Paul enthusiastically.

'Tonight?' asked Wood.

'Tonight,' he confirmed.

Wood went into his living room, grabbed his laptop from the coffee table and continued to watch the news. The engineer had repaired his computer and delivered it to Wood's apartment, 'finally,' he thought when he received it. He saw that the American stock markets had begun to fall with breathtaking speed. 'The big money across the world is starting to run and hide,' said Wood, talking to himself, as he settled his computer on his knee and logged onto Bloomberg.com to read the editorial headlines. As the website loaded on his computer, Wood watched his telly and listened to a lady in a shopping mall being interviewed by a CNBC reporter. He asked her why she thought the credit crunch had started and she replied, 'Greedy bankers I would guess. What I don't understand is what all these highly intelligent men in businesses and governments were doing. I mean, how did they allow all this to happen?'

'Intelligent?' Wood questioned and smiled. 'Lions are not required to be bright,' he thought. When the website came on display he clicked onto the news and he laughed as his eyes darted across the words that were displayed. But the irony hurt; Hoary was getting ahead; liquidity and money were being drained from the commercial world at an unprecedented rate and his bank, ITCD International had plenty of it in reserve. As the chairmen and CEOs of the world began to face their darkest fears, the calm resolve of Hoary would underline his credibility in the eyes of the elite. Wood read.

"Now that the $700 billion bailout bill has failed to pass, Paulson has said that the liquidity crisis has spread beyond Wall Street, threatening earnings at businesses from retailers to technology companies. The treasury's toolkit to protect the financial system is 'substantial but insufficient'."

"I absolutely cannot believe it,' said David Cosper, Chief Financial Officer of Sonic Automotive Inc., the third largest U.S. publicly traded auto retailer. ' I don't think the House knows what they're doing. We need this, the markets are frozen, banks are being taken over – it's a crisis. I think they're leaving it in the lurch and going on a break."

'Leaving it in the lurch,' thought Wood. 'A two day holiday. The world can gasp and despair, and unmitigated fear was about to be kindled but the lions must have their lunches. How else can they kill?' The stock markets closed with an emphatic thud and the news readers on the television marvelled with the hype that they could begin to recount. Wood flicked the channels from Bloomberg to BBC to CNBC to Fox. They were all at it, proclaiming their words, projecting their sentiments in the new climate as history was being made. The objectivity of their reports changed to the epic sentences, the legendary remarks and the hallmarks of mythology that would hook the audience and capture the numbers away from the soaps. Wood flicked back to Bloomberg where Nancy Pelosi, the U.S. House speaker was in recourse, pointing the finger of blame at the U.S. President, George Bush. The Democratic Senators were pointing at the Republicans for being non-partisan and the Republicans were saying that the bailout plan was ill conceived and useless in application. A new headline appeared on the Bloomberg website.

"Executives from across corporate America echoed the remarks…They called on lawmakers to put aside partisan differences and work to restore credit supplies and confidence to the financial markets. The Standard & Poor's 500 index has tumbled the most since 1987 and

the Dow Industrial Average slid 778 points, the most
points ever."

The U.S. stock markets had taken a hammering with the Dow Jones
Industrial index falling by 7% and the NASDAQ decreasing by 9%.
Wood realised that his predictions had been precise and he wondered
how he had been so accurate. He knew that the impact would be
devastating to the stock markets but he hadn't exactly got his calculator
out. 'Intuition,' he thought. In the aftermath of his commercial
achievements and the demanding heights of personal accountability that
he had achieved, Wood rarely doubted his ability to trust himself. Even
the idea of *doubt* was questionable. He knew what was about to happen,
how it would unfold and he saw a conclusion that only one other man
shared with him. 'Everybody else,' he thought. 'Is facing absolute
torture until this is finally resolved.'

The largest businesses in America were having their financial
resources taken from them at a speed never before witnessed in history
and their ferocious battle with insolvency had begun with venom.
Tomorrow the European stock markets would feel this impact and so
would their businesses. The frightening thing for them all was that
nobody had seen this coming. The phone rang.

'Have you seen the stock markets?' Stan asked excitedly. 'Fuck, I
just burnt my fucking finger.'

'Yes. You are not alone. I reckon a whole host of traders have just
had their fingers burnt,' said Wood, jumping on the moment, becoming
increasingly aware of the pain people would face.

'How the fuck did you get that one right? You were spot on,' said
Stan enthusiastically.

'Yes. I wish I hadn't been,' said Wood, compassionately.

'Tane, this is not the first fucking time. I'm selling more fucking
papers. Jones loves me. What else have you got?' Stan asked
desperately.

'The full story for the next five hundred years if you want it.'

'Very fuckin' funny. Look, I can write you in twice weekly. I'll
speak to fuckin' Jones in the morning but I know he'll agree. What d'ya
say?'

'Come on Stan, you know what I want. I need you to print it.'

'Too fuckin' ambitious. The fuckin' readers aren't interested,' Stan
said dismissively.

'Have you tried?' asked Wood.

'Tane, I've sold too many fuckin' papers. Come on, twice weekly, what d'ya say?' Stan insisted, sucking his finger.

'No. I want to meet you and Jones. This week?' demanded Wood.

'Wood. Think about it for fuckin' Christ's sake. Take it while you can. Life's too fuckin' short. Next month you're fuckin' nobody.'

'Wednesday, 2pm.' Wood hung up and the fax machine hummed into action. He knew that his battle would be with Trevor Hoary and him alone. Nobody else would believe him and, even if he tried, their natural reaction would be to dismiss his assertions. Stan wouldn't engage the idea. He simply needed to sell papers and keep Jones wealthy.

The page on the fax machine was from Paul. Wood sent him an email informing him that his computer had been returned and was now working fine. 'Alive and kicking,' Wood had commented at the end of his email. The message on the fax read:

> Rifling through the list. Should finish by 11am, Tuesday. Thought you'd like this one.
>
> Item 121.
>
> The ideas abound with the subject of a disruptive technology. Basically it seems to concentrate on the way in which new technologies alter and change the social order or status quo. Clayton Christensen first coined the phrase when he claimed that disruption leads to physical demands that far exceed the capacity social norms can handle. For instance, trains and boats brought a wave of immigrants to countries that were not yet comfortable with foreign cultures. The attitudes of populations take time to evolve - through death, rebirth and adoption of new beliefs – but the disruption proliferates rapidly. In this example the xenophobia would exist much longer than the antiquated means of transportation. The essence of a 'disruptive technology' is significant change, adaptation and painful shift. An emphatic disruptive technology – not cited, but comes to my mind – is the impact of the supermarket conglomerates on the corner shop boys. In the seventies and eighties the big boys used their cash power to multi-site and wipe out the competition. They still do it today.

The term 'technology' is used – in part –
metaphorically. Examples cite social and economic
change in the main, alongside technology. I guess,
extrapolating from this that at their turbulent extreme,
these disruptions could be apocalyptic. Take, for
example global warming or global cooling (whatever
they now call it) which could be seen to be a disruptive
technology. The ambitions of men run away with
themselves before the impact is realised. This
unforeseen conclusion seems less sinister than the
presumptions made by Tom Peters in his book 'The
Circle of Innovation'. He describes how Destruction Is
Cool! The Chief Executive Officer, CEO should be
aptly renamed the CDO, Chief Destruction Officer and
his primary objective is to kill; it is easier to kill an
organization - and reshape it - than to change it
substantially. Downsizing any business takes too long
and costs too much money hence the CDO should learn
to swallow it: Destruction is Job number 1 and if you
don't the competition does it to you. His book illustrates
the seemingly psychotic precedent needed to overcome
the fears prevalent in corporate survival and expansion.
For example, from chapter three; *'Treachery tolerated.
Jumping from company to company...swapping secrets
over brews or the latest-release Chardonnay...or across
the Nautilus machines...The Valley is not the home to
traditional loyalty. The ideas flow...and flow. Such
Brownian motion is one of its success keys.'*
By the way; Confucius - Got it. 'It is better to have a
lion at the head of an army of sheep than a sheep at the
head of an army of lions'. Bush or Brown? I opt for
both. PS. Do lions have brains? PPS. Have I got
something outstanding on the mortgage market? I'll get
you the detail. ITCD bank is romping it. Globally!
Hoary is the new king! Or will be. Don't agree that we
need to lock up our wives and daughters though.

'Damn,' thought Wood. 'Damn, damn and damn.' He needed Paul
on *his* side to defeat Hoary. The last thing he wanted was Paul to

commence hero worship with the wrong man. Wood knew that Paul was a great researcher – the best he could hope to have. Stan took pleasure in constantly reminding Wood that he was lucky to have him. 'You mean that you're lucky that you haven't,' Wood had thought.

Whilst Paul wasn't the easiest person to manage, Wood had sensed that he was now onside following their conversation earlier but he realised that he still needed to work on Paul. Wood decided to ring him and picked up his phone. He rang Paul's mobile number but there was no answer which was not like Paul. He lived by his phone and he seemed to need it more than he needed to eat. Wood tried it again and again, there was no answer.

TUESDAY – ANALYSTS

London, September 30th 2008

Hoary hated board meetings. The mere fact that agendas had to meet collective agreement proved to him that few men were bright. He was demonstratively fed up with the views of other men and especially those of his executive colleagues. 'If they have an opinion share it with their spouse and save us the torture,' he would say. But he would not defeat protocol and intolerably, he knew that it was the meeting of the collective view; everything must be said and everyone must say it. 'Why take the chance,' Hoary had always thought, 'It will only lead to disaster.'

There lay the opportunity, he had surmised and he had done so for many years before he had been appointed to Chairman for the ITCD International Bank. His role was a true reflection of his ambition. Few, if any, could match that. Now he was almost sixty years of age he wanted that ambition realised and he knew that it was only a matter of time until it was. Even that frustrated him. After all he had played every trick in the book many times over and he had always won. He was fed up with waiting for the glory to be splashed all over him – publicly.

The end was beckoning and he had no intention of being recycled by St. Peter and sent back down to earth. Most people feared the pending Armageddon. Hoary did not wish to suffer the same fate that resulted from the denial of men. When the going got too tough, finding someone to blame was their main agenda and if that failed, they could always blame God. It was accepted practice nowadays by almost everyone. For him, the toilet we called Earth was a shithole from which to escape and he knew that this could only be achieved if you could conquer the truth.

'How few men ever get anywhere close,' he had once said to his bishop following his experiences whilst employed by the Anglican Church.

'Don't fear the men and women who live on the earth,' his bishop had once told him. 'Fear the men and women who built what we have today.' Hoary had believed the words of his superior and his ambitions had focused on putting this matter right. He was driven to bring it all down and start again. A bright, fresh, engaging new start for everyone but whilst he got on with the task of doing exactly that, he didn't want the men and women who live today to get in his way.

This morning, at 6am, Hoary was sitting at his desk preparing for the board meeting that was starting in two hours. It was not uncommon for Hoary to do this every working day but today, for him, was crucial for the delivery of his ambitions. The pre-submissions from his Main Board regarding the agenda for today's meeting had indicated a strong bias towards a vote in favour of the disposal of their American lending company, Housefrank. Hoary could not let this happen and he knew that the sentiment was not just a paperwork expression; the rumblings had crossed his path from numerous conversations he had heard or been told about in the corridors of power that his executive colleagues frequented. Inevitably, the exposé in the Financial Tribune over a year ago had unsettled his fearful colleagues and they still referred to it now. Hoary was rifling through his records to refresh his memory of the article.

Housefrank was losing substantial amounts of money in America and it was supposed to. That was exactly what Hoary wanted but he knew that his colleagues did not see it that way. Housefrank unnerved them – shareholders needed to be answerable too - but it offered Hoary the opportunity to gain market share in the mortgage market across more countries and more consumers than any other bank in the world. And everything was going to plan. The vote today was crucial and he had to win it. Their defeat would be in the detail and this could be found in the submission his press department had made to the newspapers early last year. The detail, Hoary knew, was the tripping hazard of even the best laid plans – a place where nobody ever went no matter how much they convinced themselves that they had been there.

'Ah hah. Found the devil,' he said as he thumbed the pages of the Financial Tribune newspaper, published: March 14 2007. He folded the paper on the page displaying the article and read.

ITCD rues the result of its Sub Prime run in

Only four years ago Sir Kevin Charles, then Chairman of ITCD, presented a detailed analysis of his track record on acquisitions. His conclusion was that although ITCD had made some mistakes, its large acquisitions had proved to be successful.

It is just as well that Sir Kevin, who stepped down in 2005, is no longer around. Any presentation to ITCD's board today would have to start with an admission that the banks largest-ever deal - the $16bn acquisition of Housefrank, the US consumer finance group - has been a colossal failure.

Yesterday ITCD spelled out the damage it has suffered from its foray into lending to US consumers with poor and patchy credit records. Its North American division, predominantly Housefrank, set aside $13.2bn for bad loans last year, up 77 per cent on 2006, as the meltdown in the subprime mortgage market spread to other areas of its business. The increase meant that ITCD's North American business, which accounts for a sixth of the bank's assets, made no money.

Yet ITCD yesterday told a tale of two banks. In spite of the calamity in the US and the turmoil in the credit markets, it continues to thrive in Europe, Asia and Latin America. As a result, pre-tax profits rose 11 percent to reach a record $21bn.

Hoary, Sir Kevin's successor as Chairman, yesterday hailed the bank's geographic diversity, and its past investments into emerging markets, as a source of strength. "For ITCD to achieve another new high in earnings, despite these conditions and the exceptionally weak performance of our US business, underscores the value of the strategic focus we announced early last year to drive sustainable growth by concentrating on faster growing markets of the world," he said.

But his comments could not dispel the conclusion that, if ITCD had not bought Housefrank, it would be in a much stronger position today.

For Hoary and Michael Houndsworthy, ITCD's Chief Executive, the question is what to do now. There is little prospect of any immediate recovery in the US.

"It appears that what started as a small part of the total US mortgage market is slowly spreading to other areas as house prices fall," said Spencer Hogkard, an analyst at Nouse International. Bad debt charges for ITCD's US credit card division rose to $2.6bn last year, an increase of 81 per cent.

"The economic slowdown and the credit outlook in the US may well get worse before they get better," Hoary said. Jan Hordon, an analyst at Exane BNP, said he expected bad debt provisions in the US this year to be around $11bn-$12bn, similar to in 2007.

Arthur Kinke, the US activist investor, has argued that ITCD should consider jettisoning or spinning off ITCD Finance Corporation, as Housefrank is now called. But executives dismissed as "unthinkable and irresponsible" the notion that the bank could somehow walk away from the business, which has outstanding bonds of around $160bn.

"It would be inconceivable that one of our subsidiaries would be allowed to default," Michael Houndsworthy said.

Indeed, executives argue that the huge losses and the closure of the securitization markets on which many sub-prime lenders depended for funding, has put ITCD in a position to take advantage when the economy recovers. In particular, executives believe there is an opportunity to target Hispanic immigrants in the US by exploiting the links with ITCD's existing operations in Latin America.

Analysts acknowledge that, given the current state of the US economy and the financial markets, ITCD has no choice but to try to turn around the operations, though they think it may consider a sale in the future.

In the meantime, ITCD is likely to continue its efforts to shift its focus to emerging markets - a move that was underlined last week when it announced a provisional deal to sell part of its French retail banking operations. Yet it is unclear just how buoyant those emerging markets will be in future years.

ITCD executives acknowledge that a US slowdown is bound to affect the rest of the world, particularly countries such as Mexico and Taiwan, which are heavily dependent on exports to the US. But there is no sign of this happening so far.

"This is probably not going to be a 2008 event," Michael Houndsworthy said.

The bank is still hopeful that it can complete a deal to buy a controlling stake in China Exchange Bank, China's sixth-largest lender, even though regulators are unlikely to approve the transaction before it expires at the end of May.

If the deal goes ahead, ITCD's shareholders are likely to be paying close attention to make sure that the deal lives up to the bank's initial expectations.

'You need the vote today Trevor or you're scuppered,' said Michael entering Hoary's office spilling his coffee as he moved the door handle with his cup laden hand. Several folders under his arm had crippled the use of his other hand. 'If you lose Housefrank, the Americans will dissect it and your game is up.'

'Morning Michael,' said Hoary. 'How is Kevin today? Still fighting for King and Country?'

'Yes. Completely. Moved further up his own arse I hear and, better still, he is vehemently routing for your scalp. He'll definitely vote against you. Out of spite I hope.'

'And our allies?' asked Hoary, seemingly ignoring the jibe but he never did. Hoary held considerable respect for his friend's observations and political quips.

'Yes. Spoke to them all. You are still their King. I begged with the Gods but they merely whimpered in submission. The bad news is that you'll have their vote.' Michael sipped his drink and several drips fell onto his jumper.

'And the others?'

'Arsehole, twat and weasel. Kind statements but they summed you up quite nicely. I'm afraid that they still confuse morals with rampaging opportunity to win market share.'

'Good,' Hoary affirmed.

'Kevin is your best bet. Can't stand you at the moment though and he does enjoy his ability to hate people. Especially you it would seem. There is hope.' Kevin Fitzgerald was Hoary's Group Operations Director and Hoary held the view that his current operations were dysfunctional.

'What's his Achilles Heel?' asked Hoary. His head remained down as he spoke to Michael. He was reading the article again.

'Apart from working class grass roots and being a football fan?' began Michael disparagingly. 'He drinks as well, so I've heard.'

'Unstable?'

'Definitely. But you won't beat him on that. He's in today and he's in to vote. Against you by all account. I do hope so,' said Michael facetiously.

'Anything else?' asked Hoary.

'Yes, unfortunately there is.'

'Go on,' Hoary settled back into his chair.

'He hates analysts. More than paedophiles apparently.'

'And?'

'Young chap called…Matt. Good looking boy. Analyst for Marketing One. He's presenting the next steps to your marketing campaign. Kevin gloriously despises him; the cause of a few arguments with his wife, apparently. She was seen in town with our young analyst.'

'Wasn't Matt the brain behind my new brand design?' Hoary enquired.

'Yes indeed he was. Bright little bugger I hear. Great brand too. Focus groups said it was crap. Bound to be a roaring success. The posters are already in all our branches. They go up for public display today.'

'What time...?' Hoary looked at his watch. 'Are we on?'

'We are and thankfully, we're late. The abyss beckons.'

As they entered the boardroom the executives were all present and Hoary and Michael, after a humble bow of the head from each, took their seats. Hoary always chose to sit in an upright position with his shoulders back and his chest out. Michael was much more relaxed and draped an arm over the back of his seat in similar fashion to many of his colleagues. The analysts from the lower floor had already begun their appraisals and a young employee, Bruce, with a flamboyant pink tie, was holding the floor. The knot around his neck was wide enough to obscure his collar and it looked out of sorts against his shirt which was tightly fitted about his skinny frame. When Hoary and Michael had settled in their seats, Bruce continued.

'...And, let us take a closer look at the ITCD Bank in the trading sphere now. Since February 2007, the grey hair wisdom of our beloved Hoary has guided us to increase the market capitalisation of this company to £111,785,700; now bigger than BP and the largest market cap company in the UK. We now top the FTSE and our position in the league of world banks has risen from 5th to 2nd. By April 2008, we reported in our internal Corporate Magazine that our market share for world consumer mortgages had increased by 8% in the last twelve months; 9.2% to be more precise. Our magazine indicated towards a sharp and prolonged economic downturn. We did not indicate a 'V' or a 'U' but instead we emphasised *'prolonged'*. For the majority of banks in the US and Europe, their share price today has dropped in excess of 50% from their 12 month high. In fact, a large majority have witnessed share price lows in excess of 70, 80, and 90 even 95 percent from their 52 week high. Today, the ITCD bank share price traded at 929.00 after a 20% upward shift on Tuesday. Twelve month high 982.00 (15/10/2007). Price per earning ratio 12.84. Relative p/e 1.234. ROE 17.179. It just gets better and better. Well done, everyone. We are the pride of the City.'

'And our cash position?' asked Piers, the Finance Director, more than aware of the answer. Piers Johnson was a slender framed man barely five feet tall. His officious style was his trade mark and he had little tolerance for anything remotely emotional. 'Why use people? Calculators are more than sufficient,' he had once famously said.

'Well, we maintain a loans to deposit ratio of 0.8; the strongest in the world.'

'Please explain the ratio once again?' asked Piers. He was determined to drive home his advantage.

'For every £80 we have out on loan we have £100 on deposit.'

'In the vault, to be more precise. We may be the strongest in the world but more importantly we are the most resilient. Compared to the highly ambitious, greedy, rapidly expanding new boys who came to the party after 1997, we will not be facing the Administration of her Majesty's Insolvency practitioners. We will survive as I always said we would do. Not fall foul to the FSA like so many of the floundering wide boys who thought they owned the show.' Piers smiled with a self approval that he shared with all his team sat around the table. Only a few eyes met with his as he did the rounds.

When the sunshine finally broke through the cloud and dropped rays upon the boardroom table through the windows to the east, Hoary rose from his chair and walked to the west. He always looked out of the window by habit but this time he chose to get closer. His eyes rarely focused on the view but instead glazed and rolled in his thoughts. He didn't see the storm clouds drifting away, out of sight. The meeting dragged on and Hoary remained at the window listening to the views being expressed from those at the table. By noon he had hoped they would be further along but Kevin had spurned the time keeper on numerous occasions and she had given up her protests. He seemed to be proud of his verbal flow today and allowed all those present to accompany his glory. Time had been squandered but it needed to be, thought Hoary. The voting that needed to be cast could be hurriedly passed through. Hopefully, there would not be enough time to even cast the vote.

Matt from Marketing One was beginning his presentation and announced the success of Hoary's new brand displays. 'Mounting and display will be finalised in all stores by the end of today, in line with deadline.' Hoary saw Kevin's discomfort with this news. Kevin had opposed this implementation vehemently saying that it was too subtle and that the consumer wouldn't get it. Within the first thirty seconds, Matt had reminded the audience that the 'consumer's primary agenda was the agenda of the bank'. On the fourth occasion, Hoary cut across him.

'The consumer's primary agenda is…I suppose I must give you credit for not recycling the adage that the consumer is king. Matt, please sit down for one moment.' Hoary moved from the window and returned to his seat. This time he did notice the storm clouds disappearing beyond the horizon. Hoary felt that they had done so at his request.

'We do just tolerate things don't we? Thankfully, there must always come a time when the adversity must make us consider and marketing certainly has the edge on all of us with this earthly challenge. I think, Matt that the consumer is not the consumer that you want him…or her, to be. May be that consumer lives in a world where reasonable actions result in reasonable behaviours. I think this might be your world but the truth is that you are alone.

'Look around you. Look at our people. Rousseau was wrong. Maybe he was just an alcoholic all the time. The 'blind multitude' does not see the lie, he claimed. And what a lie was that? What could we not see?

As a young man and since, I have walked through many fields of cows and of bulls and I have trodden in their debris. They are the most inquisitive animal and when I walk amongst them they fail to leave me alone but it is easy to keep them happy. In their environment there is little to do but eat, sleep and breed. They seem oblivious to the objective of the men that farm them and of the fate that awaits them.

A faint cry of sympathy is heard for Daisy but the decisions of men choose not to hear this or they choose to hide the fate of Daisy from our children. But the truth is about us and cannot be denied. We tread in their shit and they tread in ours. Their Armageddon is universal, it is all around them and it has been for many, many years.

We can forgive them for their ignorance and we must forgive ourselves for ours because when we build norms it is our people who accept them because the faint hearts do not wish to upset the angry, affluence of our verbal and vociferous kings.

In the credit crunch, we have already forgotten how bad our fears were in April. Today, those fears have come and gone and it has become worse still but our happiness must go on.

There is no Armageddon. We have already built it and we have lived with it. It has come and nestled in. It only exists as a fear and fears have no truth.

There is only one truth and it is not that we do not know it. It is that our kings have screamed at us to forget it.

And to suppress our revolt they have built for us a world of distraction of holidays and cars, of clothes and of houses.

And they have built for us a world of repair of pubs and of clubs, of brothels and snooker halls, of golf courses, boxing rings and football stadiums. It was easy for them to distract our unhappiness. Like me, I'm sure you can smell the stench just thinking about it.

I wonder if the credit crunch was born of our revolt against the ephemeral of our distractions or of our kings' revolt against our lack of appreciation for them. Have the 'new money' merchants, the rag boys, rocked the boat too far?

It is not the material world that stands to be blamed but that the opportunity cannot be shared. The resources that we would need do not sit with the ambitions of the kings that send our cows to the slaughter. And whilst our visionaries do not surface, we are denied the opportunity to make our own mistakes and educate towards our future.

There has only ever been one God and one son, Jesus Christ. Gandhi asked to give 'India back to India', Mandela battled for freedom from Apartheid, Wallace died for freedom from the oppression imprisoning his Scotland and Luther King fought for freedom for all races. These are God's chiefs but only one man defined no boundaries and defined one vision.

I often pray, for pity's sake that somebody needs to piece this all back together. But whilst this does not emerge then there is only one truth. Consumers have no God given right. The political quip that rationalises their endless pursuit for money can take any form but in marketing you have simply mastered the art of organising and perpetrating the lie. I don't want to be told that the consumer is king. The consumer is a person and in the plural they are the people. Their one goal is to fleece the world according to their agenda and that agenda only has one language – money.'

'But surely Trevor, we are all consumers and merely by their greater number they will always win. We have to do what they say and give them what they want,' Matt gulped, having plucked up the courage to speak.

'Yes we do. Angry multitudes cannot be contained. But see the consumer for what they truly are and don't confuse that with misguided morals.'

'And what is that, Trevor?' asked Matt.

'People merely take the oxygen from the trees.' When Hoary relieved Matt moments later he told him that he had no need to finish his presentation. 'You may go and I am afraid that you will have no need to return to your employer. You will only be wasting your time. By the time you get back one of the loyal vermin that you see around me will have made a fatal call to your boss. Why give your boss the pleasure.'

When Matt had left the boardroom they broke for a coffee. Kevin said to Michael, 'What's rifled Trevor? What was all that about? I mean Matt's a spineless bugger but I haven't seen Trevor like that before. Has he been taking lessons in the pulpit?'

'If only,' said Michael. 'What fun we could have with his demise. But I fear it is no simpler than him having second thoughts on the promotional campaign. I guess you were right all the way along. I would guess further, that Trevor knows that.'

'About time,' said Kevin.

'Oh, I don't know,' said Michael. 'I think Trevor has got more time for you than you think. He is never an easy foe at the best of times.' Kevin looked Michael in the eye, drank his coffee and crumpled his cup. Kevin thought of all those people that he himself had crumpled, muttered 'right' and made for the boardroom. When the corporate council called the vote on Housefrank, Hoary's strategy was upheld by one vote. Following the board meeting Kevin rang Piers and said, 'I told Trevor from the off that Housefrank could build market share in America.'

When Matt had answered the phone to his wife, he had found it very easy to accept her demand for him to escape the office and meet her in a café at 3pm. He had decided that he would not spoil her good humour and allow her the space to break the good news to him. It was obvious from her voice that she had something to tell him. When they met and sat down with their coffee, Matt wondered when would be the best time to tell her that he had lost his job. After all, his wife had just made it considerably more difficult. Maybe, thought Matt, he could pretend to go to work every day until the news he had just heard finally came to life and the baby was born.

'Kevin is such a dream. He loves you,' said Michael, sitting in Hoary's office. He spilt his coffee on the floor and shook his hand to remove the hot liquid. 'And I was so delighted to watch you concede on the slogan. I've had Margaret memo all the branches requesting them to remove the banners. Our employees across the southern hemisphere will enjoy that being added to their shift on a Friday. You have denied thousands of people their valuable Friday night foray. You never know, you may have helped the odd desperate recession junkie landlord finally see his cash flow eradicated. The things you do for humanity. Anyway, who cares? You won the vote. Lovely Kevin obeyed you willingly.'

Hoary was and remained writing at his desk as Michael spoke. 'Designing a new slogan already?' asked Michael.

'No. Not my forte. Anyway, I want the material back up in the stores by next week. I can't let mindless executives stop me.' Hoary shook his pen and looked at it as though it had been found guilty of a crime.

'So what do you want me to do?' Michael crossed his legs.

'I don't know,' Hoary said, continuing to write. 'Get a memo in circulation saying pensions and remuneration are under review for senior executives or something?'

'And?'

'Call Flis in. Give her a substantial rise, make her pension golden and let her go. She'll go quietly and if not it doesn't matter. Either way, get her out. '

'Why Flis?' asked Michael.

'She's head of marketing. Get rid of her and replace her with Matt. I like him. Bright lad. I want my slogans back up and you make sure he has the authority to see to that,' Hoary responded without emotion.

'I believe our board has reached agreement that the slogans must be replaced? You conceded?'

'No I didn't. I merely kicked Matt out. We immediately broke for a coffee as I recall. No vote was cast.' Hoary shook his pen again and tutted.

'Ah, the wonderful prologue on humanity. And you nearly made me cry,' said Michael, admiringly.

'Get Matt in. I understand he isn't doing anything at the moment and the knock will do him well. Get him on his toes ready for his prosperous new career with me.'

'I almost sense an air of optimism. Is it Valentine's Day already?'

'Don't run away with yourself. I do like the occasional analyst. They trust themselves and they tell it like it is. They've never got a clue what is really going on but that helps.' Michael got up to leave and Hoary added. 'And while you're at it, get rid of Kevin as well. Did I recruit him?'

'You did. Gloriously, if I remember correctly.'

'And remind me not to interview board members again,' said Hoary. His pen finally ran out of ink and he tossed it into the bin, accurately, from five feet away.

WEDNESDAY – GREY STREAKS

New York, October 1st, 2008

Thirty three days before Barack Obama wins the Presidency for the U.S. the country he will inherit is collapsing. In Cibeuce, Dace is watching with his feet up, having a fag and stroking his neatly cropped, newly grown goatee beard. In the White House, President Bush is wondering how he will avoid being remembered as the worst President in history.

Jones Alwyn, a very large bodied Welshman who loved city life, moved to Manhattan, New York in 1962 and began building a media conglomerate that now rivalled Times Warner. To acknowledge his transition from his native land to becoming a fully pledged American citizen he had changed his name from Alwyn Jones. This, he believed, allowed him to recognise his new nationality in a country that had been good to him. The rolling hills and valleys of his youth had been replaced with a bustling hub of commercial energy and opportunity and he had thrived on it. 'The people are awesome,' he said, repeatedly. 'Ready to do whatever it takes – awesome.' When he said this, those who heard him thought he was Australian. His accent did seem to change as though he was role playing with his excitement and the characteristic wasn't isolated to this scenario alone. He ran his companies in a hugely active role but never took a title. All his correspondence simply referred to him as 'Al' including his business cards, letters, name plaques and the registration plate on his Rolls Royce. All of these were printed in gold emboss on a gold background as was his stationery. Jones considered it to be his personal trademark and he loved them to be visible all around him. The city networks also knew him as 'Al'. The only exception was

Stan, who called him Jones and nobody ever knew why he did this including Jones.

'This is fuckin' great,' said Stan, absent-mindedly fixing a straw between his top lip and his nose. Jones glanced at him as he did this and thought that he looked like a duck. Stan was in Jones's office watching the television sets that constantly remained on view in the office. There were twenty one of them tuned in. Every sentiment and every incident on every news station across the globe was being watched. 'Think of the sales.'

News reporters across the channels were reporting the economic woe and Jones and Stan couldn't take their eyes off them.

> 'Led by a 37% slump in car sales at Nissan, August saw similar drops at Ford, 34%, 33% at Chrysler, 32% at Toyota and 24% at Honda. Industry wide, car sales declined 26%.'

> 'Credit markets have frozen as financial institutions hoard cash to meet future funding needs amid deepening concern that more banks will collapse.'

> 'Interbank rates have soared draining cash from needy banks. Governments in Europe and the U.S. rescued six financial institutions in the past week.'

> 'Lenders are balking at offering cash for longer than a day even as central banks pump an unprecedented amount of cash into the banking system.'

> 'There are a lot of bids but no offers," said Pang Meng Yam, a money market dealer at KBC bank NV in Singapore. "There's no lending, most money markets are frozen and the discrepancy between benchmark rates and the actual trading rates are getting wider.'

'Have you heard the stiffs,' said Jones pointing at the BBC America channel. 'I think they're finally waking up to the crisis.' Jones had been in London on Monday and he had been surprised that the crisis had not been front page news and top of the television news agendas. Even the collapse of Lehman Brothers had only featured on page three of the majority of the nationals. In America, nobody had spoken about anything else for the last six months but even the U.S. citizens had not realised how defining this was about to get.

> 'That's a graphic illustration of how the horrors of the financial economy are infecting the real economy,' said Robert Peston, BBC economic correspondent. 'Like for like sales had fallen 6.1% in the 13 weeks to 27th September. In the previous quarter sales had dropped by 5.3%.This significant sales drop at Marks and Spencer meant that they would be placing far fewer orders than planned with other businesses.'

> Sir Stuart Rose, M&S Chairman said, "Our capital expenditure this year is now expected to be around £700m, compared to our previous guidance of £800 - £900m."

> Robert Peston continued, 'According to a Bank of England report, Britain's banks and building societies are set to make even more cutbacks in their lending. With economic conditions worsening, more borrowers are expected to default on their loans. In August, mortgage lending dropped to 5% of the figure reported in July and that is 98% down year on year. The amount of the UK overall mortgage debt was now beginning to reduce. Lenders reported that the changing economic outlook, their expectations for the housing market, and changes in their appetite for risk had contributed to the decline in credit availability.'

> Robert Peston went on to illustrate the economic problem as a series of cogs, inter connected and not moving smoothly.

The twenty one television sets were not arranged in any symmetrical order or hung neatly from the walls as you may expect in a Home or Media exhibition that had been installed with the particular flair of a set designer but instead they sat precariously around the room on piles of newspapers or cabinets that were too small for them or anywhere that seemed randomly out of place. Each TV was always set at the same volume as the rest and visitors were constantly amazed at Jones's ability to tune in at any moment to a particular channel and recite or exclaim at

the latest article. It didn't seem to matter which language he was
listening to; he seemed to be able to understand all of them. Jones's
office was not particularly untidy but there was no form or shape to its
layout. There was certainly no obvious reason to have seven kettles in
one room but Jones had them. 'Now the auto industry is insolvent. It's
not just the banks. Who's next? I need to get my mate, Tane all over
this,' said Stan.

'Tane? What is it with this guy? What does he want now?' said
Jones, talking in an Australian accent.

'Don't worry about Tane, I'll sort him out.'

'Why does he want to see me?' asked Jones, changing his tone to the
epic orator of an unknown Australian. 'Again for Christ's sake.'

'You're the great man. Come on, they all want a fuckin' piece of
you. We're just the fuckin' scum. I'll deal with him.'

'Yeah?' Jones said, getting louder.

'Leave it with me. I'll deal with it.' Stan insisted.

'You said that last time.' Jones lowered an eyebrow as he looked at
Stan.

'Yes, I did.'

'What does he want?'

'Probably to save the fuckin' world. What do they all fuckin' want?
You know what they're like the moment they get fuckin' published.'

'By all account this guy probably can,' mused Jones. His voice
lowered and he sounded practical.

'Yes I'm sure he can. Look, I'll offer the fucker a slot twice weekly.
What d'ya think? Leave it with me. I'll sort it out.'

Stan left the room and rang Wood. 'Excellent fuckin' news. You've
hit the big time, big time. You're on. I got you it.'

'What time?' asked Wood.

'What time! Forget that lot. I've got you a slot twice weekly. Jones
loves you. You're going places my friend. He knows great talent when
it's staring him in the face. $15,000 a week you fucker. Within a month
I'll have you all over the U.S. as the man who won the credit crunch.
Leave it with...'

Wood put the phone down and dialled out to Paul. This time Paul
answered.

'Where have you been?' asked Wood worriedly.

'Look, I'm not doing the work on Hoary,' said Paul, concerned.

'What? I..I've been worried about you,' Wood stuttered.

'I spoke to Stuart Halogen as you asked me too and there's nothing in it. You're wasting your time.'

'No, get hold of Michael Houndsworthy, Hoary's CEO. Halogen's only China.'

'You're wasting all of our time Tane. Just drop it. Stan has been on the phone. He wants to know if your column will be ready for Friday. He said he can give you 'till Thursday 3pm. Oh, well done by the way.'

'Well done?' enquired Wood.

'Yeah, congratulations. You know, twice weekly.'

'Look Paul, forget Stan. I need your help.' Wood insisted, returning to his main focus.

'I'm not doing it. I've got to go now. Bye,' Paul hung up.

Wood tried to ring him straight back but Paul didn't answer. 'Paul is Paul, and will always be Paul,' thought Wood though he was not too alarmed with Paul's reticence. Wood knew that when he spoke to anybody around him at the moment they were all talking in an aggressive, obstructive manner. He had noticed for some time now that when he asked colleagues how they were planning for the future they couldn't even plan for tomorrow. He had asked business leaders, politicians and executives. They all gave him the same answer as though all the doors of opportunity had been firmly closed in their faces. The ensuing depression was taking its toll on the people.

Wood resolved to give Paul some space and although he was frustrated by Stan's compromise with a twice weekly column, he knew that gaining more public exposure would help him in the long run. As he took a seat on his sofa with his laptop on his knee, he decided to write Friday's column and give the reader something that would seriously open their eyes.

On the television across the room he saw that Question Time, showing on BBC America, was warming up to a heated debate. A member of the audience asked the panel about the credit crunch, 'How long and how bad?' Michael Heseltine, now the elder statesmen after he was defeated in the UK Prime Minister leadership Campaign in the 1990s, answered 'Nobody knows.'

The chairperson made reference to Robert Peston's highly acclaimed news article that had been repeated several times during the day and said; 'I guess that that's the great thing about economics; nobody knows how many cogs exist in the chain, how they interact and how much oil is needed.' Michael Heseltine added to Peston's comments and described the credit crunch as 'a major problem'. His expression displayed concern and bewilderment and not the emotion that had built his reputation as a man who cared passionately about the free market principles of a thriving, competitive economic enterprise.

Wood wondered when was the last time he had heard politicians use such alarmist language. He recognised that the concern for all our livelihoods was being expressed from all walks of life. Another member of the audience said, 'The great Walter Lippman, in his greying years, once said, "It requires wisdom to understand wisdom: the music is nothing if the audience is deaf."

'Madam, are you implying that there is no wisdom?' asked Michael Heseltine.

'You make your mind up,' the woman responded. 'Or maybe God only knows.'

'God will tell you that there is no such thing,' muttered Wood who had decided that if Stan wouldn't get him a meeting with Jones, he would. 'Bugger the Friday edition,' thought Wood. 'I need a Sunday statement. If they won't listen then I'll give them something to listen to.'

Wood switched off his television and silence prevailed, disturbed only by the aimless confusion of the noise from the streets outside. He had heard enough today of the unfolding crisis and, anyway, he knew what would happen, how it would continue and how it would end. He had been there personally. He logged on, clicked on his editorial folder, opened a new document and began to type.

Kill All The Christians
iReckon
Tane Wood
Sunday 5th October 2008

Hidden within the horror of the financial catastrophe is one unfathomable truth – The fall of the Roman Empire never died. The brutal cacophony of the last seven days has shattered hopes across the whole Empire. Violently angry voices are uniformly screaming from all tiers of our establishments begging the ancient wildcats to have their blood thirsty feed in the derelict arena of the Colosseum ruin. Rome has returned, not a new one but an old state.

Hungry ravishers – wild boars, bears and tigers – are
scurrilously salivating over human fodder and no man
could be offered more willingly than Emperor Bush
after the vote in the senate and his meagre attempt to
raise a triumphant thumbs up with the declaration that,
'This Bill will return us to long term economic
prosperity'. His bailout Bill could not be further from
the truth.

It was Wednesday evening and Wood was not concerned that
he was writing about events that would take place in two days
time. By Sunday, this would be two days old and the readership
would not know that his predictions had come true. These
predictions – to his Sunday readers – would already be true.

What did concern Wood was that he was about to provoke the wrath
of a world and his darkest fears entertained wretched scenes of the
vampire pack drawing blood from his neck, the neck of their unknown
victim. This time when they would scream at him, 'who on earth do you
think you are?' he would yell back, 'It is time to act, starting now.'

'I'm off to take on the world,' thought Wood. 'And this is going to
hurt.'

An hour and a half later, just before midnight, Wood finished his
article and he had trimmed the word count below 2000. He did not
hesitate to press the send button knowing how Stan would react.

Thursday – Natural Born Killers

On the top of the memo that lay in front of Hoary, Michael had handwritten a note.

'I don't know what you're up to – well I do – but you have thrown me a bit on this one. Anyway, I know how you love the razz and matazz of Hollywood – not – so I did this especially for you. Hope you loath it.'

From the porthole by his seat on the plane, Hoary looked down from thirty five thousand feet. The cloudless sky displayed only the water trails of other jets. The sea below looked a faint turquoise and very calm. He could see the faint outline of fishing trawlers and the white surf that dragged behind them. Large dark patches seemed to be visible below the surface of the water and Hoary recognised these as shadows from the clouds that broke the sunrays. 'Hang on,' he thought, taking a second look, peering with more intensity. 'There are no clouds.' He wondered if the shadows were something different. They seemed to be moving though he was a long way up. 'Are they whales or even, sharks,' he thought.

Hoary looked up at the lockers above him that draped from the ceiling of his corporate jet. He felt that all his days merged into this spectacle. At least it wasn't the usual view he had been accustomed to in the Spectrum S-33 Independent. The company had updated these to the Cirrus SR – a smaller model and less ostentatious but much faster in the air – in line with Hoary's instruction.

Hoary eyed the memo. He had several hours to spare before he touched down in Bermuda. He sipped from his raspberry tea and began to read.

Identifying the Killer Id

'It's tough at the top'. Is this a perception from the ranks below or a truth in the ranks above?

Corporate USA would believe that it comes from above because it debates, at its very highest level, the nature of the behaviours necessary to achieve outstanding success. The Hollywood industry would agree. It has made a killing recounting the actions of powerful men and women; their corruption, their politics, their wealth and their loves.

Ask the Psychologist about this and they will refer to a myriad of internal functions that deliver a response. The commercial world has struggled to incorporate these notions into its culture but new thinking does suggest that psychology – the only academic subject with no definition – may actually be the 'Study of Human Action.'

Here the elusive, intangible debate on behaviour may well begin. Instead of looking at what causes the response, we look at the consequence of the response and, more importantly, why. In the pursuit of this, we challenge the reader to investigate several cases and, to kick off, we start with Oliver Stone's dialogue that introduces his film JFK.

Ask yourself why there is always a price to pay?'

Hoary was interrupted by a call from Brendan. 'Trevor look, we are ok here aren't we?' Brendan sounded exasperated.

'How do you mean?'

'I mean the bank Trevor. Look, don't shit with me. This thing is turning out to be a real bloody mess. Real serious stuff,' said Brendan anxiously.

'What thing is a real mess?' Hoary feigned ignorance.

'Do you not know what is going on for fuck's sake?' Brendan was starting to panic. 'There is complete mayhem.' Hoary moved his phone a few inches from his ear. It was a habit he had when the person speaking was losing their composure.

'Brendan. Calm down. What is mayhem?'

'Johnston has just upped and left. Morris and Harper have also walked out. All the hedge fund boys are leaving in droves. There's even word that Fitzgerald has taken his family, cashed in his twenty million and buggered off to the Seychelles to sit the fucker out.'

'Yes, I've heard,' said Hoary. He knew that this was only the beginning of a mass exodus of employees in the financial industry.

'What? You know?'

'Yes, I do. What else have you heard?' said Hoary, intrigued.

'They're all doing it. Cashing in and buggering off to their luxury pads. The word is that they've getting out of the country while they can; sip cocktails on the beach for a couple of years and come back when the whole fucking mess has been sorted out,' Brendan spat.

'Yes it's not good,' said Hoary in a nonchalant tone.

'Not good? It's a complete bloody mess. How the hell is the bank going to make any money with our best men gone?'

'Brendan. Calm down man. Look, I'm in Bermuda for the next couple of days then I need to fly to Taiwan. Ring Michael can you and ask him to book you two on a jet. I could really do with a bit of support when I meet Mao. Get yourself over here. You'll enjoy the hospitality. I could do with bouncing ideas off a couple of trusted colleagues. This is going to be a tough deal but if we get it we're made.'

'Made?' asked Brendan, becoming calmer.

'Yes, made. This deal could be worth £50 billion over the next five years.'

'Really?'

'Brendan, the future is in the emerging nations. Forget the West.'

When Brendan hung up Hoary wondered if Brendan would get his act together doing the job he was paid to do rather than worry about what everybody else was doing. He knew that he could be here all day thinking about this issue. He decided he would take Michael's bait instead and he continued to read the memo. Moreover, he was intrigued with the idea that the behaviour of JFK was worthy of debate in the league of the greats.

'The conjunction of an immense military
establishment and a large arms industry is new in the
American experience. The total influence - economic,
political; even spiritual - is felt in every city, every
statehouse, every office of the Federal Government... In
the councils of government we must guard against the
acquisition of unwarranted influence, whether sought or
unsought, by the military industrial complex. The
potential for the disastrous rise of misplaced power
exists and will persist... We must never let the weight of
this combination endanger our liberties or democratic
processes. We should take nothing for granted...'

Hoary sensed the irony in the words he read. He was intrigued to
understand why somebody had seemed to deny the obvious. 'Wasn't
this President Eisenhower's speech,' he wondered. 'Was he trying to
plant the seed with the military complex?' Hoary concluded that this
was the only motivation for Eisenhower to have said this. Intrigued, he
continued to read the memo without emotion and awaiting further
golden nuggets. The events turned to November 1960, when Kennedy
narrowly won the election.

'He inherits a secret war against the Communist
Castro dictatorship in Cuba, a war run by the CIA and
angry Cuban exiles out of bases in the Southern United
States, Panama, Nicaragua and Guatemala. Castro is a
successful revolutionary frightening to American
business interests in Latin America - companies like
Cabot's United Fruit, Continental Can, and Rockefeller's
Standard Oil. This war culminates in the disastrous Bay
of Pigs invasion in April 1961, when Kennedy refuses
to provide air cover for the exile brigade. Of the 1600
men who invade, 114 are killed, 1200 are captured. The
Cuban exiles and the CIA are furious at Kennedy's
irresolution... Kennedy, taking public responsibility for
the failure, privately claims the CIA lied to him and
tried to manipulate him into ordering an all-out
American invasion of Cuba. He vows to splinter the
CIA into a thousand pieces and fires Director Allen

Dulles, Deputies Charles Cabell and Richard Bissell, the
top leadership of the Agency.'

'Kennedy vows to sign his own death warrant,' thought Hoary. He
wondered why the people who were watching these establishments
couldn't see what was right in front of their face. The devious,
manipulative operative mechanisms of such institutions as the CIA
could only be established by the devious, manipulative operatives from
within. 'Killer by day, killer by instinct,' he thought, thankful that his
corporate career had not plunged him into this arena.

'The CIA, however, continues its secret war on
Castro with dozens of sabotage and assassination
attempts under its ZR/RIFLE and MONGOOSE
programs - The Agency collaborates with organized
crime elements such as John Roselli, Sam Giancana,
and Santos Trafficante of Tampa, whose casino
operations in Cuba, worth more than a hundred million
dollars a year in income, Castro has shut down.'

'In October 1962, the world comes to the brink of
nuclear war when Kennedy quarantines Cuba after
announcing the presence of offensive Soviet nuclear
missiles 90 miles off American shores. The Joint Chiefs
of Staff and the CIA call for an invasion. Kennedy
refuses. Soviet ships with more missiles sail towards
the island, but at the last moment turn back. The world
breathes with relief but backstage in Washington,
rumours abound that J.F.K. has cut a secret deal with
Russian Premier Khrushchev not to invade Cuba in
return for a Russian withdrawal of missiles. Suspicions
abound that Kennedy is "soft on Communism."

'In the ensuing months, Kennedy clamps down on
Cuban exile activities, closing training camps,
restricting covert operations, prohibiting shipment of
weapons out of the country. The covert arm of the CIA
nevertheless continues its plan to assassinate Castro... In
March '63, Kennedy announces drastic cuts in the
defence budget. In November 1963, he orders the
withdrawal by Christmas of the first 1000 troops of the
16,000 stationed in Vietnam. He tells several of his

intimates that he will withdraw all Vietnam troops after the '64 election, saying to the Assistant Secretary of State, Roger Hilsman, "The Bay of Pigs has taught me one, not to trust generals or the CIA, and two, that if the American people do not want to use American troops to remove a Communist regime 90 miles from our coast, how can I ask them to use troops to remove a Communist regime 9,000 miles away?"... Finally, in August 1963, over the objections of the Joint Chiefs of Staff, the United States, Great Britain and the Soviet Union sign a treaty banning nuclear bomb tests in the atmosphere, underwater and in space...'

Hoary was impressed with the commitment and determination of John F. Kennedy and the resolve to exercise his power to drive peace. Hoary recognised the conflict JFK would have faced whilst being hounded and confronted by the salivating military dogs who wanted to exercise their deepest, snarling, defining DNA coding – the natural born killers. 'Only natural born killers can rise to the top of the natural born killers,' thought Hoary. 'Everybody else merely gets eaten. Greedy bankers suddenly seem much friendlier foe,' he thought.

'Early that fateful summer, Kennedy speaks of his new vision at the American University in Washington. He says. 'What kind of peace do we seek? Not a pax Americana enforced on the world by American weapons of war... We must re-examine our own attitudes towards the Soviet Union... If we cannot now end our differences at least we can help make the world safe for diversity. For, in the final analysis, our most basic link is that we all inhabit this small planet. We all breathe the same air. We all cherish our children's future. And we are all mortal...'

'And we all desperately need a purpose,' thought Hoary, sensing a moment of frustration. 'Why will nobody just say it? What are we; aimlessly wandering...' He caught himself in his anxiety and calmed down. He knew that he could hardly point the finger at JFK or anybody for that matter. He had as much responsibility to do it or say it as the next person. He sat back in his seat and settled in. His intentions had just received a firm kick up the backside.

'More rumours emerge of J.F.K.'s backdoor efforts outside usual State Department and CIA channels to establish dialogue with Fidel Castro through contacts at the United Nations in New York. Kennedy is seeking change on all fronts. Bitter battles are fought with Southern segregationists to get James Meredith into the University of Mississippi. Three months after Kennedy submits a sweeping civil rights Bill to Congress, Martin Luther King leads 250,000 in a march on Washington. Robert Kennedy, as Attorney General, for the first time ever vigorously prosecutes the Mafia in American life, bringing and winning a record number of cases - 288 convictions of organized crime figures including 13 grand juries against Jimmy Hoffa and his Teamsters Union. The President also takes on Big Business, forcing back steel prices, winning 45 of 46 antitrust cases during 1963 and he wants to help everyday taxpayers by ending age- old business privileges like the oil depletion allowance and the fees paid to the Federal Reserve Bank for printing America's currency. Revolutionary changes are foreseen after J.F.K.'s assumed re-election in 1964. Foremost in the political consciousness of the country is the possibility of a Kennedy dynasty. Robert Kennedy in '68, Teddy Kennedy in '76. In November, 1963 John Kennedy travels to Texas, his popularity sagging to 59% largely due to his civil rights stand for which he is particularly hated in the South. Texas is a crucial state for him to carry in '64. With him is Vice-President, Lyndon Johnson and Texas Governor John Connally. On November 21, they visit Houston and San Antonio. On the morning of November 22, he speaks in Fort Worth, then flies 15 minutes to Love Field in Dallas, where he takes a motorcade through downtown Dallas on his way to speak at 12:30 at the International Trade Mart. Later, the motorcade takes him through Dealey Plaza.'

Moments after, John F. Kennedy is shot by the CIA, Central Intelligence Agency.

Hoary spilt his camomile tea. He had lifted his memo from his lap to place it on the table in front of him and forgot that his drink was there. He was pleased that the stewardess had noticed his misdemeanour and she seemed to leap to his rescue. He thanked her for her diligence when the spillage was cleaned up. He thought about the final statement on the memo. He wondered how long the film was and considered whether it would take two hours to state the obvious.

Michael rang. 'Being entertained my friend?' Michael knew Hoary would be reading the memo and read it in every detail. Hoary always read the detail. The subject matter was material that Michael knew, he would love. This was important to Hoary and so was Michael because without him, he would be a soldier on the front line without any bullets.

'How do I begin to thank you?' said Hoary. Michael laughed at his sarcasm.

'Please don't. I've just eaten. Anyway, for my glorious leader I will do anything to please.'

'Good. Have you got Brendan on the plane?'

'My word he's lost the plot. Of course I have. I guessed that you thought the time was right?' Michael had not been surprised when Brendan rang and knew exactly what Hoary's intentions were.

'Indeed. He's completely spineless. We can trust him now.'

'Very good. Consider it done,' said Michael.

Hoary rang off and then realised he had forgotten to grill Michael. 'Surely all hell was breaking loose,' he thought and he dialled out.

'I forgot to ask,' said Hoary. 'Unlike me to do that.'

'Good. You're losing the plot too. The world will be mine after all,' quipped Michael.

'You are very welcome to it but, all the same fill me in. What's the form?'

'Well, it's simple really. The troops are fleeing in droves, fear is rife and the commercial world will collapse. What more could you want?' Michael was sitting in his chair in his office. He uncrossed his legs and relaxed.

'I saw the figures from the Auto Industry.'

'Yep. That's a biggee gone. GM will hit the wall. Their finance division is still trying to wail on by but it won't survive.' Michael explained.

'What about the retailers?' asked Hoary.

'Be patient. They'll fall off the cliff next month. The press are already being prepared.' Michael sat up in his seat.

'Is that too early? The press will get suspicious.'

'For a scoop,' Michael jibbed with irony. 'Well they can't do anything until it hits the public arena. The Retailers need to announce their results first.'

'Yes but they skew them.'

'They do. But there are enough of them to cock it all up. The big boys are answerable to the City and the shareholders and they'd be foolish to lie. They may hide but the newspapers can be primed to feed the fears of the shareholders. The difficult questions will be asked and the truth will come out. Anyway, you concentrate on the East. We need these acquisitions for the grand master plan. The Western economies are well on their way to collapse and I won't love you for anything less.'

'Taiwan is already done. My man Mao has already agreed. His board will sign off the merger. I need to turn up. He just wants me to show my face.'

'China?' asked Michael.

'Agreed too,' Hoary said laconically.

'Excellent. Job done. Right I can skedaddle off now.'

'One last thing. What about the PM?' Hoary enquired

'Current one or new one?'

'New one.'

'Yes, it's going fine but we can't hit them with their expenses yet.'

'Why not? I need this,' said Hoary, frowning.

'David has bollocks'd up his expenses. He needs time to sort them out and re-trace his tracks. It's frightening the extent of the abuse. They've all been at it, the whole house; anything from horse manure to au-pairs. Ironically, more mortgage payments are paid for by our taxes than are lent by our banks.'

'Mortgage payments?' quizzed Hoary.

'Yes, they can claim for all kinds, second home mortgages, primary residence if they rent and so on. Apparently, half of the UK property estate is in the safe hands of our tax burden. Anyway, Davids is as guilty as the rest. I'll get it cleared up.'

'Well tell him to get it done.'

'Trevor, I'm on it. Anyway, it will work in our favour if we keep stoking the fear. I need a few blockbusters up my sleeve.'

The stewardess had been standing by Hoary's shoulder as he rang off from Michael. 'Can I get you anything Sir? We'll be landing in thirty minutes.'

'Yes please you can. Do you have a pen and paper?'

'Certainly Sir. I'll fetch it for you.'

'Thank you kindly,' said Hoary picking up his memo and reading on. He knew that he shouldn't be surprised with what he had heard. Expense claims were notoriously abused by all employees everywhere – the corporate slush fund – though he had not realised the full extent of the abuse by the MPs. Hoary recognised that the consequences could be tumultuous. Whilst employees would merely suffer the embarrassment of dismissal in the eyes of colleagues, friends and family, the MPs were answerable to their whiter-than-white public image. The press would open their biggest Christmas present ever.

> JFK's argument is clear but before we debate this, we'll throw these into the pot. (Slightly off kilter – a mere break from Hollywood - but worthy of note; Consider some of the words of the greats).
>
> 'It is better to be violent, if there is violence in our hearts, than to put on the cloak of non violence to cover impotence.' *Mahatma Gandhi*
>
> 'Those who cling to the untrue doctrine that violence never settles anything would be advised to conjure up the ghosts of Napoleon Bonaparte and of the Duke of Wellington and let them debate it. The ghost of Hitler could referee, and the jury might well be the Dodo, the Great Auk, and the Passenger Pigeon. Violence, naked force, has settled more issues in history than has any other factor and the contrary opinion is wishful thinking at its worst. Nations and peoples who forget this basic truth have always paid for it with their lives and freedoms.' *Robert A. Heinlein*

'All men die. Not all men truly live.' William
Wallace (from the film, Braveheart).

Hoary was not surprised to see this final film reference. He knew
that Michael, unlike himself, was a keen visitor to the cinemas. The
stewardess had brought Hoary a pen and paper following his request.
He had wanted to comment on the dialogue he had read from Oliver
Stone's version of JFK but he now chose to leave the paper blank.

The stewardess advised Hoary that he should prepare for landing and
after he had placed his belongings in his bag he retained the memo to
read further before they touched down.

And – back on the Hollywood theme;

The final scene from the film, The English Patient
takes place in the *Cave of Swimmers* in torchlight.
Kristin Scott Thomas, *Katherine* writes as she lies
dying, despairing for the return of her lover Ralph
Fiennes, *Count Laszlo de Almásy*.

My darling, I'm waiting for you - how
long is a day in the dark, or a week?
...the fire is gone now, and I'm
horribly cold. I really ought to
drag myself outside but then
there would be the sun...
I'm afraid I waste the light on the
paintings and on writing these words...
We die, we die rich with lovers and
tribes, tastes we have swallowed...
...bodies we have entered and swum up
like rivers, fears we have hidden in
like this wretched cave...
...I want all this marked on my body.
We are the real countries, not the
boundaries drawn on maps with the
names of powerful men...
...I know you will come and carry me
out into the palace of winds, the rumors
of water... That's all I've wanted -
to walk in such a place with you, with
friends, on earth without maps.

The lamp's gone out and I'm writing
in the darkness...

Almásy, the English Patient, begins to sing -
Szerelem, Szerelem - until that also fades and is replaced
by the woman's tender lament heard at the beginning of
the film, singing for all that has been lost.
The sound of gun fire...

The plane touched down on the tarmac and bounced violently on the tarmac. The crosswinds had not helped the descent and the pilot had dropped the wheels to the ground quickly to avoid the turbulent impact. The brakes were applied with endeavour and Hoary felt his body shift forward with the force, digging his seat belt into his stomach. The words *Szerelem, Szerelem* were ringing in Hoary's mind and he knew that he had probably sung them incorrectly, failing to recognise their pronunciation.

As he picked up the memo from the floor, having dropped it in the commotion, Hoary looked at it. He felt that he had just completed a psychometric test that had tested his wits in the identification of its hidden agenda. The underlying theme of political corruption driven by competing personal motivations had stood out firmly. He folded the memo and realised the fruitless nature of commissioning his troops to solve the 'behaviour' debate. Instead, Hoary reached for the pen and paper that the stewardess had given to him. He had changed his mind and he wrote 'God desperately needs our help.'

FRIDAY – THE REALISTS

New York, October 3rd, 2008

Wood woke at 6am, which was his usual time. After two cigarettes and a strong coffee he filled the kettle to make another cup. Whilst he waited for the kettle to boil he listened to the three messages on his mobile phone.

The first message from Helen said, 'I love you. I land at Newark on Sunday morning. I'll let you know the time. Hope you've stayed off the booze whilst I've been away. Marry me for God's sake. I love you. Ring me when you get this.'

'Marry you,' thought Wood. 'God wouldn't have me do anything less.' He was delighted Helen was returning at the weekend.

The second message from Paul said, 'Look, I can't do this for you. I'm going out of my damned mind. You're right about Hoary but I don't think you have any idea what you're getting yourself in to. Why did you get me involved? For pity's sake, just leave me out of this. In fact – sod you, I resign.'

The third message from Stan said, 'Ring me back. It's urgent.'

Wood put his phone down and poured the boiling water onto the coffee cocktail he had spooned into his mug. His phone rang and he saw Stan's name flash up. Wood was delighted that Stan was obviously eager to talk to him as this was his second attempt in ten minutes. Stan was only ever all over you when he had good news; especially at this hour of the morning. Wood also wondered whether Stan had received his article from his sub editor and read it. He had waited all day yesterday to hear from Stan and nothing had been forthcoming; he was either being reticent with his decline or he had only read it late last night. He clicked the green receive button and recognised the tension that his uncertainty had aroused.

'My mother-in-law is up for the weekend from LA,' began Stan. 'I don't have a spare room. Can you help me out and put her up for the night?'

'What?' inquired Wood, confused. For a few moments, the phone line was silent and Wood thought he had been cut off.

'You arrogant, tempestuous, paranoid, self proclaiming piece of shit. Who the fuck do you think you are?' said Stan and he started to laugh.

'What?' exclaimed Wood again, thinking that he was losing the plot.

'Your article,' said Stan, still laughing.

'What?'

'Your article *Kill the Christians.* Jones loved it. He said that you were probably the most arrogant son-of-a-bitch that he had ever come across but he loved it,' Stan said, between his laughs.

'Will Jones print it?'

'Damn right he will. He loved it. You need to half the word count and get it to the press room by five tonight.'

'Tonight? I wrote it for the Sunday paper.'

'Yes tonight. Jones wants it in the Sunday editorial. Look man, do you want the top slot or not?'

Wood felt that Stan's final comment was a distraction. 'Stan, is it going in the Sunday edition?'

'Yes. Trust me man. Listen, when they print this I am the least of your worries.'

When Wood got off the phone he was bemused; was Stan lying? Had Jones liked the article? Was it a Sunday edition? Wood sensed that Stan had been telling the truth but he remained uneasy with his conclusions. Something else was also unsettling him. Wood looked about his kitchen and into his coffee mug and when, he looked at his phone, the moment of realisation hit him. 'Shit, Paul. What does he know?' he thought, grabbing his mobile and dialling out.

Paul did not answer his phone after several attempts, and ten minutes later, Wood was roaming his electric shaver over his chin as he sat in a taxi. When Paul had started to work with Wood,

Stan had told him that Paul would entertain the most speculative
of proposals no matter how absurd or opportune. 'The best source
of the best journalism,' Stan had said. 'He's a hugely bright guy
and it has to be his idea or don't bother. He can be a funny
fucker.'

Wood had employed these tactics with Paul in all his dealings with
him except with the issue regarding Hoary. Wood knew that he had been
quite demanding from the beginning and he had steamrolled the idea. He
had kicked himself for doing so and hence he had failed to engage
Paul's commitment. However, the fearful content of Paul's message and
his unwillingness to answer his phone was now concerning Wood. Paul
could be very stubborn but these recent events were not characteristic of
him.

The cabbie turned the radio up and Wood listened. Nancy Pelosi,
was speaking in the House of Representatives and Wood listened when
he heard her name announced. 'The bailout Bill will save the middle
classes and help is needed for our hard working people. The golden
parachutes for the city executives have been stopped and there can be no
doubt that we have broken new ground with the $700 billion bill. Today
we must pass this Bill and attend to our fiscal expenditure. This is a vote
that will begin to shape the stability of our economy. This is a vote for
Mr and Mrs Jones on Main Street.'

The taxi driver said, 'we've got more hope if they write the cheque
out to God.' He turned to Wood and asked. 'My family are getting really
paranoid man. They're absolutely scared senseless. Do you think we can
get through this?'

'That's not the problem,' said Wood. 'We should be asking when all
of this will finally stop. Here we are again, in yet another crisis and by
the time the politicians have finished, we'll see nothing more than
another sticking plaster.'

'Where is the vision?' thought Wood. 'Where is the purpose and the
goal that people can aspire too?' Wood had listened to the concern and
the fury being expressed from the media channels and from all those
around him. He had consistently heard people pointing the finger of
blame at many different sources – bankers, politicians, Wall Street
traders – and he had not heard anyone raising the fist of defiance and
opportunity. This, in his mind, included him. As he saw everybody's
pain beginning to escalate, he knew it was time to act.

We are all to blame this time. This was true in all of the disasters that peppered our history books. Wood knew that he had to land this message and, more importantly, the vision that would see us never replicate this again. He needed a platform from which he could say this and be heard. At the moment, he feared that he would be dismissed and he lacked the credibility needed to announce such an audacious claim. He knew what he had to do to change this. He would find the forum by which, people would hear him, they would believe him and see the opportunity that we all had to strive for.

'I don't know where Paul is,' Wood said to Helen, standing outside Paul's apartment in the torrential rain. 'I've been to his apartment. I'm here now. There's no answer. I've rung him countless times and he doesn't pick up.'

'And he's not rung back?' asked Helen, on the other end of the line, aware that her question had only one answer.

'Nothing. He can be a stubborn arse but he lives on his phone and usually to me. I know he's got something on Hoary and I'm desperate to find out what it is.'

'Maybe he's got his head down in all the news. It's been shock and awe in England. They've finally woken up over here. My parents are wondering what's happened all of a sudden. One of the BBC newsreaders lost it when the bailout vote failed. He started pointing at the camera asking what the hell was going on.'

'They don't get it do they? Credit markets are frozen, the largest corporations in the world can't pay their wage bill and banks are toppling all around us. Even the collapse of Lehman's hardly gets them out of bed.'

'Is anybody safe?'

'Babe, don't be alarmed by their concerns. They hold to an easy doctrine and the moment the foundations rock they cry for mercy.'

'Easy doctrine? I don't get it.'

When Helen had first met Wood he could have been anybody – just another guy – in the sea of men all around her. She had dated many times but she had not found that je ne sais quoi. Wood had recruited her as his PA and his manner had begun to grow on her from the start. He spoke with an ambition she had not heard before and she admired the great esteem his workforce held for him.

At times she questioned whether she was falling for the man that everybody seemed to love and wondered whether she craved the attention he could bring her. At school, Helen had left at the age of sixteen, breaking free at the first available opportunity. She had learned to hate the bullying that her beauty brought upon her. She hated more the imposition put on her by her closest friends that her beauty had wrapped her up in cotton wool and removed her from the stark reality that most faced. She wanted to be accepted but she had learned to act in a lonely world.

Wood was different. He had accepted her and more. She often wondered whether it was because of his older years though she sensed that it was more about her beauty. In fact, he made her feel like the most beautiful woman in the world. He was very attentive to her, loving in the bedroom, willing to learn, embraced her sexual needs and was conscious of what she wanted. Sometimes she felt so close to him that he was inside her head reading every thought that she had. Wood had never given her half measures and she loved the passion he displayed to her. She knew that he demanded so much from himself and she loved to listen to his ambitions which he expressed in a language she had never heard before. She had seen him address large audiences in conference rooms and watched his passion rage, entrancing those that listened. She had never been surprised with his outstanding past commercial success. Even now, when he had recently experienced the loss of all that he had built – a lifetime of work – she knew his decline would only be ephemeral. He had been badly hurt with this loss and his depression had been short-lived with his decision to write a book in his darkest hours. His writings had jettisoned his journalistic career and the passion of his voice had returned. She could listen to him all day long and she loved to.

'In my business I always managed the cash flow. Every month I opened my doors with a $2 million cost base. I always had contracts in progress but, boy, did I have to drive hard to get them delivered. I spent every month for four years delivering this burden, often wondering what insolvency would feel like. On a couple of occasions I tried to delegate the cash flow to members of my Main Board to manage. These were FTSE 100 guys with significant CVs and every one of them ran a mile within a week.'

'They were employees. What did you expect?' inquired Helen.

'They were employees,' Wood acknowledged. 'Exactly, they earned a salary and that's all they wanted.'

'That's all they do want,' challenged Helen.

'But they expressed their commitment to my vision when they wanted their salaries and I was committed to pay it, as much as they were committed to me as long as I paid it.'

'That's the same for everyone.'

'For most, yes. But this mess wasn't started by salaried employees. The agenda here is much different. This is man pushing harder at the boundaries, started by men with vision. Whilst the employees demand their commitments to be honoured they can't have it both ways when the going suddenly gets tough.'

'They won't see it that way,' began Helen. 'That's not reality to them.'

'They are employees. They earn salaries. Men who deal in reality who haven't got a clue what reality is. Put any of these men in front of a $2 million a month cash flow and they'll run for the hills. That's the reality – life isn't a game of patience, it's not a steady eddy that needs to be well paced to retirement. Quite the opposite – it's a race for survival.'

'Survival?' asked Helen, quizzically.

'Yes, survival,' confirmed Wood.

'But you believe in God?'

'Not survival in the physical sense. We still think that survival is a position of physical strength. That's as barren as the tundras. Physical strength just keeps the species going but to what end?' Wood paced the ground outside Paul's apartment, smoking.

'I don't know,' admitted Helen.

'Exactly. This is not about physical strength. This is about vision. This is about pushing out the boundaries of mankind, reaching out to new frontiers. This is about flexing behavioural muscles in men. Not pectorals or biceps.'

'Why?'

'Look. Fourteen billion years ago, when everything began, everything was created and this included the extinction event that finally wipes out all of us. We all think it won't happen for a couple of million years or ice ages can be survived or some other daft and pitiful excuse. It's as though we've all got plenty of time on our hands. This is nonsense. It's on its way and it always has been and nothing will stop it apart from us. We need to see it and work out the solution and whilst we accept that we have time, we will always accept that we have time. We fail to commit. We are fearful of the size of the task and no bicep will stop this one.'

∞

When Wood finished his telephone call with Helen, he had told her that delaying marriage was now not an option. 'St. Peter has booked the ceremony,' he told her.

'Do I wear a halo?' Helen had asked in reply.

The taxi driver had been waiting, under Wood's instruction, whilst he had paced up and down outside Paul's apartment. When Wood had eventually got back into the taxi, out of the pelting rain, the cabbie informed him that the bailout Bill had been successfully passed at 13.22 pm. The radio boomed out the responses and America and Europe listened to the news. As the cabbie drove Wood home, they were both hooked on the words.

Nancy Pelosi said that the Bill was not perfect but it was important for the middle classes of America. She called for a full investigation into how the crisis came to be. Stan Hoyer said that we can now free up lending in our money markets. Emergency surgery has been conducted and our economy must now be brought back to full health. Another senator described the words of a businessman she spoke to this week who said that he had never seen such fear in the eyes of his colleagues since 9/11. The American public commented that this was a radical change to the principles of a free market now that bad debts had been nationalised and asked what is next; the nationalisation of equities? Michelle Buckman, U.S. senator, believed that the Bill was a $700bn slush fund. It was beyond her how this could be a good move for the American taxpayer. Lack of regulation had got us into this problem and there was no regulation to get us out. Fear was rife, the Credit Crisis was real and it was induced by fears in credit. Every member of congress had been under significant pressure. President Bush, thanked all men and women for their endeavours in completing the Bill in a timely fashion. 'Troubled assets can now be protected and windfall bonuses can be controlled. As a strong supporter of enterprise,' Bush continued, 'I believe that the government should only intervene when completely necessary. In this situation action is clearly necessary. Once the market recovers many of the assets should gain in value and the American taxpayer should expect much, if not all, the taxes we invest to be paid back. The public must understand that its effect will take some time and the economy faces troubled times. We will take the time necessary to design an effective policy that does not waste taxpayers' money. This Bill can return us to long term economic prosperity.'

Wood smirked when he heard the closing line from the President. 'It was inevitable that he would say these words,' thought Wood and he recalled himself writing this line in his article for the Sunday editorial. 'Sticking plasters by the packet,' Wood muttered.

'I didn't get that,' said the cabbie, hearing Wood mumbling.

'First the banks lent too much money. Now it's the government's turn. The world will be riddled with debt for the next decade.'

'Will it work?' asked the cabbie, desperate for confirmation.

'Yes it will. Bernanke cares. He's a good man.'

'Bernanke?' inquired the cabbie.

'Chairman of the Federal Reserve. The man who controls the money – not literally – but true.'

The radio rattled out more comments. A senator interviewed outside the House of Representatives said, 'Toxic assets are traded; *trash for cash*. This is only putting lipstick on the pig. At least we will stop the lions eating the kids on the streets of Washington'. The U.S. lost the most jobs in five years in September and earnings rose less than forecast as the credit crisis deepened the economic slowdown. Payrolls fell 159,000 more than anticipated. The jobless rate remained at 6.1 per cent, up 1.4 per cent since September 2007. Hours worked reached the lowest level since records began in 1964. Mark Zandi, chief economist at Moody's in West Chester, Pennsylvania said, 'We're in store for very sizeable job losses across many industries'. The misery index, which adds the unemployment figures to the inflation rates, surged to 11.7 per cent in August – the highest level since 1991. Wells Fargo declared their intention to take over their troubled rival Wachovia in a $15.1bn deal. A government backed rescue deal with Citiwest, provisionally agreed at $2.16bn with Wachovia, had been ditched. Scorned suitor, Citiwest, objected to the move by Wells Fargo to buy Wachovia.

The taxi driver said, 'For fuck's sake,' and repeated the phrase several times. The news channel began to report news from Europe.

'Even Europe has been hit,' said the cabbie, looking at Wood.

'The whole world has I'm afraid,' Wood said compassionately. 'We're all in this together.'

The finance minister for France, Christine Lagarde, said that the French economy risks shrinking for the second quarter in a row. The minister 'deliberately avoided using the word *recession*'. In a statement Ms Lagarde said: 'The risk of negative growth in autumn for the second consecutive quarter is now real'. Insee, France's national statistics bureau said it expected the economy to shrink by 0.1% in the third and fourth quarters of the year. The economy contracted by 0.3% GDP in the second quarter of 2008. In the U.K. a multi-site outdoor clothing and equipment firm announced that it expected a loss before tax for the first half year of £4.5m. Blacks Leisure included 260 Millets outlets and 110 Blacks Outdoor stores. Another great British retail institution, John Lewis provided us with more evidence that the impact of the credit crunch had spread to all aspects of our commercial and economic structures with an unforeseen sales drop of over seven percent. Yesterday, Marriott International Incorporated, the world's largest hotel chain, reported that their third quarter profit fell 28 per cent as US companies and consumers cut back on travel. British Airways announced that its passenger numbers were down 5.6% last month. The Netherlands took control of the Dutch operation of the ailing financial giant, Fortis in a deal worth 16.8bn euros.

When the taxi pulled up outside Wood's apartment, the driver turned to Wood and said, 'I couldn't help listening to you when you were on the phone earlier. You're that guy with the column in the papers aren't you? The guy who keeps predicting what will happen next. You're Tane Wood.'

'Yes I am,' said Wood.

'Look man. Do me a favour. I don't know how you do what you do. You're obviously a smart guy and you seem to know what you're on about. Certainly more than this lot anyway. But I've got seven kids and a wife that goes the extra ten miles every day and gets nothing but blisters. If you know something they don't, please say it and the sooner you do the better for all of us.'

'I already have,' said Wood.

Wood could not settle when he got back to his apartment. He felt restless and he knew that it had little to do with the constant feed of coffee and cigarettes that he had consumed. His concern regarding Paul's silence was growing with his powerless action to track him down or enlist a response from him. 'You dozy bugger,' Wood said to himself, looking in the mirror. 'You know how to provoke him.' Paul loved provocative prose so he decided to write a piece and email it to him.

War is Dead

In the history books, our ancestry is littered with the brutality of war. The scale of these wars escalated with the increase in our population.

By the 20th century the extent of the brutality had gained a pace that witnessed significant political change. Stalin killed six million Russians in his determination to implement communism. The First World War witnessed the death of 21 million people and the leadership of Hitler resulted in seven million lives being lost.

After the First World War, Vera Brittain in her book, Testament of Youth, described the formation of a regulatory power to prevent further atrocities arising. The maturity of this power did not gain enough momentum to stop Hitler. By the latter part of the 20th century our society had established the provision of an International security. The regulatory powers of such organisations as the European Union, the Western Alliance and more were the succession from The Coal and Steel Community cemented in 1950s. The vision was founded by Robert Schuman to create a supranational community.

Today, it is certainly true that war could not exist between Western civilisations or, at least, the ability for war to manifest itself has been significantly reduced. The possibility of war between Europe and the US, or within the boundaries of either of these two powers, has radically diminished. Its territories are now well protected against the possible onset of armed combat raging between any of their member states.

However, as a political and social species, man maintains the need to engage in power struggles, the protection and provision of resources for those people closest to us and the commercial sustainability of an economic system that meets our needs. The battles, therefore, would hardly, if at all, surface in armed combat on the killing fields.

The provision of survival today and the killing fields that safeguard power, are now played out on the commercial frontiers. Politics has been given a less visible face.

And our universal language – *money*. The chase for its acquisition could no longer be our primary cross cultural pursuit. It was becoming too obvious and the competition too vigorous. Especially now our leaders were vocally recognising that our economic markets were, now globally interdependent. We could all see the mess that it made.

The demand for resources and the necessity to establish new sources from which they could be derived now demanded that change was absolute. If it wasn't, our fearful scientists – shouting for population and energy consumption constraint – would drag us down to the depths of despair that was awaiting us with the arrival of the full force of the economic tsunami we had called the credit crunch.

A new language would need to ensue. And it will.

Wood emailed the document to Paul and waited for the response. By the time evening had firmly settled in and Wood had dozed off for the night, the airwaves remained silent.

SATURDAY – THE WISDOMITES

Taiwan, October 4th, 2008

'Yesterday,' began Hoary. 'Stephen Sackur challenged a NASA scientist during his BBC HARDtalk programme. He questioned whether the Phoenix project to explore the 'Holy Cow' ice cap on Mars was a luxury we can afford.'

Michael laughed and Brendan fiddled with his thumbs nervously.

'Do you know why it is called Holy Cow?' asked Hoary. Michael didn't answer and Brendan said, 'No idea.'

Hoary continued. 'Because of the expression of delight voiced by the scientists upon its discovery. They knew that if water existed on Mars then life probably did too and the implications for mankind could be magnificent.'

'Really,' said Brendan

'Really,' said Michael who laughed again.

'The cost of the exploration is estimated at half a trillion dollars,' continued Hoary. 'The challenge however, is not the ability to finance it but the courage to find the political will that can permit the project to go ahead.'

'Trevor, have we got time for this?' asked Brendan, crossing his legs, fiddling with his fingers and scratching his nose.

'There lies the problem,' said Hoary.

'The damned world's falling apart at the moment. Bankers are getting hung, drawn and slaughtered. We'll all be scalped by the end of the year and ITCD will be history. My wife – for better or worse – has started hoarding tinned food.' When Brendan spoke, his arms – which had been folded tightly around his chest – moved further up towards his neck. Michael noticed his discomfort and wondered whether he could remain seated on his chair. His whole body seemed twisted.

'I'll leave you with Michael and hopefully you'll feel more comfortable when he has spoken to you,' said Hoary, who rose from his seat. 'I'll be in the lounge if you need me.'

When Hoary left, Brendan said, 'Has Trevor lost the plot?'

'Many years ago, thank God. We wouldn't stand a chance if he was normal,' said Michael drolly. He had to get Brendan to calm down. This was Michael's opportunity to enlist Brendan's commitment to be one of Hoary's closest allies and join the kitchen Cabinet. Brendan had strong networks with the national press in the U.K. and America and these would be very useful for Hoary's future plans. Managing the perception of the Chairman was crucial for the success of his ambitions.

'I'm being serious. People are talking about prison sentences. Banks are insolvent. They're overtrading and they've still got their doors open. We're all going to jail when the FSA finds out,' said Brendan, becoming more agitated. Michael was uncomfortable with the direction that their conversation was going.

'Brendan, do you really believe that the governments or compliance can come down on the banks?' said Michael, calmly, hoping his manner would rub off on Brendan.

'Yes, they're already asking too many questions.' Brendan sat up, on the edge of his seat.

'Of course they are. They need to know what's going on but they can't shut us down or lock us all up. We make up 70% of the country's income, at least 50% in most countries. We hold them all together. If they close us down they close down their countries. They are more scared of us than we are of them.'

'But heads will roll in all of this. Examples will be made and livelihoods sacrificed. You can't stop that form,' said Brendan, anxiously.

'No, you're right. Sacrifices will need to happen. I guess it depends on where your loyalties lie. It always does in these difficult times,' said Michael, realising his opportunity to win Brendan's support.

'Yes and I know where Trevor's loyalty lies with me. He'll have my head at the top of the pile,' said Brendan, with heightened anxiety. Michael pounced.

'Well, we'll have to change that won't we,' said Michael, smiling at Brendan.

When Michael and Brendan joined Hoary two hours later, Brendan said, 'Trevor, I am in awe. I never realised the true extent of your ambition but I do now. I feel that I should apologise to you for my lack of commitment to you but I know that is not what you want to hear. Look, I'm with you; all the way. One hundred and ten percent. Just tell me what you want me to do and I'll do it.' Brendan took a seat by Hoary's side and said, 'God himself must blush in the company of your foresight and wisdom.'

'Thank you Brendan,' said Hoary who glanced at Michael and smiled. He acknowledged Michael's success with enlisting Brendan's allegiance to his ambitions. 'That is very noble of you and I appreciate your dedication. I do wonder though, if any of us possess wisdom.' Hoary folded his newspaper and looked at Brendan. Michael interjected, 'Woody Allen summed it up. He once said that *'life is nothing if not totally ironic.'* Hoary smiled at yet another of Michael's references to the world of film.

'We are all guilty of every crime,' said Hoary and offered his hand out to Brendan. 'We are more guilty of our failure to forgive. What wisdom exists in any of this?' Brendan reached out and took Hoary's hand who responded, 'Welcome to the Kitchen Cabinet.'

'Thank you. Anything you want just call and I'll be there,' said Brendan, pleasantly, Hoary's words going over his head.

'All in good time,' said Hoary. 'Now come and help me suck up to the man who will spearhead our merger here. Vincent Mao is something else. You'll enjoy his excellent hospitality. Now, we have an empire begging for us to build it.'

After dinner, Brendan was drunk and Hoary sipped his green tea. Hoary showed little annoyance when Michael asked him to accompany him to a private room. 'Piers needs you,' said Michael. 'He's waiting on the conference line.' Michael shepherded Hoary to a private room after he had apologised on behalf of Hoary to Mao and his audience. 'His wife needs him. Nothing urgent I understand. British weather I'd guess.'

Piers was waiting on the phone and he could hear Hoary enter the room over the intercom.

'Trevor, this is serious. I mean serious. The cash...I...it...we're running out,' Piers said, his words running faster than his voice. 'We're up carey street without...' Piers gulped.

'And?' said Hoary.

'I've never known anything like it. The cash is draining too quickly. The income's dropped off the cliff. There's no money on the overnight markets. I haven't even got a back up. We could be overtrading by next week. I can't believe what I'm seeing.'

'What about the American depositories?' asked Hoary, taking a seat and crossing his legs as he sat down. Michael took a seat next to him. 'We have plenty of cash.'

'Yes, plenty of bonds but no buyers. The yield's below three. I can't use them to raise cash.'

'No buyers?'

'Nobody has got any money and even if they have, they're holding onto it. The institutional investors won't even buy gold on a broker promise. They're asking for real gold bars. I have never seen so much fear in the market. Nothing has any value.' Piers mouth began to work at the same speed as his mind. He shuffled repeatedly in his seat unaware of the voluble rub that his perspiration inflicted.

'Recall all overdrafts on every one of the high risk accounts,' said Hoary. Michael silently recognised that this would impact over twenty percent of their customers.

'I've done that already,' snapped Piers.

'All of them?' inquired Hoary.

'Well, not quite all of them.'

'Which ones have you missed?' asked Hoary.

'Those with strong cash flows. If we were to withdraw their facilities now they will be crippled,' Piers said with heightened anxiety.

'Recall them all. Increase the recall on overdrafts to which category five and six apply. Go as low as category four if you need to.'

There was a pause in the conversation as Piers considered what he was being asked to do. 'What all medium risk businesses?' he asked, seeking confirmation, stunned by the request.

'Yes,' said Hoary, calmly.

'That'll destroy them,' began Piers. 'They're strong businesses. We need their income.'

'You told me that their income has dropped off the cliff. Look here, just recall them,' demanded Hoary, becoming irritated by Piers reservations. 'Plus the personal guarantees that go with them.'

'They won't have the cash. They won't pay.'

'Don't ask them,' Hoary began, rolling his eyes. Michael interjected sensing that Piers was about to experience the full velocity of Hoary's authority.

'Piers, Piers this is Michael. Draw the guarantees direct from their accounts. Just take it.'

'The DTI will be all over us if we do that.' Pier's voice bounced out from the speaker on the phone.

'No, they won't. Get the PG heads to write recall letters and back date them,' Michael demanded.

'Good,' said Hoary. Piers and Michael remained silent for a few moments waiting for Hoary to gather his thoughts and request further actions. 'Now cancel your provisions and delete the accruals. Realise the cash on the balance sheet. I need you to buy oil.'

'I have done that where I can,' said Piers.

'Well, do it again and do it thoroughly,' demanded Hoary.

'How do you mean?' asked Piers, reticently.

'Cancel the lot,' barked Hoary.

'What all?' asked Piers, the voluble rub returning.

'Yes and if that is not sufficient then find some more.'

'Find some more?' quizzed Piers, realising that Hoary was requesting him to perform creative accounting and *make it up.*

'Yes, you are the accountant. Get on with it.'

'What about the ISC?' Piers retained his lack of composure.

'Why does this man still quote compliance to me?' said Hoary as he rolled his eyes and sat back in his seat. Michael interjected again and said, 'Piers just do it.'

'It won't be enough.'

'How are your historical creditors?' asked Michael.

'Getting heavier,' responded Piers.

'Why?' Michael asked.

'We can't maintain the...' began Piers.

'Sack them,' interrupted Michael. 'Terminate their contracts and don't pay them.'

'They'll sue,' Piers said anxiously, dropping the pen that had been in his hand all the while.

'Yes, they will. Get Jeffers in legals on the case and have internal audit copied in with the correspondence.'

'Can he be trusted?' asked Hoary to Michael.

'Yes he is a fine chap. Quite brilliant. He'll bat them off repeatedly and by the time they have a case they'll be insolvent. He'll also put in the compliance trail. He'll use the legal correspondence. He's a clever boy,' said Michael.

'What about loan recall?' Hoary asked Piers. 'China must owe us £15 billion at least. Get it back.'

'All of it?' Michael looked at Hoary who had rolled his eyes again. He sensed that Piers was asking too many questions for Hoary's liking and not giving him the confidence he needed. Hoary wanted him to get the job done that he was being asked to do.

'Piers do whatever you need to do,' said Michael getting to the point.

'But we're contracted,' blurted Piers.

'And so are our staff. Hold them responsible for the errors in those contracts. Recall the loans, sack the employees who signed them off and blame it on admin error. We need to streamline our workforce. The markets will revel in the savings,' asserted Michael.

'All regional divisions?' Piers questioned.

'Oh for God's sake Piers,' said Michael losing his patience. 'You're the bloody accountant. Cancel the provisions, realise the cash...I don't know...sack the historical creditors. Do what you have to do to balance the books and fill the tin. Get me the accounts and your projections on my desk by first thing Monday morning. Now, get on with it.'

Michael cancelled the conference call and Hoary rubbed his hands together just below his chin. Michael let him think for a moment.

'Get him to buy oil. It'll shore up the balance sheet in the short term. Goldman Sachs is predicting $200 a barrel with all this pipeline disruption,' Hoary finally said.

Michael recognised the opportunity that Hoary was pursuing. Oil pipelines around the world were being disrupted by a burst of militant sabotage and strike actions. The sudden supply shortage had increased the value of oil dramatically and significant money was being made by buying oil at a price that subsequently rose. Hoary, Michael knew, had realised that the recent causes of the supply shortage occurred at the same speed as the large fall in the hedge funds that was in turn experienced as a result of mortgage defaults. Oil prices were being artificially hiked. 'Balance sheets have to be balanced,' thought

Michael. 'What is taken by the left hand must be given back by the right.'

'Yes, fortunate coincidence that timely opportunity presents,' Michael began. 'The poor will always be the purse for the rich.' Whatever the price of oil rose to, thought Michael, would be reflected in the price at the pumps. The public always needed petrol.

'When is the rights issue scheduled for?' asked Hoary.

'Your call. I've set it in motion. When do you want me to do it?' Michael began. 'Leave it with me. I can wobble the markets when the time is right.'

'No rush. The markets won't hit their lows until spring next year,' responded Hoary. 'Oh and make sure we keep nipping at positive swings in the stock markets. Announce enforced redundancies, a thousand, fifteen hundred headcount at a time. That should do. Blame it on the market.'

'I'll have PR on the case,' confirmed Michael.

'Good,' acknowledged Hoary. 'How was Brendan?'

'Putty, unfortunately, as you predicted. He can be trusted now and he'll feed the press whatever you want. He's very well connected. He did also mention a guy called Paul Ryder. Said he'd been sniffing about doing research for a New York paper. Quite a Sherlock so I'm told.'

'Yes, I did hear about him.'

'Anyway, don't you worry about that one.'

On the other side of the Pacific Ocean, in Manhattan, a new Sherlock was worried about an old one. 'Who was that burnt offering sitting behind the wheel?' asked a detective from the NYPD, scribbling in his notebook. 'No idea. Forensics are busy picking his teeth off the dashboard,' said the officer directing the scene. The officer told the men from the fire department that they could retire for the night. 'There's nothing else to burn on that shell,' he told them. 'Leave it to the forensics boys now.'

'What was he doing here?' asked the detective to the officer. 'We really don't know. Girl in the drug store said that she served him with some cigarettes and saw him light up in his car as he drove off. Next thing – bang – the road was alight and the car bolted across the street.' The officer waved his arms in the shape of a mushroom as he spoke. 'Look, I can't really talk at the moment. I need to cordon the street off. Forensics aren't convinced that this was an accident.'

'Why?' asked the detective.

'Can't you smell it?' said the officer, lifting an open palm into the midnight air and crunching his nostrils. 'That's not petroleum. That's LPG. The poor sucker's driving a diesel and he's been zapped by a gas cloud.'

'But you have to know what you're doing to ignite LPG in the open air.'

'Yeah. Well, you're the detective. Smacks of professionals to me. Anyway, I must get on.'

'Any other clues, belongings or anything?' beckoned the detective.

'Not really. The guy's mobile phone survived, just. Pretty useless though. Forensics have it.'

When the detective inspected the mobile phone he gleaned very little. The explosion had damaged the access to the menus and the glass on the screen had been shattered. However, when he looked closer and moved into the drug store to utilise the light he could see that the screen was frozen in the call log. He read, '15 missed calls: Tane Wood.'

Sunday – The Visionaries

New York, October 5th, 2008

'They told me that he was a great visionary,' said Helen, pouring the water from the kettle into two mugs of containing the ingredients of coffee, sugar and milk for Wood and herself. She had forgotten to check if the kettle had boiled and listened for the fizz as she filled the cups. The steam accompanied the sound and she was satisfied. 'I could have got more from Arthur,' said Helen, sipping from her cup. 'That's what I call vision,' she said pointing to a picture illustrating the first moon landing with an inset picture of President John F. Kennedy. Below the picture, the inscription read, 'In a real sense, it will not be one man going to the moon it will be an entire nation. For all of us must work to put him there.'

Helen took a seat on the sofa in the living room, flicked off her shoes and rested her feet on the cushion she had placed on top of the coffee table. She took another sip of her coffee and said. 'I missed you. It's great to be home.' She stretched, making a dominant purring noise and curled her body into the sofa. Wood looked across and she looked submissive. He liked that. 'Did Paul get back to you babe?' she asked.

Wood smiled when Helen called him 'babe'. He always did. It took him some time to get use it after they had first met and he liked it. She used it to emphasise her affection for him and Wood recognised that his hesitancy with it – he had hitherto associated it to women – was merely a prejudice he had inherited from his youth. Helen was from a newer generation.

'No. I've tried him twice this morning and still no answer. He did tell me to stuff my job.' Wood had tried to ring Paul on several occasions since visiting his apartment on Friday but he had received no reply. Neither, had Paul, returned his messages.

'He's always telling you that,' said Helen, flicking through the pages of a magazine.

'Yes, but it explains his silence. Maybe he meant it this time.' Wood did not believe this. He had surmised that Paul was avoiding him and that, given a few days, Paul would ring him.

'I doubt it.' Helen said faintly. Wood looked at her and realised that she was just making conversation. He decided to change the subject.

'I think he has what I need to know on Hoary,' said Wood. He was not impressed by his attempt.

'Are you sure? He seemed to be spooked by your fixation with him. So was I,' said Helen, folding back a page in her magazine. A fashion article entitled *It's a Bling Thing* caught her eye.

'Please baby,' Wood said becoming assertive. 'You must trust me.'

Helen dropped her magazine to her lap and looked at Wood. She knew how powerful his trust was in himself. 'Sorry,' she said aware that she had been flippant with him. 'You know I do.' She had come to learn that when he said it, the future had an awful knack of unfolding what he saw.

When they had been in Tokyo, nearly two years earlier, Wood had read about the unfolding crisis with mortgage defaults in America. He had told her that his business would be badly affected by this and that the eventual fallout would depress world economies. Later, when they had moved to Poland, Wood told her that his business would topple within six months but that he had to trust himself in his need to pursue his ventures abroad. True to form, his cash reserves had dried up, half of his senior team had resigned and Wood had returned to support the demise of his business; he had not wanted to miss the disastrous events that would unfold.

She had questioned his motivations and sensed a masochistic demand that he put up on himself. But, as his business was torn to pieces, so was he and she realised that he had not wanted to bring this upon himself. She concluded that he had had no choice and that he would not shirk his responsibilities. Helen had remained very close to him as the events unravelled. She watched him face brutal legal enforcement, the fear of jail, the threats of violence, the repossession of all his worldly belongings and the rejection he faced from his peers, his family and, eventually, everybody. At the finale of the whole episode he had become a very lonely man. She had asked him why he did it and he had told her that he did not know but he had to trust himself.

He had done so, emphatically, throughout the whole episode. This was one of many examples of his fortitude and she had come to admire his persistent resolve and his unflinching determination. Neither Helen nor Wood ever discussed the purpose and the future demands his trust would make of him. Inwardly they both knew. Helen was always afraid of the consequences that she could foresee when it finally did arise and she knew that, one day, it would.

'You need to read this,' said Wood, passing a copy of the Sunday Times to Helen. 'The *lead* is on the front page and it continues on page two.' Helen cautiously took the paper from Wood and read the title *Kill All The Christians – The Fall of the Roman Empire Never Died* by *Tane Wood.*

'You hit the Sunday papers,' said Helen with reservation. Wood was not surprised that she had not commended his achievement.

'Darling. We need...' began Wood. Helen leapt from the sofa, threw the paper on the coffee table and went into the kitchen. 'Give me a fag,' she demanded from Wood who had followed her. He lit a cigarette for her and when he passed it to her she caught his eye. 'I know,' she said and turned her back on him.

'Babe,' Wood began – he used the same term of endearment. 'I have to do this. Nobody else will.'

'What is this damn fixation with Hoary? He's a banker for God's sake.' Helen said adamantly.

'Yes, he is. But he's not God's banker. He's got ambition and vision.' Wood lifted a hand to her shoulder and she rebuffed him. 'The credit crunch is as much his baby as it is mine. They just don't get it.'

'Who are *they*?' asked Helen, her back still turned to Wood.

'Whoever you want them to be. Journalists, bankers, heads of states, entrepreneurs,' responded Wood. 'Everybody – Joe public.'

'What don't they get for Christ's sake?' asked Helen, sharply.

'The world that is about to evolve,' said Wood. Helen turned her head towards him. 'This is out with the old and in with the new. The king is dead, long live the king. Everything's about to change and the change will be dramatic.'

'This is crazy,' said Helen, running a hand through her hair. 'It sounds like world domination and all that crap.'

'No. It's much bigger than that – much bigger. You can't get bigger than this.'

'Than what?' Helen said and looked at Wood. She saw determination in his eyes and she had seen this many times.

'The *Basileia tou Theou,*' said Wood. Helen threw her cigarette out of the window and put both of her hands on the window sill. She gazed out into the New York skyline and lowered her eyes to the people in the streets. There were hundreds of them in her view and thousands of apartments rising above them. She recognised the Greek term and its reference to the greatest empire of them all.

'How can you be so sure?' she asked, timidly. 'I need another fag.'

'Because I know,' said Wood, reaching for the cigarette packet and passing it to Helen. 'In 2004, I finally saw the opportunity and I took it. I didn't hesitate although it had been brewing for a while. I had no plan. I just went for it. I let providence guide me. You know how much I trust myself.'

'But why Hoary?' asked Helen.

'It seemed to happen too easily and too quickly – faster than I had anticipated. Then I realised that somebody else was playing with me.'

'What did you see?' Helen sensed that there was no rhyme or reason to her questions. She felt confused.

'How to get what we all truly wanted,' said Wood, opening his palms in front of him.

'Everyone?' asked Helen, frowning.

'Yes, everyone,' said Wood. He hesitated. 'I realised that we had got God completely wrong. It was blatantly obvious when I saw it. It had literally been staring us in the face all the time.'

'How can you be sure that it was Hoary?'

'I wasn't at first but it dawned on me in Tokyo. He is the only one that could have seen it. I knew exactly what he was up to when I read the article in the Financial Tribune. His American venture, Housefrank gave it away. He knows how powerful balance sheets can be.'

'Balance sheets?' Helen said, impatiently.

'Yes, they are very easy to manipulate wealth. You can generate whatever you want on paper and if it's credible enough you can gear against it, raise money from it, all kinds – effectively printing money. How do you think the cities of the world get built?'

'I get that. But why?' Helen asked, contorting her expression, looking confused. 'But why do any of it?'

'I can't speak for Hoary. I'd guess he wants social change. So do I. I want the mess sorted out. But I know Hoary is not the man he thinks he is. His DNA is not balanced and the result will be catastrophic. The world is waiting for Armageddon and they assume that a meteor or a gamma ray or some other physical event will take us out of the universe. This is all myth and speculation, scientific hypothesis at its best. If I am right and Hoary is the man I think he is, our lives will face a serious threat in the near future. He doesn't know the real truth to man's political advantage.'

'How do you know? How can you be so sure?'

'Trust me,' said Wood, softly.

'I do,' said Helen, raising a hand to her forehead.

'I need to do this my way and I'm committed to it,' said Wood looking for his newspaper. He couldn't find it. 'Read my column.'

'Babe, I'm scared. I'm scared for you,' said Helen, stubbing out her cigarette. She knew what Wood had been looking for and she went into the living room to retrieve the newspaper.

'I know. So am I. But I must trust myself now,' said Wood.

Wood left Helen sitting in the living room reading the paper. He went into his study, switched the television on and grabbed the other Sunday newspapers that had been delivered.

He glanced through the myriad of economic gloom that was being painted by all the media. Hypo Real Estate, the second largest bank in Germany, along with the powerful European Fortis bank were nearing collapse. The whole Icelandic banking system was facing the same devastation, if their government's negotiations with the trade unions to repatriate pension funds failed. Gordon Brown had recalled his notorious adversary, Peter Mandelson to head his Economic War Council. 'It's War already,' thought Wood continuing to read the U.K. Prime Minister's comments, 'We will do whatever it takes' and 'We will get through this.'

'Have they told themselves that they might not?' thought Wood.

Alistair Darling, the U.K. Chancellor of the Exchequer, was being blamed for not acting sooner and leaving it too late. The same business editorial of the U.K. Sunday Times was shedding accountability on other institutions too. J.P.Morgan was blamed for the fall of Lehman's by its Wall Street rivals for dealing the final hammer blow that forced them to collapse. Wall Street traders, soured with the attacks upon them by the American taxpayers, were forming into two camps; those that want to give it up and those that were trying to trade a way out of all this mess.

The Sunday Times also ran a front page article entitled 'Britain Spirals into Recession this Winter'. The banks had torn up their forecasts because of the rapid deterioration in the economic climate. Robert Barrie, an economist with Credit Suisse, said the "downside risks" to the economy had increased significantly. "There are colleagues talking about stockpiling tinned food who think that it's going to be a lot worse than that."

In the News Review editorial of the Sunday Times, David Smith, Economics Editor, asked, 'Are we heading back to the 1930s?' His headline read, 'Depression of 2008'. He asked if 'despite all the economic advances of the past half-century' depression will return. He painted the picture of the 1930s when 25% unemployment existed, production levels fell sharply and resources such as coal were stockpiled. America was hit hardest with the collapse of its banking system and an economy that shrank by 33%. It suited Hitler's political ends to call it "the Wall Street Depression" but Herbert Hoover, America's President insisted that the European disease had contaminated the United States. Americans faced not just unemployment but starvation and poverty, economic refugees in their own country. Smith quoted the words of John Steinbeck's memorable observations in the great migration on Route 66 from the 'Oklahoma dust bowl to California'

"66 is the path of a people in flight, refugees from dust and shrinking land, from the thunder of tractors and shrinking ownership, from the desert's slow northward invasion, from the twisting winds that howl up out of Texas, from the floods that bring no richness to the land and steal what richness is there."

Smith described the causes of the 1930s default that saw banks hoarding cash, government bailouts and depositors withdrawing funds, albeit too late in many cases. In America and Europe, their governments began to hoard capital. Every country looked after itself. It was painful and disruptive.

Smith drew on the parallels between then and now and quoted from the foresight of men who warned us it was coming; Bill White, former economic advisor to the Bank for International Settlements and George

Magnus, a veteran City economist with UBS. Smith argued that the most significant parallel with the previous era had come in the past few weeks with a domino series of events. "It is when the unthinkable becomes routine. That happened in the early 1930s".

Smith concluded that the forecasters were already pushing out their predictions of recovery to 2010 and 2011. 'It looks like two to three years of cold turkey'.

International sources meanwhile pursued an understanding of the problem. Ben Bernanke has devoted a life of study to examining and researching the causes of the Great Depression. 'Understanding it', he had written, 'is the holy grail of economics.'

'Wrong holy grail,' thought Wood and he recognised that the hysteria of the events of the last seven days had begun to re-shape the modern world. He knew that these events would be the beginning of the making of this world and they would eventually give man a reference point from which it came. Today, the economic advances would support world trade in a manner which had not been apparent in the 1930's and these would stave off the resource starvation of that time. Quantitative easing programmes in Europe, substantial increases in money printing and flooding World Markets with U.S. dollars would appease the effects of a depression. But these would only provide short term solutions that would fall under the eye of a microscope in comparison to the colossal vision that had realised our adversity. Wood got up from his seat. He had read enough and he walked into the living room. He sat next to Helen as she read his article.

Kill All The Christians
iReckon
Tane Wood
Sunday 5th October 2008

Hidden within the horror of the financial catastrophe is one unfathomable truth – The fall of the Roman Empire never died. The brutal cacophony of the last seven days has shattered hopes across the whole Empire. Violently angry voices are uniformly screaming from all tiers of our establishments begging the ancient wildcats to have their blood thirsty feed in the derelict arena of the Colosseum ruin. Rome has returned, not a new one but an old state.

Hungry ravishers – wild boars, bears and tigers – are scurrilously salivating over human fodder and no man could be offered more willingly than Emperor Bush after the vote in the senate and his meagre attempt to raise a triumphant thumbs up with the declaration that 'This Bill will return us to long term economic prosperity'. His bailout Bill could not be further from the truth.

The truth in economic terms remains elusive in the political arena for now until our North Atlantic battlements provide these answers for us in this trimester. The charters are already scrolled and favouring approval in the powerful European territories where the great U.K. orator, Brown is actively building his western council.

Unmitigated challenge will demand significant compromise for our democratic principles. The fury concerning the permissible tolerance within our free market conditions will echo within the public sphere until we submit to the harsh reality that we don't want to be thrown to the lions. Nationalising banks, after all, is not singularly conducive to state control and we can comfortably compromise – for the sake of the mob – by relinquishing management control in favour of shareholder ownership.

Hold Bush back from the prey. He is forgiven for his attempt to imply truth in bailing out the banks because he is not alone in ignoring that this truth is nothing more than economic diversion. If he is not forgiven, we're all facing a hideous mauling in the Flavian amphitheatre.

Here we are again. We face a significantly repetitive theme in mankind's seemingly insatiable desire to fall after the rise; clearly the fall is not dead.

Rome is hardly alone in our history books, which are littered with Alexander, Khan, the British and – the list is more extensive than the vociferous slaughter of Christians – everywhere and for everyone.

Today's fall – the euphemism we call the financial crisis – finds its blame on the failure to detail our hedge funds or the failure to secure robust compliance – the devil is in the detail but clearly not us – or the fact that a minority of scoundrels swallowed the capital reserves in a drunken orgy of copious wine acquired from "Bonuses 'r' Us".

At least if we can spear the intoxicated rogues we can stop it happening again. I mean, ask the Romans or the British and whilst you are wasting your time sharpening the spear, remember that the bonus boys have already scampered before the spears have been thrown. They will be the last to be fed into the arena and after all, our democracy signed off their party. Let us waste our time instead on raising the question with Emperor Bush and asking him what we really want him to do for us.

Heaven forbid the sight of the senate stealing from the state, procuring taxes to pay for their villas. In central Rome or the provinces, who in our civilised world has refused this complicity? Ask Bush to divert us once again – distract the mob – pile in the beasts and announce an unprecedented 100 days of gladiatorial slaughter.

Has the devil a new disguise? In our Dynastic Constitutions we ask our Emperors to get our politics right but we fail to ask them what the right politics are. How can we expect Bush to call this one when clearly nobody can? Let's face it – riding a fall after the rise is our favoured pursuit and all our philosophy has failed to get a grip on this one, throughout time.

Surely the only way to sort all this out is to finally understand *who we are*? What does lurk behind the colossal pillars of success waiting for that moment when it is time to rock the foundation and in doing so, bring about the fall? How dark is the shadow that drapes behind those pillars; dark enough to obscure anything from view? Let us blame the shadow because I guess that he is brighter than the bonus boys. After all, he has eternally eluded all of our spears.

In the last seven days, the depressive, emphatic fall of the 21st century has become frighteningly visible throughout the world. This time, we may be forced to

enter the dark. The free market has entertained this fall –
governments whether democratic, socialist or even
communist have failed each time to choose the right
politics. What if it is simply more fundamental than this?

Let us keep helplessly begging the wrong question.
With each fall, we fearfully pray that we will not become
the ravished victim to this new scarcity and have to face
our darkest fears; not us and not those in our closest
territories – we do not want the barbaric hoard on our
doorstep.

The truth is that our politics, our intellect, our
reasoning and our wisdom has let us down and not for
the first time. We are defined by these values and more –
more intelligent, empowered by sophisticated
communication skill, driven in our pursuit to reproduce,
strong in survival capacity. This, it would seem, *maketh
the great Homo sapien.*

How exhausted is our trust in these avenues, forever
beholden to the ultimate test of resilience. We are on a
journey and eventually, maybe if we endure it we will
arrive and this will only become visible in the distant
generations of our future children's, children's, children.
Meanwhile we send our Christians to the slaughter –
again.

Our religions permit us to endure the journey ahead
and allow us to believe that we can survive it although
many won't and the suffering will be abhorrent. But then
the conundrum of science is less entertaining because
most species don't – they become extinct because they
fail to adapt.

How confused and lost we are; a species that swims
in the dark and still fails to identify the shadow that has
remained obscure throughout history, distracted by our
politics, our intellect and our wisdom – distracted from
the truth.

iReckon we need to redefine man; a species that
cares, exceptional in its expression of this with love, the
emperor of all DNA. We care compulsively to solve the
problem but dismiss the purpose; dismiss it as absurd;

dismiss the opportunity; dismiss the truth –
demonstrative to the answer, even the question, that will
make the fall finally fall.

First of all, I will look behind that pillar and I won't
find the devil because he is dancing now. The detail is
his joke and I have beckoned him to come out and
dismiss me for that is his purpose.

iReckon that I need to redefine man. Yes, *I do*. God
gave us free will and how fearful we have become to
exercise it. We wait for the chosen one forgetting all the
time that we have the choice. I don't know what you are
waiting for but I no longer can. I have chosen and I
repeat, *I do*. After the learnings from Jesus Christ, God
has committed me to do it better this time and, more
importantly, I have committed to help him.

'Babe, I'm scared,' said Helen when she had finished reading. 'What
kind of man could be driven to write such a thing?' Helen fixed her gaze
on Wood and in her intensity her eyes flickered, searching for answers
in his. She needed Wood to give her an answer but one that she wanted
to hear. She knew that if it wasn't, she did not want his words to fill the
air. In her confusion she raised her hands to her ears and momentarily,
felt the need to scream.

'One evening, past midnight in late 2006,' began Wood, taking a
seat. 'I was sat in my Porsche which I had parked up in the garage block
on my estate. I lit a cigarette as I sat there. I knew that I didn't want to
go into my house because Karen didn't love me anymore. I had fallen in
love with you. I was in despair thinking about the consequences on my
kids if we split up. Only a year earlier, I had been concerned that life had
been too good to them. I wondered how they would get the knocks in
their life that would shape them for adulthood.

My thoughts turned to the memories of my life and the horrors of my
youth and the constant imprisonment I had felt with my relentless
internal drive. I sensed that I had never had the opportunity to relax or
enjoy the pleasures in life which so many did. Tears rolled down my
face as I recalled the grief of all my experiences. I looked about the
grounds of my mansion and I saw the millions of pounds worth of super
cars that I owned. I thought of my £300 million wealth. My tears grew
harder and harder and faster and faster until I choked with my

unhappiness with it all. That night, I asked God what I had done to deserve his pity.

The next day, I spent the evening getting drunk. At midnight, I got into my Lamborghini and drove home ignoring all the traffic lights. My foot was hard on the accelerator and I deliberately drove on the wrong side of the road on every corner I entered, on the busy, lorry laden A420; every corner – with no exception – for eleven miles. When I arrived back at my estate and pulled up in the same garage block, I got out of my car. I looked up to the stars and said, 'Ok God. My commitment to you is that I will absolutely tell them the truth about who you really are. Your commitment to me must be that you show me the way.'

Helen was sitting on the sofa with her knees and her hands tucked under her chin. She saw a tear gently roll down his cheek as he had spoken. 'They always said,' Helen began. 'That you had the most horrific youth. What did happen?' Helen began to search harder, reading the expressions from the movements in his face. 'And what the hell is going to happen now?' she asked.

Wood returned the gaze. He was trying to read her feelings for him as she spoke, conscious that he may have pushed her too far. She did not portray any demise. It was too important to him that she did not. The softness in her radiance and the gentleness in her eyes suggested to him that she loved him as she had always done and he said to her, 'Which question do you want me to answer first?'

PART THREE

THE FELLOWSHIP OF MAN
THE MAKING OF THE SON AND THE ADVERSARY

THE LEGACY OF TANE WOOD

Nobel Prize Awards - Peace
Brussels 2084
Speech by Gallardo Wood

H ere we are in 2084 and it is a wonderful thing being alive today. The behavioural world we now recognise is such a far cry from that of my youth. In those days, I constantly sensed the physical conveyor belts that our politics had built – a pill popping medical profession, an education system streamlined to the economic churn and a world of social science that failed to recognise our personal impact. It was a world smothered by its fascination with the internal id. We simply allowed the damage to grow. How I wish my father could have seen this. I marvel to think that terrorism and war are now historical events but how many more lives could have been saved. What could these people have achieved?

By next year, I do hope to recognise the completion of the lock down of our criminal systems. I must implore the West to keep pace with the Eastern Continents with fulfilling the delivery of the Repair Stations. Sentencing for all damage must conform within the maximum repair programme of six months. All school curriculums globally have reduced their education programmes by half to schedule emotional coping awareness. Our children today will not need the extensive repair as they enter adulthood and Corrective programming should be halved again. Impactology will continue to integrate the sciences and deliver a framework for man. We may recognise psychology as the senior partner but the DNA debate will conclude the clarity of the Homo sapiens when the Drivian level is proven with evidence. Maybe we shall no longer need to retreat thousands of years to find and know the truth.

TOWARDS TODAY
WHERE WE CAME FROM

35,000 Years Ago
Seiranoisiv – The Tribe with One God

'**B**ggbgbggb,' grunted Sheara, pouting hard and breathing rapidly.

The sound was familiar to the people in her tribe and lost in 35,000 years of heritage.

Her mate, Tanin darted his eyes across all aspects of the landscape before him. He had a good view across the tundra from their mountain vantage point but this gave him no comfort. He knew that they would not be able to survive this latest threat. The ice had covered the land for many years. Food was scarce though this was nothing compared to the threat that they now faced from the men who had come from the south.

Tanin and his group had known from the start that the others were savage. They had not even seen the wild cats act with such brutality. Tanin's brother, Manjil had watched these men kill each other in what Manjil described as 'Fuglhl' (Seiranoisiv for *sport*). Ahersha had seen them sacrifice their young by fleecing their skin and boiling them whilst they were still alive. Tanin also knew that the men from the south had murdered, raped and slaughtered all his kindred within the range of mountains that he had known all his life. He had visited the sites of his friends and seen the decapitated corpses and their scrotums hanging upside down from the trees. It would only be a matter of time before they found Tanin and his tribe of twenty one and his numbers were no match for the invaders from the south.

'Snikw Addrah Cir,' Manjil had called them – *natural born killers*. Nerosu had disagreed with Manjil and named them instead 'Niwrad Sel Rahc.' – *men with no purpose*.

'Bggbgbggb,' Sheara grunted again and again, sweat pouring from her forehead, her hair drenched in the agony of her labour. Tanin had sensed that their baby would be born today. He had asked his relatives to keep the fires burning to make the cave warm. A stack of rug skins lay by her side and the water was boiling, waiting for the happy event.

The whole tribal group would work together and be very attentive to the family need when labour began for any of their women folk. Julooh, Kyrth and the other men in the tribe would normally have been preparing the flatland areas for the feast to celebrate the birth but the threat of attack had made this impossible. They would be too vulnerable from attack in the open fields.

Tanin was sat at the mouth of his cave watching the women folk attend to Sheara. He recalled the feast they had had following Hgdfra's birth, his first born daughter. The evening was spent by his father recalling the legends of their tribe. He had told them that the earth was 6,000 'tulas' *years* old and that people used to live for 1,000 tulas. The younger men had teased his father because he had always claimed that the moon rose every eighty 'mangees' *days* but everyone knew it was sooner than that. Tanin had not corrected his father for his error and they had tried for many years to find a counting system that could keep accurate records and prove him wrong.

The whole tribe shared his father's beliefs about their ancestry and all of them enjoyed the mysterious manner in which he always told them. They loved more the tales of the future in which he described tall manmade structures that would reach to the skies and vessels that would travel across the ice and water. They all joked and thought him absurd but he loved to watch them be merry. Tears would well in his eyelids as he watched the men rolling in laughter whenever he spoke. They had sat for hours that evening by the wooden pole that the men had carved for their God, Ecad. The younger children had asked Tanin why fresh leaves were tied to it each day by the elder women and why new animal skins were hung from the strings tied around its girth. Tanin told them that Ecad had given them all life so that they could find him and help him. The leaves were a thank you from all of them in their tribe to Ecad for giving them their lives and their lands. The skins were their message to their God that they ate well in order to preserve life until one day they would find him.

Tanin placed more wood on the fire by the entrance to their cave. Kligjh, Tanin's nephew sat beside him. He told Tanin that he had promised Ecad that Sheara would give birth to a healthy child. As his cousin, he could teach the newborn to be committed to finding Him.

Tanin had grown to love his family more and more as the years rolled by. He was constantly warmed by the gentle manner and the care they gave to each other. As he watched them work unselfishly for Sheara, tears ran down his cheeks but he could not be sure if they were as a result of the joy of what he saw or the fact that he knew that the Sevissimid tribe would attack them at any moment.

Sevissimsid – The Tribe with Many Gods

Ravga's child would be born today. The Gods had told the tribes people so.

The Sevissimsid tribe had walked far from the south before settling near the mountains. Their camp was basic and functional and the women went about their work in an orderly fashion. They knew that the Gods had spoken the truth because Ravga was close now. They had seen the blood stained water mark where she lay.

The men stayed away when they heard the Ravga's labour cries. They sat by the trees sharpening their spears wearing their hats weaved from leaves and bark to protect them from the 'Santra'. They always stayed away from their women during childbirth. When the woman's screams began they knew this was the God's signal and if they interfered, his wrath would strike them on the head with stones thrown from the skies. They had already sacrificed two boars that morning to appease the Gods.

Ravga had seen the sacrifice and she had begged her mother that this would be enough to give her a child that would live. Her mother was not beside her now, the elders would take care of Ravga and her mother had told her that she would only return if the baby lived. It was not uncommon for the mother and the daughter to be sacrificed if the child died and Scollt, Ravga's partner, knew he would have no place at the ritual if the child did not live. 'Jas geryhu nasdf Gborw,' Scollt had said to Ravga as he had left, *it's in the lap of the Gods.*

The Sevissimsid men had many Gods, they expressed every fear in their lives through them; Duga *sun*, klaa *moon*, fgil *winds*, sghle *lightning*, bregj *thunder*, sbonk *war*, gfhy *birth*, lpoki *death*, esaelp *predatory animals* and many more. When the ice had come and settled they had made more Gods. The God of ice was Geuhy and the God who was making their resources of food, fuel and clothing scarce was Hjaanm. They were now making more and more sacrifices every day to Llufyttip. Their God of truth was called Eil and their God of all Gods was called Gnorw.

For the last two days the skies had shouted their thunder and lightning strikes had floored several trees. Scollt had sensed the unrest in the men and several of the elders had looked to Ravga saying that all was not as it should be. Scollt had got the ear of Hsertyl and begged him to gather the men for a war on the last tribe that lived in the mountain caves. He had told Hsertyl that the lightning had been a sign and he convinced Hsertyl that this was a message from the Gods for him to rouse the men and prepare for battle.

Hsertyl was aware that the Gods always called on him and not the other men in their tribe. All the men knew this and when Hsertyl had commanded them to assemble, they had gathered their weapons.

The women knew that the battle would happen today. They were preparing for the injured men who would return and need their wounds healing. Their workload would be demanding but they had become accustomed to this and efficient with it. Ravga's labour had come early and added to their burden.

The Sevissimsid tribe had much greater numbers than their enemies in the mountains and they knew that they had better technique. They had learnt so much from their travels and they had spears that could be thrown from a distance whilst the mountain men had heavier spears that could not. As the men gathered to begin the war they started with their war chants, gnarling their faces with the cacophony. The noise and the grotesque sounds made the women cover their ears and Hsertyl told the men to paint their faces in red to appease the Gods.

The Last of the Seiranoisiv

Scollt had been killed in the fight but the Seiranoisiv tribe had presented little resistance to the highly experienced Sevissimsid men and they had all been slaughtered in a matter of minutes. Ravga had not had time to grieve the loss of her partner and she was glad that the women had been distracted with the injured men who had returned from the battle. Before Ravga had fled she had disposed of her stillborn child by throwing it from the cliff beside their camp.

Ravga had fled to the mountains and nearly been spotted by several of the men returning from the battle. The mountains were the best place to find shelter and she believed that they would not look for her in the enemy camp. When she had seen the heads of the Seiranoisiv men and women hanging from the trees she knew she was close and it wasn't long before she was climbing into the desolate caves.

The fires were still burning when she arrived and the rocks were heavily stained with the blood of the men. She gathered several limbs that had been severed in the battle because she would have to eat later. Now, she wanted only to shelter in a cave. The pains from her labour and her journey had left her exhausted though she still had her life.

As she entered the cave, she dropped onto a pile of rugs to lie down. There she rested but her moment was distracted by faint whimpers from the rear of the cave. As her eyes adjusted to the dark, she rose and entered further towards the noise until she could make out the image of a woman holding a child with her hand over its mouth. Ravga looked hard into Sheara's eyes and she knew that the blood all around her was not from the battle. The newborn boy was wriggling intensely in his fight with his mother's restrictive hold.

When Ravga removed her foot from Sheara's throat, the Seiranoisiv woman had taken her last breath. Ravga had used every ounce of strength that she had left but Sheara had not the know how to put up a fight. As Ravga looked about the cave she sensed that their lives were more settled than her own. The cave was full of their industry and this accumulative endeavour presented comfort that was stark in its contrast with her habitat.

For that second, Ravga allowed herself to drop her shield. She was alone – away from her tribe – and now she had her child. The solitude allowed her to relax from the grief of her day and amidst the warmth of the surroundings in the cave she felt a new dream unfold in her mind that she had not experienced before. As she looked upon the animal skins, the rugs and the water that was still steaming, she muttered *'hope.'*

Ravga took the baby from Sheara and she could see that the newborn was not the same as her own but she had immediately felt a bond when the baby had taken to her breast. Ravga was very aware that her kin folk would dismiss her new child and denounce it as one of their own but she knew that she could challenge their assertions when she returned; there were many rumours from their ancestral past that they had met other tribes similar to them and fostered their children and Ravga could be equally dismissive if she had to; this was the way of her people. She sensed that her new child would not behave as her tribesmen typically did and she feared that he would need to be protected more than the child she had just lost.

Ravga named him Susej and Sheara may never have known the significance of her infant to their God, Ecad. As Ravga became more and more accustomed to the warmth of her new environment she wondered if she could ever have this in the life that she would soon return to amongst the Sevissimsid. Helplessly, she felt powerless in her desire and tears grew into pools on her eyelids before they rolled, inclemently down her cheeks. She also knew that she had no choice but to go back.

ASHTRAYS ON MANTELPIECES
THE HISTORY OF HOARY 1

Family and University Years (1969-1970)

'**D**addy,' said Maggie, as he tied her shoelaces. 'Why is mummy so horrible?'

'I'm not horrible,' shouted her mother, Audrey from the hallway. 'I heard that. Now get ready for school. We'll be late.'

'Your mummy is the boss,' said her father, William, quietly. 'Somebody has to keep us all in line or nothing would ever get done.' William finished tying her laces and kissed his daughter on the head. As she rose to her feet he patted her bottom and said, 'Quick, quick. Don't keep mummy waiting.' He smiled to her and she smiled back.

'Trevor,' his mother hailed from the ground floor in an attempt to catch the ear of her son in his second floor bedroom.

'Yes Mother?' responded Hoary.

'Make yourself sharp young man. I'm leaving right now.'

'Yes Mother.'

'They'll never amount to anything. Lazy pair,' said their mother to nobody in particular and held her tone so that all in the household could hear. 'It's a bloody good job that Churchill didn't behave like you two when he sent the men to Dunkirk. We'd all be dead now.' She had raised her voice again as she had said this.

'Darling,' said William to Audrey. 'Shall I get the groceries after work?'

'No. Don't bother. I want ripe fruit and fresh produce, not the rubbish you accept. If you want the job done properly you have to do it yourself.'

'Is there anything you need me to do,' said William, placing his hand on her waist and giving her a kiss on her cheek.

'No, just have a great day at work,' said his wife.

In the evening, the dining table was set in immaculate fashion when the family sat down together for their meal. The napkins had been ironed by the maid and Audrey had inspected the silver tray that the condiments stood on. Yesterday she had found dust on the tray and she had spoken to the maid. When they had taken their seats, Maggie waited for her mother to help herself before she ventured towards the serving dishes of sautéed potatoes and the array of boiled vegetables. Hoary was less hesitant and willing to challenge his mother's gripe when she would curse him for not waiting his turn. 'I eat to be strong mother. You wouldn't want me facing the rigours of the world without proper sustenance.'

William was telling them how his hospitals were coming along and his plans to commission a much larger build programme that would encompass the whole of London and service the health of all the people. Maggie said that her father's plans were magnificent and she was very proud to be his daughter. Audrey had cut across her daughter and said, 'The poor are undeserving. They need to learn to get off their backsides and look after themselves first.'

Hoary said, 'there is money to be made in enterprise, Mother.'

'Not from the poor,' Audrey said, firmly.

'Especially from the poor,' retorted Hoary.

'You'll learn,' said Audrey adamantly. She gave Hoary a stern look.

'Indeed Mother. That's the plan.'

'Can I learn too Mummy?' said Maggie.

'You'll never learn young lady. Finish your food.'

'Are you still going to the University New Year ball,' said William to Hoary changing the subject deliberately.

'Yes Father. I'm going up the day before. The Halls are opening for the weekend and I've agreed to meet Fosters and Smithers early.'

'Sounds like fun,' said William.

'Sounds like a riot,' said Audrey sardonically.

'I do hope it is a riot,' said Hoary. 'That's the intent Mother.'

'What's a riot?' asked Maggie.

'Be quiet and eat your food,' said Audrey

'Will you need an allowance?' asked William

'I do hope you're not condoning this foray,' demanded Audrey.

'Not at all my dear. I just don't want our son stranded,' said William

'I am fine Father but I would welcome a donation Mother.'

'Charity is only for the beggars,' said Audrey. Hoary stood up from his chair, knelt down on one knee and placed an open palm towards her. William sat rigid, with his mouth slightly open and his lips pinched. He gazed at Audrey.

'Don't be so silly Trevor,' said Maggie.

'Eat your vegetables,' Audrey said to Maggie. Audrey gathered a mixture of potato, beef and mustard on to her fork and ate it. She sat back and unfolded her napkin to pat the corners of her mouth. 'No man will amount to anything whilst he remains self indulgent in the mindless world of intoxication.'

'Your Mother is quite right Trevor. Don't overdo it.'

'I won't Father. Heavens forbid that I should encounter the devious world of enjoyment,' said Hoary.

'The house of feasting is for...' said Audrey, failing to think of an adequate term to complete her sentence. 'For...for aimless bums,' she finally said, surprising William with her choice.

'Yes Mother. I will ask for forgiveness after every sip of alcohol,' said Hoary, not rising to his mother's turn of phrase.

'Daddy, what's a bum?' asked Maggie.

'I won't tell you again. Eat your vegetables,' said Audrey to Maggie. William smiled at Maggie and picked up the bottle of red wine to read the label.

'A bum, sister, is a thing that should remain alert at all times,' said Hoary. William kept his eyes on the label.

'One day,' said Audrey holding up her knife and looking down the handle as she pointed it towards Hoary. 'The world will teach you not to be so smart.'

That evening when Audrey and William were preparing for bed, Audrey had commented that she did not know what to do with Hoary. 'He is becoming very petulant,' she said. 'He should have grown out of it by now.'

'Jim's death wasn't easy for him,' said William. Hoary's twin brother, Jim had fallen whilst climbing three years before and his body had never been found.

'He must be over that by now,' began Audrey. 'He has to make his way in the world. He'll amount to nothing acting like a victim.'

'Come on suckers,' said Smithers, downing his pint of beer in record time. 'Pay up and get them in.' Fosters confirmed the record time of seven seconds to the table and Smithers asserted, 'It's all in the throat my friends.' It was New Year's Eve and Smithers was going for a new record for the New Year. They were mastering the art of drinking down a pint of lager in the quickest time possible. Smithers had fathomed that he simply opened his throat and did not swallow as he poured the beer into his mouth.

'My shout then,' said a youthful Hoary rising from his seat to go to the bar. 'I bet he drinks for a living.' He had lost a shilling in his bet with Smithers. The pub they called 'The Rat Box' was jammed with the New Year crowd. Most pubs in Cambridge were and their venue had been popular with the undergraduates for over a decade since it had opened in 1959. The tables were wooden, so too were the benches, the oak flooring, oak panelled walls and the oak beamed ceiling. The floor was always covered in sawdust so that the landlord could sweep away the spillages and the sick effectively at the end of every evening.

Hoary was telling Fosters, who had joined him at the bar, about his boarding years at Eton. He went on about how they had avoided the attention of their house master for nearly a year when they had smuggled in liquor and sat up by candle night laughing into the early hours. 'We eventually got caught. The slipper did its job. We didn't do it again but I hated the detention; eight frightful weeks. I could have hung myself for Waugh and Joyce by the end. I read Dubliners a dozen times and I could have written 'A Handful of Dust' word for word. Briggers was a hound. Forever clipping us behind the ears if we dropped off.'

Fosters listened to Hoary as he spoke. The time was just past eleven in the evening and Fosters was too drunk to talk. Hoary had been holding him steady with one hand but when the drinks arrived, Hoary needed both hands so he released his grip and Fosters toppled over.

'Come on sport, crawl over to heaven,' said Hoary to the limp mound of Fosters nestled at his feet, pointing towards their table with both hands clasped around three pints of lager. Hoary sensed that his words had not landed and said, 'Oh dear. Asleep already. Excellent form.'

Fosters body jolted back into action and he threw up, which seemed to do the trick as he got to his feet, returned to the table and, after several minutes, challenged Smithers to a 'down in one' dual.

Minutes before midnight, they headed out of the pub into the street with the crowd of thirty thousand others – at least it felt that crowded to Hoary. He had a bottle of wine in one hand and a pint of beer in the other. A cigarette hung from his lips as he coughed the smoke from the corner of his mouth. Fireworks were bolting into the sky and a poorly synchronised chorus of Auld Lang Syne sang out into the air. Hoary didn't know the words though everyone else seemed to, especially Fosters who had his eyes closed singing as loud as his voice would carry. Two men in suits with small briefcases approached Hoary. They had been trying to get the attention of many people in the crowd though they had failed until Hoary acknowledged them – he had alcohol in his hands, everybody else had everybody else in their arms.

They introduced themselves as George and Oliver and asked Hoary if he would donate to their charity. He didn't hear much of the detail. The New Year spirit humoured the air, its vociferous jocularity ramming down his ears. He lifted one arm and nodded to his waistline. Oliver caught on and took a crisp green pound note from his trouser pocket. In return they gave him an amulet and they left.

Hoary noticed that they did not attempt to catch the attention of anybody else. It appeared that they finished their job for the night. As he watched their backs shrink with distance, their final words to him began to register after ringing through his mind for several rehearsals. 'Please tell everyone that he needs their help.' Hoary saw the once clean pound note trodden into the muddy ground below him.

The church clock hurled a beat into the midnight sky. The crowd recognised the annual symbolic chime. By the third beat the whole crowd were uniform in their countdown. Their voices cried out the cheer to bring in the New Year. As the cheer of 'eight' was followed by 'seven', the singular voice of the happy gathering raised its harmony to deafen the faintest of hearing and with the final chant the people hurled and jumped and cheered and kissed and hugged and gallons of alcohol was spilt. Hoary saw the romantic dance of lips meeting lips all about him but he was surprised when Fosters kissed him, held his face in both of his palms and followed his gesture with the words, 'I love you. I always have.'

In that moment of intense endeavour, Hoary sensed the pain that had found courage from Fosters' drunken spirit. Fosters eyes drilled deeply into Hoary's thoughts as he followed his words with a desperate search for acknowledgement. For Hoary the moment turned to silence for a few seconds amidst the deafening fever of the joyous crowd. He too searched hard within the physical signals of Fosters face following the sudden imposition but Hoary was not able to return the same level of intensity. Fosters grabbed the bottle of wine from Hoary's left hand and he held it upright above his mouth until the content was drained. It must have been nearly half a minute before Fosters lowered the bottle, wiped his mouth with the back of his hand and smiled generously and widely at Hoary.

Fosters seemed to leap from his feet as he left Hoary's company and mingled with the crowd. It was hardly ten minutes later when Hoary noticed that Fosters had already reached the sixth floor of the town hall offices, scaling the outer walls up the drain pipe. Hoary was entranced by Fosters' kiss. He joined the gawping crowd as they became alerted to Fosters' heroics. Fosters screamed out that the cape of Superman was his rightful claim. Hoary was already walking towards the building when Fosters lost his grip of the drain pipe with his left hand. The crowd was beckoning Fosters to come down. They thought that his failing left hand was a taunt to their fears but when the right hand followed, Fosters fell with a thud that lacked resonance and belief.

Within several steps, Hoary was close enough to his victim and he had no doubt that death had been instant. As Fosters lay impaled on the railings, several spikes pierced his body. His thigh, his chest and his face were severed by the iron weaponry and the wounds were severe.

Within moments the fountains of blood lost their energy and the jerking stopped. Hoary looked at Fosters face. The spike had ripped through his lower jaw and exited through the top of his skull. Hoary could see his eyes and his lips and he sensed no sorrow in the dead expression. In fact, Hoary felt he was looking at a child who had encountered the embrace of his mother when he had wanted her the most.

'Trevor?'
'Yes Father,' responded Hoary from the other end of the phone line.
'I need you to come home. Your mother is not well.'
'Is it serious?' asked Hoary.

'Yes, I'm afraid it is,' his father replied, sensitively.

Hoary returned to the family home and found a household scene that was unfamiliar to him. Maggie was sitting on the sofa in the living room, in the arms of her father and she was crying. The maid was sitting beside his mother in the master bedroom where his mother was lying in bed asleep. After surveying the house, Hoary descended the stairs and chose to take a seat in the living room.

'But I love my mummy,' Maggie said. 'She is horrible, but she is my mummy and I love her for being that.'

'Your mummy isn't horrible,' said William. 'She just loves you very much and she wants the best for you. We all have our way.'

'But why does she shout at me?' asked Maggie

'I sometimes wonder. I guess that that is what everybody does. It's what your mummy knows. It is her way of telling you that she cares. She loves you very much.'

Hoary had asked his father about the illness when he had spoken to him on the telephone. William had told him that his mother had cervical cancer and it has highly advanced. When Maggie got up from the sofa to fetch a drink from the kitchen, Hoary had asked his father how long she would live.

'Matter of days,' said William. 'The doctor was surprised that your mother had tolerated the pain thus far. She has painkillers now thankfully.'

'How has she been?' asked Hoary.

'Worried about you and Maggie.'

'Does Mother know?'

'Yes. She hardly gave the doctor a chance. You know your mother; he was made to tell her the truth.'

'Is she sleeping a lot?'

'Yes. Best way I guess. Plenty of rest.'

'Can I go up and sit with her.'

'Yes do. Mother would like that.'

Hoary went into the bedroom and asked the maid to leave them. He pulled a chair close to his mother's bed and he took her hand. Her hand had lost its softness over the years and the skin felt hard and coarse. Hoary held her hand in his palm and rubbed his other hand gently over the back of hers. He wondered when had been the last time he had held her hand and he could not recall. The nostalgia about the bedroom presented Hoary with a history of his mother and he began to sense that her passing would not just be the loss of her but the demise of a life. He wondered how others had seen his mother and he guessed that a gruesome view would be held. Even as she slept her mouth looked grim and the wrinkles about her face fused together to present an unapproachable image. His father had told him that she had been a very handsome lady in her day. The pictures beside her, stood on the bedside table, the dressing table and the wedding photographs on top of the tall boy, showed that in her youth she had been a beautiful woman. Even then, Hoary thought, she looked formidable. Her chin was raised in all the photographs Hoary had in view and she did possess a strong jaw line and a thick neck. The contours of her mouth had always seemed to draw down towards her chin.

Hung above her bedside table were two pictures from Audrey's youth and as Hoary viewed them he sensed that his mother had not always been the person he knew today. In both photographs she had a very large smile spread across her face. She looked very happy, mischievous, bright and full of energy. As he saw them now, he thought that she had been born to take the world on and maybe that was what she had always done. Throughout his life, his mother had become a constant challenge to all his motives and his actions. As his years had grown he had come to recognise that he admired her stoic presence about him with the influence of the aura she presented him with. Since leaving the household and living in the halls of residence at Cambridge University, he had enjoyed returning home to her company; especially if he had good news regarding his academic achievements. He had come to know that he very much loved his mother and he was proud to be her son. In all his social interaction he had never encountered an unpleasant appraisal of her. Whilst she had taken a self appointed air of authority she had constantly remained committed to it. He looked upon her now, raised his hand to her forehead and gently stroked her hair. He could not hold back the tears that rolled down his face and felt the choke in his throat.

The following morning, after the doctor had confirmed her death, Hoary couldn't help but recall her words when she had awoken as he had sat beside her.

'You look tired Trevor,' Audrey had said, yawning.

'I am fine Mother.'

'Yes you are my son,' Audrey had said and raised herself up from her lying position to sit upright against the headboard. 'What an awful affair for you.'

'Don't be silly Mother. Please rest.'

'I will very soon.' Audrey had asked how Maggie and William were and Hoary had told her that they were bearing up. 'Maggie will need the support of her older brother now. She idolises you. Heavens forbid.'

Hoary had smiled. 'I will do my best Mother.'

'And more. I hope,' said Audrey. She hesitated for a moment and took a sip of water from her glass besides her. 'Your father will be fine. He has his writing and his hospital programme to keep him amused. The maid will look after him.'

'Yes, he is certainly making his mark,' said Hoary.

'His mark,' said Audrey gently lifting her eyes to the ceiling. 'The whole world seems angry nowadays. Thrusting the blame everyway it can. I often wonder why but I can't fathom it out; work that one out son and you'll make your mark too and more.' Audrey took another sip of water and placed both her hands beside her on the bed.

'I can't help but wonder though. Even as I lie here knowing that I am about to die, what it would all look like if we had another view.'

'Another view?' asked Hoary.

'Yes, I am dying and even now I want to help God. I hardly feel the need to beg for mercy. I never really understood why he got all the blame.'

'He is the almighty. Surely his wisdom is everything?'

'Is it? The hardest thing about motherhood is the knowledge that your children need all the help they can get. As a mother, it is very difficult to give them that and even if you do, you never know if you are doing the right thing.'

'You have always been the most wonderful mother. I would never have wanted for more.'

'Then make sure that you give it all back to the world son, no matter how many times it tells you not to.'

In the afternoon when Hoary was alone with his father he had spoken about his conversation with his mother and William had said, 'That is your mother, no doubt.' William had lit a cigarette and asked Hoary to pass him the ashtray from the mantelpiece. Hoary did as his father asked. 'Audrey was barely affectionate in all her manner but I never doubted how much she loved me. She had her way in everything she did. I did my bit and she did hers. She was truly magnificent and she loved us all very much.'

'Father,' began Hoary. 'I have been wishing to talk to you and mother about something for a while now and I do think that the time could never be more pertinent.'

'Please, go on.'

'It's regarding my future and my career.'

'Yes.'

'Well. I want to join the church; the Anglican Church.'

'What a splendid notion.' William puffed at his cigarette. 'Did you tell your mother?'

'Yes I did. She was very much in favour.'

'Excellent. And you have my endorsement too.'

'Thank you Father,' said Hoary looking at Maggie as she lay asleep with her head resting on William's chest. 'I can't help thinking that mother had a point. When I told her she had laughed. I sensed that she had always known.'

Walking Draglines
The History of Tane Wood 1

The Entrepreneur (2004 – 2007)

O n the 21st September 2004, Wood opened his first property stock holding intermediary retail store. His team of thirty had worked throughout the night to get the store ready and when he cut the tape in the morning he told his tired and weary crew, 'This is a highly ambitious project; possibly one of the most commercially courageous ventures of all time. Today we start the journey that will eventually transform the mistrusted culture of the property industry and change it. In forty years time our children's children will move house without ever knowing that all this stress and hassle ever existed. In our own way, we will put a large slice of trust back into the fabric of our society.'

As his team cheered him and themselves, Wood sensed the mountain he was peering up to. He was not concerned about the height of the snow capped summit and he was not fazed by the epic demand. He could never have known how much this would hurt him and others.

In his business plan he wrote;

> The company has been formed to deliver a fundamental shift in the way the property industry treats customers. The vision therefore is **To Redefine the Delivery of Housing in the UK.**
>
> This company has been incorporated to develop the customer offer and open a retail store to market the proposition. This format bucks the trend. The mission is to

provide the customer with the easy way to buy and sell their home and hence the aim is to deliver what the customer actually wants, unlike the existing non customer focused and fragmented agency market. Service delivery to the customer is the key building block. This can only be delivered via a value set that delivers for the consumer. The company sets out to break industry norms.

Our values: -
Trust: reduced chains, guaranteed completions to the consumer's timescales.
Ease: we will take responsibility for all the components, removing the stress.
Transparency: no hidden costs or agendas. The Price you see is the Price you pay.
Reliability: the fact that the stock is owned by the company, and that the chains are small, means that we can deliver to the customer's requirements.

The current house buying and selling process is neither customer friendly or focused, with many varied and unforeseen pitfalls. A house purchase or sale tends to be a very stressful and frustrating experience for the customer and in excess of 38% of chains fail before completion. Those that do proceed are usually fraught with issues and take, in excess of, six months. This develops an arena of uncertainty for the consumer which delivers a stressful experience second only to death and, in the U.K. £350 million is spent in aborted sales annually.

By creating a stockholding company which will buy and sell properties to the consumer in a retail environment the majority of reasons for delay or failures in chains can be eradicated. The company will buy property from customers at a discount and sell on to another customer with an incentives package. The discounts are based on a RICS valuation and not on an agent's market appraisal. The valuation will be independently instructed by our facility provider – a blue chip bank.

Our targets:-
Reduce failure rates to below 5% (Industry norm 38%)
Completion timescales reduced to 42 days (Industry norm 157 days).
Longer term reductions to sub 1% and 21 days respectively.

The offer to the consumer will be that completion of the purchase will take place within a timescale that works for them with full visibility of the deal from the outset. The fact that the chains are in most cases only two or three in length enables a very tight control over the variables that can affect the process.

The conclusion stated;
This enterprise has all the ingredients to succeed. A team of highly motivated, committed people determined to deliver on a mission that consumers not only want but are already starting to demand. Clear unique selling points within a commercially viable prospect are market leading and innovative.

Prior to the concluding statement, the business plan had stated the ingredients of the proposition; the development of the product range; taking the product range to the retail format; the financial expansion plan; a competition report; a marketing plan; the facility requirements, funding sources and shareholder input; a S.W.O.T. analysis; strategy format; market research and a management synopsis detailing the board of directors.

His plan, his team, his idea, his ambition and his courage were admired by bankers, businessmen, colleagues, employees and friends. Then the battle began. 'The ambition is excellent and admirable,' Wood had thought. 'Now the people get involved.' He felt that all the variables to success were now facing significant impacts. At any one moment, people have the opportunity to act in a million different ways. 'There are a lot of people,' thought Wood. 'And many more moments.' He sensed his anxiety.

Seven days before opening, Wood sacked the company he had employed to fit out his retail outlet because of escalating costs. When he smashed the phone down on them after telling them of his decision, he begged a new company to complete the job. With the help of his team, the new store fit crew moved the earth with Walking Draglines to meet the opening date.

Two weeks earlier, Wood had learned that his major investor, who had committed £1.1million, was pulling out. Wood was contracted to buy ten properties which demanded a financial outlay of over £400,000. To meet this cost and his six month cash flow he needed the £1.1million.

When he heard the news of his investor's withdrawal he knew he was facing failure before he had even begun. Reviewing this potential disaster with Heath, his Managing Director, he paced about his patio garden, raiding his cigarette packet. 'Fuck it,' Wood said between puffs, 'I'm doing it anyway. I'll find a way.' He lit another cigarette and realised he was still smoking one.

Heath did not respond. He decided to give Wood room to think. When Heath had first met Wood, he had arranged several mortgages for investment properties that Wood was buying. Heath scraped a living as a broker and Wood had opened the door of opportunity for him. He had offered Heath a senior position in his company and Heath had trusted his vision and his judgement. His loyalty to Wood had been cemented at this time and they had become good friends. They had spent many hours in the pubs talking through their plans for the business and developing their ideas. From the start, they both recognised that the journey would be demanding. 'What have we got to lose,' Heath once said. 'The mansion or the park bench?'

Heath left and Wood went into his house. Karen his partner had overheard his conversation. 'I don't know why you bother,' she said. 'Nobody wants to help you. They certainly won't want you to be more successful than they are.' Karen's words drifted past Wood's ears. 'Where do I find half a million pounds,' he thought and recognised that he did not know. 'Keep going. Build it and they will come,' he resolved, finding solace in his well used phrase. His colleagues could offer Wood no advice. He felt the loneliness of his pursuit and he knew that they all looked to him to find the solution.

Wood and Karen had met when they were both on the rebound following failed relationships. They had made each other happy in their unhappiness. When Cameron, their first child was born Karen had been delighted to become a mother and Wood had loved his fourth child. Sarah had followed two years later and Karen was well on her way to her ambition of having four children.

She knew, early in their relationship that Wood had a different ambition. The adversity that he had experienced in his youth and the death of his father when he was only thirteen had cemented his drive. Karen was aware that his pursuit was very determined. Neither really knew where his ambitions would take them. She sensed that when it finally came, the action would be significant and she had not been surprised to witness the success of his empire building around her. She recognised that he would not be content with anything less but it frightened her. She had simply not wanted to get involved. She didn't want to know how he did it or what he did because it scared her.

For Karen, she wanted her children and she was determined to have them. Sex had been an awful experience since her very first encounter. It had never improved and when she met Wood she had no desire for it to do so. It was purely a means to an end. She did not realise that Wood knew this about her and she showed him her love in different ways. She did everything for him. In the house she ticked all the boxes and busied herself with running the household. It was her way and she knew that this allowed Wood the freedom to do what he needed to do.

When his empire began to grow, Karen was busy giving him the space to do it. The first six months were very demanding for Wood. He was often on the phone begging to investors. He didn't have the money to pay his employees and they fought with him to gain what they were due. Bills mounted up and lines of credit did not materialise. He was often to be found sitting at his desk with his problems, running his hands through his hair.

The sales fell well short of the projections and the income was poor. 'Fuck him,' said Anthony. 'If he doesn't pay me he can stuff his sales up his arse.' Wood heard the concerns being expressed by his staff. Anthony was not his only dissatisfied employee. 'Sod them,' he thought in the heat of the moment.

'How do I keep this lot together?' he thought when he had time to consider his dilemma. 'I'll lose the business if I don't.'

'Get me appointments in London,' he demanded from his directors. 'Canary Wharf and the financial square mile. Get me in front of their banks and their brokers.' Wood felt that he had to open doors and ask questions to build opportunity. 'Act, act and when all else fails, act,' he told Heath.

'Your staff think you've have abandoned them,' Heath told him. 'You don't pay them and now you shoot off to London every day.'

'Tell them to trust me,' said Wood. 'I have to build the cash.'

'But what about the vision? Consumers are being neglected.'

'We need cash and I need to get it. Tell them to trust me,' insisted Wood. He felt that it wasn't just Heath who was breathing down his neck. He wondered how much longer he could hold them together. 'What choice do I have,' Wood thought. 'I have to raise cash.' He knew that if he didn't, he would lose everything; his employees, his business, his house and nothing would be left. Furthermore, he sensed that he was running out of time.

Facing failure, Wood opened up networks in London and established bulk purchase deals direct with developers. Brokers in Canary Wharf had provided him with the leads. He agreed to buy the houses, from the New Home Developers, which they had bought as part exchange from their consumers. Wood lined up buyers and negotiated finders' fees. He also agreed deals for their new build properties and lined up investors to purchase these. He investigated legal contract structures to assign the purchases to the investors and found permissible methods.

'Drive volume and increase sales,' Wood demanded from his team and sales began to be lined up. He approached high net worth broker firms to supply lending to his investors and he bought funds from banks in excess of £20 million. The banks were concerned about the legality of these purchases. Wood got his contracts onto the tables of the Main Boards of the firms that he had requested the funds from. Wood got his funds. By February 11th 2005 his first sale came to fruition and by the end of April he had amassed over £2 million in finders' fees.

To his team, the deceiver, the liar and the optimist became the hero. 'Bugger me,' said Anthony. 'Did you get a bonus too? Wood is a genius. I hear we're getting company cars.'

Karen had told him that he should show no commitment to his employees. They were hard at it now, but when Wood had needed them most, they had not been. 'They will as soon as let you die,' Karen told him. She knew what they had been saying about him when they had been asked to make sacrifices. They had hated him, Karen told him. When Karen had left the room after telling him this, Wood felt that he had hurt his team. He knew he had hurt Karen. He recognised that they wanted him to share the pain that they felt he had brought upon them. His ambitions were demanding sacrifices from the people close to him that only he was prepared to face.

Wood felt that it was not his accountability to motivate them. Their responsibilities in their lives, he believed, needed to be owned by them. His responsibility was to give them choices to make and to lead them in the direction he believed. He would not make the choice for them. He knew this would present them all with difficult challenges.

'Now, let's sort out our consumers,' Wood demanded, relieved that he had raised the cash and kept his vision alive. His business was now performing. He decided to focus his team on the successful delivery of his vision. He needed them to forget the hard times they had faced and move on with ambition.

Wood returned his focus to the principle of changing the housing market. They had completed their first transaction and done so in line with their marketing campaign, 'Sold in 21 days'. Wood knew that this was achieved, more by enthusiasm than infrastructure, but the challenges had been reinforced.

'I've got you it,' Heath said, strolling confidently into Wood's office. 'The funding from ITCD has been agreed.' Heath clapped his hands together loudly and punched the air. He had secured a lending source from the commercial bank for £6 million which allowed the business to buy houses into a stock holding format. Furthermore, a service level agreement with the bank and the solicitors made it feasible to buy houses within seven days.

Wood got up from his seat as Heath told him the news. 'Consumers will love it,' he said, sensing his relief that his plan was coming together. He knew that Heath had excellent relationships with local bank managers and he had tasked him with raising the funds. Heath was a jovial, larger than life character and people trusted him. He was consistently generous in his approval of people and they warmed to him. Wood was not surprised that Heath had achieved the success with the banks because Heath was very good with people, especially bankers. 'You are no threat to them,' Wood had told him. 'They warm to you and trust you.'

Wood had opened the door of opportunity for Heath in his life and Heath strove to win his approval. At this time, Wood knew that he could trust him, implicitly.

By May, with the property market stagnating in poor economic conditions, house sales declined. His retail format achieved the sale of 16 properties in a region which sold 31 houses in total in the whole of May. Wood was delighted with the impact he had gained in market share even though he had faced significant attack and dismissal from the local estate agents and faced political trip hazards. Surveyors deliberately down valued his consumers' properties motivated by their positive relationships with Wood's competitors. Wood had simply turned to national surveyor's companies through his networks in London to combat this.

The investment arm of his company structure was performing well and fuelling the cash flow. Wood had built his stock holding up to 32 properties with individual values ranging from £75,000 to £500,000. His consumer offer was widening. The ITCD funding facility was working for his consumers and he was removing the stress from the experience they encountered when they moved house.

But bombs were about to be dropped. 'Have they taken our entire network?' asked Wood, hearing explosions go off in his bank account. Heath was adamant. 'Developer, broker and investor networks,' he confirmed. 'What do we do?' Wood put his head in his hands and considered the impact. The directors who managed the Investment arm of his business had decided that the finders' fees they could earn were more lucrative than the salaries they received from Wood. They had broken away and decided to go it alone. They had planned their exits months before, established their own companies, built their own networks and before Wood had noticed that his income had dried up, they had drained them. 'This is disastrous,' said Heath.

Wood felt Heath's despair. Heath did not recognise that Wood was constantly being faced with dilemmas. Instead he was confused with Wood's next action. 'Trust me. I'll find a way,' said Wood deciding on his resolution. Heath was glad Wood had said this. It was exactly want he needed to hear. Heath did not doubt him.

At the same time, Wood was struggling to deliver his commitments to his consumers who were buying and investing in new build properties and building property portfolios. Their mortgages were taking too long to materialise. Both problems impacted on his cash flow and the bank account was, once again, empty. Wood was frustrated and the burden was his. Again, he knew that his colleagues looked to him and with every hurdle, he faced his potential humiliation.

With the consequences of his personal ambitions nearing disaster, Wood positioned his existing employees to fill the gaps created by his breakaway ranks. He personally went back into his networks to draw his income streams in line. By 2006, after surviving the second terminal attack on his cash flow, Wood built his cash again and began to open more stores. Now, he was becoming more visible. His success was exposed in the Plimsoll industry report in which his turnover was competing already with the three largest estate agent chains in the country. His networks of surveyors and bank lending relied on the associated networks of his competitor. They did not like his success. He was becoming a serious threat to their future plans and obstacles began to increase. Again the cash was being dealt fatal blows.

Karen knew that he was bringing the pressure home with him. He was beginning to drink heavily and he made little conversation with her. Often, she watched him walk the dogs around the lake on the grounds of their estate. For long periods he would do this, alone, and he was spending little time with the children. 'I still don't know why you bother,' Karen told him. 'Nobody will love you for it.' She sensed that he sought the hero status of the man that had conquered the property market and put the trust back into the industry.

When Wood walked around his lake, it gave him the time to think. He often chose to do so. He needed to find solutions to his problems. He felt inspired with the peace, the quiet and the beauty of this environment. Here he could realise what he needed to do though he was unaware of the demands his actions placed on the people close to him.

Wood decided to investigate Europe. He knew that his competition did not operate beyond the shores of the U.K. He decided to enter these markets and build a financial resilience from them. His competition would not see his manoeuvre and he could build the financial strength to compete with them. They would not see his expansion into Europe.

In the U.K., the delays involved in obtaining mortgage offers for his consumers and investors were impacting on deadline commitments contracted with the developers. These developers acted to get Wood to comply with his commitments which resulted in the threat of lawsuits. Wood knew that this would bring down his company. He could not afford the financial penalties and they thought he could not deliver.

Wood drove forward and increased sales to lift incomes and introduced innovative products to gain an advantage over his competition. He drew more property investors to his offers. The mission statement of his portfolio investment company was, 'Making Every Property a Possibility for Anyone'. To achieve this he had to support his investors in the serviceability of their debts, should times get tough. He introduced loan systems to support his investors in a market where his competition merely focused on the derision of lucrative commissions and left their consumers to fend off the financial consequences they would inevitably encounter. However, Wood was to learn that his consumer offer had many takers and created many enemies.

Wood put every penny he had into the company and rose several million from his personal assets to support cash flows and enable expansion commitments to be met.

'You are pushing too hard,' Karen told him. 'You'll lose everything.' Wood knew that his ambitions were frightening Karen and she feared for the security of their family. Karen was scared and hurt and he knew that she was telling him so. When he tried to console her she did not want to listen. Karen was not alone in telling him that what he wanted could not be achieved.

Karen loved him and she wanted him back. Her constant rebukes were the greatest challenge to the success of Wood's ambitions. She was not alone with this. He held to the doctrine that when people told him that it couldn't be done, there lay the opportunity. He had to hold his nerve and take it. He had to trust himself and he was learning that he did. He felt that his greatest challenge was to get his people to trust him. Whilst he did this, he felt the pain that this evoked in them.

Wood chose Poland to begin his European expansion and he merged with a small operation in Nottingham providing him with an outlet in Krakow and also in Sri Lanka. He wanted to explore and learn the Asian market.

Sri Lanka proved to have little promise because the country offered no funding for house purchases and he did not have sufficient cash to support a business build programme. The demand would have cost several million pounds. Yet Poland was very promising.

Funding for consumer mortgages was available, it was aggressive and the country was experiencing the highest capital value growth for property of any of the European countries and the highest growth in funding levels. Polish residents could consistently achieve 100% loans on properties and their appetite for buying their own home was significantly increasing in a country where individual real estate space was, on average 54 square meters. One of the smallest living space figures in Europe.

Their people, simply, wanted more room and the demand for new housing was surmounting to a 40,000 properties, annual deficit in its housing estate.

He established an international team to begin building an estate of 42 store outlets over a five year period. It would commence in June and Wood decided to live in the country to aid the development. Before doing so he had embarked on a visit to the city hosting the largest population on the planet and the capital of the world's second largest economy, Japan. 'What opportunity exists in this powerhouse?' Wood had asked and he wanted to find out. His focus on his ambitions would entertain no cost.

Tokyo was magnificent. The streets, the cars and the buildings were all so clean that Wood felt he had arrived in toy town. The environment didn't feel real to him. The city looked new and it thrived with people, high rise buildings and neon lights. In all his travels, Wood felt that this was the most sophisticated place he had ever visited. His optimism for the opportunity he sought would be realised. Again, his trust in himself would come true although he would not suspect the devastating nature of it.

In Tokyo, Wood's accountant rang him to inform him that the cash flow position of the company was seriously under threat, more so than at any previous time. A number of sources of income amounting to several millions of pounds were being stalled. The deadlines, agreed with the banks, were being delayed.

Feiger and Solander, an Icelandic bank had committed to securitising the £4.1 million funding Wood had used to support his portfolio investors. The Citiwest had revalued Wood's personal residence and agreed to remortgage and release cash of £1.1million.

Investbuz had reviewed an Own Lending source for Wood to enable him to provide a mortgage offer direct to his customers. The fund of £200 million would reduce the completion timescales for the consumers who bought houses from him. This would significantly remove the stress induced by the uncertainty of house moving. Similarly, ITCD International was still reviewing its commitment to extend Wood's stock purchasing facility from £6 million to £20 million.

The discussions with the banks had commenced in the early part of last year. Their commitment was to a three month timescale. Wood had provided all items of due diligence material requested by the banks and yet, the decision making processes at these corporations were stalling, resulting in unforeseen delays and a significant lack of adherence to the commitments they had given. The decisions were with their credit departments undergoing risk assessments.

Wood was not new to these delays. Constantly, this issue arose. 'Constant cash flow threats,' Wood thought. 'Constant reluctance to commit.' He knew that their agreement would take another six months at least. His fears of failure were being imposed by the banks' fears to lend and he wondered if the consumer would ever get his solution. 'They will as long as I keep hammering at their door,' Wood told Heath. 'All of them, banks and consumers.'

More importantly Wood was caught in the same cycle of uncertainty as the consumers in the housing market. In all his internal literature with his team he had insisted that the words of William Murray should be sung from every page;

'Until one is committed, there is hesitancy, the chance to draw back, always ineffectiveness. Concerning all acts of initiative, there is one elementary truth, the ignorance of which kills countless ideas and splendid plans. That the moment one definitely commits oneself, then providence moves, too. All sorts of things occur to help one that would never otherwise have occurred.'

'Providence and trust,' Wood had thought and he would not allow himself to be defeated. 'My ingredients to success,' Wood had told Heath one evening in the pub. They were increasingly to be found in the pub and it was a Friday night. The venue was full of the jocularity of people looking forward to their weekend. 'I'll get the beer in,' Heath had replied, going to the bar, barging his way through the crowd.

Wood had experienced the dilemma that the banks were faced with. He had, himself, looked at the potential to invest in other institutions and felt the reticence that could ensue. Risk always demanded an assessment, intuitive or factual but the risk assessments conducted by the banks with their consumers were historically affluent. The hesitancy from the banks was not in risk evasion but in bureaucracy and commitment.

Both, for the consumer, were wanton and malevolent. The corporate beasts that had arisen to deliver the consumer lending offer had evolved into inefficient process management and decision making structures which were cumbersome, unsympathetic and subjected to countless levels of analysis whilst creating emotional turmoil in the public that craved for them.

They were decadent and uncommitted and attracted fantastic margins. At least they had done.

The next morning, whilst at breakfast Wood picked up the Financial Tribune newspaper and read an article entitled, *ITCD Rues the Result of its Sub Prime Run in.* It was March 14th 2007 and one of the largest banks in the world, The ITCD International was experiencing unprecedented mortgage defaults in its American operations and fears were now arising that this trend would hit the whole of America, Europe and beyond

When Wood finished reading the article, he smiled; his personal and business financial exposure was significant and he had learnt that movements in markets, no matter how minor they appear initially, could present serious challenges.

He sensed that this sub-prime deficit would have substantial consequences for his trading market. He knew that his competitors would falter and his future survival would undergo a serious threat. But he also sensed that the consumer could win from this; that corporations would be presented with threats that would demand adaptation in a market that needed this reform. He welcomed the potential and believed the challenge for him was to position his business for the consumer.

In the property market, the redefinition could only be achieved if the banks were to undergo significant change; if the levels of their commitment to their consumers became a concern that questioned and threatened the status quo of their analysis and resultant bureaucracy. However, Wood also felt that a sub-prime crisis would not be sufficient in itself. The reform would only arise as a consequence of cataclysmic threat to the balance sheets of the banking corporations and all those with a consumer offer. A colossal landslide was needed, the size of which would jettison a raging tsunami. 'It is already on its way,' thought Wood. 'This is going to hurt.'

The balance sheet of these corporations needed to be torn up and thrown in the bin. However, there was another way. Wood knew that if God himself was defined in his truth, the economic, political and social world we knew could survive, even though the turbulence would be dramatic and the reformation would be universal.

The problem was, look what happened last time somebody told the truth about God. Christ had destroyed the beliefs of his contemporaries, hurt them too much in the process and exposed himself to the crucifixion.

Wood winced as he recalled the brutal scenes from 'The Passion of The Christ'.

For two thousand years we had been in debate with Christ's words and, at our best, we still remained in conflict about the interpretation of the detail. This time, the delivery of the truth needed to find a different method of influence.

The tsunami had left the shores and it was on its way. Could this present a window of evolution to Wood? Could he build a credible platform from which the world would listen? Could he land his vision and deliver the confidence that would allow people to listen? He knew that he had to entertain the dismissal that he would encounter and combat this.

Tokyo had presented him with the true realisation of his ambition. The adversity that mankind was to face in the future had begun. Nothing could stop the tsunami landing. It was on its way.

Here was his opportunity and from the article he had just read, he knew that he was not alone in his ambitions.

BUSKERS & TSUNAMIS
THE HISTORY OF HOARY 2

The Priel (1975)

Throughout his degree in Politics and Philosophy, Hoary had
sought relevance in his life. Now, in his priesthood he seemed to be
searching harder every day. It all made sense – he did not doubt that –
after all what didn't? The question he now asked was *why*.

'Robot Hands – Nightmarish Future,' Hoary read on page nine of the
Daily Mail. The head line was qualified by the first paragraph that read
'Horrifying events have blazed the movie screens of a science fiction
future governed by robotics but now they are coming to a person near
you, soon. Scientists have created a robot hand that can be attached to
the human body and controlled by the brain. The SmartHand can allow a
man to walk up to you unnoticed and effortlessly squeeze the life out of
your body.'

Hoary wasn't certain whether he should be smiling or grimacing as
he read this. 'Great story if you are a one handed man who needs two
hands to strangle yourself,' thought Hoary. He chose to smile and then
felt guilty that he had not recognised the practical application for those
who had lost a limb. He looked about himself, along the high street, as
though he was checking that nobody had been able to read his thoughts
or, at the very least, that nobody had seen the expression of mischief that
had been written across his face.

Frequently, on Saturday afternoons, Hoary would be in Newport
high street. After his midday ceremony he would walk through it on his
way to his apartment and he would shop, mainly for books, as he did so.

He had moved to South Wales in the summer to take up his new parish appointment and he had gladly snapped up the opportunity to live in, what he considered to be, a beautiful part of the world.

When he finished his sandwich, he rose from his seat, folded his newspaper and walked further along the high street. His hunger was beginning to pass and he realised that it was nearly four o'clock in the afternoon before he had eaten. The buzz of the high street seemed to be winding down and he noticed the extent of the litter all about the pedestrian thoroughfare. Discarded food cartons, sandwich wrappers and food packaging were all about his feet. Even broken ice cream cones, beer cans and brown paper bags – he didn't recognise the source – seemed to be everywhere. Men and women were sweeping up the debris, almost invisible amongst the shoppers. Hoary noticed groups of girls and boys hanging about the benches. He was conscious that his white collar attracted dismissive comments – not always, but enough to make him aware. He noticed young men and women entering and exiting the clothes shops dressed in average sized clothing, exhibiting a multitude of body shapes. Plumbers, builders, carpenters, painters and more were mingling with the crowd, dressed as though they were stained from their days work and unashamed of a standard that had become over looked because of its regularity. At the bottom end of the high street, this was more evident outside the crowded pubs. The men who could find no room inside were spewing onto the streets. They stood in groups or sat on the wooden garden tables smoking, laughing, joking and often loud.

Voices could be heard emanating from the street from those who wanted to be noticed; predominantly, youthful and aggressive in their pitch and determined in their message. The voices screeched above the hum of the shopping crowd.

The nineteen seventies had witnessed a recession that saw the high streets display as many 'commercial let' signs above the first floor windows of the buildings as it did brand names. Amongst the array of household names, every other board suggested times were hard for the retailers.

Shops shouted out sale prices with window length posters proclaiming bargains as aggressive as '50% off'. The commercial drivers appeared to be all around the shoppers enticing entry and the graffiti on the walls between the shops shared the same enthusiasm. It was hardly legible but its tone was clearly different. Buskers sat outside either, singing or strumming their way to a hatful of cash, confusing the crowd as to why they were resorting to such meagre pay as opposed to the spotlight.

All about Hoary, as he walked, he saw the result of a busy Saturday and the voice of a shopping crowd. Against the beautiful, precise, manicured wealth of the branded shop windows firing at us all 'buy, buy, buy,' was the repugnant, unglamorous rebuke of our care. 'Release me from the spell that you have cast upon us all,' thought Hoary as he consciously looked upon it. 'I cannot shout at you because it is not I who is the wicked witch.'

As Hoary reached the end of the street, the bustling crowd had – in the main – gone home and the bright lights from the shops proudly shone out into the streets displaying the garbage that they had painted onto the pedestrian causeway. The debris would take an evening to clear. 'Every fucking Saturday night,' said a woman pushing a broom and getting on with the job. 'What a palaver; nothin' but animals, the lot of 'em. Ooi, Priest,' she continued, seeing Hoary. 'Teach 'em some manners at tomorrow's sermons.'

'If they attend,' he thought and replied. 'I think more rubbish bins may stand a better chance.'

'That's the last thing they use. The ones they got are always empty.'

Hoary sipped at his tea as he took a seat in his living room, shortly after he had arrived back at his apartment. He opened his bag from the book store and read the back covers of 1984 and Blott on the Landscape. Then, after a moment's hesitation, he recalled his find from last night and realised what had been niggling at him all day. Yesterday evening, he had broken his calculator by mistakenly standing on it. Whilst he had searched for a new one – digging ever deeper into drawers he had not ventured into for some years – he came across the amulet that he had been given on the New Year's Eve of 1969, five years ago. He got up from his seat and went to retrieve it now that it was fresh in his memory.

The amulet was attractive; ruby leather casing, distressed effect with cotton shredded, edged pages about six inches by three inches. The front cover was leather and the look and feel was beautiful; the words 'The Step,' were etched in brilliant, opulent gold upon it. Hoary opened it and began to read. When he had finished the twenty pages of its content he wished he had not lost it for a moment, let alone for all those years. He knew he should have read it sooner and despaired that he had not, especially when he read the last page.

∞

'How could God take a man in his prime?' asked the widow after the burial of her young husband, aged thirty seven. Hoary had held the burial ceremony in the absence of a priest being employed in the parish.

'If I had a pound for every time I've heard that,' thought Hoary, smiling and nodding at the woman speaking to him. He recognised that, in pain, we all need somebody to blame but, for Hoary, doubt was starting to set in.

'If Jesus gave his life for us then why do all the good men die so young,' said the mourning wife holding her two children close, either side of her.

'The Lord works in mysterious ways,' said Hoary. 'And you can be assured that your husband is in a better place now.'

Hoary did not tell the woman what he really wanted to say. He could not remember the last time he had buried anybody under the age of fifty-five and he was convinced that our maker would be delighted that he suddenly had.

Priests were being expelled from their parishes more than ever before. All the priests were aware of the current trend of modern times. A parish priest was now becoming a scarce commodity. Many village churches were opening on a rotation system owing to the lack of numbers available to conduct the ceremonies. Orders from their hierarchical superiors asked the priests to maintain greater vigilance in an increasing climate of exacting diplomacy. Recently, the church had begun to draw priests from abroad with more regularity. Their previous history was less visible and local numbers had run too low to provide enough priests.

An act of discretion, or a misplaced comment seemed to have less room for forgiveness in the people who inhabited the parish communities. The clergy found themselves increasingly beholden to the onslaught of raging commentary, holding them to account. Drawing new priests from abroad did incur the added expense of relocation but it was a lot easier to remove them quickly should diplomacy be compromised. The Anglican Church had recently surmised that the shelf life of a Priest within any given community was no greater than two years.

Hoary, himself had come under severe recent criticism from the wrath of several members of his congregation. They had been concerned with a newcomer to the village being seen drinking in the local pub. The man in question had recently moved into the large Manor house on the estate to the east of the church. The parishioners had expressed their disgust that the lord of the Manor should be drinking with the commoners in the local tavern. They had asked Hoary to visit him and put him right and Hoary had made the visit but their new lord had been seen in the same local the following weekend. The parishioners had been concerned that Hoary lacked the authority to keep order in the parish. By way of compromise, Hoary had asked his new neighbour to make a reading in the church. After the morning sermon the congregation had met their new lord and decided that he was a 'very nice man' after all and they had forgiven what they had seen to be his misdemeanour.

However, when the very nice man had introduced two Rottweiler dogs on to his estate the villagers had said that he was housing a vicious pack. Local youths had spread rumours of sheep being killed by the dogs and by-passers being bitten. Fury had quickly grown in the village and although Hoary had attempted to take a low profile, he found himself being drawn in from many angles. He was soon the source of every solution that the parishioners wanted to be implemented. Hoary was increasingly beckoned into the fury they held for their new lord. Soon this grew to fever pitch. The local nursery school teacher had recounted a story in which she had been pinned down by the two dogs whilst her Jack Russell had been torn to within an inch of his life.

Hoary visited the new lord and asked him to maintain a low profile and to keep the dogs away from public view until the heat had died down. But the rumours began to gain momentum and the police became increasingly incredulous with the volatility and violence that was reported to them. At the request of his parishioners, Hoary was visiting the newcomer every other day and reporting back to them. Hoary consistently maintained a non-alarmist stance in the hope that his local community would calm down eventually. When the local farmer applied to have a slaughter house built adjacent to the village which included laying a new roadway to accommodate the increased traffic, the parishioners turned their fury towards the farmer but Hoary – for reasons he could never fathom – was not drawn into this foray.

That evening, following the ceremony, Hoary was sitting in his study thumbing through the book that George and Oliver had given him, entitled 'The Step'. For several moments, Hoary reflected on the events of the day until he closed the amulet and eyed the front cover. He sensed that his optimism for his faith was being forever tested but he chose to open it and he began to read. The first page said, 'I beg you all – please help Dace.'

Hoary turned the page and read more.

'By George and Oliver. 'As it is Now,' - these words are taken from much narrative by modern man – special thanks to theologians across your industry. 'As it will be with Dace,' - we speak for Dace. He desperately needs your help.'

The next page gave a listing which read;

1. *Trust; True Purpose*
   The Truth – The Forcefield – The Lie – The Obstacle
   – The House of Mourning (Solomon)

2. *Faith; Not a Tangible Thing*
   Longsuffering – Adversity – Forsaken – Value –
   Immortality

3. *Belief; Truth v Dismissal (Dace v Satan)*
   Brutality – Mercy – Death – Purpose – Translation –
   The Debate

Hoary frequently read the contents of the amulet since fortuitously finding it after so many years. Often when his faith was being tested. His belief in God was absolute. He was concerned that his religion could not stand the onset of more, new generations. He sensed that his fellow men were becoming more and more prone to the distractions of modern life and less concerned with the potential of a purpose to our lives. At no level in the social fabric of life did he hear a whisper of a vision for mankind and, quite the reverse, he believed that it was becoming increasingly unacceptable for any such whisper to even grace the airwaves. He wondered what had become the purpose of power if it was not to lead and provide ambition and foresight. Such was the judgment of the populous; his best resolution was that it had become too dangerous to do such a thing. The incredulous leagues of rejection would not permit it. 'So what are we here for?' Hoary asked himself. 'Just to die.'

His mother's words to him as she lay dying were being challenged by a hardened and hurting voice manifesting from every media of modern life. Only in 'The Step' could he find solace and again he read the first chapter.

The Step

1

Trust; True Purpose'.

The Truth

As it will be with Dace

'There is at the bottom only one problem in the world and this is its name. How does one break through? How does one get into the open? How does one burst the cocoon and become a butterfly?' – *Thomas Mann.*

First of all, look to the question – 'How does *one*' – and choose.

'Render unto Caesar the things which are Caesars and unto God the things that are God's' (Matthew 22:21). When Jesus said these words, was he making a statement or asking us to make a choice?

The Forcefield

'All life is given the opportunity to thrive. The journey of any species depends on its awareness of its true DNA. The challenge is to discover this before the extinction event that is already on its way.'

The Lie

'Everything beyond purpose is transient – language, materials, resources, money and so forth.

Are territories defined by power or purpose? Does power control the transient? Where are the real territories? Do you need to be defined by the resources you fear may never be stockpiled?

In a world full of sand you do not have to ask where the beach is.

The Obstacle

As it is now

In 1983 the cast of the Monty Python team told cinema going audiences that The Very Big Corporation of America has an urgent agenda of the realisation of just how much there is still left to own. Harry, fields item six on that agenda, The Meaning of Life. His team have established that there are two fundamental concepts;

1. People are not wearing enough hats

2. Matter is energy. In the universe there are many energy fields which we cannot normally perceive. Some energies have a spiritual source which act upon a person's soul. However, this soul does not exist ab initio, as orthodox Christianity teaches; it has to be brought into existence by a process of guided self-observation. However, this is rarely achieved owing to mans unique ability to be distracted from spiritual matters by everyday trivia.'

The debate moves to the concern for hats and is distracted by an attack from the Crimson Permanent Assurance leading to the loss of lives.

The House of Mourning

The Bible, Solomon: 'It is better to go to the house of *mourning*, than to go to the house of feasting: for that is the end of all men; and the living will lay it to his heart. *Sorrow is better than laughter*: for by the sadness of the countenance *the heart is made better*.'

Modern Narrative – These statements are God's words about how He views man and how He actually *designed* their life. If one is mourning, it is usually because something *terrible* has happened – serious illness, painful divorce, death of a child or loved one, loss of property through a disaster or bankruptcy, or something similar. Therefore, this passage seems absolutely backwards to the human mind. This is why Solomon states that "the end of all men" (the goal of the average person) is to make life one long, never ending party or 'feast'. *(David Pack)*

As it will be with Dace

From adversity man takes strides forward. From
feasting we merely awake – a little heavier and a little
more aware. Are we predisposed to be unbalanced?
Excesses of either give little recuperation, moderation
can provide essential regeneration; we learn to care and
that we love and these deepen.

What behaviour do we need – routed deep in our
DNA – to answer the questions? If we lived in a world
in which we did not care would our answers merely
demand from us that we feed, we breed and we survive?

What is the motivation of the Darwinian scheme?
Am I to be judged for my physical prowess – like them
– my supreme adherence to my dominant characteristic;
the natural born killer? Or do I propose a choice born of
more purposeful balance?

For Hoary, the Christian methods of his church did not ferment his
disillusionment. Quite the contrary, he believed in God and he was
credulous with its verse. However, he was beginning to believe that the
commercial world offered a greater stage for influence and he had
already begun to seek the realisation of his ambitions in another social
manifestation. Today, money mattered and its voice had the loudest cry
and entertained the widest audience. He had already accepted a post
with McCinley & Company Incorporated, a management consultancy
firm which had assigned him to employment in Europe, North America
and the Middle East.

'The church has lost its vision,' said Hoary being challenged for a
reason for his resignation.

'Hoary you have jurisdiction for Wales and I am prepared to extend
this to Western England,' said his superior, Thomas. 'In a couple of
years, who knows? I do not doubt your ability.'

'Thank you. I very much appreciate your recognition. However, you
are trapped in the same diplomacy that now infiltrates all ranks.'

'Why do you say that?'

'Basically you are begging me to stay – maybe begging is too severe.
Across the estate we struggle to retain good men and women. They are

being slaughtered by their communities. We spend our time sorting out the mess as opposed to driving forward the vision of Christ.'

'But our sermons do that. What is our estate if it does not represent this?'

'Do they? Do the public consider that true? Do they not doubt our words? When we are challenged about the doctrines in the bible do we not fail to convince our followers?

'In what way?'

'Genesis states that the world is 6000 years old. That people lived for a thousand years. Can we not resolve this contradiction with science? Modern congregations cannot resolve this and neither can we. Instead we internalise our struggle within our ranks.'

'God moves in mysterious ways.'

'I cannot accept that. God is the standard – he is an excellence of man. There is no mystery to this just a lack of understanding. I am sorry Tom, but I do not believe that the church can help me fulfil my ambition.'

'And what is that?'

'The world must become the place that God wants it to become. Christ must be heard. Our damage and our pain must reside with the onset of the truth. I do not believe that the church is now best placed to do this.'

'What an awful indictment,' said Tom, leaning forward on his chair, resting his chin in his hands. Tom was not confronting Hoary with this comment. He was searching the room with his eyes, glancing out of the windows, seemingly beleaguered. 'That it should come to this.'

'It didn't. You let it.'

'And what would you have me do?'

'Find the courage. Assert your vision – the vision of God. Let providence pursue, not your fears, not decline. You have forgotten how to gamble. You won't rock the boat; denying the future for a nearsighted present.'

'And you?'

'I need to rock the boat and not in stormy seas. God needs a tsunami.'

VIPERS PIT
THE HISTORY OF WOOD 2

Employment (2001-2004)

'We are not Frank Sinatra,' demanded the senior voice shouting at his team from the conference podium. 'Only he can do it *my way*. You do it our way.' The company was struggling to maintain compliance and discipline in its ranks, and profits were falling as a consequence.

Wood knew that he had a reputation for being a maverick. He sensed that many eyes in the audience were homing in on him as these words rang out around the hall. 'Get your own house in order first,' Wood thought challenging their stares with a grimace. He knew that they would enjoy witnessing his demise. After all he was the golden boy in the eyes of the Operations Director and that made him too good. There were far too few places available for promotion. Wood was in their way.

In these early years few knew that Wood was on a journey that would see him eventually exert great influence over the future of mankind. As his life unfolded and people crossed his paths, some dared to wonder. Something in his words and his demeanour made them stop and think. Socially dismissive norms did not permit these thoughts to grow. They had little foundation in a world that had not yet identified who man really was.

'What did you think?' asked Kyle seeking feedback, in the coffee lounge, following the conference.

'It all went right over their heads,' Wood replied. 'Your junior management still dream of the promotions they will never get. You boys at the top need to get your act together. If you want them to comply, force them.'

'Was the message too subtle?' asked Kyle.

'By far. They're too thick skinned to be shouted at and told,' said Wood lowering his eyes to the floor.

'What do you suggest?' asked Kyle.

'Threaten to sack them,' said Wood kicking a plastic cup with his foot.

'What will that do?' asked Kyle looking at Wood.

'Well, they're far too lazy to go and get another job,' said Wood flippantly, returning his gaze to Kyle. 'You never know. They may do some work.'

Kyle Ghana was Wood's Divisional Director and by far the best boss he had ever come across. He had built his career in the Marks and Spencer's retail business and everybody in the industry knew that they were the best. They built cultures of responsibility in their people who prided themselves in being the best in all their systems, products and procedures.

Kyle had left to build a more lucrative career in a less established retailer that could offer greater opportunity for him and he was determined to exploit the potential. The current regime of Barrow Boys would not stand in his way. They couldn't. They didn't have the expertise, the vision or the behaviour that was necessary to grow a maturing company.

Kyle fiercely held Wood to account and Wood didn't expect anything less. Wood did do it his way; with his staff and with his bosses. Kyle knew that he couldn't control Wood because nobody could. However, Wood hadn't always been the man he was today. Kyle respected that Wood had learned the hard way.

Several years ago, as a young General Manager, aged 32, Wood became a real life Gung Ho. He inherited a problem that those before him had failed to conquer and his solution had to be in the success of his team of employees. He needed the Gung Ho spirit that would drive them to work together in the pursuit of one goal, as one harmonious group.

The Watford store was a disaster. His seniors, fearful that he would not have the courage to take on this task, did not tell him the size of the problem he was to inherit. It didn't take Wood long to establish the position he had found himself in. The employees were aggressive, militant and unproductive; they had been demoralised and then kicked some more. The store was ranked at the bottom of every corporate league table and there were plenty of those. The bosses had expressed their complete dissatisfaction on many an occasion when they had visited the store and the grief and anxiety had dripped down every rank and file in the workforce.

'Today is the big day,' Wood had said to himself on the morning he had set off to start at his new store. 'State of the art grandeur, four football pitches in length and the beast is all mine.'

On arrival, the small, old and tatty unit reeked of neglect inside and out. When he introduced himself to his team and punched the air with enthusiasm, his gestures were not motivated by his despair. 'How the hell do I survive this one,' he wanted to scream. Within two weeks he was given his answer when his senior management gave him their ultimatum, 'Sort it out or find another job,' Wood was told. In his gloom he decided to get the job done and he had liked the people he met in his team. They were resilient.

At his first staff meeting he chose to inspire his staff. 'Do you know about Gustav Eiffel and the Frenchman's experience in building the Eiffel Tower?' asked Wood only to be met with unenthusiastic silence.

'Gustav loved his country and he wanted everyone in the world to love his country as he did,' Wood continued bravely. 'So he built the Eiffel Tower to tell the world how magnificent Paris and France were. The tallest tower ever built became his statement.'

'You want us to build a tower,' shouted a disparaging voice from the crowd. Wood was encouraged that he had a response even though the tone was challenging.

'If you like,' he answered. 'More importantly, like Gustav, we are going to build the most magnificent achievement of modern man.'

'Out of this shithole?' came another shout.

'At least it's our shithole,' said Wood apprehensively.

'Why doesn't the company spend some money on this place?' asked another concerned voice. Wood sensed the unrest before him. He could hear bums rustling in seats and the sound of murmuring started to increase.

'They will eventually,' began Wood fearing a riot. 'How long do you want to wait? How long do you want to put up with this hell?'

'Why should we?' shouted an aggressive mouth. The employees were one by one rising from their seats. Wood could see his audience moving as a tide towards him and the wave was looking gruesome.

Wood shot from the podium and moved quickly in front of them. 'Who here thinks that they can make a difference? Who here has got the courage to say that enough is enough? Which one of you will be the first to tell me that it is our time and it starts now,' exclaimed Wood passionately. The tide fell short of the beach and slowly retracted into the sea. Silence fell for several seconds.

'I will,' said a timid voice from within the calming waters.

The team began revamping the store by moving every fixture and painting every inch. As the work became more visible, his staff bought into his ideas and the enthusiasm grew. So too did Wood's other concerns. This was not the way in which managers were allowed to manage.

'If a senior manager walks in here you'll be sacked,' Wood's lieutenant told him. 'You need Main Board sign off, sales projections, layout plans, detailed cost analysis and uncle Tom Cobley an' all before you can do what you're doing.'

'I haven't got time,' replied an anxious Wood. 'While they work all that out, they'll sack me for the poor performance of this place. I have one choice and I'm exercising it,' Wood stated adamantly. His revamp plans were in front of him and already he was behind schedule. He recognised that this would test his resilience.

'Yes, but we'll go down with you,' said his lieutenant challenging him back. Wood wanted to verbally tear into him but as he looked at his lieutenant he realised how scared he was. His eyes were wide open. Wood thought for a moment.

'Next week is the Divisional conference. I need to be on stage,' Wood said looking at his lieutenant. 'I need to get to them before they get to me.'

'How will that help?' said his lieutenant dismissively.

'It may not. It's the only chance I have,' replied Wood assuredly, running his fingers through his hair swiftly.

Wood smuggled his name onto the conference agenda. He chose to deliver a speech on *Employee Engagement* and used his psychology degree credentials to bargain with. Normally, Speakers were handpicked so Wood spent an hour on the phone commending his Human Resources Director for his vision. He sanctioned Wood's speech.

He knew that he was taking a significant risk and the consequences for him and his store team could bring a new highlight to the history of pain that crept down every orifice of the store. The conference was being held to recognise divisional achievements. 'If I fail in this forum to celebrate success,' Wood told Karen, his partner, 'I will be seeking a new employer.'

'That will please your staff,' replied Karen worriedly. Wood did not believe her but he knew she was not alone. Many feared for the outcome.

He finished his preparation for his presentation in the hours before dawn and after a couple of hours sleep he wearily drove to the conference in Greenford, London. On arrival, he found that his material was a problem. He had written it on acetates and there was no over head projector in the building. But the Conference had begun and Wood was scheduled to speak in twenty minutes time. 'Am I destined to fail,' he wondered, anxious with his predicament, surveying his 200 strong audience. 'The viper's pit beckons,' he said to himself.

Wood knew that his political acumen was in need of nurture. What he didn't know was that the resilience he had learned in his youth after the loss of his father when he was aged thirteen was to become his strongest ally. He didn't know that he was beginning a journey that would challenge the working class values that he had learned from his parents. He didn't know that the pressures that had been applied by his father and continued by his mother, to gain a good education, would now come to his aid even though he had struggled throughout his early educational years. It was only later with the advent and fortitude of self discipline gained by the maturity and ambition that he realised in his early twenties that he achieved an excellent standard of degree from university. Prior to this, he had experienced a string of failures and retakes in his 'O' and 'A' level exams.

Wood looked about the conference hall. He knew all the delegates would assess him on his performance and his lack of a projector would not help him to win them. 'I can either perform or I can worry,' thought Wood digging his nails into his palms, concentrating on the pain to distract him from the horror that awaited him. Wood was yet again to see that his childhood had destroyed his confidence. Now, all his efforts to *trust himself* would be called.

Wood was called to the stage. After his introduction, he apologised to his audience and insisted that he improvised with his material because it was crucial to his message. He met raucous laughter when he stood on stage holding the acetates above his head for all to see. He told the story of Eiffel and of his plan to establish the greatest retail store in the world.

After several minutes, the audience was beginning to listen. What followed was emphatically illustrated by his seniors - highly ambitious men and women - ignoring incoming urgent phone calls from their Main Board. At one point, the most senior manager in the conference, on his mobile phone to the MD, asked him if he could ring him back.

Wood took 45 minutes to tell the conference. When he finished the room was silent. He had told them how he had inherited a store that he had characterised as a **silhouette of a man with his head hung down below his shoulders**. By the end, the audience had the Eiffel Tower imprinted on their minds. In that audience, Wood had demobilised any ambition that may have challenged his passion to succeed. He had acclaimed his company as the finest and begged his seniors to help him.

Pins could be heard dropping after he landed his final sentence. He could not recognise their response. 'Have I frightened them into submission?' he thought. 'Did I shove it down their throats?' During lunch, his audience shook his hand and recognised the inspirational drive of his ambition. His Divisional Director asked him, 'What do you need?'

'Right,' said Wood. 'Let's get on with it,' he told his team the next day. Wood was delighted and he was more eager than ever. Now, his team knew he would get the job done and they had to join in. Failure was no longer an option. He had driven them to choose.

Wood achieved his ambition for Watford. The Main Board, who had previously been too embarrassed to face the riotous store team, began to flock to see the new found success. The store marched up the league tables. He had fought battles with his bosses who couldn't accept his maverick ideas. Those seniors had lost their jobs. The bosses that survived were those that offered Wood more resources than he had ever needed. The Chairman of the Group, on hearing of this episode, had remarked, 'We have a problem. We have one manager of this ilk. We need 320.' He was concerned about the falling share price that his company was experiencing.

Wood had never checked the details of Gustav Eiffel's journey in the pursuit to complete his Tower. He knew that he had not recalled the story in truth. 'I got them to own the problem,' he told Karen. 'If they had been in the Garden of Eden, they would have admitted to God that they had eaten his fruit and not blamed the serpent.'

'All of them?' asked Karen.

'More than enough of them,' Wood replied. The success of his team had given him time to recuperate from the pressures he had felt in the pursuit of his ambitions. Karen had also been relieved. The family was now more secure although she sensed that Wood would embark on another challenge in the future. Her foreboding would not settle.

Over the next ten years, Wood achieved increasing success, but not without its trials. He won company events and competitions. He became the company employee of the year. He won the title as the U.K. National Retail Store Manager.

He delivered the highest workforce engagement score ever recorded, either side of the Atlantic; the comprehensive survey, conducted by Gallop, included participants from several thousand corporations and his score was double the standard identified as World Class in the bestselling novel called *First Break All The Rules. What the Greatest Managers in the World Do.*

Wood had experienced the power that vision could deliver when it was supported with the physical iconic imagery of the Eiffel Tower. Serious episodes would now follow which would challenge this learning and lead him to greater solutions.

The Mona Lisa presented people with the *ever* elusive answer to the question *Is she smiling?* For centuries they had asked. Wood was about to learn what the answer was and that it was the single most important piece of art ever. First, he was promoted. A bigger problem had arisen.

The new manager that replaced Wood at Watford was not happy with what he inherited. 'Get this lot off the walls for a start,' he demanded, picking out all the images of the Eiffel Tower that Wood had placed around the staff block. 'And all these inspirational quotes. I don't want the staff filled with rubbish. Let's get a sense of reality back in this place. Feet on the ground and good old fashioned hard work are the only order of the day.'

He told Wood's old team that change was necessary and he made similar noises to the directors of the company. His verbal affluence began to build a stage that would bring in a network of significant support from his colleagues and seniors. 'He's certainly out to get you,' Wood's old lieutenant had rung and told him. Wood came under significant attack from this vociferous influence. It was necessary; after all, Wood had been too successful and who could follow that? Wood was also aware that it didn't necessarily matter how credible the source was, bad news could kill your career and even, your job.

Within months, the Watford store had collapsed and it was languishing back down the league tables from which Wood had removed it. The new manager claimed that Wood had hidden key issues from his seniors and that his success had been superficial not real. Wood did not want to go back even to visit the store. He did however compromise and return and his old team told him that life had returned to the bad old days. He saw the anxiety on their faces and the return of the demoralised, beaten workforce that he had initial inherited. He was empathic with their concerns and also with his.

In the West Midlands, Wood was wondering if his ambitions had upset others as he settled into his new isolation after being sent to Coventry. The notorious town was infamous for being inhabited by people that no one wanted to talk to. He had been at Watford for only ten months. A new store had now sunk to the bottom of the league table.

'How bad do these stores get?' Wood asked his new lieutenant, walking the shop floor of the colossal mess he had inherited. Wood now had an even bigger problem in Coventry and he was again, telling his new team about the virtues of Gustav Eiffel. The next two years were difficult for Wood. He was concerned about the performance of Watford and the gunfire that was coming his way. Within a year, the replacement manager had been dismissed from the company. His seniors had been concerned about his competence and were actively pursuing a disciplinary path when the store's HR manageress claimed sexual harassment against him.

However, the dilemma for Wood did not go away. He couldn't understand why the store had fallen from its standing so soon after his departure.

His peer group did not share the optimism of his seniors. They felt that the guy who replaced Wood was incompetent and that it was only a matter of time before the company kicked him out. Wood knew of this but it did not ease his mind. Coventry began to perform and again it climbed up the league tables. However, fate was about to intervene.

'One million five hundred and ninety seven thousand pounds, Mr Wood. That, my friend, is the worst stock take result this year by far. I will talk to you again when you have had time to provide me with an explanation.' The golden boy had just become the black eyed pea in the eyes of his Operations Director. Wood knew the reason for his horrific result. He had been stitched up. This did bother him but not as much as the fact that he couldn't prove it.

'Did you get to the bottom of the million pound addition on my stock line?' Wood had asked the analyst on the other end of the phone.

'I've never seen anything like it,' said the analyst alarmed.

'What's the reason?' asked Wood tapping his pen on his pad.

'You've had a million quid just added to your purchases,' said the analyst in high pitched excitement. Wood wondered whether he had been bitten by a dog.

'I know but why?' asked Wood holding the phone from his ear.

'Beats me. You need to ask your Ops Director?' said a calming analyst.

'He's the one asking me,' exclaimed Wood aware that getting information from anybody in head office was like climbing Everest.

'I'd talk to him. He's the only one who can authorise that.'

'Did he authorise it?' asked Wood. His new lieutenant was sitting opposite Wood listening to the conversation on the speaker phone. He mimicked a pair of pliers pulling at his teeth.

'I wouldn't know,' said the analyst in a deep voice.

'Who would?' asked Wood.

'The Ops Director.'

'OK but who would input it?' asked Wood. The new lieutenant was writhing on the floor pretending to strangle himself with his tie.

'Me,' said the analyst.

'Did you?' asked Wood directly.

'Yes,' said the analyst. The new lieutenant couldn't hold out any longer. He burst into laughter and darted out the room to the toilet.

'Why?'

'The request came down from the Ops Director. Most do. I just input them,' said the analyst regaining his excitement.

'You're not being helpful here,' Wood said sarcastically.

'I can only tell you what I know,' said the analyst abruptly.

'Thanks a lot,' exclaimed Wood.

Silence remained on the phone for a couple of seconds.

'Look. All as I can say is that this input is highly irregular. And I didn't tell you that. Goodbye,' said the analyst hurriedly and hung up.

Wood's dilemma was now complete. He could either tell his Operations Director that he knew that he had authorised the loss and get sacked for the accusation or he could admit that he didn't know and he'd get sacked for his ignorance. What worried Wood more was, why had his Operations Director done it?

Meanwhile, word had spread that Wood had delivered the very worst result that year, in the 320 strong store estate of the company. He came under significant pressure and colleagues thought he would not survive. They were enthusiastic to learn of his problems and empathic with them when they spoke to him. Relaying the details to their colleagues was much more fun. Wood had taken the focus off their results and afforded them the pleasure of anticipating that the next promotion slot would be theirs and not Wood's.

He decided to provide his Operations Director with a recovery plan for his store to rectify his stock loss and he took responsibility for the poor result. One of his action points was a weekly control and review of head office purchase costs.

'Are you happy with his response?' Kyle asked to his Operations Director after reviewing Wood's plan. Kyle was sitting stationary in heavy traffic.

'Yes, it was very good. I liked the detail,' replied the Operations Director forcing his foot down hard on the accelerator to overtake just before the bend. He was running late. He always was.

'Did you see his comment on purchases?' said Kyle looking up to the bright sun and blinding himself.

'Yes, he certainly is a bright little bugger. That was a shot across our bows from him. I like his style,' said the Operations Director, ducking in just before the bend and receiving the horn from the drivers coming in both directions. He just missed each of them.

'He knows about the addition to his purchases but he'll get the job done. He'll remain focused,' said Kyle rubbing his eyes.

'I'm sure he will but hit him back for that - hard.'

'I think the networks are already on the case. He's the current laughing stock. Leave it with me. I'll get him wriggling more,' said Kyle poking himself in the eye with his knuckle.

His Operations Director was concerned that the focus in his business on stock taking was poor. He had manipulated the loss in Coventry to drive home his message. Wood had been an excellent choice. He was a very high profile manager having recently won a national industry award for his management skills. He knew that if Wood was seen to fail, all his other managers would be questioning their ability to deliver. Wood was his pawn and if he dropped his head in face of his disaster, his career was over. If he didn't the door would be widely left open. Now it was down to Wood.

Wood did survive and he remained at Coventry for a further eight months. The store began to perform well, but Wood had not driven it to the successes he had achieved in Watford. He had remained pre-occupied with the fall in Watford after he had left and the speed in which it had happened. After his departure, his seven store managers had been promoted from Watford under the surmise that they could impart the success of Wood in other stores. However, this had not materialised and Wood's success was now being seen as luck or something remote that didn't really exist and could not be replicated.

Wood questioned his abilities at this time and wondered if his success was purely down to him. He believed it was and he had been attacked by colleagues for the arrogance of his beliefs. His concern, however, focused on his ability to lead people and he knew that he was doing something wrong in the way he led.

Wood was moved from Coventry and sent to Luton. This made little sense to his peer group because Luton was a store categorised as a Red status; one of the five worst performing stores in the company. Wood was frustrated by his failure to climb further up the seniority ranks and he was disillusioned by the repetitive requests for him to sort out problem stores. He knew he was being used as a pawn by his seniors for their survival. He never implicitly understood what their motives were but he had a fairly good idea. He was more concerned with how long all this would go on for. How long would he languish as their pawn? For now, though, he was engrossed in his need to deal with the weaknesses in his ability to lead.

'What have I got to lose,' Wood said to Karen the day before he started in his new store in Luton. 'My goal now is to get sacked. I reckon that I can last longer than a year.'

In Luton, the store had suffered a poor stock take and the problem was so serious it had become the talk of the company. The entire twenty seven strong management team had been dismissed for fraud.

'Human Resources have sacked the whole team,' his brand new lieutenant told him after they shook hands and sat down for a coffee. 'I'm the only manager left and I think I'm next.'

'No you're not,' said Wood adamantly. 'They will need to knock me down first to get to you. If they sack you I'll walk.'

'The staff are still leaving in droves. The only ones left are the militants,' said his brand new lieutenant worriedly.

'Excellent,' said Wood. 'We need an army.'

'There's not enough for a troop let alone an army,' he replied wiping his forehead with his sleeve.

'Excellent. Why waste money on staff costs,' said Wood glibly.

'There's hardly anyone left. The store's falling apart.'

'Brilliant. Who needs a store,' Wood exclaimed excitedly.

Wood was starting to enjoy himself. He took a new approach and he dropped the principles of Gustav Eiffel and iconic vision. He believed that this was insufficient because Watford had returned to languish in the despair that he had inherited after he had left.

When he started at Luton the store was so out of control, so poor in every aspect that Wood saw a wonderful opportunity. He didn't hold meetings with his staff. They held meetings with him.

He was frequently told that the 'fucking' company didn't know what it was doing, didn't 'fucking' care, and had created this 'fucking' mess in the first place. Wood repeatedly painted a short term picture of stability and told his team to trust him; it would take him time, but he would sort it out. The team threw this back at him and told him that was exactly what every previous manager had 'fucking' told them and they had 'fucked off' out of the door at the earliest opportunity.

Wood recruited a management team with volition. He was not too concerned about the calibre of the team. He would shape them. He just wanted numbers. With no authority to spend money for recruitment and incurring huge expense, Wood was aware of challenge he would face when the bill came in. Unperturbed, he got his team. The consequence did not worry him. He was firmly committed to his ambition that the only success in his career with this company would be in the demise of his livelihood with it.

'Have you seen these figures,' said Wood's brand new lieutenant, showing him a performance report for the store. 'We need to lie or we'll all be dead. They are horrendous. The bosses will kill us.'

'You are quite right,' said Wood who changed the figures and handed the report back to his lieutenant.

'What the...' he began, realising that Wood had made the figures considerably worse. 'We'll be...they'll...ton of bricks...and...' his lieutenant stuttered.

'Send them,' said Wood. 'And put my name on them.'

In the store, he exposed the truth, he dug deep into the detail and the facts about the nature of the store were very poor; the performance was under considerable threat. The further he dug, the more painful the truth became but he was intolerably persistent and he was looking forward to the war he was beginning to wage. Luton was such a mess, his seniors wanted it kept quiet and swept under the carpet. Wood had other ideas.

With his team in place and the truth hammering in the corridors of power, Wood instructed his management team to write the rules and follow the company guidelines to the letter. He gave them two weeks to do so.

'Now communicate it to them all, every detail, nothing must be left open to interpretation,' Wood told them. 'I want the company mission statement indelibly imprinted on the heart and soul of everyone employed by me.' His team did as he asked. Wood sensed that his previous tolerance levels may have resulted in his lack of leadership. He had to find out, even if in meant that he would get the sack for his actions.

'Now sack anyone who isn't compliant,' Wood demanded. Again, his team did so. On one 'Bloody Sunday' twenty seven staff lost their jobs. In total, over 170 staff were dismissed whilst Wood built the store back to full strength. There was absolutely no tolerance.

In the staff and administration office block, he wrote in large bold black marker pen, 'When you identify with your company's purpose, when you experience ownership in a shared vision, you find yourself doing your life's work and not just doing time'. He positioned this statement by the door that separated the staff block from the shop floor. Nobody could miss it.

Kyle spent most of his time shouting at Wood and Wood spent all of his time agreeing with Kyle. Wood was told to sort the mess out and he promised he would. His promises however did not conform to his actions. Kyle dismissed the good results of the store to luck and hammered Wood for the poor ones. Wood was remorseless and single-mindedly on his own agenda.

After six months, an engagement survey (a measure of an employee's satisfaction with their workplace), recorded the lowest result in the Southern Region. Luton was bottom out of seventeen. Wood called his whole team together and apologised for his behaviour. His seniors converged with their divisional Human Resources teams and surveyed the problems within the store personnel. Wood was told that they would be removing him from the store.

Feedback groups were held in all departments and they were asked for the positive and the negative aspects of their boss, Wood. One hundred and twenty one negative points were identified and seventeen positive. His bosses gave him the feedback directly and the young ambitious Human Resource managers added their concerns vociferously.

Wood watched intensely as the chaos reigned around him. He studied his actions and the effects of these on the people around him. He was conscious that his ambitions now had no boundaries and no limitations. He did not feel the pain of those around him, or their joy. He simply watched and observed and kicked himself when he got it wrong and cheered to himself when he got it right.

Wood apologised to his seniors for the demise in his store and convinced them that he could learn from this and deliver a great store for the customers of Luton. He was also confident that they would not sack him because, like him, they knew that nobody else could sort this mess out.

In his career, he was demoted seven times and promoted on twenty one occasions. He never learned how he survived this personal onslaught and what conclusions his seniors had surmised in their debates about him when their doors had been closed.

Behind these doors, senior voices drew their conclusions from the observations gleaned from Wood's team. In their meetings they summarised the most recurrent comments.

'Paranoid, arrogant, demanding, schizophrenic, passionate, single minded, gregarious, ruthless, committed, bold, irritable, keen, receptive, obsessive, lusty, prosperous, thriving, expressive, idiosyncratic, reserved, reflective.'

'I think we may have more to fear in losing him than in keeping him,' said Kyle. His mouth was full with food. He had a plate in front of him with fifteen slices of heavily buttered toast. 'What is he guilty of?'

'Madness, looking at your summary.'

'Most of my time I find that I am asked to judge my juniors because they are fearful to act; their performance is mediocre at best.' The butter dripped from his toast as he ate and spoke simultaneously. 'Madness eh. It will be interesting to watch this madness unfold. He must be mad to have survived this shithole of a store that we gave him.'

'You think he should stay?'

'Who else could run this place? When we put Wood in here, hell had already been unleashed. Discipline him, remove him from your Succession Planning and tell him he forfeits his salary review. Poor bugger.'

'And he is forgiven?' Kyle was challenged. He laughed.

'Only God can forgive this dump. We should pray for Wood.' He replied. 'Somebody get me more toast?'

'But he is off his head.'

'Good. Thank God. Now, toast please.'

Wood changed his tolerance and twelve months later, Luton climbed up the league tables and this time it achieved the highest accolades. Wood's results broke company records in many areas, including his stock take result. It was at this time that he was recognised as 'The Best Manager in the World' following the Gallup survey of employee engagement.

Wood realised that tolerance was not the key to leadership. He now trusted himself that he did know and he did not want to test it out any further in the environments that his employer could offer him. This, he now knew, had been his implicit mistake. Now he wanted to seek a new, much greater challenge.

Wood had concentrated on behaviour. His maverick style had drawn him to take risks from which he had survived. He had raised the bar with his team and won their respect. They had learned to trust him and they were proud to be *Lutonites*. On September 1st 2004, Wood walked out of the store and that completed his thirteen year career with the company. He did not go back. He had survived for over a year and he had delivered his goal.

Years later, the team stood by the values that Wood had installed and new managers were held to account by variations from these values. The store dropped from its heady heights of success under Wood but it performed well. Wood had installed a discipline into the fabric of the store which demanded from the team that they dig deep into the detail and fight for every penny and when he was asked by his seniors to quote the company mission statement he could and so could his team. 'Nobody else can do this,' his MD had remarked. 'The mission statement is too long and too complicated'. Wood let his MD express this observation but when his staff had challenged him with the same view, Wood answered, 'When in Caesar's palace, you pay Caesar's taxes. If you don't like them, change them.' Wood knew he was going to change them.

Wood was interviewed by the group Chairman after his global accolade and asked how he did it. Wood explained to him that he did not know how he had achieved it; he just did it. Wood told him, 'I suppose that I had tried iconic vision but I learnt that it had no sustainability. I felt that I had forced it down the throat of my team.' He thought for a moment and said, 'I recently saw an icon of Jesus on the cross. I sensed that that was what the church had done to its congregation. What other purpose could such a negative symbol serve,' Wood said. He learned from this and turned to behaviour. 'I made nothing visible, I never connected anything I did or said to anything physical or tangible. I had no grand plan. I just started one day and I kept going. I guess that I simply trusted myself to do what was asked of me and in fact, I trusted myself to do it a whole lot better.'

'I suppose, it was about trust, faith and belief. I trusted myself to achieve the very best, I believed I could do it and this trust and belief gave me the faith to go for it.'

The Chairman walked the store with Wood and he spoke with many of the staff. When he left he said to Wood, 'Whenever I speak to your team, they tell me what they are doing and what they are going to do next. They didn't tell me what they had done. Earlier, I asked you if you had any problems that I could help you with and you gave me no answer.'

Wood had seen a greater opportunity outside of his employment in retail. He would set up his own business and determined his objective; *To Redefine the Delivery of Housing in the UK, Europe and Beyond.* Wood had picked up David's stone and he was eyeing Goliath's forehead. Here was a market for Wood to assert who he had become. The emotions of his youth – the pains of his early adulthood – the ambitions of his middle age had shaped a new man. Life had been murdered in him but he had barely ever been more alive and kicking.

In September 2004, Wood opened his first outlet, designed to begin the evolutionary process that the property market desperately needed, and in doing so, he commenced a journey that would see his personal wealth climb to in excess of $300 million, fall into personal bankruptcy four years later with debts in excess of $175 million and rise to redefine economic, political and social reformation.

In the commercial battlefield he would be forsaken, hounded, ravaged and hung. Wood was not yet aware that none of this would matter. He had already learnt to trust himself and nothing mankind or the world could do would stop him decoding the greatest mysteries that remained obscure.

The physical world was the testament of his aggressors but the behavioural future was everybody's immunity. He knew how to deliver this for everyone. Here forgiveness was a given.

GRAVES AND MR HENDERSON
THE STORY OF HOARY 3

Pre-Banking (1982)

Learning a trade would be a ten year plan. Hoary had too often heard the dreams of men and women who had expressed their desires and wished for the delivery to happen instantly. He would not cave into the demand to have it now. Too often he had seen those men and women fail, invariably, because they lacked the need to get their hands dirty.

He was focused primarily on wealth generation and the influence it could deliver. If credibility and confidence were the ingredients that asserted influence – and Hoary had decided that they were – then these would be his game plan. With McCinley & Co, he was being exposed to the balance sheet of some of the largest companies in the world and over the next few years he knew he would be exposed to some of the most lucrative financial avenues available to man. And he was.

His flight to Dubai had departed on schedule and Hoary decide to relax for the seven hour flight. The stewardesses were busy seeing to the passengers that accompanied Hoary in the first class cabin. Beverages, canapés and coffee had been offered after they had given out the handtowels. Following take off, it was customary for the passengers to wipe the anxiety from the palms of their hands. Several of the travellers wore eye masks to allow them to sleep. Hoary nestled into his seat. He wanted to read.

He read the brief for his undertaking to review the balance sheet of Henderson's Middle East venture in real estate. The assignment proposal consisted of a four week review, possibly six but Hoary was confident he could finish the appraisal in two. He was typically impatient at the best of times and even now, twenty minutes into his flight he had already begun to fidget for something to do. He decided that he could never be too well prepared and considered reading through the Henderson review once again. He knew that it was always too easy to miss or over look valuable detail. He reached for his bag and as he thumbed through the contents he noticed that he had brought with him his ruby red amulet. He had not realised that he'd packed it but he was delighted to see that he had. He removed it from his bag along with his review document. He peered over his shoulder and, noticing the seat behind him was vacant, he reclined his chair and placed both documents on the table in front of him.

Hoary was constantly compelled to read and re-read the final page of the amulet. He clearly remembered the impact it had had upon him when he had first done so – nothing had ever come close – it had changed his life.

Furthermore, the text had consolidated the truth behind the words his mother had said to him before she died. Hoary recognised that they provided him with a unique opportunity to define a world that he knew his mother had wanted. From her perch in the heavens, Hoary yearned to witness the smile that would unfold upon her face when he found the courage and the way to expose it publicly.

He did not doubt the size of the task that lay ahead of him. He would be challenging the social structures, the politics and the inherent belief systems of the world that had come to be. If he merely said what he knew, it would be dismissed as absurd or, at best, languish in the debris of silenced genius. No, this knowledge was a panacea of opportunity for a world and it needed a world stage from which it could be deservedly announced and heard. With this platform, a new, exciting vision for mankind could be delivered to a population that would vehemently fall in love with its principles.

His seniors in the church had stated that, following the episodes and the crucifixion of Christ, God would find a better way to deliver his message next time, two thousand years later. Hoary did believe in the virtue of providence and he also knew that providence could be best placed on a credible, world stage from a voice that people had confidence in.

As Hoary eyed both the amulet and the Henderson review, he pondered his choice until he opened the pages of his new religion. Over the years, Hoary had developed a habit of having alternative material close at hand so that he could swap between them when he felt the desire to do so. In his house he always had at least six novels he was reading at any one time. During an evening he could comfortably change between several of them. Now he was on a plane, he felt no urge to change his habit.

The Step
2
Faith – Not a Tangible Thing.

Longsuffering

As it was told

'But the fruit of the Holy Spirit is love, joy, peace, long suffering, gentleness, goodness, faith, meekness, temperance…' (*The Bible; Gal. 5:22-23*)

As it is now

God describes His Spirit – his divine nature – as 'longsuffering'. Most can understand that God is love. Many can also recognize that God experiences joy and happiness and certainly, none would doubt that God has complete faith in His own plan and purpose. But why does God list suffering (actually suffering *long*) as part of His character? How does God suffer?

Before the world was in Noah's time, "it repented the Lord that He had made man on the earth, and it *grieved Him at His heart*" (Gen. 6:6). Does it surprise you that God felt pain (grief) at what mankind had chosen—and become? Was the Flood to put mankind out of his misery?

In Numbers 14:18, God plainly says, "The LORD is longsuffering. God wants no one to misunderstand that even He suffers.'

As it will be with Dace

The fruits of the Holy Spirit – are these not the behaviours inherent in men and women that enable them to consider?

Is love not the most passionate of our energies? Man was designed to love; deliberately because man had to care, to create action. I would not like to be locked away for over 14 billion years and nobody cared. Nobody would come and get me. I would have no salvation. Does God need our help? Has he been waiting for a long time – 14 billion years – for us to come along and find Him? Are we destined, in his master plan, to be his gatekeeper? Does he not suffer for a long time until we do?

Does suffering demand us to consider? Does it not make us yearn harder to be free? Does it not allow us to appreciate how powerful and precious our ability to love is?

In a universe where opposites create the balance of nature, suffering is the baseline from which our love strives to be freed. There is only one key to our salvation and Noah despaired that we may never realise that we have to go and get it.

Hoary wondered how the church would respond to this view. He sensed that in all his learning as an Anglican priest he could find no counter argument to dissuade him of the words in the text he had just read. Quite the contrary, Hoary concluded that he was being presented with a different view of God. In this new context, many of the interpretations of the texts from the Bible that had perplexed scholars over the years, were now given a framework that enlightened their meaning. For all our time, in many of our religions, God was the almighty wisdom, sitting on his throne in his kingdom, governing our actions. Hoary was beginning to realise that we had got Him wrong. Dramatically so.

The captain's voice spoke out from the internal PA system informing the passengers that the plane had reached 38,000 feet. Whilst the captain continued to relay the flight information, Hoary closed the amulet and placed it on his table. When the PA system went quiet, Hoary chose to pick up his Henderson review.

Synopsis

The Henderson Group was born by the passion of one man, Jim Henderson and his ambition to provide a commercial estate accessible to all factions of our industrial networks. The estate focused upon wholesale, distribution and factory warehouse space and latterly it moved into the acquisition of office and retail buildings. Jim believed that he could make these premises more accessible to a growing but frustrated entrepreneurial demand.

The demand was clearly evident in the market place and Jim considered that if he could develop longer lease terms, the benefit of the longevity to his cash flow could reduce the overheads cost, i.e. the rent, he would need to charge to his tenants.

By the mid 1970s, the Henderson estate had reduced its non-tenanted buildings (void periods) to an average below 5% per annum with yields well within industry norms. This performance gained significant interest from finance houses that provided Jim with sufficient funds to increase his holdings and by the end of the decade, the Henderson Group had purchased over £17 billion of commercial estate.

Two years after Jim's death in 1983, a review of his Estate found that the repair bill for the buildings had grown sevenfold. This had predominantly arisen owing to the mismanagement and poor enforcement of the 'Repair and Leasing' contracts held with the tenants. Since this review, the group has struggled to deliver a sustainable financial performance and the estate has undergone retraction. The opportunity is to reverse this trend. Since Jim's death, the City has been critical of subsequent management stating that 'Jim Henderson had commercial buildings routed under his fingernails. The group has lacked this essential ingredient since his untimely departure.'

Hoary reached for his pen and wrote in the left margin of the page he had just read, 'Lacks vision – needs strategic direction and milestone planning. Review mindset of personnel – engagement at risk.' Before Hoary put down his pen he crossed through the word 'strategic'. 'Horrific word,' thought Hoary. 'Needs banning from the dictionary.' He noted his usage of the word 'mindset' and decided that he would introduce this into his new environment in Dubai. He was confident that he could have everyone in the offices using this word by the end of his stay – this would not be the first time that Hoary had done so. He was amused with the ease by which people could be influenced.

Hoary placed his review document on the table and decided to swap it for the amulet. He realised what he had done and thought that it would be far easier for him to constructively work through the Henderson paper if he could continually replace it with 'The Step' after every section. He had read the document several times and on each occasion he had found something that he had missed previously. This would stand him a better chance of reaching the end with a clearer understanding of his task ahead.

The Step
2
Faith – Not a Tangible Thing.

Adversity

As it is now

Most people have no idea what God's purpose is for mankind. Many assume that life is probably about "getting to heaven," but have no more understanding than this.

King Solomon was inspired by God to record one of the great principles in the Bible: 'In the day of prosperity be joyful, but in the day of adversity *consider*: God also has set the one against the other, to the end that man should find nothing after him.' (Ecc. 7:14).

God designed life so that we would face 'adversity' and be forced to 'consider' the circumstances we are experiencing. Certainly, adversity is no fun. It is sometimes *very* difficult, hard, painful, even traumatic, to endure. Yet, God said He engineered the human existence to include adversity. This seems strange to the human mind that wants a free pass to sail through life, experiencing only the good life - good times.

As it will be with Dace

'...face adversity and be forced to consider.' Choose your politics – dismissal or salvation? There is only one purpose and the adversity that will conquer your dismissal has not been significant enough for you to choose it – yet.

What is salvation to you – a world in which you are saved? A world in which you are free?

And, how is man engineered – in Vitruvian style?

Hoary swapped narratives once again. The stewardess seemed to sense that he had just concluded the section he had been reading when she interrupted him to ask him if he would like another beverage. Hoary opted for a tea and a Mars Bar.

Corporate Structure

The Henderson Group has a simple company structure. A top co. Plc retains all assets, and incomes are distributed amongst nominal divisions relevant to the category of building. For example, rental income from retail outlets is paid to the retail division. Payment of overheads conforms in the same fashion. The Plc is retained off shore in Dubai where decision making has been centralised.

The current senior management view the business purely as an asset retention and management vehicle, with strict financial performance of the portfolio managed by cost to income ratios, capital growth targets and net and gross yield delivery.

Quarterly reports are submitted to the stock markets. They define the above performance with turnover measured by year on year growth/decline.

The last two years have witnessed double digit decline with the share price dropping by 37% during this period.

Cost cutting criteria has seen the workforce numbers decrease by 24%. A compliance management team have been introduced with an additional head count cost of 2.5%.

However, annualised projections for the forthcoming full trading year indicate a further decline of 11%. At the time of writing this report, the assumptions for this erosion were based on the first four months trading of the year.

The Henderson Group will not maintain solvency without successful action and, the implementation of this, being realised within six months. Moody's will conduct a credit rating review, as per guidelines, following McCinley's report.

Hoary did not deem the task ahead of him to be exacting. The decisions before him would be fairly normal protocol and, in this, he would establish his diplomacy. However, the balance sheets had been a challenge for him to decipher and Hoary knew that this presented him with his most serious hurdle. Large insurance premiums were being paid and deemed losses had been hedged and yet, no claims were evident. If the management team had displayed the foresight to bet against potential losses which had now become true, why were they not claiming their winnings?

The Step
2
Faith – Not a Tangible Thing.

Forsaken

As it is now

The world gives much attention to the suffering of Christ. God's answer to this question: "Though He [Christ] were a Son, yet learned He obedience *by the things which He suffered*".

Christ was sinless. If He was otherwise, we have no Saviour. So, of course, He *was* without fault, blameless, sinless. Yet, this passage reveals that even Christ learned from the suffering He endured. Pain kicks the mental learning mechanism into gear. We have to answer the question, 'why has this happened?'

For instance, physical pain of sufficient intensity stops people in their tracks. They search for the cause of the pain. Whether it is the discomfort of an on-coming heart attack, an acute headache or the inflammation of arthritis, people want to know why their body hurts.

The apostle Paul begins to relate suffering directly to the process of God's purpose in making sons who reflect His character. Notice: 'For it became Him [Christ]…in bringing *many sons* unto glory, to make the Captain of their salvation *perfect through sufferings*' (2:10).

Christ's suffering actually perfected Him—made Him full, mature, complete, as God's first begotten, and later firstborn, Son. This is what it says. Hebrews 5:9 continues by adding, 'And being made perfect, He became the author of eternal salvation unto all them that *obey Him*.' Christ qualified to 'become the author of eternal salvation' because He was willing to endure and learn from God's prescribed suffering process for all who are His sons—those who 'obey Him.'

The salvation process involves obeying Christ. But let's see more plainly exactly what this means. The apostle Peter explains, 'For even hereunto were you [Christians] called: because Christ also suffered for us, leaving us an example, *that you should follow His steps*' (I Pet. 2:21).

As it will be with Dace

There is truth that pain and suffering matures learning. In the final hour, Christ suffered at the hands of the politics of dismissal, from men who followed a different faith and chose a different power.

Sin can easily be misinterpreted. In many circumstances it is transient and values change. Christ was certainly unequivocal with Gods purpose – an excellence of behaviour we are yet to know or, at least, not yet ready to practise by our norms. However, we cannot confuse this issue with sin. Would sin exist in a world governed by forgiveness?

If Christ was forsaken to cleanse our sins then what does this tell us about the value of his life and hence the value of ours? Christ did not choose to be displayed as a crucifixion on a cross. Is this the negative symbolism we wish to shape our future pursuits? Christ would argue that it is not.

Christ did argue that we must have faith in our true pursuit – to find God. A pursuit that is the most intangible of things, or so it would seem – it is engraved on our DNA. The church that was designed before our birth yet remains to be built. Faith doesn't exist in a physical world; it is a behaviour, an action governed by choice – one day it can become a simple yes or no.

Christ is the resurrection. That is the truth.

Hoary closed the amulet, lent back in his seat and closed his eyes. The words written in the amulet had touched the sentiments he had come to believe. How the symbols, the statues and the art which was housed within the churches he visited had begun to frustrate him. 'Jesus,' he thought, 'would turn in his grave if he could see what we have done. All his glory displayed in an act of brutal violence, nailed to a blood stained cross.' Hoary could hardly justify the church buildings themselves and he had questioned their significance and mans' motivation for building them. 'Had Jesus wanted us to see them as our symbol to God and by attendance alone we would acknowledge His presence?' Hoary had said to his superior, Tom. 'Or are they a house in which we can exercise our choice to believe in him? If they are the latter, why do we need a house?'

'We are indebted, through our choice, to express our obedience to Him.'

Hoary had not challenged Tom when he had said this. Diplomacy was a consistently practised art for all those who held office in the church. Modern day challenges and contradictions presented this demand upon them. Hoary did, also, admire Tom's seemingly unnerved commitment to God. Tom was always the first to rise from his seat for psalms. Hoary did not believe that obedience was a demand from God. Since he had read 'The Step,' he had realised that God did not want our obedience. Maybe this word had a different context two thousand years ago. Maybe the translation had lost its true value. Whatever the case may be, Hoary had surmised, the opposite was true; God needed our help. He needed our help now.

Hoary flicked through the pages of the Henderson document and reviewed the financial data presented on a series of balance sheets, and portfolio schedules. He noted that the estate had been geared heavily in the early eighties with the financial commitments to the external lenders – predominantly Canadian banks – being in excess of 88%. However, since this time, the lending commitments had dropped below 62% owing to the value of the estate growing. Hoary noted this observation on the corresponding document – if the company needed cash, this presented an opportunity, even though, Hoary thought, the current management would not have the appetite for this. On current performance, they would certainly have a challenge to raise cash from re-mortgaging the estate. Hoary wrote a note on the page, 'commitment and appetite'.

The Step
2
Faith – Not a Tangible Thing.

Value

As it was told

Paul said, 'I do not like to suffer. Neither do you. But it is *only* through suffering that we can learn what God intends in order to achieve salvation. Paul also wrote, 'It is a faithful saying: For if we be dead with Him, we shall also live with Him: *If we suffer*, we shall also reign with Him…' (*The Bible, II Tim. 2:11-12*)

As it is now

Suffering is absolutely essential to the character-building process. Because it is a process, time and experience are involved.

Paul recognized that suffering was tied to the resurrection of the dead, and actually looked forward to it, seeing it as a way of drawing closer to what Christ endured—as literally 'fellowshipping with Him.' Here is how God inspired him to record this connection: 'That I may know Him [Christ], and the power of His resurrection, and the *fellowship of His sufferings*, being made conformable unto His death; if by any means I might attain unto the *resurrection of the dead'* (Phil. 3:10-11).

As it will be with Dace

The primary reason for suffering goes hand in hand with the dismissal of purpose; our failure to see it and our failure to take the actions and the responsibility to deliver it. True, suffering intensifies learning which matures ones politics; eventually, you get the point. But the suffering is not essential, it is a by product. The fellowship and conformity to the faith of Christ, when you exercise this choice, allows you to see the resurrection as a truth. Suffering can and will stop. We may dismiss the resurrection as a mythical ideal but how can our science answer this if we are not prepared to engage the question?

Hoary believed that the resurrection of Christ was the truth. Who were we to denounce this as a possibility? What would we face at our death if we could give the same commitment to God that Christ did?

When we did die and face St. Peter at the Pearly gates, Hoary thought, we would be given the account of our commitment to God and the purpose of mankind. For the majority, the lack of this, would see them rejoin a lengthening queue of recycled people being sent back to earth until they finally got the point. How long that queue would be, thought Hoary, possibly Christ was the only one given a greater task – a new dimension to tackle – and the resurrection had purely been his cheer to us that he had conquered the challenge that all God's children faced. 'This is the way. This is what to do,' Christ had been telling us and we had not heard the context of his words because we could not see what he had.

Hoary wondered what level of commitment he would find in the existing management team of the Henderson Group when he arrived in Dubai. Would the survival of their company be upper most in their drive and determination? Would he see through their lip service, if this is what he was to encounter? Or would he meet an inspirational voice setting a new pace for a winning team to act upon? Hoary closed the document and put it into his hand luggage.

The Step

2

Faith – Not a Tangible Thing.

Immortality

As it is now

: Can evil come directly *from God*?' God answers: 'I am the LORD, and there is none else…I form the light, and create darkness: I make peace and create evil: I the LORD do all these things' (Isa. 45:5, 7). Satan is often the vehicle that brings it.

In Corinthians 11:24-30, Paul's ministry required him to endure astonishing discomfort, pain and suffering – he saw the purpose of God.

Yet, in the grand scheme of things, when compared to the reward God has in store for all His begotten sons and daughters, how difficult was the suffering? Paul answers, 'For I reckon that *the sufferings of this present time* are not worthy to be compared with the glory which shall be revealed in us. For the earnest expectation of the creature waits for the manifestation of the sons of God'. (Rom. 8:18-19).

Nothing we endure even remotely compares to the immortal life in God's kingdom in store for those who serve Him.

Nevertheless, suffering can be very difficult for the moment—for 'this present time.' Job knew God's supreme wisdom was at work in all that happened to him. After he acknowledged God's sovereign power over his life, he was blessed vastly beyond what he had before his trial. Faith in God's wisdom paid off in the end.

Recall that Solomon explained that God, throughout our lives, alternates 'days of prosperity' with 'days of adversity' (Ecc. 7:14). Put another way, either condition you are experiencing will be followed by the opposite condition. If you are enjoying good times, difficult times lie ahead. If you are enjoying difficult times, good times will soon follow. David, Solomon's father, knew that, 'weeping may endure for a night, but joy comes in the morning' (Psa. 30:5). This is God's promise.

If you submit to God, this will be fulfilled in *your* life, both now and eternally.

As it will be with Dace

God does not want you to submit to him he wants you to find him. He does not have a hand that can beckon or influence the world we live in. Our world is his platform from which we are given the opportunity to exercise our destiny. The choices we make determine that destiny. You and I decide on our fate. You and I are responsible for our actions – not God or anybody else. With faith in God, our actions will lead us to a wealth that we cannot even imagine.

When we dismiss God, we will lead ourselves repeatedly along roads that we have already walked, repairing the wear and repairing the wear, frustrated by this constant affliction, destitute that it is the actions of others, beholden to an empty escape, vocal towards your satanic fellows, unaware that we are the satanic fellow.

God does not want you to fear him, to be submissive to a dream. He wants you to demand his

company, act, find him and in doing so you will have
to conquer all your fears – a journey that only courage
can pursue. He wants you to deliver your political
truth. He wants you to build new roads on new
territories.

Beyond fear, beyond all of our limiting beliefs,
what exists; immortality? Which is our life – our DNA
or our organic human form?

Hoary knew that he had made the right choice to leave the church. In
it, he could not act as he believed he needed to. The church evoked his
fears and confined his actions. His ambitions could not permit this. He
felt strangled and oppressed. In the five years that had now passed,
Hoary had learned that the commercial world would release them and
already he was beginning to see how he could evoke the tsunami that
would devastate the shores across all of our lands. He felt alive and
excited by the challenge. Whilst the anxiety he felt from his trepidation
could constrain his actions he knew that he could manage this. It would
not hold him back.

In Dubai, he would encounter a clearer path to this ambition. His
commitment was absolute and his actions now needed providence.

Popcorn and Uncles
The History of Wood 3

Childhood - October 13th to October 31st 1978

Tane Wood loved his dad. He was his king. Everything his dad did was brilliant.

'Zip,' his dad would say, his cuteism for his son, 'I've nearly finished your castle. I'm going to crack on with it. It's nearly Christmas.'

'Dad, can I watch? Can I come with you?'

'No. When I've done, it will go to Santa. You'll spoil the surprise.'

'Oh Dad. I know there's no Santa. I'm thirteen.'

'If there's no Santa, then there's no castle.'

'Dad?'

His dad shut the front door behind him and disappeared behind the garage door. Wood went into the kitchen and found his mother. His mother had just opened the post and one letter remained in her right hand whilst her other hand was clasped around her forehead.

Wood wasn't alarmed by this, at first. His mother was very expressive. Whilst Wood played in the street, kicking the football continuously against the wall that ran the full length of their garden, he often heard the loud, screaming voice of his mother in altercation with either of his two brothers. Wood often kicked the football around with one of his friends from the street and when they played in front of one of their houses, he never heard their mothers do the same. He was alone this time but the embarrassment he had learned to feel from it had grown to follow him everywhere, whenever he heard his mother's raucous shouts. And if she wasn't shouting (and she usually was) she was crying about something, usually her sister Casey, who was a prostitute (Casey's husband didn't know). She was always in trouble and always dressed to kill. Gerry often laughed that Casey could nick anything from anyone. Casey told Gerry she nicked her clothes and her jewellery, their food, the clothes for their children, the petrol in their car – everything. They had three children and none of them were Gerry's. Wood's mum cried often when they spoke of this. So they all tried not to mention it.

Aidan was in the kitchen with his mother when she opened the letter. They had been talking when Wood walked in and Aidan said, 'Don't tell him. Just bin the letter.' Aidan, five years older than Wood, was sitting at the kitchen table, legs across it, brandishing a hockey stick. When Wood entered, Aidan swiped the stick at Wood and said, 'Fucking lucky, boy. I'll get ya next time.'

'I can't just bin it. He gets so angry and frustrated waiting for the damn thing. If only he wouldn't bother.'

'Well, the shit's gunna fly,' said Aidan who sprang to his feet. 'I'm off to see Smithy. He owes me a tenner, the fat twat.' When Aidan passed Wood at the kitchen door, he poked the butt of the hockey stick towards his face and pulled it back before it made contact. 'Lucky again boy. One day.' Aidan opened the front door, leapt across the garden and ran down the street, kickboxing his way as he went, triumphantly cheering as the hits defeated his imaginary foe.

When Aidan left the kitchen, so did Wood. He went into the playroom to find Mark, his younger brother, who was always in there. Their dad was so pleased to own a house with a playroom. 'I never had this when I was a kid. Slowly but surely, my son.' He would say and he bought them a ping pong table and a table football and a Scalextric and a train set and a whole lot more. Mark had once told his father that his friend had more toys than he did. His father hadn't liked this comment. He had risen from the dining room table, lifted his plate of food and thrown it at the sideboard, smashing an engraved, lead crystal decanter as it hit. The moments of abuse that hailed from his father lasted only as long as it took for him to leave the room. 'You've got more fuckin toys than any kid in any street,' he said. When he had left, his mother spoke to Mark in a torrid, scolding voice, repeating what their father had just said and telling Mark that he would get no lunches for a week, he was banned from the playroom and he could not see his friends.

It had been easier for them then but that was six months ago and tempers had got worse. Wood was sitting in the playroom with his brother and they could hear the sound of angry voices coming from the garage that sat below the playroom.

'Dad's 'Top of the League,' has been rejected by Waddington's,' Wood told his brother. He had read the letter before he had left his mum. The voices became very loud and very angry. His mother's voice, they were used to it now, turned from anger to a high pitched screech as she became more intense. Their father's voice always ruffled and boomed in his anger.

Wood went to the window and looked either way down the street. He was glad that the street was empty and none of his friends, or their parents could be seen. He looked more closely at the windows to see who was about.

'I'm going to my bedroom,' said Mark. He had started doing this recently, since he'd turned eleven, whenever he heard his parents argue. He had come to know that that was where he always ended up. 'Don't worry. I'll go down,' said Wood.' Mark looked over to Wood and then left the room.

When Wood began to descend the stairs, he saw that his mother had come back into the house and she was sitting at the kitchen table. She wasn't crying this time but the blue of her eyes had faded behind the pools of tears that had settled on her eyelids. Wood went to the front door and his mother saw him. 'For God's sake Tane, stay indoors. Go to your playroom.'

Wood moved from the front door and slipped out the back instead. His mother did not see him do this and when he got to the garage he peeped through the slot in the side of the door to watch his father. His father was sawing a piece of wood and he seemed to be doing so with some venom. His eyes were fixed and his teeth appeared to be biting his lower lip. He suddenly rose and threw the saw and the piece of timber to the floor. He stood back and put his hands on his hips for a moment and then raised his hand to his forehead whilst he sighed and sighed again.

He looked over at the door and his eyes moved towards the slot from which Wood was peering. Something seemed to catch his eye and he looked harder and then moved toward the door. He flung the door open and Wood stood before him. Wood didn't speak and when his father grabbed him he didn't say a word but the cries emanated from his anguish and from his pain as his father removed his belt and repeatedly whipped it across his son in frantic, absurd fashion.

'Clever shit are we? No Santa eh? I'll fuckin' teach you there's no fuckin' Santa', his father had kept repeating the words.

'Fuckin' teach ya, you little shit. No fuckin' Santa'.

The next day, Monday, his dad left early for Cambridge to attend the Annual General Meeting for the company he worked for. He returned from it the following evening. He was standing in the kitchen whilst his mother heated up a pan of stew for him to eat. 'I never saw the bloody thing coming. I had to swerve and the car went up on two wheels.'

'Bloody hell.'

'Bloody hell? I nearly lost the damn thing. I thought I was going over.'

'Wasn't the roundabout signposted?'

'It must have been. I just didn't see it. I don't understand it. Damn thing. I'm lucky to be here. I really thought…I was doing a hell of a speed. I...well.'

Wood had heard their conversation. In school the next day, his classmates were talking about the time Jake had lost his father and Wood froze with these words. He was shaken and glad by the fact that it wasn't him they were talking about. He couldn't contemplate life without his dad. What would they do? He began to cry. He couldn't lose his king. He knew that life wasn't good at the moment but it would get better and his dad would love him and know his son was a great son.

When Wood returned home that night his mum seemed anxious throughout the evening and she was angry with him and Mark as they played in the kitchen whilst she peeled the potatoes in the sink with the usual red handled knife that dad had blunted for her. They knew she was about to get very angry with them because the shouting had started. They quickly tidied up their toys and went to their bedroom. Their mother screamed after them.

'The playroom. Now. No toys in the bedroom.'

When their dad arrived home from work, he nearly stood on the dog by mistake. Genghis was only a puppy, just over four months old and the Golden Retriever was lying on the floor, half hidden by the armchair, chewing a toy bone. 'Nearly stood on his head, the daft git,' their dad said it in a funny voice, as though he was drunk, and the boys laughed. Wood had been asking for a puppy since he was eight and his dad had always thought it a good idea for the boys to have a dog. Their mum had been reticent because of her allergy to dogs but when Wood was thirteen, his dad and mum had told him they needed to talk to him and called him into the kitchen. 'If you promise to look after him, feed him and walk him every day, you can have a dog.' It was his thirteenth birthday and Wood had climbed on to his father's knee, flung both arms around his neck and told his dad that he was the best dad in the world and the best dad he could ever have.

The following day, Wood was standing outside the school waiting for his mum to pick him up. She didn't usually pick him up and she was twenty minutes late. Most of the time he walked home with his friends and saved the bus fare his mum gave him every day. But today, his mum and dad had some news that they wanted to talk to the boys about and she wanted them all home early before their dad got home. Wood knew that his dad had got his promotion but they hadn't told him or his brothers about the big six bedroom house they had bought in Cambridge and the car that their dad would get with the new role, a Daimler Sovereign 4.2 litre. Their dad had always wanted one, 'An Emperor's dream', he would call it and their mum knew that they would all be excited when they found out.

Wood's housemaster tapped him on the shoulder as he stood outside the grounds of the school by Ashleigh High Street, waiting for his mum. 'Come on Tane. I'm taking you home. Your mum has rung and asked a favour from me.'

As Wood walked with Mr Hughes to his car, his housemaster began to tell him why his mother had rung him and asked him to take him home. Wood began to cry and when they arrived at his house, the ambulance men were carrying his father on a stretcher down the steps from the front door to the ambulance. His father was wrapped in blankets and as Wood looked at his dad, he couldn't recognise his face and he couldn't understand why. He ran over to the stretcher and told his dad that he loved him and he couldn't wait until he got home because he was the best dad in the world. His mother was running around the house trying to find certain items which she was placing in a bag. She kept shouting at Wood and Mark telling them to stop getting in the way and, 'where is Aidan, for God's sake. I'm sick of him always being late.' When she stopped, the ambulance left.

Wood wasn't allowed to see his dad in hospital for nearly a week. 'He's very poorly and he needs to rest. We don't want to disturb him now, do we?' When he finally got to see his father, his uncle told him before they went in, that his father was different from when he had last seen him. Wood didn't understand what his uncle meant by this but he had overheard his mum say that his dad had been reacting badly to the medication.

When Wood entered the room and saw his father, the shock ripped through him with the gusto of a new experience deployed by a lightning strike. For the five minutes that he stood holding his father's hand he did not cry. He would not allow himself to and he told himself this before he'd entered the room. The large heavyset sixteen stone frame of his 6ft 2in father had been stolen and replaced with the slightness of a young skinny boy, about to enter his teenage years. The theft was made more unreal at the sight of his body covered in black and blue bruises, his mouth wide open and his lower lip and tongue, gone. His father's defiant breaths and his unconscious silence did not stop Wood holding his dad's hand and finding the strength in his voice to tell his father calmly that he loved him and he couldn't wait to get his castle from Santa at Christmas.

The GP, Michael Jamieson, could not stop apologising to their mother a week later, on the day their dad had died. 'If I had gotten to him a couple of days earlier it may have been a different outcome.' Their mum had thanked him for his honesty and asked him to leave. But this was an honesty that left her uncomfortable in the same way that she had always been uncomfortable with her GP. He had hit on her a year earlier and she had spent nearly a month refusing his advances before he had finally backed off. To a large extent she had become used to these advances. She worked contract hours modelling for labels that sold their clothing through the Littlewoods catalogue but the GP had been more persistent than most and she had found it odd that he had not responded more promptly to her anxious phone calls and her desperate concern for her husband.

Wood was in Liverpool with his auntie on that day. She worked in a chemist and Wood had often helped out at the shop when he had stayed with his uncle and auntie in Childwall. The pharmacist had asked Wood if he would accompany him on his rounds that day because he would be delighted to have his company. Wood had been excited by this and the pharmacist had added that they would see Ken Dodd on the round.

When they visited the people, they were all old and each of them was in bed with an oxygen bottle by their bed. 'When you see an old person in bed next to a cylinder it only means one thing I'm afraid,' the pharmacist had said when they had left the first house. When they met Ken Dodd he had asked Wood why his favourite fan was making a personal visit to his home and Wood had told him that when his dad got better, they too were moving to a magnificent house just like his. Wood had laughed constantly for the half an hour he had been with Ken and he later told everyone that he had seen the Diddy Men. In fact he did not stop telling everyone until his uncle and auntie decided that they had better sit him down and tell him that his father had died.

Wood was in Liverpool with his relatives because they had no choice but to take him away with them. Two days earlier, his mother and her three sons had argued severely, shouting and screaming and blaming each other for their dad's illness. Wood had come off the worse. Aidan had cracked a golf club over his head and at the hospital, the doctor had applied seventeen stitches to the wound. 'This is not the first time that this wound has been reopened but it must be the last. Skulls were not built to take this,' the doctor told his mother.

They often blamed Wood for everything and it had started after he had failed his eleven plus exam. His father had accused the headmaster of favouritism. 'That bastard begged me for a mortgage to save his family and I gave it to him with a lot of risk attached,' Wood's livid father had said to him after he had visited the school and told the headmaster to expect a sharp increase in his monthly payments. 'Policy, I'm afraid. New policy. A lot of people will be unhappy and it could ruin some'.

'Don't worry son. You are bright enough OK? I'll put you in Prep school and you can pass your thirteen plus.' Wood did pass this exam and he got into a grammar school, but his brothers had thought him a 'posh twat' and a 'spoilt shite' and even his mother had thought that he had changed for the worse, gone above his station and demanded too much from their dad. 'Skateboards, school trips to Marseille and quad bikes. Who the hell does he think he is? Your dad can't sleep with the expense.' Since then, Wood had mostly paid the price when the family had argued.

When Wood was being driven away in the car, he had asked his uncle why he was going to stay in Liverpool again and his uncle had answered 'because you wouldn't have survived, son.' Wood had stayed often with his uncle since he was nine years old, mainly in the summer holidays. Aidan and Mark had stayed with his mother's relatives in Huyton and Bootle. Their mum and dad always sent them off during the holidays and Aidan had told them that their dad was angry with men always hitting on their mum.

Wood had come to hate it. He would often question whether Aidan had been telling them the truth or whether it was an excuse used to hide their hatred of him. Wood could never understand why his father's relatives had not liked his mum. Every night when they ate, his auntie would complain that she did not understand Wood's mother. 'She was born a scouser but she thinks she's above it all now with a big house and fancy curtains. There's more to life than that you know.'

In much the same way, Wood always felt apprehensive when he stayed in his uncle's house because the tension in the household was too often very uncomfortable. Angela and Alfred were always arguing and she occasionally went to work wearing dark glasses or neck scarves and Pip, his cousin, was often being reprimanded by his father. The screams from his bedroom could be heard above the sound of the television. Wood knew that his uncle had used a belt buckle.

He didn't like being away from his dad either but he hated more, much more, the man who lived next door to his uncle. His auntie, Angela had always told Wood and her son Pip, to stay away from that man because there were rumours about him which she could not talk to them about, but their uncle had laughed at these claims and often said, 'Any man with a limp nowadays gets accused of the worst.'

On the Saturday, three days after his father died, Wood was playing football with his friends in the park, whilst his dad's funeral took place. Wood was good at football and today he was running rings around Gordon Durie, who would go on to play international football for Scotland. The five boys had decided on two-on-two with one goalkeeper and as Wood side stepped Gordon once again and banged the ball passed the goalkeeper he shouted 'forty-seven' to taunt his opponents with his goal tally. Milky, playing alongside Gordon, told his teammate that he was crap and he'd never play for Liverpool School Boys.

When the boys noticed the next door neighbour limping his way towards them they were quick to begin shouting their taunts at him. Milky told the man to go home and play with himself and Gordon shouted to him that there were no sheep in the fields today but they would round some up if he was desperate. The man got out a gun and started to brandish it at them but Wesley, the goalkeeper, ran up to him grabbed the gun, put the man in a head lock and shouted, 'you can't kill kids with popcorn'.

This made Wood recall the tragic events that had impacted his life in the last two weeks and the other boys noticed that he was sitting on the floor with his head in his hands. They tried to tell him that everything would be ok but Wood told them that he should go home. His uncle had told him that it was his choice whether he went to his dad's funeral or not, and that if he didn't want to go everyone would understand. His uncle had been concerned that Wood would suffer more abuse if his family got too upset and he told Wood that they would do. His uncle knew that Wood always got the blame and that he always took the brunt of the misfortunes that happened in their household.

His uncle had often spoken to his brother about Wood and they both described him as a survivor who would always land on his feet. Wood had heard them say this but as he walked back to his uncle's house he found it very difficult to believe that they were right. Before his uncle and auntie left the house that morning they told Wood that they had got seats in the directors' box at Anfield that Saturday, to watch the big game with Ipswich Town. 'Title decider,' his uncle had said. They would tour the ground first, meet the players and see the trophy room. They had arranged it all with Kenny Dalglish, who had invited Wood to eat with the team after the game. His uncle had been excited and lifted Wood and thrown him over his shoulder playfully, when he had begun to smile. 'Remember son, your dad always was and always will be very proud of you,' his uncle had said as Wood had left the house before Angela and Alfred left for the funeral. As Wood returned to the house now, he could not find the desire to smile and only wanted to go to his room and sit alone. As he walked up to the house and pushed the gate open he was surprised to see his uncle's car sitting on the drive. It seemed early and he was disappointed that he was not to be alone. No lights were on in the house but it was only early evening and as he got to the door it was slightly ajar. He knew Trixie the dog would have escaped and his uncle would be angry but a smell that he didn't recognise distracted him. He pushed the door open and when he saw the blood stained hallway, his uncle crumpled uncompromisingly on the floor and his auntie bent in half in an impossible position, his mind did something it had never done before.

∞

His eyes were open but the police could not wake him. They had decided to take him back to the station and call for a doctor. At the station, the sergeant told them that he was suffering from shock and they should get him to a hospital right away. In hospital, they gave him medication but Wood remained silent. The police had assumed that the hospital was tracing his next of kin and the hospital assumed that the police were doing it. The doctors decided that they could do nothing more for Wood and so they moved him to the Whiston hospital for Psychiatric patients. It was several months before Wood began to express any signs of emotion, he had still not spoken a word and the psychiatric nurses were becoming frustrated with him. They left him when he wet himself and kicked him when he wouldn't eat.

It was not until Wood reached the age of forty four, thirty years later, that he could recall what happened to him the moment after he had witnessed the gruesome scene at his uncle's house. But he finally did, and when he did, he cried with joy.

FROZEN OECUMENICAL ENGINES
THE HISTORY OF HOARY 4

Becoming a Banker (1982-2004)

'What are you going to do?' said Kline, the CEO of the Henderson Group. The anxiety on his face matched that of the Chairman, Geoff Hope sitting next to him. 'Are you going to tell them?'

'No. You are going to tell me the truth,' said Hoary.

'I have done,' said Geoff.

'And then,' Hoary continued undeterred, 'you will hand over executive control to me. Not strictly speaking. I wouldn't want you to relinquish your titles and why would I need to be associated with this shambles? I'm sure you get the point and if you don't, I can spell it out.'

'What makes you think you can sort this shithole out?' asked Geoff. Kline was busy wiping his brow.

'At this juncture, I do suggest that the truth is forthcoming to me before my intolerance sees me walk out through that door and get on the next plane out of here.'

'I have spent ten years building this company and I...' began Geoff.

'And the last two, severely destroying it,' interrupted Hoary. 'Now the truth?'

Kline and Geoff looked at each other. Their anxiety changed to submission and Hoary was pleased that they were going to concede earlier than he had anticipated. 'We lost the files,' said Kline.

'No you didn't,' said Hoary. 'The truth please?'

'We did,' Geoff said, glancing at Kline, seeking his affirmation.

'I spent two days in your accounts department. There never were any files.'

'Oh fuck it,' said Kline, sitting back in his chair, rolling his eyes up to the ceiling. 'There weren't any files.' Kline looked at Geoff and shrugged his shoulders. 'What's the point?' he said to Geoff who also sat back in his seat when Kline said this.

'Good,' said Hoary. 'Already you are gaining my utmost regard for you both.'

'Don't patronise me,' said Geoff.

'I'm not. I mean it. Now let me tell you what is going to happen.'

By the time Hoary had set foot through the door at the Henderson Group, he had travelled extensively across the Western nations and the Middle East. He had lost count of the companies he had assessed and the balance sheets he had reviewed. Invariably, the entrepreneurial spirit behind all of them, displayed an ambition that had sailed close to or broken the compliance and legal criteria in which they operated. Good entrepreneurs did. Vision and commitment seemed to be the ingredients that governed growth and they superseded all other requirements. His assessment of the Henderson operation had presented him with little more than most but now the timing was different. Hoary was due to resign his position at McCinley's on his return from Dubai and his observations whilst here had presented him with a lucrative opportunity to score a political advantage with his new employer, the ITCD International Bank.

Hoary knew that he was building the future he wanted. He felt stronger as each day passed. His vision of the opportunity that his mother had presented him with was already taking shape. He knew what he had to do. In all of our pain and desolation, the church had lost its courage to deliver its vision. Hoary felt that he would not. The church had been distracted by the physical representation and iconic idlery of its purpose. For two thousand years, this did suffice. Now mankind was growing a new maturity and it was time to finally learn how man could really behave.

Today the church was simply there to take the blame and Hoary knew that this would not do. It needed to be reshaped, repotted and downsized to a core influence giving the sole message of forgiveness. The commercial world had arisen from its wake. This was the modern influence and it would provide him with the public distraction whilst he cemented his milestones. From this foundation, he would build his stage and his vision would be delivered.

The Henderson Group would need a minimum of two years of Hoary's commitment but by the time it was back in full swing, he would firmly have his foot through the door in his new venture. Whilst his initial position in the bank was fairly senior with his responsibilities to corporate planning, Hoary needed a scoop that would jettison him into Global Operations. He knew that he could make the Board of the ITCD bank from here.

'When the files are complete, draw down the claims from the insurance company,' said Hoary, summarising their 'to do' list. 'This will give you at least 3% of turnover and, when you have completed the backlog, you will get a further 2%. Your cash flow will be secure for twelve months even if your projections deliver the worst case scenario. The insurance company will pay – I've checked the contracts – just consolidate the files.'

Hoary took a sip of water from his glass. 'And you need to sack Frederick. If council find out about his non-exec position with the insurance company they will throw you two to the lions. Suspend him today – here is your evidence.' Hoary handed Geoff a file. 'You can get anyone on their expenses.' The file contained Frederick's expense claims for the last two years and they were more than excessive and certainly outside the parameters of policy.

'How the...' began Geoff, thumbing through the paperwork in the file. 'The cheeky bastard. How was he allowed to get away from this?' Geoff asked Kline.

'I would suggest that you both check your own records before you point the finger,' said Hoary.

'Are you suggesting complicity?' demanded Geoff.

'Yes I am,' said Hoary. 'Check your whole workforce if you want proof. And by the way.' Hoary pulled a page from his briefcase. 'Here is mine.' He handed the page to Geoff.

'It's blank, what the...' said Geoff rolling the page over between his fingers.

'Precisely,' said Hoary. 'The solution is staring you in the face.'

Hoary had formulated a series of turnover projections, cost savings and financial targets that he talked through with Geoff and Kline and outlined a critical path of actions. 'My report will win Moody's favour.

You two get the job done. When I've found the competent man at the bank, we'll refinance the estate. You'll both be able to retire.'

'What do you want?' asked Geoff.

'Nothing,' said Hoary.

'No hand out? A bonus?'

'No. Nothing. I'll be in touch.'

Geoff and Kline looked at each other, bemused and relieved. 'Nothing?' asked Kline incredulously. Hoary thought for one moment. He was not interested in the financial benefits of bribery; the opportunity to acquire a £15 billion fund into the ITCD bank – when he had time to find the internal men and women who could manage such a task – would be his prize. He did not consider their morality and it hadn't even entered his mind. He was concentrating on the kudos and the realisation of his ambitions.

'Well, just one thing,' Hoary began. 'On my return to England, have a mission statement drawn up for your group and please don't delegate this. Fax it to me. I need to be inspired, as do your personnel. You never know, we could realise double digit growth.'

Hoary felt that it was only a matter of time before the Henderson Group achieved success. He was encouraged by the opportunity. Another milestone had been achieved and he sensed that his future was moving closer to his goals.

Three years later, in 1985, Hoary secured the position he had sought and in 1992 he was promoted to the Treasury department of ITCD Holdings plc with responsibility for their treasury and capital markets businesses globally. Before the millennium, Hoary was appointed to the Main Board and subsequent years saw him increase his responsibilities before taking office as Group Chief Executive on 1 June 2003. The stage for his ambition was nearing completion and in less than a decade he would release a colossal commercial tsunami. He had already put many of the pieces in place even before his appointment to Chairman of the Holdings Group. His understanding of world trade, financial markets and the extents and limitations of global commercial networks could hardly be more comprehensive than any individual alive at this time and he had always been highly conscious that he needed to be fully aware of the completeness of the political oecumenical engine.

Geoff and Kline had delivered their mission statement on time and in line with Hoary's request for them to do so. They had stated that, 'The Tenant is the King' and driven this mission into every office and every staffroom within their administrative control. Kline had qualified this statement with staff training and awareness programs and the company had returned 11.2% growth that year. When ITCD bank acquired the financing of the Henderson estate, the fund had increased to £21 billion, the largest acquisition in banking history and the deal required 70% of this fund to be raised from external global investors.

For Hoary, his learning at McCinley's had been paramount for the realisation of his ambitions. He had seen an array of good and bad practices in corporations across half of the globe and he had come to understand the inherent weaknesses in business cultures. He had never witnessed sustainable good practice and whenever he entered a business in which the senior team expressed a level of pride in their operational establishment, Hoary had invariably dampened their enthusiasm with his findings.

Workforces could not manage detail, and resources were always too inadequate – usually by perception as opposed to truth – to handle demanding workloads. Whilst senior staff statements, aimed at increasing the engagement of their personnel, smacked of optimism for the future and excellent profit and productivity performance, the resulting impact was merely conducive to the increasing onset of complacency. This only made matters worse and Hoary had no doubt that painful consequences were insidiously and invisibly fermenting below.

Fear was undoubtedly the panacea of all corporate deaths. Once fear had cemented in the staff culture of a corporation it could rarely be reversed and the only solution was Voluntary Administration or insolvency.

'Define your exit strategy before you even begin,' Hoary consistently advised. 'And if you haven't, then destroy what you have built with the least amount of damage and start again. You have the advantage that you will probably do it better next time round.'

Of course there were exceptions to the rule but these were the heroics that hit the media. The industry was plagued with text books, self awareness manuals and strategic advice. This simply told Hoary that there was a large market for people desperately trying to work out the solution to their problems but if the solution was evident in any one of these books, why hadn't the problem gone away? This was a bit like our heroes – but they had gone away – here today, gone tomorrow.

For Hoary, however, all his observations were essential. He had looked harder and deeper than most, if not all, of the men and women in his industry. At McCinleys, he had developed a reputation for his insight and the people in his profession recognised his talent. The devil was in the detail and that was where he went every time with a diligence and a discipline that his colleagues did not exercise.

He was driven to do so by the size of his ambition and he had already observed certain given principles that he began to exercise during his activities with the ITCD International Bank. But it wasn't until 1997 and the unique advent of the credit default swap that Hoary saw the opportunity to raise the seas from the ocean beds and begin the fermentation of a colossal wave. He had felt his mother's grave leap into his heart.

The New York markets were the first to announce the unique insurance scheme. The derivatives market, in which a price would be set for a product and the gain or loss would be borne by the person who set the price, had lost its vociferous hunger. Its excessive wealth generation in the early 1900s had consumed investment traders and their agendas. The commercial and investment markets had hungered for a new event that could induce such incredible wealth generation and now they had found it. Hoary was excited by its inception. He knew that its potential for disaster was absolute. Most traders did too though Hoary's anticipation had not purely been lucrative earnings.

The credit default swap was basically an insurance policy placed against a mortgage. If the borrower was to default the credit default would pay out for the loss and hence the lender could hardly lose. The price of this insurance policy was easy to determine because the norm with mortgage defaults was less than 1% of global lending in the western markets and therefore, premiums could be set quite low. The return to the insurance companies from 99% of the performing loans meant that they would make considerable money with minimal risk exposure and hence, default payments.

The borrowers, finance houses and banks, were delighted to receive this insurance policy because effectively – no matter how much they lent – they were guaranteed payment.

In the late 1990s lending growth was escalating with this new found confidence and new and ingenious methods of lending were arising. Similarly, the stringent criteria that had previously been applied to borrowers began to diminish. The banks were secured by their insurance policies. No one could lose.

Within less than a decade, total global mortgage lending had increased by over 400%. In certain nations, growth escalated to over 1000%, Poland being the prime example.

Hoary had seen this growth pattern emerging even before the turn of the millennium. He had also seen the opportunity it presented him with and he watched it unfold for him, keen to see it all advance. In his role with the ITCD International bank and his responsibilities for Capital Markets Businesses Globally he was very well positioned to see this new impact in lending confidence. He had sensed the opportunity that corporations had witnessed and the future they would explore. Volumes of mortgage lending would increase substantially. As the confidence had set in, so had the volume of transactions and the advent of complacent senior management practices and over worked administration centres.

In the detail, the devil was beginning to dance for joy. In America, the ITCD acquisition of Housefrank – a U.S. consumer finance group – the devil was surfacing before Hoary. He watched it grow, amazed by the oversight by his counterparts.

Hoary had been the founder of the proposition for ITCD International to acquire the American bank. He had negotiated and concluded the $16 billion purchase. Hoary had personally overseen the operation of this acquisition. In 2005, when Hoary was promoted to the Chairman's role, the bank had been positioned to relinquish its stringent lending criteria. A substantial increase in its lending volume resulted. Housefrank was well positioned for its destruction. This event of self implosion gave Hoary the tool that would jettison the advent of fear across global financial markets.

The credit default swap had entertained a joyous period of excessive prosperity. The world population would soon be considering an unprecedented adversity. Hoary saw it and many of his counterparts in the industry did too. They had been looking at their bank accounts whilst Hoary had seen the advantage it would give him.

Hoary had dropped a meteor in the ocean and the wave was on its way. His press department had been instructed to distribute the message throughout financial markets. Substantial losses had been incurred by its American lending acquisition, Housefrank. Mortgage defaults by borrowers were rapidly increasing.

As the volatility grew throughout 2005 and 2006, banks across America and Europe began to wonder if the markets could stabilise, but the reality was only just dawning. The lending volumes had been wrapped up into large bundles of loans which offered lucrative returns – hedge funds. These bundles amounted to hundreds of millions of dollars and there were hundreds of bundles. They had moved from New York to Frankfurt, to London, to Tokyo, to Shanghai and so on, being sold each time, and as they moved, the files – mostly incomplete or never in existence – could not be traced.

The borrowers who were defaulting on their loans could not be found, and hence the insurance premiums could not be claimed.

Hoary watched the people of the world encounter the turbulence. As it grew and became more visible, he noticed that his trepidation did not. This was what he had wanted to happen and now it was doing so, he felt ready.

The financial markets panicked in early 2007 and two French banks BNP Paribas and Societe General froze the money markets. Lending from all sources was about to cease and when Lehman Brothers collapsed in September – the largest failing of a corporation in the history of commerce – the world was not yet aware of the devastation that was coming. Corporations across the Western Markets could not pay their staff at the end of the month. Nobody had any money.

On the Monday that followed the Administration Filing of Lehman Brothers – September 29th 2008 – the world populations would wake up from the party and the depression would land in all their living rooms. The adversity had dawned and everybody would have to question their excesses. By the end of the week our media channels would spread the panic and with the onset of this fear, all our internal conflicts would begin. Hoary knew that the advent would change our behaviour forever. He felt that now, he had to work harder than he had ever done before and he was looking forward to the challenge.

But how would all this mess end? After all, Hoary had only just begun. His plan was beginning to work but it had not gone unnoticed by one man. The mastodonic vision of both of these men was about to cross swords. This time, 2000 years after the first event, God was not sending one son on his mission. He was sending two.

PART FOUR

LOVE
THE EMPEROR OF OUR DNA

HELEN

In the March of 2006, Wood first saw Helen. Wood had left the office early with his Managing Director, Heath. The Wood Group of Companies was performing well and undergoing significant growth. In the first eighteen months of operation, turnover had risen above £150 million and the pace of change was demanding.

'Fancy a drink?' asked Wood.

'Fancy one? I need one,' quipped Heath.

'Where do you want to go? Local?'

'Very local. Across the road,' said Heath rubbing his hands together.

They entered the Crown and approached the bar. Helen had just finished serving a customer and saw Wood and Heath waiting. She made her way towards them and it was then that Wood saw her. She asked Wood how she could help and he gestured with an open palm towards Heath. Wood could not speak. His whole body had become engulfed in paralytic anxiety.

Heath ordered the drinks and Helen served them. Wood took his drink and, in the dozen or so steps he made on his way to a seat, he did so in his best efforts to avoid drawing attention to his affliction.

Wood and his younger brother Mark had often been described as complete opposites. Mark had worked for Wood in the early days of the business for several months. When Wood had been away from the business for periods of time, he had left Mark in charge but he constantly returned to a disruptive acrimonious team, forged from the emotion that Mark evoked. Mark had a propensity for the opposite sex that frequently became the pre-occupation of his agenda.

In private, Wood had spoken to Mark about his behaviour. Too often he had observed Mark run his hand gently across the hips or the buttocks or the thigh of his female employees whilst immersed in a conversation which had little to do with work. Predominantly, Mark did this outside the office, mainly of an evening when the team were in the pub, winding down after work. But Wood knew Mark, and he knew that Mark had an insatiable need for women. A need Wood had seen for many years as he had witnessed the sea of bed post notches that Mark had totted up with precarious intent and bewildering consequence.

'Try not to shag the payroll.' Wood had asked.

'I don't,' rebuked Mark.

'Mark. You've been shagging Tracy and Maddie,' said Wood persistently. 'They work in the same office. Their desks face each other. Girls talk.'

'I am not shagging Tracy or Maddie,' Mark kicked back. He put both his feet on Wood's table and crossed his ankles.

'Your hand was constantly on Tracy's thigh last night. You were lucky Matt was there to keep Maddie distracted,' Wood said exasperated.

'I like Tracy. She's cut up about Craig. I was just comforting her.'

'With your sperm?' said Wood sarcastically.

Jim and Stuart – work colleagues - joined Wood and Heath at the local.

'Who is the girl behind the bar?' Jim said as he saw Helen. 'God, she is gorgeous.' Jim took a seat next to Heath. 'She started here about two months ago. Her name is Helen. That's Matt's bird. The one he never stops talking about,' said Stuart also taking a seat.

'That's her?' asked Jim, excitedly.

'Yes, that's the *sixty-nine* times a night girl,' confirmed Stuart emphatically.

'In his dreams,' retorted Jim.

'In her dreams. It's Matt we're talking about.' Heath said, joining in, thankful for conversation. He had been watching the football before Stuart and Jim had entered. He had given up trying to talk to Wood.

'Hang on,' continued Heath. 'That's not the Helen that Nigel has been seeing?'

'Nigel? No chance,' said Jim.

'Nigel showed me two tickets for a Green Day gig. One was for someone called Helen,' confirmed Heath, seeking clarification.

'So?' said Jim shrugging his shoulders and taking a sip of his drink.

'Look what she's wearing,' said Heath pointing towards her.

Helen was wearing a vest with the bright, emanating, graffiti style font of Green Day displayed.

'Heath, Green Day are massive,' Stuart said, joining in and also shrugging his shoulders. 'It could have been anyone.'

'She fits the description. The hair, height, styles everything. He never stops talking about her,' Heath said, trying harder to convince his friends.

Wood could understand the attention Helen had evoked in his colleagues but it had not made him anxious, even though Stuart, Jim and Nigel were closer in age to Helen than he was. They were all in their mid twenties and Helen looked no older than eighteen. He also knew that his colleagues were liberal with the truth. They always had been. They had more fun that way.

Wood had not considered the age difference. He was captivated by Helen as much as they were. Wood knew that Helen had hardly noticed him and she wouldn't notice them. She had no need to. In this context, Wood could never be more than a customer to her and this demobilised him more.

There was something about her, something that he had not seen before, and he couldn't put his finger on it. At the same time he tried to recall the last time he had experienced the impact that Helen had made upon him. He knew that he could not.

Stuart said. 'My God, she's *fit*.' He went to the bar to order more drinks. All the glasses on the table were nearly full.

On one occasion, shortly after the New Year of 2005, Wood returned to the office after spending a week in London. When he arrived, Wood sensed that the workplace was tense. Very tense.

Leslie, a junior director, caught Wood at the door and said, 'Come outside. Join me for a fag. Here's a coffee.' Leslie was a lesbian. Everybody knew because she made sure they did.

'Guess?' quizzed Leslie.

'What?' said Wood, suitably quizzed.

'Guess?' Leslie repeated.

'You and Polly have split up.'

'No chance. She's crazy about me,' replied Leslie, nudging Wood with her elbow. Wood knew Polly wouldn't leave her. He just wanted to provoke her and get to the point.

'What then?' Wood asked, hoping it would be for the last time.

'Tracy's found out that Mark has been shagging Maddie,' said Leslie. Wood looked at her and frowned.

'Oh dear,' Wood's sarcasm was foreboding.

'I know. But it gets worse,' Leslie said, maintaining the grim topic.

'Go on,' prodded Wood.

'Mike doesn't know and he's in the office downstairs from Maddie.'

'Who is Mike?' asked Wood.

'Maddie's husband. Come on keep up,' said Leslie and she shoved him again.

'What's he doing in the office?' asked Wood, sipping from his mug.

'He works for you,' Leslie said in a matter of fact way.

'Since when?'

'Aziz recruited him two weeks ago,' Leslie said and looked at Wood. 'You didn't know?' she quizzed.

'Is Aziz mad?'

'*You didn't* know,' exclaimed Leslie.

'Oh dear,' said Wood, despondently.

'Oh dear. Anyway, Tracy's going mad and she's not exactly keeping it quiet.'

'That's Tracy,' said Wood. They both knew that could be Tracy highly emotional when she wanted to be. Everybody knew when she had a problem.

'Yes,' Leslie confirmed and puffed from her cigarette. 'And just to top it, Carol is waiting in reception to see you. I think Mark dumped her last night. She's in tears.'

'Why does she want to see me?' asked Wood, alarmed.

'Beats me,' Leslie threw her cigarette on the floor and stamped it out. 'I'll sort out Tracy. You sort out Carol. Have fun.'

When Wood entered the building he could hear the commotion that was erupting on the second floor.

The day after Wood first saw Helen, he knew that she had consumed all his boundaries of restraint and rationality, consequence and confidence. He could not stop thinking about her. He suggested to Heath that Heath should approach her and ask her to an interview. Heath knew that Wood was looking for a PA who demonstrated excellent interpersonal skills.

'She has a great smile,' Wood told Heath. 'She is warm and attractive and she looks bright and cheerful. She has the credibility.'

'Bit young,' said Heath.

'Dress her up.'

'Dress or undress?' asked Heath raising an eyebrow to Wood. Wood thought he saw both eyebrows lift.

'Heath?' Wood said, dismissing Heath's intent. Wood wondered whether his infatuation with Helen showed.

'Sorry. I guess you are right. She would look very credible accompanying you to the powerful boardrooms that you frequent,' said Heath carefully, aware that Wood was besotted with Helen. He saw it written all over Wood's face and her name had entered their conversations regularly since she had served them at the bar last night.

'Heath!' snapped Wood.

In the coming days, Wood became anxious by the lack of action from Heath. Heath had deliberately stalled any action on his behalf. It was more fun for him to do so. He thought that Wood seemed quite pathetic with his infatuation. Wood decided to give the task more momentum and so he delegated it to several of his personnel but reticence had gripped them all. Wood then forced the issue by visiting the pub with his MD and insisting he asked her there and then. Heath finally did and Helen attended the interview later that week.

Wood instructed Heath to interview her and offer her the job, regardless, but Wood did not want this episode foiled so he gate crashed the interview, took over the conversation and tried his *calmest and persuasive* best to influence Helen to join. Wood rang Heath shortly after the interview.

'Well?' said Wood.

'Well what?' asked Heath, very aware of the subject matter.

'Has she rung you? Fuck,' the thought occurred to him, 'has she got your number?'

'Yes, I gave it to her.'

'And?'

'And what?' asked Heath, enjoying the moment.

'Has she rung?'

'Give her time to consider for God's sake.'

Ten minutes later when Wood rang Heath to ask him the same question, Heath gave Wood the same answer. Ten minutes later when Wood asked again, Heath told Wood to bugger off and leave him alone.

After five o'clock that evening Heath rang Wood to tell him that Helen had agreed to take the job.

Wood was unaware that when Helen had left the interview she had been captivated by him. His impact did not leave her thoughts.

Wood asked Sonia to make two cups of coffee and bring them up to his office. Carol accompanied Wood to his room. Mark had recruited Carol to deal with the interior design requests by their consumers and even though Carol was sub-contracted, she spent all of her working day in Wood's business. Almost all of her waking day.

'Tane, help me please. I'm desperate,' Carol sobbed.

'Carol, I told you he would dump you,' said Wood being direct.

'I love him. I love him. I can't help it. I love him,' Carol repeated pathetically.

This had become a regular event in Wood's life with the fallout from Mark's girlfriends. Wood was no longer amazed by the level of despair that Mark consistently evoked in his lovers. Too often he had sat with them in the early days of the relationship proclaiming to Wood that they knew all about Mark's womanising past. They claimed that they could change him. They were the one that would finally conquer him, get him on the straight and narrow and sort him out once and for all. Wood had heard these proclamations too often. Often enough for Wood to wonder how Mark had attracted so many women, where had they all come from and why had they always been so intensely besotted with him.

'He's confused. He's like a little boy. He needs help and only I can help him. You must speak to him. Get him to see sense,' Carol pleaded.

'Carol. I told you not to get involved. I told you he would do this. What do you want me to do?' Wood retorted.

'Talk to him please. He needs me.'

'He does this to all his girlfriends. He doesn't seem to need anybody.'

'He needs me. He doesn't realise it. Tell him,' Carol insisted. Wood was pleased that her tears had stopped. He was already frustrated that his agenda was being neglected as he had a busy day ahead of him. Another of Mark's ex-lovers had only increased the anxiety Wood had with his workload.

'Carol, you are wasting your time. You have been from the start,' Wood insisted.

This final comment had not landed in the manner that Wood had intended. Wood was confused with what would. Carol's eyes had opened and she was immersed in her tears. Wood knew that his unsympathetic approach was not helping her in her despair but he had tried every approach he could think of with Mark's previous girlfriends and he had not yet found an appropriate style. Wood was also becoming weary of this ridiculous and constant demand upon him. 'Why,' he wondered, 'do they keep turning to me?'

Helen started working for Wood as his assistant on March 21st 2006. He made every excuse he could think of to avoid sitting at his desk because his desk was next to hers and he couldn't bear to allow her to witness the paralysis she brought upon him. Helen, meanwhile, arose from her seat to look out of the window every time she heard a car, excited that Wood had arrived. They rarely met for more than several minutes each day, and spoke for less. Neither could find the nerve to break the deadlock and Wood was concerned that he was twice her age. He could not see what she could find attractive in a man old enough to be her father.

Helen tried to find the moments to get them alone so they could speak but Wood made his excuses quickly; he was too paralysed to talk and too concerned that he would foul up in dismal silence or be embarrassingly boring.

Helen, naturally, began to attract the attention of the other male employees and this attention gathered pace. 'Jet engines don't fly faster,' thought Wood, witnessing the speed of the interest in her.

Helen was regularly and invariably top of their creative league tables. Within the office environment it seemed to be the only topic of conversation. These tables considered every part of her body and her behaviour but the behaviour usually resulted in acts of sexual deviation. They eventually gave up their pursuit of the leagues of their despair when they concluded that Helen would be the only entry in the universe for the 'Would You Die For Her' table.

Jim repeatedly asked Wood for his permission to ask Helen on a date and Wood repeatedly refused.

'I don't want her poisoned or dumped. She's a good kid and she has great potential,' Wood would answer. 'Anyway, I don't know what you see in her.'

'She is absolutely stunning.'

Jim was not the only male employee that was liberal, vocal and repetitive with his besotted compulsion with her beauty.

Wood had asked Leslie why they didn't approach Helen and ask her out for a date. 'Why does Jim seek my approval?'

'Helen is stunning. She is bright, charming, innocent, graceful, sexy and incredibly beautiful. I've rarely seen a girl who has what she has. In fact, I'm not sure I ever have or ever will for that matter,' Leslie told him. She knew that Wood did not have a clue about women. She liked that he asked her and she enjoyed trying to piece together his thoughts to help him make sense of his predicaments. The women in the business and Leslie's heterosexual friends found Wood attractive. He wasn't threatening to them, although his status was, to some. They liked his innocence. His position as Chairman, the top man, allowed them to publically entertain lewd acts of sexual feasting with him being the subject of their joint laughter. Leslie doubted that Wood would ever notice this, even if she told him.

'So, why doesn't she get asked out all the time?' Wood asked.

'Because she is the dream. Helen is the ultimate dream for all these men. Whilst they don't ask, she can't say no and the dream stays alive.'

'Would you?' asked Wood.

'I fear not. If I got her into the bedroom, I don't think she would survive.' Leslie said. She had never been shy with sharing her sexual exploits.

Helen's impact was unique and for Wood, he could not subdue the anxiety he always experienced in her company. Wood retained his own council with his affection for Helen and she did the same; the situation was made more complicated because both Wood and Helen were in long term relationships but both had also recently broken from long spells of fidelity with recent affairs.

Neither Wood nor Helen was vastly experienced with the opposite sex. Wood had always been a highly driven individual and Helen craved happiness but both knew that their current relationships had come to an end.

Helen realised that she was living with her best friend and he was not the man she could see by her side as the father of her children. Wood, however, had shared a vision with his partner; he had always talked of building a future of opportunity for his children and she wanted four kids. As the years had passed, both supported each other in their pursuit of their goals but when Macy had been born, their fourth child, the game suddenly seemed to be over and they began to grow apart.

When Helen's current partner, Simon had asked her to get engaged, Helen had been taken off guard and she had angrily agreed. When Wood had heard about this, he could not contain his despair. Wood had received a more romantic version of the proposal from a girl in the office who held her own feelings for Wood. Following this, his nerve was less forthright in the decisions that he was making with the business and his closest colleagues noticed. 'Nothing ever fazes Wood,' Heath had said. 'I don't know what's wrong with him.' Heath realised that Wood's infatuation had not resided.

Wood had stood and watched as other men had always been more forthright with the girls that Wood had been attracted to. This frustration had gained over the years. Wood had become increasingly plagued with his ineptitude with women.

But with Helen it was different. He had quickly forgotten or overcome his other infatuations. The frustration he felt over Helen was deeply more heartfelt than his previous encounters. He was desperate in his deemed loss, frustrated by his reticence and angered by his timidity. This time, he resolved, nothing would deter him and he would find a way. It was at this time that Helen asked Wood if, like all his fellow directors did, he would take his PA to lunch.

The day following Wood's ordeal with Carol, the ordeal with Carol continued. She rang Wood and pleaded with him to meet her away from the office for coffee.

Wood used every tactic he could think of but his life endeavours had been intensely exercised with the pursuit of his drives and his ambitions. Personal relationships, as Leslie concluded, 'are not your forte.'

When Wood met Carol she continued with her desperate claims to Mark and Wood tried to resolve the situation as bluntly as he possibly could. But his efforts had little effect. Carol became more vociferous and her behaviour more concerning.

Several days later Wood began to wonder how he could subdue Carol and get her to move on. The days rolled into weeks before Wood realised that he may be the subject of her stalking. Carol had followed him home one night, she had found Wood's home telephone number and her pursuit began to manifest in several calls a day to him. The subject gradually became more about Wood and less about Mark.

Wood, becoming increasingly concerned, rang Carol and told her
that he would meet her that evening at her apartment. When Wood
arrived he was forthright with Carol with his concerns. He told her that
he had no feelings for her. Carol was unperturbed by his sentiments and
said, 'I know this doesn't come easy to you.'

'What doesn't come easy?' Wood asked, aware that she was drawing
him in.

'Asking girls what you want from them,' Carol flirted, rolling her
eyes and moving closer to Wood.

'Carol, I don't want anything from you,' asserted Wood determined
to be resolute.

'Come on. I know you Tane. Better than you think,' hissed Carol,
moving even closer. Wood knew he was not very good at allowing
people into his personal space and her tone did not encourage him to
learn fast.

'There is nothing to know,' he said again.

'I know what you want,' Carol ignored his reticence as she raised her
hand to the back of his neck.

'Yes. For you to leave me alone,' Wood said, remaining rigid,
determined not to move back on the sofa.

'No you don't. There's no need to be coy. I hear these desires run in
the family.'

'What?' Wood said, confused. He looked at the perfume shop image
of Carol. He wondered if she had set the spotlights.

'You only need to ask and you can have whatever you want,' Carol
said, widening her eyes, cupping his chin with the palm of her other
hand.

'Carol, I don't want anything,' he said noticing how orange her
complexion was.

'Your brother was crazy for it.' Carol's voice was becoming softer
with each breath.

'What are you talking about?' Wood retorted, half laughing, half
scared.

'You can have it too,' she said, her voice hardly a whisper, attracted
to Wood's resolute stance.

'What?' Wood was increasingly confused.

'Just ask and you can do it to me.'

'Do what?' he said innocently, completely mystified.

'Anal sex.'

The week prior to Wood's luncheon with Helen, he had taken her to view a couple of office buildings for the expansion of his business. In the car, they were alone. Wood asked Helen if she had finished the summary of his personality report that had been conducted by an outside agency for the bank.

'Yes. It's done,' said Helen. Wood had the roof down on his Ferrari and Helen was struggling with her long dark hair. He noticed the shine in her hair as it blew about her.

'Anything interesting?' he asked, as if matter of fact.

'Yes. Quite a lot,' she said in the same tone.

'Anything stand out?'

'Yes. The piece about you not liking to be touched,' she said, looking for a response.

Wood looked at Helen and she looked at him. He was uncertain at Helen's intent. He wondered if she had a reason to say this. They *were* alone. Or was Helen genuinely and simply just making conversation. Wood replied, 'Yes, that's right, at least not in the workplace.'

Helen had been surprised with herself for the forthright nature of her question but had seen Wood's answer as a firm 'don't go there, this is strictly professional.' Wood kicked himself for the stupidity and abruptness of his response.

However, Wood was encouraged significantly when he learned that day that Helen was 27 years old. Ten years older than he thought and ten years older than she looked. Perhaps there was hope after all.

Another afternoon, when Wood returned from London, he once again found a trail of emotional debris that Mark had created in the office. Mark had gone on holiday and it was two weeks before Wood could challenge him with the event. Wood had not forgotten. It was impossible to forget.

'Mark. Maddie is off sick, Tracy has resigned and Carol is stalking me. Will you please stop shagging the staff?' Wood fired at Mark.

'I have not been shagging Maddie or Tracy. Matt has, not me,' Mark fired back, huffing as he sat back in his seat.

'Then why are the staff telling me that it's you,' Wood enquired.

'They hate me. I'm their boss, they hate me.' Mark shrugged his shoulders as he spoke.

'Could that be because you treat them like shit?' said Wood, reluctant to let the matter lie.

'I don't. They just hate me,' Mark said, sticking to his line.

'I'm their boss too. Do they hate me?'

'You are too soft. They walk all over you,' Mark said dismissively.

'Do they hate me?' Wood repeated.

'Of course they do,' said Mark, his eyes opened wider with the improbability of his answer. His tone had been adamant.

Wood decided on a different approach.

'Mark. I don't want to lose Maddie. Heath raves about her. She does all the work and holds the mortgage arm together. Tracy is one of the brightest we have got. She will be brilliant in a few years. Please persuade Tracy to come back and please, do your utmost to keep them happy. We need them.'

'I am not shagging Maddie or Tracy.'

Shortly after, Wood spoke with Leslie.

'I see Mark is back,' she said, smoking her cigarette.

'How do you mean?' asked Wood, taking the cigarette that Leslie offered him. 'Thanks.'

'He's already pissed off half the workforce with his attitude. Maddie must have dumped him. She would if she had any sense. He is such an arsehole.' Leslie put her packet of cigarettes in her pocket and picked up her coffee mug. 'That reminds me. I forgot to tell you that when you were away, Mark called all the senior guys into the boardroom. I don't know what was said but I know Martin stopped the meeting and asked everyone to leave.'

'Why?' asked Wood.

'You need to talk to Martin but I understand that Martin told Mark, when the others had left, that if he ever spoke to them like that again, he would personally remove him from the business.' Leslie's tone was not its usual chirpy self.

'I don't get it with Mark,' said Wood, leaning on the railing next to Leslie. He looked out at the skyline.

'I guess Martin didn't tell you?' asked Leslie, looking at Wood.

'That's not Martin's style. He tells me nothing unless I ask him,' Wood said reflectively.

'Martin's a good guy.'

'Very straight. I'll talk to him. He always tells me the truth.'

Wood met Helen for lunch at midday. Within five minutes the conversation had converged to their respective partners and both Helen and Wood agreed that they could never be unfaithful to them. The food arrived and Wood took a mouthful of steak and a large piece of gristle caught in his throat and he started choking. Wood attempted to hide his embarrassment and Helen attempted not to notice and she averted her amused gaze.

An hour later, Wood said that he had little to do that afternoon and he was going to stay for another drink and would Helen like one too.

'I can't. I need to go back to work in a minute and I'm driving.'

They spoke for a moment but when Wood got up to order himself a drink, Helen changed her mind and said, 'go on then. You are the boss after all. Get me a pint of lager.'

Several hours later, they were still drinking, smoking and talking merrily. Helen kissed Wood on the lips after he had told her, with drunken courage, how beautiful she was. She did it again. And again. Wood sighed with the conflict between his desires and the consequences. He thought for barely a moment. He opened his mouth to Helen and they didn't stop kissing for the next couple of hours.

For a few days after, they avoided each other but following an evening session in a local pub with several of the business team, Wood and Helen were the last two to leave and they embraced again.

∞

'Mark you need to do something about Carol,' Wood said to Mark, wondering if he was wasting his time talking to him.

'Why?' Mark asked, lifting a foot onto a dwarf wall and resting his right elbow on his knee. He lowered his mouth to his right hand to take a drag from his cigarette and looked out into the street.

'I think she's stalking me. She won't leave me alone,' Wood stated.

'She's a stupid bitch,' Mark said dismissively, flicking his left hand through his hair.

'Mark just tell her straight that it's over,' Wood said impatiently.

'I have. She won't listen,' said Mark.

'Is she stalking you?' Wood wondered how he could engage Mark's endeavour, aware that little ever did.

'No. I haven't spoken to her. Looks like she's moved onto you,' Mark smirked.

'What?' asked Wood screwing his face up.

'Stop worrying. Just give her one,' said Mark finishing his cigarette and flicking it into a bush.

The following day Wood saw Carol and Mark. They were walking hand in hand towards the office. Carol kissed Mark, got into her car and drove off. When Mark walked into the office Wood said, 'I thought she'd moved on?'

'So did I. Stupid bitch,' Mark replied.

Later that evening Wood bought Leslie a drink and said to her. 'I don't get it.' He took a seat next to her.

'Fuck me, I do. Polly won't leave me alone. She's crazy about me. She loves my tongue.'

'No. I don't get Mark.' Wood said, laughing.

'You never will. Especially you.' Leslie looked at Wood and he folded his arms.

'What do you mean?' he asked, uncertainly.

'I guess you are referring to his womanising?' Leslie cocked her head towards him.

'Yes. That and his aggression with the staff.'

'You two are complete opposites,' Leslie began, sitting forward and taking her drink. 'You'd never get it.'

'Why not?' Wood copied her and took a sip of his drink.

'Did you know that many people in the business have questioned your sexuality?' asked Leslie, prodding the slice of lemon in her spritzer with her toothpick umbrella stem.

'In what way?' he said sitting back. He had heard this said of him before.

'Quite a few think you might be gay. But you're not. They just confuse your gregarious style.' Wood looked at her to seek confirmation of what she meant. 'Like when you hug other men and make comments about how good looking Jamie is,' Leslie said and Wood nodded his head thoughtfully. 'But you are the definitive heterosexual man. It's no surprise that you have seven kids. And it's no surprise that you don't get Mark.'

'Go on,' said Wood looking at Leslie.

'Women love Mark. They can't help it. Even though they know that he is a complete womaniser. They can all see that, well most of them. But have you ever asked yourself why he stays with Lindsey?'

Wood saw Leslie had looked him in the eye. He held her gaze and said, 'She's his wife.'

'Yes and he shags everything that he can and she does likewise.'

'I have wondered. Lindsey treats him like crap,' said Wood, sitting back in his chair, folding his arms and watching Leslie.

'Have you ever wondered why Mark dumps them all and he isn't remotely bothered, whilst they tear themselves up in despair for weeks after?' Leslie was looking up to the ceiling as she spoke.

Wood was silent. He didn't know what Leslie was about to tell him. He let her continue. 'I have been in the gay scene all my life. Gay people are, on the whole, an emotional bunch and it is not surprising,' Leslie began, rolling her eyes from Wood to the ceiling repeatedly as she spoke. 'Throughout their lives they are ostracised and bullied and when they do find somebody to share their lives with they are faced with challenges that most couples never even think of. Gay men get the toughest ordeal.'

'Are you trying to tell me that Mark is gay?' asked Wood as he lent forward to pick his glass up.

'No, Mark isn't gay,' said Leslie cupping her glass with both hands. 'He is heterosexual. At least I think so but that is not his problem.'

'What is his problem then?'

'Mark once told me that on the first date he makes them laugh. On the second date he tells them about his father's death when he was a young boy. On the third date he gets his way and has sex,' Leslie said, hesitating for a moment, whilst she drank her spritzer. 'Works for some but as they get to know Mark, they sense that Mark has been hurt in the past. Maybe they read this in his manner. I guess that many of them attribute it to his father's death but Lindsey is the only one that has truly touched a nerve.' Leslie sat back and sipped from her glass. Wood thought that Leslie had finished. Wood urged her on.

'Yes. And?' he waved his hand in a gesture to support his request.

'And it's the same for gay men and often gay women,' said Leslie, gesturing herself, as though Wood had set a new trend.

'What is the same?' said Wood screwing up his face, looking puzzled.

'The hurt manifests itself in an acceptance of degradation,' she said, looking at Wood. 'They hunger for it.'

'How do you mean?' Wood said remaining puzzled.

'You don't get it. I don't suppose you would,' she said, slumping back in her seat looking into her glass. She thought for a moment as though she was contemplating her next sentence. 'Lindsey demands anal sex from Mark. She likes it,' she said flinging her arms open before her. 'He dumps all the others as soon as they have agreed to do it with him.' Lindsey's arms remained outstretched. 'He has to persuade *them*. Lindsey and Mark were made for each other.' As Leslie retracted her arms, she knocked Wood's glass of beer off the table and it crashed to the floor.

Later that year, Helen accompanied the team that Wood took out to Poland. The visit had been planned as part of the initial stages of Wood's proposal to expand his business abroad. Whilst there, they learned how deep their affections for each other were.

Wood told Helen that his relationship with Karen was over, that he knew that it had been for nearly a year and that he was ready to tell Karen as much. He asked Helen if she would not try to hide their relationship. 'We can't hide this. People will know.'

Helen was uneasy with this and said that she didn't want Simon to find out before she had told him.

'How will Simon find out? Nobody in the business knows him or his circle of friends,' Wood exclaimed.

'I know, but I don't want to take the chance,' said Helen thoughtfully.

'Helen, you can never hide. And anyway, I want to take you to Tokyo with me,' said Wood looking at her. 'How will we explain that?'

'We can't yet. It's too early. It's not fair on Karen or Nige…' Helen fell short of finishing her sentence and Wood finished the word for her.

'Nigel?'

Helen had taken a cigarette from her packet but she decided to put it back and she walked away, back into the office.

Wood cleared the broken glass from the floor and bought himself and Leslie another drink. He returned to his seat and said to her, 'Many years ago, in secondary school whilst attending a Religious Education class, we were visited by a local priest. During his speech he told us all about the couples in his congregation. He often visited them in their homes and he was welcomed in for a drink and a chat. He told us that the relationships of the couples in his parish were a colourful array but that he had mainly observed two types. Those that sat together and never spoke and those that argued with each other relentlessly. He spoke of one couple that were very vocal and vociferous and acrimonious with each other. The priest told us; "The strangest thing was that we all knew of their constant arguing and none of us complained. I think that we sensed that they cared about one another more than most couples." The priest told us that he believed that they had loved each other passionately.' When Wood finished, Leslie thought for a moment then said. 'No doubt about it. I see it all the time.'

In the last two years, since Wood had begun building his own business, he had moved from the highly protective brand environment of his corporate life. The endless corridors of support functions, more support functions and counter support functions were no match for the commercial lioness called self employment.

The ambition that had engaged his determination to redefine the housing market had demanded from him the establishment of his management team, the raising of initial investment funding, and the opening of his first outlet.

Within a year, Wood had grown the business from its humble opening and driven its growth, which had surpassed thousands of pounds, tens of thousands and then millions. He constantly lived with the pressure of delivering income, generating cash, driving the business forward, surviving political hazards and living with the looming potential of losing everything. With a cash flow raging and the business booming, more staff were needed. All these saw rapid growth. His team grew from a small group of thirty to a demand for over two hundred and fifty staff. Within a year, Wood experienced many challenges and the pressures began to show with the changes in his behaviour. Fuelled with the dissolution of his long term relationship, Wood turned to alcohol. He was starting to become very unhappy.

He enlisted the support of a psychologist to help him understand and be aware of these pressures, how they would manifest themselves and the solutions he could adopt to cope. Cracks were beginning to riddle his pavements and several incidents had already become visible. On one occasion he had driven home after drinking heavily and he had written off a brand new Ferrari.

Wood was certainly finding it difficult to overcome the denial of his march towards alcoholism.

Wood made several trips to Poland in his ambition to start the business in a country that he considered to be full of opportunity. The visits, gained in frequency and by the end of November they took place every fortnight. Each visit lasted for five days.

The team always included Wood and Helen and, most of the time, Nigel accompanied them. Wood noticed that Helen spent most of her time with Nigel. He felt that Helen was more comfortable with Nigel because he was the same age as her. The other members of the team were older. They were also more serious in their dealings with the business agenda. Wood had surmised that Helen was more comfortable with Nigel away from this intensity.

Helen, often, was seen huddled in laughter with Nigel. Wood knew that she enjoyed his wit and humour. He believed that Helen was too obvious with her friendship with Nigel to fancy him. He concluded that her fondness of him was that of an older brother.

On two occasions Wood was scheduled to conduct meetings with Helen but Helen declined, feeling unwell, and remained with Nigel.

Back in England, Nigel pursued Helen with a series of texts messages in which he asked Helen's council regarding a girl who was chasing him. Wood felt that this act by Nigel was too close for comfort but surmised that Helen would not be sucked in by this.

However his tolerance began to change. One afternoon, Wood was outside his offices with a small group of employees, having a cigarette break, and his anxiety with his suspicions of Nigel intensified. Jim and Heath were discussing Nigel's fortune in being included on the international team alongside Helen.

'I bet if you got half a chance you would,' Jim taunted Nigel.

'Who said I needed a chance?' retorted Nigel, who looked over at Wood as he spoke. It was obvious that he knew of Wood's relationship with Helen.

Wood found himself asking, 'How the hell does Nigel know? After all, nobody else seems to have a clue.'

∞

Helen, since leaving school at sixteen had tried everything. She had started her employment as an IT assistant but she had spent these days in disillusionment. Helen tried various courses at night school, vocational schools and eventually university in her search to find a future that would engage her. But one evening, watching her partner throwing the same set of darts at the same dartboard on the same Friday night, Helen decided that she had to leave all this behind. Helen felt very lonely and unsure about her future.

When she had joined the Wood's company, one of the other directors had seen promise in Helen. 'She is very bright and she doesn't suffer fools. She is certainly capable of taking on key agendas in the business.' Helen was encouraged with his support and before the New Year, she moved on from her role as Wood's PA and she was promoted to junior director working on the international team, negotiating and purchasing housing stock in volume.

Wood's suspicions of a relationship between Helen and Nigel was growing with insidious acrimony. At first, Wood held his own council. He knew Helen was young and adventurous. He felt that he should not confront Helen and chose instead to let the passage of time allow Helen to make her choice.

But, it wasn't long before Wood was unable to hold his silence. Wood spoke to Helen about his suspicions, in particular when she had failed to finish the sentence with Nigel's name in it. She told him that she had just come off the phone to Nigel and it had been a slip of the tongue.

Wood spent the evening drinking in the pub with Heath. Heath was surprised he had been asked by Wood to join him for a drink. Heath and Wood had spent many evenings drinking together for nearly a year now and become good friends. When Helen had arrived on the scene, Heath had felt neglected and found other drinking partners. Heath had enjoyed the kudos of being Wood's right hand man. Wood was the top man and everybody agreed that his charisma was highly engaging.

When the late evening settled in, Wood was drunk. He decided that he wasn't convinced about Helen's fidelity and wanted to know the truth. Earlier in the evening he had asked Heath if Helen was having an affair with Nigel and Heath said that there had been talk of it. Wood was surprised at Heath's answer. He had heard no other talk of this and it was not the answer he wanted. He also knew that he was unlikely to hear about it. He would be the last to know.

Wood sent a text to Helen. It was 11.30pm. Helen was usually to be found sitting in front of the television, reading a book.

Text. Wood to Helen. 'Where are you? I need to talk to you.'

Text. Helen. 'In Chicago's with Nancy. Where are you?'

Text. 'In town. Stay where you are. I'll get a taxi.'

Text. 'Be quick. I didn't know you were out. I'm dying to be with you.'

Wood found a taxi, asked for Chicago's, arrived and paid his entrance fee to enter the nightclub. He couldn't find Helen at first and looked all around the floor several times. He sent another text message to Helen.

Text. 'Where are you?'

Text. 'Near the bar, looking for you.'

Text. 'Where? I have been round and round for five minutes.'

Wood looked again but could not find Helen. He sent another text.

Text. 'Where the fuck are you?'

Text. 'I'm at the top. Look for the signs for the toilets.'

Wood found the sign and made his way over. He saw Helen coming towards him. She was wearing a long cashmere coat and a long woolly scarf that hung down to her boots. The club was warm despite the frost that had settled outside in the winter morning. Her long, straight hair cascaded across her shoulders and down her back. Wood was choked with her appearance. He knew he had never seen such beauty. Helen would never have told him that her appearance did not come without effort. She had been in the toilets for over ten minutes making herself look her very best for when Wood arrived.

'Where the fuck have you been?' said Wood aggressively.

'What? Tane?' said Helen, confused and concerned.

'I have been over this place time and time again. You were nowhere to be seen,' he said, searching her eyes.

'Tane, stop being a prick. I was looking for you.'

Nancy drunkenly interrupted Helen and asked her to dance with her and Wood went to the bar whilst Nancy dragged her off. When Helen returned, Wood asked her to kiss him.

'Not in front of Nancy. She doesn't know,' said Helen, struggling free from his grasp. Nancy went off to the toilet and Wood kissed her. They were joined by several friends that Wood had met on a stag do. They had all got to know each other quite quickly during the event and Wood had won their approval when he had stood on a table in the bar in the middle of an Irish bar, told them he was English, and offered to take them all on. The audience that night, in excess of a hundred Irishmen and Irishwomen, had joined Wood in a barrage of jibes that had brought the place down in riotous humour for over an hour. The following day, people had walked up to Wood and said hello with a large smile. Wood had asked 'Why do people keep saying hello to me? How do they know my name?' he had been very drunk and he could not recall any of the events.

He was becoming very drunk now as the evening progressed. One of his friends had seen him kiss Helen.

'Fair play to you Tane. Brains and beauty. She is stunning. You deserve it mate. I have heard about the people in your business. They love working there. They all say that it's wonderful. I have never seen so many people so optimistic. Enjoying themselves so much. You deserve your luck.' His friend's words seemed to drift in and out of Wood's hearing. Wood finished his drink and grabbed a full glass from the table. He had no idea if it was his or not.

Later, when the club closed, Wood took Helen to the taxi rank. 'Did he see us kiss? Does he know we are together?' Helen asked anxiously.

'You can't keep hiding,' said Wood searching her eyes again.

'I need to tell Simon first.'

'Helen. How the hell will Simon find out? Nancy won't tell him. What are you hiding from? What the hell is going on? Tell Simon it is over,' he'd begun shouting.

'Tane!' His tone was concerning Helen and she knew he was drunk. 'Nothing is going on. I can't tell Simon yet.'

'Why the fuck not?' said Wood impatiently and aggressively.

'Tane!' Helen looked at Wood and he saw her concern. He grabbed Helen and held her by her upper arms. 'Helen, what the fuck is going on? What can't you tell Simon; about me or about Nigel?'

'What? Tane, stop it. You're hurting me. What are you on about?' Nancy had seen the altercation, she came over to them and grabbed Helen away from Wood.

'You touch her and I'll kick your head in. Leave her alone,' Nancy said. Wood shouted after Helen as Nancy guided her into a taxi. 'Where were you when I arrived tonight?' slurred Wood as he stumbled and fell over. 'Outside, saying goodnight to Nigel?'

Wood was very drunk. He got a taxi back to his house and sat in the snow, outside the magnificent gated entrance to his estate. He wrote a text to Helen.

Text. 'You bitch. I know you have been screwing Nigel. Everybody knows. Why did you lead me on? Do you think that you are so superior that you can just tread all over the rest of us? Bitch. Tomorrow I will build a mountain of lawyers and instruct them to hurl a million rocks of despair at you. You fuck with me. I'll fuck you over. Bitch.'

Wood spoke to Helen the following day and apologised. Two days later she forgave him. But this was not the last time. Helen had always attracted the attention of many of the men in the business and Wood's alcohol propensity was getting worse. It was not until they had left the U.K. that Wood went too far.

After they returned from Tokyo in early 2007, Helen and Wood agreed that they would move to Poland and live together.

They had both told their respective partners, which had caused terrible anxiety and despair for both of them. They found it difficult to cope with. On several occasions they fiercely argued with each other as the guilt had manifested itself.

Wood remained resilient and focused in his pursuit in Poland. But he was becoming increasingly aware that the demands upon him were changing his behaviour. His psychologist told Wood that his resilience was very high and she warned him that his drive could lead him to falsely ignore the physical detriment that he may endure. Wood sensed that all was not well. He was unaware exactly how bad his state of unhappiness had become. He knew that he was hiding certain truths from Helen. He feared telling Helen and he despised himself for not dealing with his fear.

Wood was also aware that his departure from England had the potential to put his companies at risk. He resolved that he needed a year to sort out his personal life and in Poland he would have the space he needed to find out why Helen was so important to him. He had been besotted with her from the moment he first saw her but, unlike his counterparts, Wood had not been intrigued by her stunning beauty alone. There was something about Helen that he could not fathom. This too, he was about to learn.

Wood and Helen spent an inordinate amount of time arguing and Wood told Helen that they should take more precaution during sex. 'We have both been under too much pressure. A child now may break us.'

Helen had her suspicions that his request was too late. Later that day, after taking a test to confirm it, she met Wood in the restaurant of the hotel where they were staying. 'Baby,' she began. 'I *am* pregnant.' The delight was written wide and radiant across Helen's face. Wood hesitated and said, 'Look, I love you. If it's not mine, I don't care. I will love the baby.'

Helen stared at Wood, aghast. She got up from the table and left. She did not say anything but before she rushed out of the restaurant, her tears were falling without restraint.

Hugh was sitting in his office when he rang Wood. He had recently joined the Main Board to deal with the mountain of PR that had built around Wood. Hugh was the court jester who embroiled himself in school boy politics believing he was playing with the big boys. For Wood, he was the best PR director he could have hoped for.

'Magnificent interpersonal skills. He has always been in the wrong job. Should have brought him in ages ago,' Wood described Hugh to his senior team, introducing his new appointment. Since that day, Hugh was always on the phone.

'Tane, I can get Colleen McLaughlin to your wedding. Wayne will come too and I'm working on Beyoncé. I've found a fantastic castle in Suffolk. Helen will love it. I need a date from you?'

'It's not so easy at the moment,' Wood responded.

'Christ. Are you two still arguing? You know my views.'

When Wood interviewed Hugh for the job, they had known each other for almost ten years. He had always felt that Hugh was very talented and had been wasted in his corporate career as a retailer. Wood offered Hugh the break and although Hugh was very reticent, his brother had convinced him that it was his one big chance and he should take it.

Hugh had arranged to meet Wood in a local hotel bar. When he arrived for the interview, Helen was sitting with Wood. When she left, Hugh asked Wood how long they had been seeing each other.

'Is it that obvious?' said Wood, embarrassed.

'My God, you two have splattered love across the eighteen storeys of this hotel. Obvious? Bugger me, my grandmother knows and she is away in the clouds over the Himalayas. Marry the girl and have twenty children.'

'It's not that simple.'

'Oh dear. I detect acrimony?' Hugh said looking at Wood over the rim of his glasses.

'One of many problems,' said Wood thoughtfully.

Wood offered Hugh the job and pressed him to take it. Wood knew that Hugh did not rise to challenges with the same nerve as he did to his comforts. But Hugh had heard of the vibrant atmosphere in the business, 'It is all over town,' Hugh remarked, 'I have met The Queen, Margaret Thatcher and Tony Blair. But there is something about you Tane.' Hugh accepted the job and the conversation returned to Helen.

'Is she just after the money?' asked Wood

'Maybe,' Hugh began. 'But you are a pretty good looking guy and it has not gone unsaid, by quite a few in fact, that your success is not a surprise. You are a very charismatic guy.' Hugh was sitting forward with his elbows on the table, sipping shandy.

'But she is tearing me apart,' Wood was sitting likewise.

'Yes she will. She is absolutely stunning.'

'It's not the looks – and the age difference,' said Wood.

Hugh told Wood about an affair he had had several years ago. She too was stunning and she was fourteen years his junior. 'She was magnificent, young, and adventurous. She was the most unnerving experience of my life,' Hugh concluded.

'What did you do?' asked Wood, drinking from his glass.

Hugh told Wood how she had repeatedly asked him to leave his wife. How he had promised her many times that he would but that, after nearly two years he had still not done so.

'Anna eventually got fed up,' continued Hugh, remaining on the edge of his seat. 'She loved me madly but she wanted more. She left me and met a younger guy. When I see them together today, it breaks my heart. But I am happy for her. She is a great girl.'

'Why didn't you leave your wife?'

'I'm glad I didn't. Lisa is the most wonderful girl. She is a great mother and she works so hard. There is something very nice about sitting in front of the television every night with your wife. After twenty seven years, I guess I know everything there is to know about Lisa. I can even fart in her company and it doesn't matter.'

∞

By the time Wood held his first board meeting in Poland, Helen had finally forgiven him. His remarks, following her announcement that she was pregnant, had needed considerable apology. It had taken Helen nearly two weeks.

On the evening before the meeting, the English team, chosen for the Polish Main Board, flew out to Krakow to meet their new, Polish comrades. Wood assembled them at the Redolfi Restaurant, on the atmospheric and beautiful market square that made the town famous. Wood wanted his team to celebrate their future endeavours in Poland and he wanted his English guys and their new Polish recruits to bond.

Jacek, his Polish Operations Director, told Wood that this restaurant served the best food in Poland.

The restaurant could only provide small tables and therefore the group was not able to sit as one. At their table, Wood and Helen were joined by Hugh and Heath.

Before they entered the restaurant, Hugh told Wood that Heath had been moaning constantly on the two hour flight from England. 'He thinks that you have pissed off to Poland with Helen and your interest in building the business out here is a disguise.'

'Why?' asked Wood screwing up his face.

'I don't know. Have you upset him?' asked Hugh.

'Not to my knowledge.'

Helen was dressed casually and in accord with all the team. No matter what she wore she looked stunning and tonight was no exception. At the table, Wood spoke about his ambition for Poland and said, 'I want the very best for our Polish friends and recruits. We must drive forward with commitment, endeavour and providence.'

Hugh said, 'I hear that the Polish don't do commitment.' Heath laughed heartedly and Hugh joined him. Wood looked at Helen, she was laughing too.

When they finished their meal, Michał invited them all to his brother's night club, Showtime and they all agreed to go. Michał had been recruited by Wood. When he had first met Michał, he had liked him instantly and he'd told his team that Michał was a man he could trust and would be a great manager for their new store.

Wood had been drinking during the meal and when he walked to Showtime with Helen he said to her, strangely, 'Was Hugh playing footsie with you under the table?'

Helen did not join them at Showtime. She walked away from Wood
in disbelief when he made his accusation. They had moved into an
apartment the previous day, a short walk from the square on Pijarska
Ulica. Helen had made her way home and wrote a text to Wood.

Text. 'I love you; I trust you and I always will forgive you for
anything. It's only you and it always will be.'

Wood was fuming and he left his party telling them that he would be
back shortly. He had not got the text by the time he arrived at the
apartment. When Helen met him at the door he was very angry and he
grabbed Helen and threw her against the wall. He accused Helen again
and she denied it. He told her that Hugh had admitted playing footsie
with her. Helen refused to believe this. Wood slapped Helen across the
face and silence and stillness followed for several seconds. In the next
moment, Wood ran out the door.

An hour later, Helen sent Wood another text.

Text. 'I still love you despite your problems. When you calm down
I'd like to know exactly what's going on. There was no footsie with
Hugh. If he told you otherwise then I'd like to know why. You put our
baby at risk. And you hit me. That won't mean anything to you at the
moment though, I know.'

Wood had rejoined his team and he was drinking whisky. He read
Helen's text and he said to himself, 'slut.'

Text. Helen to Wood. 'Good night. Take care. I love you.'

Text. Reply. 'Fuck you, you whore.'

Text. Helen to Wood. 'Goodbye Tane. It was good to learn
forgiveness from you. At the very least I can forgive what you did
tonight.'

Wood switched his phone off. The team had noticed Helen's absence
and they had noticed the mood of Wood.

'Are there whores in Krakow?' Hugh asked.

'Inspirational idea,' Heath said and looked at Wood.

'We have everything,' said Jacek, cheerfully.

'Cheap. They do anything you ask,' said Michał joining in.

'Have you ever looked into the eyes of a woman and it has made you
come?' Wood asked, stopping their conversation. They all looked at
him. 'I have. It was the most loving experience I have ever had.'

They left him and found a brothel. As they were leaving Wood shouted after Hugh and said, 'Why didn't you leave Lisa for Anna?'

Heath answered, 'For fuck's sake Wood, go back to your wife, Karen.'

The following day Heath and Hugh turned up late for the day's work agenda. Hugh arrived first and Wood asked him where Heath was.

'I only saw him briefly. He was smiling at his dream,' said Hugh, sitting on a small wall surrounding a lawned communal garden. He lit up a cigarette and offered one to Wood.

'His dream?' enquired Wood, taking a cigarette.

'He spent the night with a girl. Cost him a fortune but apparently she stayed all night and she did everything. He felt awful when he woke. Guilty I guess. He felt that he had to tell his wife,' Hugh said and puffed on his cigarette.

'Bridgette?' asked Wood senselessly seeking confirmation of what Hugh had just told him. They both knew the name of Heath's wife.

'I convinced him to just think of the episode as a fantasy. Park it as a dream and just remember the dream. He calmed down. He said that she was amazing; sucked his dick, the works.'

'Where is he?' asked Wood taking a seat on the wall.

'Don't know, sat in the hotel probably. That's where I left him smiling like a Cheshire cat.'

Later that day Wood received this message from Helen.

Text. 'You know, in my more paranoid moments I've thought that your menacing message after the New Year - saying you're going to fuck me over this year - might actually be true. That all this is some way of paying me back for something. What did I do that could make any person treat another like this?'

When Wood had returned home the night before, Helen had gone. He sent her a text,

Text. 'Where did you stay last night?'
Text. Helen. 'I need to get my things. Let me know when you go out. Please leave the door unlocked.' The text conversation continued.
Wood. 'Where are you?'
Helen. 'Waiting for you to go out so I can get my things.'

Wood. 'Where are you?'

Helen. 'You care now? At a hotel, didn't have much choice.'

Wood. 'Tell me where you are.'

Helen. 'No. Tell me when you've gone out.'

Wood. 'Are you with somebody?'

Helen. 'Never been more alone in my life Tane. And it's saying things like that that gives me no choice but to leave you.'

Wood. 'Please tell me where you are?'

Helen. 'I'm at the Stary. Where fucking else would I be.'

Wood. 'I'm sorry.'

Helen. 'You always are Tane. Tell me when you've gone out. Make sure you leave the door unlocked.'

Wood. 'I love you.'

Helen. 'Do you? Did you have fun after you hit me and threw me out last night?'

Wood. 'I'm sorry.'

Helen. 'That means less than sod all to me at the moment. So did you have fun? What did you do?'

Wood. 'Got drunk.'

Helen. 'Gone out yet?'

Wood. 'Helen please I'm sorry. Please come to the flat. There was no arrogant behaviour last night after you left.'

Helen. 'To quote you Tane. Fuck off. No arrogance? Showtime good? Whores? Have you gone out yet?'

Wood. 'Yes, I left ages ago. No Showtime wasn't good. I sat in the corner and drowned my sorrows.'

Helen. 'Thank you for having the decency to allow me to get my things and leaving the door unlocked. Meetings ok?'

Wood. 'Sod the meetings. I need to see you.'

Helen. 'Let me get in there by myself. You are a horrible person.'

Wood. 'Helen please I want to talk to you.'

Helen. 'If you don't leave me alone I'll get Michał or Jacek or someone to come in with me. I'm not going to be alone with you.'

Wood. 'I have asked Jacek to meet you at the flat. He has the key.'

Helen. 'Why is Hugh ringing me asking to come round for a chat?'

Wood. 'I asked him to. I thought he could talk you into meeting me.'

Helen. 'What was all that crap about last night? Why did you try and manipulate a situation with him?'

Wood. 'I lost the plot. I know I pushed you too hard; I don't want you to leave. I'll do anything. Please.'

Helen. 'I'm going to Tane.'

Wood. 'Please.'

Helen. 'And that is what you planned. By the way, thank you for your concern about me and the baby. I think we're both fine apart from a few bruises and a slight swelling around the stomach.'

Wood. 'I don't know why I did what I did. I only know that I love you and I need you.'

Helen. 'That's ok Tane. The answer is in alcohol. But you already knew that.'

Wood. 'I know. I have denied it. I need to get a grip and I will. I love you and I want our baby. I will sort myself out.'

Helen. 'How could you do that to me? I take it your arm is still intact?'

Wood. 'If you come back I will cut it off.'

Helen. 'How does that work then? Why the silence over what you did last night? Asking me if I was with someone? Guilty conscience?'

Wood. 'No. Nothing but drinking. They all buggered off. I sat outside in the square until 2am with Christine talking about you. Baby I love you. All as I wanted to do was comfort you, say sorry and tell you that I love you.'

Helen. 'The only person who could've comforted me is the person who inflicted the pain. You either still don't know me at all or choose not to believe it for whatever reason. You didn't love me last night.'

Wood. 'I did. I don't know why I said what I did.'

Helen. 'I want to know exactly what that was about last night. You told me you'd told Hugh to play footsie with me. He didn't. Why did he tell you he did?'

Wood. 'He didn't. I lied.'

Helen. 'Why did you come back from the bar in a rage saying you'd just spoken to him?'

Wood. 'I don't know.'

Helen. 'Why would you do that? To give yourself an excuse to come back and bully me? Were you drinking spirits after I left?'

Wood. 'No. I need to see you.'

Helen. 'No. I hate to say it but I'm too scared. Were you drinking spirits after I left?'

Wood. 'No.'

Helen. 'Well at least you've identified spirits as the cause for your violence. Have you told everyone that you hit a pregnant woman and threw her at a chair and into a wall?'

Wood. 'They know. I didn't know why you had walked off.'

Helen. 'I walked off? I didn't tell you I love you a million times and that it didn't happen only to be told to fuck off, that I'm a liar and to fuck off back to England? I don't really get your point.'

Wood. 'Please forgive me.'

Helen. 'I could forgive you again. But it's not just myself I need to look after now. I never ever thought you could do that to me whilst I was pregnant. Your thoughts on the baby? Did you have any at all? Apart from questioning its paternity again of course. Was that what made it acceptable to you?'

Wood. 'Baby the denial is over. I love you. I will sort this out and I will get help.'

Helen. 'And the baby? Or is another miscarriage fuck all to you?'

Wood. 'I will get help.'

Helen. 'It can't be me that helps because I'm the person you attack. If it was just me I could handle it but it's not now. By the way I have a massive need to punch your fucking face in. But that won't change anything so there's no point.'

Helen asked to be left alone for the rest of the day and told Wood that she would remain at the Hotel Stary for the night. Wood rang her later and asked Helen if she would join them in the evening but Helen said that she could not face anyone and that she couldn't be out with him and have to pretend that each other wasn't there.

In the morning Helen's mood had changed. Wood rang her. 'I love you. Are you ok?' Wood was sitting in a dark room with the curtains closed.

'I love you. I am a mess,' Helen said, lying in bed drawing the duvet up to her neck.

'What are you doing?' asked Wood

'Nothing. Lying here. I don't want to leave this room or this bed.'

'Why?' asked Wood, aware that his question was leading.

'You'll get angry with me and call me a victim. I don't know what to do. I'm so lonely,' said Helen. Wood slowly ran a hand through his hair.

'Baby. Let me come round,' he pleaded.

'I can't. You don't understand.'

'As soon as I have finished the board meeting I will be over. Please let me see you,' he pleaded again.

'Glad you're happy and out enjoying yourself.'

'Baby. I must hold the meeting.'

'Just carry on as if nothing happened,' said Helen sadly.

'No. That's not fair.'

'You don't understand what you've done to me do you? You carry on as if nothing's happened,' said Helen folding her arm around her chest.

'Baby. I can't think of anything but you but I need to be with the team,' said Wood, throwing an arm out in front of him, gesturing with his open palm.

'Of course you do. Where else would you be. Sitting in a bed crying your bloody eyes out?'

On the 21st December Pace was born. Wood and Helen were delighted. Helen endured a long and painful childbirth and Wood told her that he was proud of her and he had never seen anybody show such courage.

When the baby was born and she held Pace she felt as though she was the happiest person in the world. When Wood kissed her she had not wanted him to stop.

They had continued to live in a whirlwind of acrimony but the tone had gradually changed and they had grown close. Wood learned what it was about Helen that had captivated him, engulfed him in paralysis, and conquered all his restraint.

Wood had been very unhappy but that had now changed. He had failed to notice its manifestation because the onset had begun so early in life but he had faced his fears and told Helen about the abuse he experienced in his youth.

He recounted the death of his father and the violent murder of his auntie and uncle. When his relatives had been killed, he had spent over a year confined in a psychiatric ward for children. The male nurses had been brutal with him, frustrated by his inability to speak. He was consistently bruised and healing broken limbs. The nurses claimed that he was mad and that he threw himself off tables and out of windows, to disguise their mishaps.

Wood told Helen about his distraught cries of anguish and despair to the elder nurses when he finally could speak again. They had suppressed the gruesome ordeals he had tried to recall. He had concluded later in life that their denial had resulted because they did not want it to be true. They did not want this horror to be in their lives. They wanted life to be normal, like everyone else.

He told Helen how one day the male nurses had been taunting and arguing with a gang of college boys who had been passing their sports field. The nurses were supervising a football match with the children and they had been distracted by the raucous shouts of the boys from the sixth form college across the road. The altercation had turned violent and stones had been thrown. Afterwards, when the nurses were laughing and joking about it, they began to curse the children and call them spastics. One of the nurses grabbed Wood whilst he was playing football and butted a gun in his neck as he forced him to follow him to the pavilion. The other children had seen the incident, the gun and heard his cries for help. He had been certain this time that help would come. He had been forced at gun point to climb into the loft and then jump back down to the ground. He awoke to the intense pain of a broken pelvis as the nurses had left him where he had fallen. He surmised that the other children had not wanted to report the crime because they feared that the nurses would be found innocent and would be set free. If he remained the victim, then they were not.

Helen helped him to recall much of the detail that he had suppressed over the years and Wood finally laid the ghosts to rest. Wood learned earlier that year that the man who killed his auntie and uncle had been found, at his home, rocking in his chair with the body of a young man at his feet. When the police found him, the dead body was in decay and the executor was close to death. He had not eaten for five weeks. He had just sat and rocked - bemused, worthless, senseless, silent and inert. He had pleaded with the police to execute him and send him to hell when they took him away.

For years Wood had wanted to speak of these ordeals but he had feared the disgust that he perceived he would face from his audience or the dismissal that he had experienced earlier in his life. The death of his father when he was thirteen had broken all his resolve. He recalled the day he learned of his father's death and his absolute despair; an emotion that had no resolve. Subsequently, when he saw the lifeless bodies of his relatives, he simply switched off his emotions as though a plug had been pulled from a socket. It was the only way he could survive and cope.

Helen did not dismiss a word. She loved Wood and gave no judgement. The affection she showed him was the response he had yearned for, for nearly thirty years and he loved her for it. Helen asked him about the nurses and whether he wanted retribution. Wood told her that he hoped that they had learned to forget. He knew that the nurses would face the consequences in later life. They would have their own children. If they did not forget, their conscience would find no release and their behaviour could manifest in many ways; always seeking rationalisation for their actions. Constantly, a shadow cast by a dark cloud on the landscape of acceptable norms.

When Wood learned of the fate of his relatives' murderer he was surprised with the ease with which he was able to forgive. He felt that Helen had enabled him to repair the damage.

Wood stopped drinking. His psychologist told him that the only solution was to avoid any trace of alcohol for at least a year. 'When alcohol has gripped you, it will take control and there is no limit to the change in your behaviour that it may enforce.'

The manifestation of many of Wood's experiences may, the psychologist told Wood, have resulted in paranoia and schizophrenia. The key was finding the 'maggot', the trigger of his psychosis, and recognising it when it came. Helen had helped Wood find his maggot. When Wood visualised the acts of infidelity that accompanied his suspicions with his partners, including Helen, he did not see love and affection but instead, passionate scenes of sex. He surmised that he felt inadequate in the bedroom and considered that all men were spectacular compared to him.

Helen taught him how to overcome this. She found him to be very loving, very attentive to her needs. Her affection assured Wood that he was conquering his ignorance.

Helen had always reacted bitterly and defensively to his accusations and hence her reaction went a long way to proving guilt.

However, Helen was defensive because she had learned to be. She was the dream and the dream was constantly under attack. In a world that looked over its shoulder and witnessed savagery, war and poverty, how could we escape from ourselves to anything but the drudgery that immersed us?

Helen was truth. She was beauty. She was everything we wanted the world to be; all that we wanted to have around us. Until we choose to go and get it, whilst we choose not to, we will become the victims of our own inaction. We will get what we give. Beauty is what we all want but we fail to act. We fail to go and get it because we deny our purpose. And until we see it, Helen will be the person who would has to pay for all our inaction; the poverty of our cry, the pitiful acceptance that *we are only here to die; be a good person; be happy.* Unaware always what any of this looks like.

The people of the world hurt Helen because it is easier than to blame themselves for their inaction. And the hurt is the motivator of our denials and our dismissals.

They do not know how to act. Few do, only the visionaries can take the pain away. She is the politics that man has learned to accept.

For Helen, she could only ever find happiness with a man of vision. It is her only form of escape from the pain. She had been defensive when Wood attacked her because without him she knew that the wolves would gather in their packs and the loneliness would engulf her, pitilessly.

Helen was the truth and we were denying it; a denial that had gathered acceptance. A denial that would build for us a crisis we would have to endure, a proposal of Armageddon that would distract us and provide us with a haze from which, when the midst began to clear, we could hope that something or someone would hold his hand up and say.

'I'm sorry. I did not act sooner. All this is my fault. Please forgive me and join me because I know which way to go. I know how to make all our lives beautiful, all our dreams come true, all our opportunities become real; for everyone. Now is the time for action, in our future, in our political truth.'

Helen needed Wood and Wood needed Helen. Wood realised what he had seen in Helen from the moment he had first seen her. Beyond her stunning looks, Helen was the truth, a truth which was the most beautiful place Wood would ever encounter.

They both needed to find this place, locked away in a foreign land, that they had dreamt about. When they were together, they were staring it right in the face.

Wood had still not recalled what he had seen the moment he witnessed the gruesome death of his relatives. He could not have done so. First of all he had to see the world that could deliver the greatest dreams and fondest loves for everybody who would ever live.

PART FIVE

VISIBILITY
CHAIRMEN OF THE EMPIRE

MUFFLED STORMS

June 2006

'Is Alex still head of our Press Office?' Hoary ate a biscuit as he spoke.

'He is,' Michael answered sitting the other side of Hoary's desk.

'Why haven't you sacked him?' asked Hoary.

'Because I enjoy having fun at your expense.'

'I'll sack you then.'

'If only dreams did come true,' said Michael as he dialled out on his mobile phone and asked for Miranda, when a voice answered. Michael was put through to Miranda and he asked her to be in Hoary's office within the hour and she agreed.

'Who is Miranda?' asked Hoary.

'She is the death of Alex,' said Michael

When Miranda arrived, Michael introduced her to Hoary as his new Press Officer from Lords Media. 'We will be outsourcing in the short term,' said Michael and instructed Miranda to organise a series of Press Releases to promote Hoary's activities in Europe, America and China. Prior to this, Michael wanted the articles to hit the London papers and their internet sites, later this evening to ensure visibility before close of play at 6pm.

Miranda left the office before midday and confirmed that she would get the job done.

'Now you have two,' said Michael

'I don't need two. I only need one good one.'

'Your wish was my command before Miranda ever walked into your life.'

Hoary looked up from his desk to eye Michael. He murmured and returned to his workload on his desk. Hoary always had his head down in his paperwork regardless of which of his internal team was sat in front of him. He also did this in the boardroom since he had become Chairman of the Group.

'Have you reduced my salary?' asked Hoary.

'Yes,' answered Michael.

'And my bonuses and conditional awards?'

'Yes and your pension,' confirmed Michael. 'All in line with your requests. Your bonus has been capped at 10% of your earnings. I was of a mind to award you 20%, but why should I let you enjoy life?'

'Good,' said Hoary. 'I suggest you do the same. Earnings will soon become a hot topic, especially 'golden hello' payments. Get the Main Board in line – all of them. Don't concern yourself with the Investment boys – they're dispensable.'

Hoary was initiating an internal cultural programme of ethics into his senior team based on the premise that *values are key to value.* For him, he knew that his position as Chairman would bring substantial focus to his actions, as it did for any high profile individual in society. However, for Hoary's true ambitions to materialise he could not be dragged down into ethical arguments that others of his status would simply challenge on the premise that there were abundant fruits in the gardens of high achievers. He needed to be whiter than white and this applied to his entire audience, whether this was his internal networks, his employees, the public or the press. Especially the press.

His Press Office was predominantly focused on delivering a corporate brand awareness programme called *Key People Delivering for Key People.* Alex used grass root personnel as the efficient voice of the company to attract grass roots customers. Hoary had thought the programme quite ingenious and it had certainly increased their customer base. However, this would do nothing for his personal agenda of building his profile in the networks of influence that Hoary particularly wanted to target. Hoary needed to be well connected with the decision making personnel of the large corporations. He knew that, when the timing was right, these were the people who would react with the most volition when he needed them too. These were the people at the top of the tree and they had further to fall. After all, the drop from the top always looked considerably more frightening than looking down from the lowest branch.

Alex was excellent in his role but he had to go. He was very passionate about the effort his team put into the programme and his success with it, but this would not do for Hoary.

At 3pm, Michael walked into Hoary's office and handed him a file. 'You can open it if you are feeling curious but I shouldn't. You'll be in danger of being impressed and I can't have that. To see you smile would have me tie a noose around my neck. Anyway, it's all in there, including your speech for the Institute of Directors foray this evening. Must go. I have the Beano to read.' Michael left the office and closed the door behind him.

Hoary picked up the file and read the phrase on the front cover, written in thick, black felt tip pen. The handwriting was unmistakably Michael's and it read 'Love from Miranda.' Inside were the contents of seventeen articles that had reached publication that day and a detailed PR programme for Hoary's public profile with a fifteen year agenda. The executive summary said;

> *Goal*
> Hoary reigns paramount on the lips of the elite
>
> *Objectives & Themes – message delivery*
> 1. Values are key to value
> 2. ITCD International Bank is globally #1
> 3. Financial Meltdown
> 4. B20 President

The file contained significant volume of article copy for press release with numerous interview briefs and specific reviews that covered key milestones that Hoary had planned. As he thumbed through the pages his eye caught a press release for a forthcoming IPO awaiting official approval from the Hong Kong Stock Exchange next month. Hoary read.

$3bn IPO Approval for Chinese Bank

> Bank of the Public Ltd., China's third-biggest lender, achieved approval from the Hong Kong stock exchange to raise as much as $3 billion in an initial public offering next month, Reuters have confirmed today.
>
> The Shanghai-based company will start briefing potential investors about the IPO today, said Reuters.

The bank will sell 11 percent of its shares in the offer, they said. ITCD International Group, the owner of a quarter of the bank, will buy 25 percent of the IPO.

Bank of the Public would be the first lender owned by the Chinese government to sell shares overseas. The transaction probably will be used as a gauge to measure investor interest in state-owned lenders. China Commercial Bank plans to sell $4 billion of stock in an IPO later this year.

'Investors want banking exposure in China, but they will be selective because there are more Chinese banks coming to market,' said Sam Ho, who helps manage about $200 million at AKG Asia Ltd. in Hong Kong.

After the approval, the Hong Kong Exchanges & Clearing Ltd.'s spokesman Geoff King declined to comment on the transaction.

Goldman Clearance

Goldman Sachs Group Inc. and ITCD International Group were hired by Bank of the Public to arrange the IPO. Spokesmen from Goldman's in Hong Kong and ITCD declined to comment.

Bank of the Publics' Chairman Mao Tuoliang didn't return calls. Mekyi Mau, a spokeswoman at Citidoor Ross Dewerson which works for Bank of the Public, declined to comment.

London-based ITCD, Europe's biggest bank by market value, plans to buy a quarter of the IPO (4.6 percent of the company's shares) to maintain its stake, the officials said. Bank of the Public is selling 6.8 billion shares.

Bank of the Public reduced its 2004 profit by 71 percent after the government cancelled a 10.14 billion yuan ($1.36 billion) tax credit. The decision cut the company's net income to 1.8 billion yuan from 5.1 billion yuan, according to filings from the bank.

Expanding China

China's economy expanded 9.4 percent in the first quarter, after growing 9.5 percent in 2004. The

> government is trying to reorganise its banks so they can
> better compete with international competitors, which
> will start offering domestic currency services at the end
> of next year to tap $1.56 trillion in savings held by the
> nation's 1.3 billion people.
>
> Founded in 1899, Bank of the Public is one of 15
> commercial banks with a national banking licence,
> allowing it to operate without geographic restrictions.

Hoary smiled. The Chinese economy would generate more income than the U.S. by 2020 and become the largest global economy. Hoary needed a significant presence in China whilst it was priced for entry. In a few years, he would need to pay four to five times the value he would today. He also knew that any investment he placed in China, would be worth double his whole estate in America by the time the emerging nation took the world title.

Hoary flipped through the rest of the pages in the file. His eye caught sight of a note on the back cover written in the same style as the front page. It read, 'Hugely bright girl. She loves me.'

The taxi arrived at 7pm at Hoary's apartment in Little Venice, London. He had decided to stay in London overnight, conscious that his evening would be a late night affair. When he arrived at the Halls of the Institute of Directors, the courtyard was busy with cars ferrying in the arrivals that made up the 400 strong audiences for the dinner that evening. Hoary was pleased to be sitting on a table with the most significant men and women in the room, which included royalty, politicians and chairmen and women from the commodity giants in oil. The event was the annual highlight of the Institute. However, they had not expected Hoary's speech to be on the issue of corporate ethics in a business climate which was experiencing unprecedented commercial growth.

Many in the audience wanted a more relevant topic, geared to the genre of financial boom but Hoary's sources had pulled the right strings to get him in front of the influential crowd. He wanted to be remembered as being the figurehead who had brought this topic to the agenda when most were still unaware that it would soon be. In a couple of years it would become the hottest topic of all their debates, and in the media.

When Hoary was introduced to the podium, he was pleasantly surprised that the host had incorrectly announced his bank as the largest in the world by market value. Hoary knew that most of his audience would not be able to refute this claim from their personal knowledge and it gave him greater credibility. Hoary introduced himself and then continued to read the speech that Miranda had prepared for him.

> Ethics in business is often regarded as the most disparaging imposition on the boardroom agenda, even in a climate today that has given the subject significantly greater endorsement than ever before. Maybe we need to think again.
>
> First of all let me deal with God.
>
> Recently I was talking to a colleague in New York. She told me that God wears a tunic. I told her that God was an American. She rebuked me and told me that God is our excellence. I told her that God lives in Queens. She asked me where the temples of wisdom are in Queens. I told her that he is buying a CD in a record store. She then said to me, 'Next thing you will be telling me is that he smokes.
>
> 'At the moment, eighty a day,' I replied.
>
> I think that it is definitely time for us to rethink our values and on this thought let me recall to you the words of Orson Scott Marden.
>
> 'The greatest trouble with most of us is that our demands upon ourselves are so feeble, the call upon the great within us so weak and intermittent, that it makes no impression upon the creative energies.'
>
> What do I stand for today? At ITCD we stand for *Values are key to Value* and we, like all companies, need to nurture our ethics to flourish commercially.
>
> To achieve sustainable profit growth, companies need to underpin their business model with a set of values which is embraced in every aspect of their business, and that will gain the respect of the public. Business strategy needs to be based on clear competitive advantage; it needs to be executed energetically and efficiently, obviously. But a culture of values is

essential to long-term success, too; or, to put it simply, values are key to value.

But this begs the question: how does a company — indeed, how does it's board — ensure that the company really aspires to the values it espouses? This is, in some ways, a very difficult question to answer, and in others an easy one.

If you take ITCD, for example, we are a company with more than 11,000 offices around the world, in 87 countries and territories, and we employ 315,000 people. ITCD feels like a meeting-place of the world, a crossroads of different cultures, of people from different ethnic backgrounds, and religious and other persuasions. The diversity of my colleagues — collectively we speak more than 81 languages — reflects the diversity of customers we serve around the world, and of the people on the planet.

In some respects, this might seem to make it difficult for a company to adhere to a single set of principles. Yet, for all the obvious cultural diversity, one thing that constantly strikes and impresses me is the extent to which my colleagues share the same desire to work for a responsible and respected company.

ITCD is a company made up of people of many different faiths, and people of no faith, but there is an enormous amount of common ground in terms of their value-set and their aspirations for the way the company that they are a part of, behaves.

I believe this is true of most organisations, large and small. Corporations are a human endeavour, and the majority of the people who work for any given institution want to work in an honest environment, and for a company in which they take pride. As the economist, John Kay has observed: "Companies have no immortal soul, but, like human beings, they live and die. While they live, they prosper by the attributes of their personality."

A company's personality, its culture, if you like, is a central component of its ability to be successful over a sustained period of time. One of the most important tasks for any board or management must be to nurture and strengthen the corporate culture.

It should be the subject of explicit discussion at board level: how the corporate culture has evolved; how it is contributing to sustainable shareholder value; how it can be nurtured for the good of future generations and not in self-congratulatory mode, but with an uncomfortable-at-times spirit of self-analysis.

Nurturing a company's personality, its values and ethics, is not an exact science; it can't be represented in figures on the profit and loss account. But it is no less important for that. It is nothing less than an essential leadership task.

Values are not something that can be prescribed smugly by edict from the centre; they run much deeper than that. Every individual has the power to live by — or to abuse — those values, and to influence his or her colleagues to do likewise, however many or few people they have reporting to them on any organisation chart.

So, I consider that every one of my colleagues has a leadership role in this respect. Companies will be seen as responsible and a force for good only to the extent that each and every employee lives the company's values.

'A culture of values is the key to long-term success.'

A company's brand is an important standard-bearer for those values, internally as well as externally. Companies that seek to position themselves as committed to treating their customers fairly — and which companies do not at least say that they strive to do this? — create brands that resonate with colleagues, as well as with the wider world; a company's aspirations are understood internally as well as externally. So it is a real challenge truly to *live the brand.*

This is easy to say, but so much harder to deliver — mainly because it cannot be easily pinned down to a single action. It is a multitude of smaller things that add up to a bigger whole: how people are recruited; how training programmes reinforce the values; how a strategy articulates a company's aspirations to be a responsible, sustainable business; how these values are buttressed by guidelines that spell out the way business should be conducted, and processes such as objective-setting and compensation.

Indeed, we consider our values to be of such critical importance to our long-term success that, if we are considering an acquisition that makes sense on the numbers, but that is not compatible culturally, then we will walk away from it.

It will never be perfect. Corporations are a human endeavour, with all the possibilities and frailties that are intrinsic to human beings. Maintaining values and culture is a task that needs perpetual renewal.

In 2004, the former Chairman of the Federal Reserve, Alan Greenspan, forecast that business would see a 're-emergence of the value placed by the market on trust and personal reputation in business practice.'

How a company makes money, as well as how much money it makes, is becoming an increasingly important part of its investment proposition. In this environment, there is no conflict between sustainable growth, value, and values. To repeat: values are key to value.

Before Hoary stepped down from the podium, His Royal Highness had risen to his feet and walked over to him. When he approached, Hoary was very pleased to shake his beckoning hand.

From the rear of the hall, Michael was studying the reaction of the audience. The dark haired, rum faced women next to him, who had earlier professed that she was a new age entrepreneur, asked Michael when ethics had entered the debating arena. 'Surely in today's moment of money madness – we're all making pots you know – we need an industry in itself to deal with all that stuff,' she grabbed Michael's knee under the table – endearingly as opposed to a sexual advance, (Michael surmised this was her manner) – and continued to say, 'I'd help fund it. What d'ya think?'

'There lies the opportunity,' responded Michael and he smiled knowing that Hoary was alone in his pursuit. Clearly from the meagre reception Hoary had received and the looks of envy on those that had desperately wanted to council his Highness, the sentiments of the lady sat next to him were a fairly good indicator of the level of ownership shared by all those within the audience regarding this matter.

PLANTING SEEDS

November 2006

'It was the best of times, it was the worst of times'

The quotation shone out from the screen visible to the audience that Wood had chosen to attend. More people had turned up than had been invited. It was November 21st 2006.

Many years ago, when Wood was 17 years old, he had been sitting in the student union bar with his psychology lecturer, Stuart Wattom. After listening to Wood for some time, Stuart stopped him and said.

'You're a bright kid. Very bright, despite your endless list of academic failures. You talk in a maverick, compassionate, determined fashion and you paint many pictures in your debates. One day you could be brilliant, maybe more. But can I give you some advice? Today, you are nothing. Hardly anyone knows who you are and, fewer still care who you are. Get your head down, work hard and shut your mouth. In many years to come, build yourself a stage and when you do and only then, open your mouth and tell the world what you have to say.'

Twenty five years later, Wood had built his stage. He was the company chairman and his conference was held in the grounds of his estate, a fifteenth century Jacobean mansion that had been restored with the affection and the care with which it had been initially built.

When Wood entered the stage to begin his speech he had not dropped a nerve. There was no time for worry. Now was the result of his ambitions, his pursuits, his endeavour, the countless sacrifices and eternal conviction. The audience was made up of senior bankers, solicitors, accountants, businessmen, media, brokers, investment brokers, hedge fund managers, investors and many of his employees. They would advocate witness to all he had ever promised – even though, Wood knew, they would not hear, they would not care to and they would dismiss. But, for now, that was not his concern.

Before he stepped onto the stage, he arose from his seat. Sitting next to him was his partner, Karen and her mother and father. At the back of the hall, Helen was at her table with her colleagues from his company. Wood and Helen had first embraced two weeks earlier.

'It was the best of times, it was the worst of times.'

Wood verbally repeated the words displayed on the projector and continued.

> 'The immortal words of Charles Dickens who inspired us with his observations of the French Revolution; the awakening of new dawns arising from the brutality and savagery of oppression and the need for change.
>
> Those words, today, have no less meaning than they did for the time for which they were written. Now, more than ever, they beg for a greater significance. Now, more than ever, they can become true. The opportunities we face over the next five to ten years can define us for hundreds of years.
>
> My sixteen year old son said to me recently that, "Man is failing to evolve because man has become preoccupied with evolving his environment". There is providence in our youth. My responsibility is to nurture my son, to equip him with the courage to open the doors of providence and walk on through.
>
> If his words are true then we must recognise how they apply. When our early ancestors bravely ventured to uncharted lands and hosted the findings of their new fruits, their education must have propelled a desire for a better politics. But was the intention of that promise an evolution from the spear, to the gun, to a dearth of a corporate and economic spirit?
>
> A lawyer once said to me that the opportunity for us lay in a universal structure for all, in which each

and everybody's *limited company* defined its trust with its contracts.

Today, consumer surveys tell us that the Estate Agent is the most mistrusted commercial profession and that the brokers and the lawyers come second.

Maybe it is not the mistrust of these professionals that is the issue but that the products they work with are broken. In the norms of the Real Estate industry, the agent is faced with the management of the consumer's expectations. The expectation they have of the value of their home. These are invariably high but the eventual buyer has a different value and only conflict will result. When this conflict is resolved, the consumer is then faced with the diversification of the mortgage industry and the complexity of the Conveyance process. Control and expectation is replaced with anxiety and uncertainty. And just to add to the disaster, the initial conflict can return with demands from the buyer to reduce the price that was agreed for the house in the first place.

There are solutions to these problems but lying beneath this is a more serious issue. We know it is wrong. We all know it. We welcome the idea and the man who can put it right. But we fear the price we may have to pay during the period of correction and we fear on whose territories we will have to trespass.

But there is no trespass. There is only redefinition. Legends forgive those that redefine. Coffins and graveyards are filled with unknown men who have already asked for forgiveness.

And of the men we trespass against? If they protect what they deem we will take. If in their protection their behaviour is violent or aggressive, then forgive me, the frontiersman, for failing to find the political advantage – for failing to share my success, for failing to gain your trust, for failing to persuade you of my vision.

Vision is the rarest of resources and rarer still to perceive.

There is no evil. There is only the failure of our political advantage that manifests in conflict because our social, economic and political structures have yet to evolve to find and guide our visionaries into power.

Visionaries don't take power, they cannot command it. They only see the world that must become not the world that is around them and ready to trip them up. They may be the fools of today but whilst we suppress them we engage our biggest folly. In doing so, we deny the essence of us - our political advantage - of its real destiny. *Of truth, of unity and of purpose.*

Deny our visionaries, denounce their oppressors to evil and we languish every day, all of us, lost and upset, confused and fearful, oblivious and insecure, crying and ashamed, desperate in our quiet pursuit; *please, I beg you – why am I here? What is all this about? What is the meaning of life the universe and everything? Please tell me?*

And this fear manifests into distraction; momentary wins and goals, small blessings of happiness – of holidays and cars, clothes and chocolate - of material gains and more.

Fuelled by money and the greater the petrol tank and the greater the potential we have to fill the petrol tank, the greater is the level of distractions we can obtain and the more we can fill our lives with small blessings and fill the days on our calendars with happiness and not loneliness. All the while wondering if this is right or wrong and if the critics of the material world really have a point or whether the seemingly boring quips should be silenced.

Whilst our goals are subjected to the momentary blessings of happiness, we confuse ourselves in finding the true visionaries. Our shelters have evolved into something more and our architects can design the greater and the bigger opportunity. Their beauty is subjective to the observer but their vision is inconclusive, whilst our purpose is opaque. Is the beautiful house a beautiful house or a brick in the wall of destiny?

Our political states are not of capitalism or socialism or communism. How can we define our politics when we don't know what the end goal is? In a capitalistic state we maintain that we need conformity to individual and property rights. Why? When the politicians tell me this, are they seeking my approval or telling me that I must forgive them?

Did George Orwell not tell us of the folly of socialism whilst he witnessed the rebukes from its adversaries when he fought in the trenches of the Spanish revolution. Was 1984 not a vision of communism in its true political manifestation?

How can we know if any of these are true without knowing our real purpose? How do we know if freedom is a true value, an ideology or even – please forgive me - a show stopper?

In all our political states we talk of the distribution of resources and yet we still haven't learnt to stop killing the best resource known to man – *mankind.* Does this not hint to us the types of the men who define our political states? The same men who talk of the evil of terrorism. Terrorism can only exist where boundaries exist and boundaries are defined by fearful men, concerned about limited resources, adverse and dismissive of the ideology we need from our visionaries to multiply our resources.

Peter Goldmark once said;

'Businessmen tend to grow old early. They are committed to security and stability. They won't rock the boat and won't gamble; denying the future for a nearsighted present. They forget what made them successful in the first place,'

Find our visionaries, define who they are and protect them. Did not Elizabeth I commence the build of the most far reaching territory – The British Empire? Was her pursuit not protected by the strength and politics of Walsingham? She reigned for sixty

years and if her visions had been maintained by her
successors, the Empire may have become the globe
and, today, our pursuit may be unrecognisable. I fear
the pursuit would have been a different historical
episode if the roles of Walsingham and Elizabeth had
been reversed.

The visionaries will shape our future and find our
purpose. Give them the rope to hang themselves and
when they do, before their breath fades away, untie
the knot.

Heath stepped onto the podium and announced a five minute break.
Wood stood down from the stage and spoke to Heath for a few moments
before walking to the bar and asking for an orange juice. He was not
drinking today. He wanted all his wits about him. He met Helen and
when they moved to one side, he looked at her. Helen moved her eyes
from his and said, 'I hate this.' Wood let her walk away from him
without his reply. He felt helpless when he was with her and helpless
when he was with Karen, no matter how rational his thoughts seemed to
be or the strength of the imposition they put upon him. His dilemma was
not in knowing what he wanted to do. It was how he was going to do it.
He finished his drink and re-entered the stage. Heath announced that it
was time to reconvene and when the audience settled, Wood continued.
The word 'vision' was displayed on the screen behind his stage.

Vision

My ambition for my Group of Companies, the
details of which you see hanging from the banners
displayed about you, is to *Redefine the Delivery of
Housing in the UK, Europe and Beyond*. To achieve this
goal, I need more than the best laid plans. Although for
the bankers amongst you, I do need the best written
business plan and a well fed cash cow.

Essentially, I need the best laid culture. I stand in
front of you begging your recognition of me as a
corporate servant. Today you have witnessed my
achievements in the lands that I own and the company I
have built. Let this stand as testament to who I am.
From the humble beginnings of the red brick terraces of

Eccelsie Street in Liverpool, many of my ambitions and achievements have been fought and won.

But the defining moment in my life was as a thirteen year old boy and the day that I lost my father.

I think of my father as a good man. He was an ambitious man who had an ideology beyond the working class foundations of his youth. He achieved a good education and after a couple of fruitless jobs he found employment with the Nationwide Building Society. He dragged the family around England in pursuit of his ambitions, with each promotion he received, but he became increasingly uneasy and disturbed. I believe that when he died, aged 39, he was exhausted; not by endeavour but by disillusionment.

I recall him once telling me, just before he died that 'remember one thing in life, son. Everyone is only out for one thing; *Themselves'*. He was angry at that moment and I believe that the values imposed by his working class roots had created a conflict that he could not resolve as he progressed further and further up the ranks.

I have worked in these cultures. In the ravenous pit of personal accountability where your colleagues are vocally visible in their pursuit to actively prey on your mistakes. This tension builds the politics of action. Kill or be killed. The killing delivers the results.

My father failed to absolve his values and adapt. I believe that the result would have been the destruction of his ideology and his fear that he had to give up. On his death certificate they diagnosed his death as cerebral thrombosis but I believe he became exhausted by his disillusionment and hence, susceptible to his fate.

However, after his jibe at 'themselves' he followed this statement with, 'I can never sort this out in my lifetime but I pray that my children's, children's children will.'

My dad had not given up. He had simply seen the potential and the truth of its manifestation.

My father's death and the impressions he left with me, defined me then. Amidst the grief of my loss, I had become the victim of the damage that he had endured and I had to stop this. I had to succeed where my father had not. I had to go further and deliver his ambition; his mission.

Inherent to the values of my father, was his propensity to apply discipline via his leather belt – a norm of his lifetime. Today, my children are disciplined verbally or by alternative means, but I cannot cast the first stone. Norms have changed because values are transient, they change with time, but vision does not. My dad was and is, the best dad. He gave me purpose and I was and am committed.

Today, I see around me a host of experiences and skills in the people who are helping me deliver my mission. But talent is not the result of this. Talent is inherent within us. Everything we do and say and build is a result of our talents. What is implicit is the need to build an environment in which the talent can flourish; to build an environment of opportunity and forgiveness, an environment in which we can behave and act.

Of opportunity in which we believe we are the best and our purpose is great; to pursue this purpose and to love it. To kick ourselves when we lose sight of it but to commit and venture with courage.

An environment where mistakes are recognised, not by tolerance, but by the journey to new frontiers and the unforeseen trip wires that provide us with an invaluable education that results from our initial blindness.

An environment in which we recognise that we need each other for support, debate and balance. That we stick together in our pursuit and as our numbers grow, so too do the opportunities abound.

To recognise that we will love it more and more when we pursue the future and strive to determine and shape it. The future being the place where we spend all of our time in the actions we take and the decisions we make, aware always that the further the journey takes us

into the future, the more we can build for everyone.
When we choose and act in this time, we choose to live
in a place that is not hounded by our mistakes. That
does not repeatedly choose to recall our faults. We
choose to commit, to let providence ensue, let doors
open, ventures be ventured and forgiveness be a given,
rigid in our culture.

The one overriding lesson that we are taught by *time*
is that we cannot go back. Time is not a dimension. It is
a reason. It teaches us that we can only move forward.
We can only live and survive in our future. It is where
we must go. We can look back and criticise ourselves or
we can look forward and act and exercise our choice
and our purpose.

In forty years time, I want my children's, children's
children to be oblivious to the dismay and the hassle
that exists in the stressful demand of moving house
today. I want them to never have to realise that it had
ever happened. I want them to take on bigger and better
challenges.

I want my actions in corporate cultures to redefine
those businesses that build ahead of me. For businesses
to exist that deliver for consumers and recognise that the
consumer must win because they are greater in number
than any one corporation and that the corporation is
nothing more than a servant to all of us, a place to
provide us with opportunity in a world where we are all
consumers to each other. Where action is not tainted by
fear and where inaction is not hidden amidst the faint
excuse of bureaucracy.

I believe my team have the talent to build this
opportunity, the talent to redefine the housing market.
To redefine the cultures inherent in our corporations and
when the pathway is cleared to recognise that
corporations are servants to the consumers, that the
consumer is all of us, let my father have his day and
recognise him as the man that redefined mankind, that
gave us a future with purpose and a world of action and
that I was *his* son.

I leave you with two thoughts.'

Wood had finished his speech and as he moved from the stage he presented to his audience these two quotes.

> *"Choose your plane, get in it and fly. Values are like clouds and planes cut straight through them. All your fears will disperse when your truth becomes singular – forgiveness." Tane Wood*

As his words faded from the screen, Wood made his final statement and when it appeared on the screen behind him, Wood looked up into the audience and found Helen.

> *"Love is everything it's cracked up to be and more. It really is worth fighting for, being brave for, risking everything for. If you don't risk everything, you risk even more." Erica Jong.*

DAMAGED BOWLS

August 2006

Hoary was worried. A rare event in a man with such colossal plans, such was the extent of his mastodonic vision. 'Has someone else seen what I have seen?' he thought.

In early August, 2006, Hoary observed a significant increase in mortgage lending in the UK. His market share was declining rapidly and although it had been for nearly two years now – that was the determined pattern he expected, as he exercised his plan – the nature of the increase had been rapid and it seemed to be coming from one specific source. The growth that Hoary observed was unprecedented throughout all global markets.

He had always felt that nobody else would share his vision because he had never met anybody who he considered to be a worthy challenger. Few, if any – in his mind – could see past the next twenty years and if they did, the language they used to illustrate their vision never had any element of truth. Invariably, they pictured a utopian world of joyous feasting or a world in which Armageddon would finally arrived. 'And what causes all the conflict today?' Hoary had thought, bemused when he had heard these views. 'Is the whole planet in denial?' He resolved that it was worse than that. People simply did not explore the courage that was needed to travel down the unchartered routes, the unlaid roads, explore the new frontiers and challenge the norms that perpetrated the almighty social mess. Few men in history ever had. Those who did were deemed to be, 'the greats'. Men that were mysterious and men that intrigued us all because we couldn't really understand them. They had

had to be 'great' because, Hoary had concluded, it gave us all an excuse to not have to follow in their footsteps, make the difficult decisions, and face the awful consequences of their fates. The psychologists argued that we were a species that was driven by our gregarious needs, seeking acceptance within our peer groups so that we could feel better about ourselves and dispel our insecurities that arose from deemed loneliness. How wrong, Hoary thought, the words of the idealists could be.

And to protect their claims of the ideal, those in the minority had been deemed to be adversary, militant, anarchical or – better still – mad. These views silenced the enterprise in people that was necessary for them to explore their lives, suppressing their actions and leaving them sweating and fearful in that moment of cold turkey when they would say, 'phew, that was close.'

And for those that sponged down the sweat, punched the air and shouted, 'come on, let's do it'. These were the risk takers – the irresponsible men doomed to a fate of failure and there was a whole library of introspective views confusing us on this subject. The occasional risk taker would break through and our media would climb all over their personality and intrigue the audience with the X factor debate. Those in the spotlight could enter the majestic ballroom in muddy wellington boots and set new trends. For the rest, such action would have them thrown to the dogs by the overzealous actions of the security guards.

The powerful elite would marvel in this distraction; a global blaze of trivia that provided intrigue in a half hearted attempt to absolve and abdicate the misery of our unhappiness. And sunk within the distraction was the curious world of the soap dramas providing us with the pitiful message that we weren't alone in all this mess – everybody's life was fucked up – or the lifestyles and glamour of the other half – parked in the most distant of dreams, soaked in a golden wealth of trinkets that did not exist on the shelves of mainstream retailing only to reinforce the elusive cry of the unattainable.

Whilst the majority remained distracted, the elite could sort out the impossible task of distributing the grossly insufficient and limited pool of resources that they knew would merely result in a plague of suffering and death for many. At least for the elite, their control secured their fate for a more ambitious feast and whilst the majority remained distracted, it would keep the baying mob from their front doors.

The brighter boys and girls would not sit with this. The resources could be managed and deployed. They would dream of efficiency and production and fight for it. But few had the courage to expose the limitations in our current systems or see far enough along them to correct the mess.

The distraction kept the populations of the world immersed in the lie and the political bureaucracy silenced the passion of those who tried to expose it. And the few who did break through – their souls could be bought for knighthoods or the prestige of some other national recognition. The alternative, as Nelson Mandela had discovered, was – at best – the foregoing of their personal freedom. Locked up and silenced until they would shut up. And if this had not sufficed, the natural born killers, who reigned in our Darwinian time, could exercise their dominant desires.

Occasionally – literally on the rarest of occasions – the visionaries would arise and drive towards a world where man would sacrifice its nearsighted future to fill a fruit bowl for all our children. Very few survived and most were thwarted by the universal language of dismissal. A mean cry, *'nonsense the task is impossible,'* dismissing the ambition as absurd. They had to be mad. This was the penalty that would justify the release of the bullet that would silence their souls; perpetrators fused in their broken politics; finally regretful on their deathbeds; scared that their soul bared significant plight to fearful doom.

In life, people needed to be silenced and their explorations needed to be dampened. Their propensity to risk could be muffled by a language of disdain. To prove the point, their counterparts – the responsible men and women – would join the crowd in the easiest commercial win of all time – the insurance policy. We were encouraged to protect everything and to put our winnings in accounts and ISA tax efficiency schemes with poor returns which drained the liquidity from the masses and distributed it to the elite.

People put on this mask – it was the right thing to do – and put up the fence around their territory – they would survive into the dream of a retirement that would never materialise because, like the two week holiday, they forgot that they were taking themselves with them. There could never be any escape from choosing the easier path to walk along, niggled by the lie, vociferous in the distraction, rationalistic in the deemed morality of death, *'he was a good man. She was a good woman'.*

Andy Warhol had said that, 'most people treat life as a dress rehearsal for the real thing'. Hoary did not want the event to return. Whilst everybody feared the pending potential of Armageddon, Hoary knew we were merely in denial of the world we had built. What could be worse than all this mess? Armageddon was already here. Hoary knew that he could find the pathway to get us all out of it and he knew what the alternative could be.

What concerned him now was that he sensed that somebody else knew this too. Hoary was not worried that this person would share his vision. He was concerned by the fact that he did not know what their motivation was. What was driving that person on the inside, his invisible truth?

Hoary was sitting in the lounge of the Reubicans Hotel, a stone's throw from Buckingham Palace. This was one of a select few, of his favourite haunts. He very much liked the country-house style of the decor. The floral sofas and chairs were garnished in plush cotton fabric as were the drapes and the warm, strong velvety reds, greens and yellows were rich and calming. Hoary never craved company. He found adequate company in himself and he was not pleased to be greeted in this obscure venue by the perturbed expression on the face of Alex.

'Trevor, can I have a moment?' asked Alex directly.

'What a pleasant surprise,' Hoary lied. 'Please do take a seat,' gesturing to the chair beside him.

'I won't if you don't mind. I just wish to inform you that my resignation is on your desk.'

'Whatever for?' asked Hoary, aware of Michael's scheme.

'Don't play that game with me. Your name is all over the tabloids and the viral sites,' barked Alex.

'Yes, I hear it is,' said Hoary calmly.

'You hear it is. You damn well know it is.'

'Please do calm down,' requested Hoary calmly.

'I intend to. I only came to tell you to stick your job up your fruitless arse. Goodbye and the worst of all possible luck.' Alex left the lounge and before Hoary had lifted his china cup of raspberry tea, Michael appeared.

'The fortune of genius timing. I nearly missed the encore but I heard every word. What would you do without me?' said Michael chirpily.

Hoary lifted his cup and took a sip. He looked up from beneath the rim of his reading glasses and acknowledged Michael but he did not speak.

'Miranda starts on Monday. Tuesday week she will present to the Main Board the new corporate strategy for the press office. I take it you liked her file?' said Michael taking the armchair opposite Hoary.

'Yes, very good. Have you gained council on it?' asked Hoary.

'Done already. The board hated seeing Mr and Mrs Jones all over the telly. Spoilt their social status being associated with the masses. You will have commendable support from the table.' Michael crossed his legs and placed an arm on either side of his chair.

'Have you seen the latest reports on the money markets?' asked Hoary.

'I have,' said Michael assuredly.

'What's the source of this growing spike in U.K. mortgage funds?'

'Not sure yet but I've got my team on the case. Apparently, it's outside of London,' said Michael, fingering the sleeve on the arm of his chair.

'It can't be,' said Hoary surprised. He sipped from his tea.

'I see before me a worried man. There is hope yet. Calm your nerves. This provincial enterprise can only be a nomadic drift from the financial square mile or Canary Wharf at best,' said Michael confidently.

'These new boys are muscling their way in. I wouldn't want to be unseated by red brick ambition,' Hoary said, wondering if Michael could sense his concern and where he was going.

'Talentless, greedy and confused morality. Don't worry about them,' said Michael. He knew what Hoary was worried about.

'I hear their hurt factor is gaining credibility with investment circles?'

'It is, but only because their ambitions are the easiest to steal. Anyway, I already know that the lending source is in Bravills Private Finance. A bright young chap is breaking all company records by all account. Lending for fun, I'm told. Very gorgeous girlfriend with hugely expensive tastes,' said Michael intent on allaying Hoary's fears.

'I want him out,' said Hoary adamantly.

'Yes but not yet. Think about it. He can help you get the job done without you hardly lifting a finger. He's perfect for you. Don't worry. I'll take him out when the time is right.'

'It's not him I'm worried about. It's the potential nutter raising his profile in circles that easily get scared,' said Hoary getting flustered.

'Look,' said Michael. He decided to be more definite to ease Hoary's concerns. 'I have already initiated a £20million scandal to derail Bravills. The solicitor is in place. When the money is drawn down, the agent will skedaddle out of the U.K. with it.'

'I don't get it,' said Hoary, confused.

'All I need is an ambitious young bum with no talent. He sources property stock and raises the £20 million via mortgage funds to purchase it,' explained Michael.

'How can a young bum raise £20 million?'

'He doesn't. He simply provides the files for 40 investment buyers. The files are for clients who don't exist.'

'How do non-existent clients get mortgage lending?'

'It's easy and it happens all the time – even to us. Anyway, his solicitor draws down the funds from the lender and sends it to the young bum's account who promptly disappears whilst the property developer is left screaming for his money. The lender sues Bravills for negligence because it has given away £20 million and received no charge against any assets.'

'And compliance is brought into sort out the mess?' said Hoary fathoming Michael's plan.

'Not only that, but compliance will bring the brand down. The FSA won't tolerate it, they can't. The glamorous young kitten will need to seek another chap to fund her jewellery.'

'How long will this take?' said Hoary impatiently.

'A year maybe. But they'll all fall. It's done.'

Hoary folded up the money market reports he had been reading and put the file on the table. He felt more relaxed now he understood Michael's plan. Michael was the very best politician in the industry – in any industry for that matter and Hoary knew this. In the city, everybody did. If they did not and they had influence, Michael got rid of them very quickly. 'Would you like a tea?' Hoary asked Michael.

'Ground coffee would be nice,' requested Michael.

Whilst Hoary caught the eye of the waiter, Michael asked him, 'How are the acquisitions in the East? Your disruption in the U.S. markets could cost us $25 billion.'

'Small change,' replied Hoary. 'China, Hong Kong and Taiwan are secure. Mao has agreed in Taiwan. I will need a foot hold in Tokyo if I can get the Japanese to concentrate on anything but their sex trade.'

'Failure Trevor. You encourage me,' Michael said facetiously. 'I'll get you in front of Mituzure. He's been chasing me recently. May be they do want U.K. assets after all.'

'I doubt it. Though, Mituzure may be an excellent choice. I hear he sees fewer merits in the protectionist ideals of his countrymen?'

'Yes, I've heard that. I'll arrange it,' confirmed Michael.

When Michael's coffee arrived he hardly had time to drink it. He had a busy day ahead with his company secretary reviewing the mounting debt of litigation. Wong Chin, Head of their Shanghai Banking, was arriving in the mid afternoon. As Michael swigged back his coffee he said to Hoary.

'By the way, Miranda has commissioned a novel to be written for you. She needs to organise a series of pre-release events. One or two will need to be attended by you. I'm sorry but they like to meet the author.'

'Do it, just let me know when and where,' agreed Hoary, sipping his tea.

'Miranda is very good. You'll like her,' Michael said confidently.

'I'm sure I will. What title did you choose in the end?' asked Hoary.

'Miranda chose it. In fact she came up with it – *Honouring God, Honouring Money.*'

'Very good. I do like this girl,' said Hoary uncrossing his legs and placing his newspaper on the coffee table.

'Sleep at night Hoary. By the time the elephant's turd hits the fan, she'll have you crowned as a commercial God. You'll be untouchable.'

'I need to be the loudest voice,' said Hoary adamantly.

'Trust Miranda. Your saintly wisdom will be the only voice.'

When Michael left the lounge, Hoary noticed his discomfort return. He had learned to trust his intuition. Despite Michael's confidence, he recognised that he remained uneasy with the supposition that his voice would be the only one. 'Who is this red brick rogue,' thought Hoary.

RUSTY HUNKS

January 2007

J essie parked up and flung the door of her car open. She jumped out of her seat and held a sign up against her chest and shouted, 'wow, what an achievement.' The sign said '700%' and as Wood approached her he smiled. Jessie was making reference to the growth that had been achieved by Wood's company in the last year.

'Has anybody ever done that?' asked Jessie looking at the sign and pointing to the number. She was excited about meeting Wood and her new employment with him. He was eager to let Jessie loose on his senior team. His business had grown at an incredible pace, as Jessie had acknowledged with her sign, but it was now struggling with the challenge of expansion. He had increased his Main Board to ten individuals and whilst they brought valuable skills and experience to the table, their talents were not – in his opinion – flourishing. Their behaviour needed help.

Jessie was driving a 1960's Aston Martin DB6 and as Wood approached her, he stretched out his open palms to acknowledge her car. 'Beautiful,' he said.

'I just love it. It's always in the garage being repaired but I can't bring myself to part with it.' Jessie was a surgeon by trade but she had studied extensively throughout her thirty five year career. Her business card displayed 57 letters after her name, accolades from degrees, post graduates, doctorates and practice predominantly in the disciplines of medicine, physiology and occupational psychology.

'I haven't got a clue how it works,' Jessie said. They were standing by the James Bond memorabilia and Wood noticed how the rust had corroded a series of holes above the wheel arch; in fact, all four of the wheel arches. 'I think the engine is at the front. But isn't it magnificent?'

'Talking of magnificent,' Wood began. 'Can you repair my men?'

'Did you know,' said Jessie – Wood sensed by her tone that she was about to change the subject and his expression displayed a man confused by her manner – 'That the Greek definition of an apocalypse derives from *apo* – away and *kaluptein* – to hide. Therefore an apocalypse is an event from which people run away and hide. I have a friend – he is not my only one but he is important – Matt, notorious by the fact that everyone considers him to be better looking than Elvis Presley. He believes that you can't run away – integrity demands it. He tells me that if he is in a nightclub with a friend, he will ask them if their girlfriend is in the room. He is completely indiscriminate with whom he will approach. If he asks their girlfriend out and she says yes, he will sleep with her. Matt tells them that he does not want to hide. He simply wants them to know exactly who he is.'

Clearly Jessie had not changed the subject. Wood said, 'Will Matt work for me?'

'No. We don't need him too.' Jessie linked her arm through Wood's.

'My men need this integrity,' said Wood, picking up Jessie's walking pace quickly.

'I've met your team and they're ok. Let's get started. Who's first?' When the kettle had boiled and they had made their drinks, Jessie took a seat in front of Wood in his office. She picked up her pen and pointed to her note pad. 'Come on. Let's get on with it,' she said. They spoke for a while and Wood asked Jessie to spend a week in his business to get to know everyone. When the week had passed they spoke again.

The first objective Wood gave to Jessie, would eventually defeat her but no crystal ball stood amidst their belongings on the table they were sitting at. Wood explained that a member of the Main Board, Scott, was gay.

'Is this a problem?' asked Jessie.

'Yes,' said Wood adamantly.

'Why?' asked Jessie chewing the end of her pen.

'Did you know he was gay?' Wood was sat back in his seat.

'No,' said Jessie leaning closer towards him.

'Does anyone in the business know?'

'No. I don't think so,' said Jessie thinking and shaking her head.

'Is he vocal about it? probed Wood.

'No. I didn't even know he was gay until you just told me and I didn't even suspect he was. In fact, I'm a bit surprised. Well, *very* to tell you the truth.'

'Did you know that he is an alcoholic?'

'No,' said Jessie beginning to wonder where Wood was heading with these questions.

'Raging. I took him with me to Poland. He started drinking at five in the afternoon and finished twelve hours later, every night. When we got the flight back, it was ten thirty in the evening by the time we were out of the airport and driving home. Scott drove like a maniac and asked me to join him for a drink. We got to the pub five minutes after closing time and Scott begged the barman for two bottles of wine. He paid over the odds but he got them. Half an hour later, Scott was ready to drive me home. Both bottles were empty.'

'Ok,' said Jessie tentatively.

'Ok or not. I need this exposed,' said Wood opening up his arms before him.

'Ok.'

Jessie decided to try to deal with the alcoholism first before tackling his homosexuality. A few weeks later, Wood asked Scott what he thought of Jessie. He said, 'I'm struggling with this psychology stroke behaviour stuff. And as for Jessie, she's a nutter. She's off her head. I think she thinks I'm an alcoholic.'

Wood was pleasantly surprised with the ease with which Jessie made herself comfortable in his business. At least, with most of his team. Scott was not the only person to doubt her validity. He was vocal about her value to the team and derogatory in his assessment of her. She was aware of this, and she seemed to handle this dismissal.

Jessie rang Wood one day, 'Where are you right now? I need to speak to you,' she said, flustered.

'Where do I need to be?'

'I'll meet you in Lombard's in one hour,' Jessie said adamantly.

'*Lombard's?* Ing House?' said Wood seeking clarification.

'Yes.'

When they met, Jessie was visibly agitated.

'I have looked at this data time after time after time. I can't fault it. Well I can, nothing's perfect. But from every angle I've looked at it, from every manner that I've torn it apart, I constantly draw the same conclusion.'

'What conclusion?'

'My assessments of your team; the people you have around you – who they really are.'

'And?'

Nearly fifteen years earlier, Wood and Karen began dating. In their early courtship they both went to extraordinary lengths to surprise and please each other. They both craved happiness and they made extra efforts to give this to each other.

One evening, Karen had driven for over fifty miles, with no brakes, worn tyres and one head lamp. Her Rover Metro had been condemned after a failed MOT two years ago. She did not see the value in getting it repaired and she had learned to use the gears to compensate for her lack of brakes. Karen had never driven this far before. She had got lost in her attempts to find the retail store where Wood worked. Tomorrow was his thirtieth birthday. She wanted to surprise him and give him the presents she had saved up to buy for him after they had first met two months ago. When she finally arrived at the store, she asked the checkout girl if she would call him to the tills so that she could surprise him. Karen explained her reasoning. The checkout girls had a soft spot for Wood because they knew that his wife had recently left him and taken their three children. When the loud speaker announcement was made in the store, the girls hid behind their checkouts so that the area appeared unmanned to deliberately wind him up.

When he arrived, he was angry at first but he saw Karen and his surprise momentarily overwhelmed him. The checkout girls appeared from behind the tills and laughed at their joke. They enjoyed Karen's ploy and her romantic gesture. Wood handed over the store to his assistant and left early with Karen. When they had returned to Wood's flat, Karen had told him she had booked a table at a restaurant in the city centre. She could stay the night. As Wood showered and changed to get ready for the evening, Karen organised her surprise so that Wood wouldn't see it until she gave it to him on the morning of his birthday.

During the evening, when they were dining, Karen asked him if he was over his ex-wife. 'The divorce is going through and it should be complete this month. They seem to reel these things off of the conveyor belt nowadays,' replied Wood. 'I'm more bothered about the fact that she took all the money after she agreed to split it in half.'

'Why did she do that?' asked Karen. By habit, she held her knife and fork in the opposite hands to the norm. All her life, she had had problems cutting her meat. She was struggling now. She hoped that Wood hadn't noticed.

'I don't know,' began Wood. 'I only found out on the day we finally sold the house. Her solicitor told me that I wasn't entitled to anything because she had to care for the children.'

'That must have hurt. How did you feel?' asked Karen, finally separating a piece of meat.

'Destitute. My bank account is still frozen. I still don't know when I can pay them back.'

'Change your account,' she said.

'No point. My salary only just covers child maintenance and my loans. I needed this promotion. I got the flat with it. I couldn't bear sleeping in my car for much longer,' said Wood. She looked at him and noticed how matter-of-fact he was being as he recounted his experiences.

'How long has it been?'

'Six months,' he said.

'Well, I'm impressed. How many people could secure a promotion when they're going through what you've just had to endure?'

'You'd be amazed at the simple things you miss when you have to bed down in your car. The lengths I have had to go to,' said Wood with his eyes looking over her shoulder. Karen had been fighting with her meat again. This time she lost the battle and her knife flew off the table.

When they finished their meal, Karen caught the eye of the waiter and requested the bill. 'My treat,' she told Wood. 'You're poor. Come to think of it, we both are.'

The Crown and Puppet had a bar extension until midnight and Karen and Wood decided not to go on to a night club. As they drank their last orders, Wood said, 'This whole mess has taught me one thing. This is my life and I don't want to live it this way. I've seen the real value of money and I want the choices it brings.'

'You're already getting back on your feet,' said Karen crossing her legs and making herself comfortable.

'Yes but that's not enough.' Wood took a sip of lager. 'What am I waiting for? When you're at your low nobody really helps. It's not that *they don't care. They just haven't got time to. They've all got their own problems to deal with.'*

'That's not strictly true,' she said looking at him.

'Maybe, but the point is that you have to decide what you want and you have to go and get it,' he said and looked at her.

'And what do you want?' she asked, circling the rim of her glass with her finger.

'I want to be on the other side. I don't like being below the poverty line. I want to know what it's like to have more than enough.'

'Do it then,' she said finishing her drink.

'I'm going to. I want the million before I'm forty.'

'How?'

'I don't know yet but it's time to start asking the question,' said Wood watching the flickering neon lights dart across the ceiling.

In the morning, Karen awoke first and Wood remained asleep whilst she prepared his surprise. When she brought him a tray with a cooked English breakfast, orange juice and a coffee. She couldn't fit his birthday cake on it. Karen had made several trips before her surprise was fully complete, on the bed before him.

He loved the watch she had bought him. He told her that it must have cost her a fortune. It had and it meant a lot to her that she had given up so much to afford it. Karen was delighted that Wood was so pleased with everything she had done for him. She hoped that he would be happy with her efforts but she was taken aback when tears ran down his face and he told her that, 'this is certainly a birthday I'll remember. I've never had anything like it before.'

That afternoon, when they were sitting in a cafe drinking coffee, Wood asked Karen what she wanted in life.

'I was crap in school. My teachers thought I was useless and I got out as soon as I could.' As Karen spoke she cupped her hands around her coffee mug. 'My dad never seemed to know who I was. I know that I want kids; four – no less and no more – I want to give them what I didn't have. I'm not really sure why, I just know that that is what I want to do.'

Ironically, Wood had been Karen's boss in a previous role and they had despised each other. She had thought he was a tyrannical boss and he had found her to be militant and lazy. After Karen had lost her first child at birth, she had changed. She had come to admire Wood. She had no longer deemed his behaviour as oppressive. Instead she saw determination and sincerity in his actions that, hitherto, she had learned to despise.

She came to sense a maturity in him that she would not have previously recognised. She knew she was falling in love. Her previous boyfriends and ex-husband were not handsome men. She had been attracted to Wood and she was pleasantly surprised when he had called her. She had offered to be there for him if he needed a friend to talk to. They had briefly spoken about his divorce. He had rung her and taken her up on her suggestion. That had been their first date and they had got on well.

She told her closest friend that she was delighted that somebody that she actually fancied had also been attracted to her. Karen had been swept up in the joy of their encounters. 'I hate to use this word,' Karen had told her friend. 'But I actually think he's a bit of a hunk.' Karen never told Wood that she felt this way about him.

Wood began to recognise that Jessie's influence was seriously shaping the culture of his business. Simple principles began to become rooted in the language used by his teams. Jessie told him that she was not exerting the influence over his senior team and getting the results that he had asked of her. She told him that she needed to get stuck in more, be more forthright, get in their faces. Wood told Jessie that this was the last thing she needed to do.

'Just be yourself,' he said sitting very relaxed.

Wood maintained with Jessie throughout, that patience was the call needed from both of them.

'Why?' she asked sitting on the edge of her seat.

'Cultures take time to develop, to overcome resistance and to accept change. This could take us two to five years.'

'Even with a small team?' she asked writing on her note pad.

'Even with a small team; bright as they may be. We will need the executive and the management to share the principles. The vision will only be delivered when our team can truly understand the aspirations of our consumers. We need to know who we are first and, eventually, we must evolve this to our customers.'

'How?' she asked continuing to write.

'I don't know. We'll find a way,' said Wood encouraged by Jessie's endeavour with her notes. He knew that she worked hard.

'I guess you're right. Dale Carnegie once said that those convinced against their will are of the same opinion still,' said Jessie, sucking the end of her pen and looking up to the ceiling.

'There you go then,' said Wood.

'The Greeks said it first,' said Jessie, changing the subject in mid flow. Wood was getting use to this by now and he was beginning to understand that Jessie had her own way of explaining herself. 'Nearly four thousand years ago. They claimed that humans were defined by four specific types. By the mid part of the twentieth century, their ideas gained attention once again. Pioneering Psychologists were in agreement that simple principles governed our moods and the types of people we were. Being aware of these allows us to know more about ourselves and how we react to different situations. I think that the potential could be highly significant for balancing the dynamics of teams. It will permit the players to deal with emotional states such as high anxiety and fear.'

'Ok. Can this be applied?' asked Wood.

'Yes. The challenge is mine. Can I get them to understand it, do they want to and can *they* apply it. If they do, I can get you a team that is self aware and delivers exceptional performance.'

Wood was convinced that Jessie could repair his men. Following his initial interview with her, Wood told Jessie that he wanted her to present her ideas at the next board meeting. If she gained the acceptance of the team, he would give her a job. Jessie agreed and asked for the early slot, '9am please, whilst they are alert and still awake.'

Before Jessie met the team at the board meeting she asked if she could conduct one to one interviews with each of them, to carry out a series of assessments. Wood thought that this was a brave move and he agreed.

During the assessments, Jessie took each member of the team through a series of simple scenarios which delved into their styles of behaviour, their coping mechanisms, their emotional responses and more.

Their reactions were surprised and positive. Clearly these were men and women who had achieved a relatively high level of success. Yet they had acquired a series of *limiting beliefs* throughout their lives which had presented them with negative doubts about their potential. For example, mediocre and poor achievement in their education exams, feedback from superiors about poor performance issues, breakdown in personal relationships leading to separation and divorce. She concluded with each of them, that they sat within the top 2% of society in regard to performance, capability, competence and a host of other measures that she applied.

'Think of it like this,' Jessie told them. 'You have a cuddly, warm monkey on your shoulder. He is your best friend and he will help you no matter what happens. Every time you beat yourself up because you have done something wrong, you beat up your monkey. Look after your monkey. He is your best friend and the one chance you have got to get it all right. The last thing you need to do is piss him off.'

'Self talk is good. Listen to Tane, he often talks about himself and his conversation is positive. He is stroking his monkey and feeding him with peanuts. His monkey is happy. Tane's profile puts him in the top 0.1% and above according to my assessments. That is probably why he is the boss, the entrepreneur and he has achieved his success. In this sector, he has significantly more challenges, more threats and more fears to face than almost anybody. The happier his monkey gets, the greater is his chance of survival and the greater is his chance of achieving his ambitions and his goals. Your monkey is the best defence you have. Make him happy.'

Back at Lombard's, Jessie was starting to make more sense. 'When I originally assessed your team I concluded that you had a good balance of people across a range of types,' Jessie began. Wood sat up and looked at her. 'Scott was social/sensitive, Tom was robust/individual, Christine was sensitive/robust, and Martin was social/sensitive and so on and so forth. I think I got it wrong. The more I get to know them, the more I see beyond the surface that they present and delve into the people that they really are, the more I realise they I was wrong in my initial assessments of them. Take Scott, he comes across as a man with considerable empathy. But, I think you are right – this is not really him. It is a mask he presents to us because he is afraid that if we know the real Scott we will reject him. I get the feeling that with his empathic efforts he is over compensating for something. When he was demoted six years ago, he told me that the feedback from his boss was very negative regarding his social skills.'

'You still have to deal with his homosexuality. You have to show him that we know, that we are not bothered and that we love him whatever.'

'I accept that,' said Jessie.

'Yes, but you are shying away from it. You are not dealing with this issue. I know it's tough. Many of these guys have come from senior positions in FTSE blue chips. In these environments they are constantly being attacked. They learn to guard themselves to survive.'

'OK, but that is not the real problem.'

'What do you mean?'

Five years after Wood and Karen had met, she gave birth to their son. They called him Cameron. Wood had chosen the name.

'Why Cameron?' Karen asked holding the newborn whilst she sat on her bed in the maternity ward.

'I was in my car, driving to the hospital and I thought, sod it. Cameron it is going to be,' said Wood, moving closer to Karen's bed.

'And?' she asked, surprised with his answer.

'I was very unpopular at my last school. When I left and entered sixth form, a number of the guys from my school did the same. They had not liked me previously because they were the popular crew, especially Cameron Lewis who we called Lui. At sixth form Cameron and I became the best of friends.'

'How come?' asked Karen

'He fell in love with a girl and she had previously been going out with a guy called Kinsey. Everyone thought Kinsey was a dork and Cameron took a lot of stick for falling for Louise – the girl with the dork,' explained Wood shrugging his shoulders. 'Cameron had been concerned and he'd asked me what to do. I told him that he was a very popular guy and that this impact wasn't significant enough to taint that. A year later, when she accepted his proposal to marry her she had been delighted and Cameron was over the moon. He was crazy about her. He told me then that if it hadn't been for what I'd told him, he doubted he would have had the courage to ask her out. Ten years on, he is married to Louise and they have three kids. He's still madly in love with her.' When Wood finished his sentence he sat back in his chair.

'Why are you concerned about the name?' Karen was puzzled. She thought that the principle behind Wood's decision was a wonderful accolade.

'I've thought about it ever since you got pregnant and I've struggled with the idea,' said Wood sitting forward again, placing a finger on the baby's cheek.

'Why?' asked Karen.

'Cameron had everything that I wanted and I told him that. I always sensed, from hints that he dropped, that we got on so well because he felt the same way about me,' said Wood looking puzzled.

'He obviously did.'

'Yes, I finally decided to believe that today, when I was driving to meet you today. I just always wanted him to say it. It was pretty horrific being as unpopular as I was.'

'Cameron is a great name,' said Karen, reaching out a hand to Wood.

Cameron was Karen's first child following Jane's death and Karen was overly protective in her manner with him. Wood understood why she acted the way she did with Cameron. Jane had only lived for four days. Karen had recounted the appalling events of the death of her first child when she had first met Wood.

Jane was born at the John Radcliffe hospital in Oxford. Karen was the second mother to try out the new birthing pool procedure that the doctors had recently implemented. The previous week, on their first attempt, a Spanish girl had given birth in the pool and the baby had died. The doctors had concluded that the death was due to medical reasons and not the procedure.

Following Jane's death the national newspapers had pounced on the event and Karen's loss had been exposed on the front page of the newspapers. They implied medical negligence and ignorance on behalf of the mother.

Karen had been distraught with her loss and the exposure in the public eye had intensified her grief. 'I had been useless at school, I never got on with any of my bosses at work and my dad didn't have time for me. My boyfriends just wanted to shag me and I never really knew what my husband wanted. I eventually worked out that it certainly wasn't me. The only thing I felt I stood a chance at, was being a mother. Suddenly, I learned that I was disastrous at that too.'

'Oh dear,' said Wood, holding his head in his hands.

CHICKEN & MILK

November 2006

'**C**hicken fodder,' said Michael. 'Compared to the $13 billion you have written off in Housefrank.'

'Whose idea was it?' asked Hoary.

'It pains me that you have to ask.'

'Mine?' said Hoary facetiously. He knew that it wasn't.

'Of course it was. Miranda merely co-ordinated it, established the partnership, organised the event launch at the Rochester and ensured that everybody left the party knowing that the great Hoary was the man who would save the world. After she had finished sorting that lot out for you, the feisty, sexy minx gave you a blow job and – my guess is – you can't even remember that either.'

'Who did you say launched the event?'

'Read it. You were great,' said Michael, placing the press release on Hoary's desk and pointing a determined finger in the direction of it.

ITCD International announces a US $120 MILLION program to combat climate change worldwide.

ITCD has created a five-year, US $120 million partnership to respond to the urgent threat of climate change world-wide with the support of The Climate Group, Earthwatch Institute and WWF.

The ITCD partnership will help some of the world's great cities – Hong Kong, London, Mumbai, New York and Shanghai – respond to the challenge of climate change creating 'climate champions' worldwide who will undertake field research and bring back valuable knowledge and experience to their communities.

They will conduct the largest ever field experiment on the world's forests to measure carbon and the effects of climate change and help protect some of the world's major rivers – including the Amazon, Ganges, Thames, and Yangtze – from the impacts of climate change, benefiting the 450 million people who rely on them.

Speaking at the London news conference to launch the programme, Sir David Attenborough, one of the world's best known broadcasters and a pioneer of the nature documentary, said, "As we increase the production of greenhouse gases, we face the very real prospect of causing irreversible damage to the Earth's more fragile ecosystems. We are not powerless if we act now, collectively and decisively. We can significantly reduce the causes of climate change and greatly improve the chances of safeguarding for future generations, the spectacular diversity of life on Earth."

ITCD Group Chairman Trevor Hoary said, "The ITCD Partnership will achieve something profoundly important. By working with three of the world's most respected environmental organisations and creating a 'green taskforce' of thousands of ITCD employees worldwide, we believe we can tackle the causes and impacts of climate change. Over the next five years ITCD will make responding to climate change central to our business operations and at the heart of the way we work with our clients across the world."

ITCD's US$125 million partnership – including the largest donations to each of these charities and the largest donation ever made by a British company – has significant programme targets and offers transformational support for the environmental charities. The donation will help to deliver increased capacity, help the charities to expand across new countries and research sites, and increase their access to more people.

Mary Harding, CEO of The Climate Group said, "Climate change is an increasingly urban issue. High summer temperatures, storms and rising sea levels will have more extreme impacts on city life. We have a short period of time left to take action. Many of the solutions lie in cities – concentrations of capital, decision makers, opinion formers and population. Through the ITCD Climate Partnership we will accelerate our programme in five world cities, engaging the most influential businesses and city governments to lead a 'coalition of the willing' against global warming."

Windser Frazer, Executive Director of Earthwatch (Europe) said, "People need positive solutions to help them tackle climate change rather than messages of doom and gloom. Earthwatch is committed to inspiring action, not apathy. We will do this by involving ITCD's global workforce in online education and climate change research in forests worldwide to leave a powerful legacy."

Langford James, Director General of WWF International said, "WWF is pleased to be continuing its collaboration with ITCD. Climate change, poor management and waste mean that water supplies around the world are more and more stressed. The ITCD Climate Partnership will help WWF work towards better management of global water supplies, improving water security for about 450 million people.

The ITCD Partnership will train 200 scientists and send 5,000 ITCD employees on conservation research projects world-wide benefiting some 50 million people.

'Very good,' said Hoary, finishing the article. 'Quite pathetic really but Miranda certainly milked it for every penny.'

'She has just produced your fourth book by the way,' said Michael.

'Fourth? When was the second one launched?' said Hoary surprised.

'It wasn't and neither was the third. Amazon provides the only listing priced at £149 a copy. No one orders them. Miranda uses the titles to define you as the moral lord and master.'

'What if someone were daft enough to pay?' asked Hoary.

'Trevor, do you really believe that anybody would part with £150 to buy a book on morality and banking? Sex, murder and mystery struggles to get £8. By the way, who is this new guy – Brendan...O'Murphy, I think.'

'Brendan O'Sullivan. He's a Manhattan boy who was posted by me in Shanghai. I've promoted him to Main Board.'

'Any good?' asked Michael crossing his legs and folding his arms. He scratched his nose.

'No, not really. He's gets right in your face. I've asked him to head up the North America Holdings. The defaults have risen fivefold since 2004 and we are piling in provisions from Shanghai to compensate for the loss.'

'Is it visible?' asked Michael.

'Yes, but well under the radar. Group profits should remain strong for another two to three years before all hell breaks loose. I need a feisty fighter to bat off the analysts when it all breaks. Brendan will be my man.'

'Miranda knows him. She says he's a snake.'

'Interesting. I've not heard that but it wouldn't surprise me.'

'Piers tells me that the depositories are at an all time high.'

'That reminds me. I need all heads to drive margin and lower volume.'

'You've already asked me. I implemented it by policy last month. Do I sense senility settling in? There is a God,' said Michael chirpily.

'Yes, there is. That's the problem,' said Hoary playing on the irony.

Hoary needed to strengthen his cash position. When the tsunami broke, liquidity would cripple companies. The saying that 'Cash is King' would redefine the meaning of a king.

'I see that U.K lending is still escalating. Have you found the source?'

'Yes we have. He is all over the tabloids. The Express claimed he was Britain's New Tycoon, although The Mail dismissed his enterprise as subversive.'

'Why?' asked Hoary.

'He has ambitions to redefine the housing market but he is asking for 20% discounts from vendors. The journalist surmised that the ethics had potential but like all new frontiersmen, the cowboys always get there first.'

'Bright?' asked Hoary. Michael eyed Hoary to see if he expressed his concern and he did. Hoary fidgeted with the papers in his hands.

'Courageous definitely but no indication that he has a brain,' Michael said uncertain of the truth but having nothing to suggest otherwise.

'Take him out. I don't need the imposition.'

'As luck will have it, we have his account – personal and business. Fourteen million went through his personal account last year alone and his business account saw £125 million in transactions in the last ten months.'

'Are his filings strong?' asked Hoary.

'Companies House register his turnover as the third largest in his industry in Europe,' confirmed Michael.

'Take him out. His credibility will be growing,' said Hoary adamantly.

'I have initiated the fraud. Bravills are plagued by compliance as we speak. The legs of his lending source have been taken away.'

'Watch his account holding with us and...'

'I've already highlighted his industry as high risk by policy,' interrupted Michael. He had this matter under his control and he recognised that it was unlike Hoary to probe so deep into his efficiency. 'The regional team are all over his business as we speak. I can pull his liquidity whenever we need to. Leave it with me, I will get it done.'

'Make sure you do,' Hoary said passionately.

People Eat Fruit

February 2007

O n the day of the board meeting, Jessie had already won over her new colleagues. They were feeling better about themselves following her initial consultation with each of them. The idea of the monkey had come under satirical attack. Wood unhooked the toy monkey from its noose, hanging from the ceiling, before Jessie had arrived. Generally her ideas were accepted and Wood knew it would take some time.

After Wood opened the board meeting, he introduced Jessie and spoke of his intent with her employment. He wanted the very best for his team. To deliver the agreed objectives and the vision, they would need the very best in team performance.

'Ultimately, our brand must become a universal success in the world. Our team, from the top down, must live and breathe the values we want for our customers. To achieve this we must know how to listen to our people and to our customers. We must strive for the very best and seek no compromise to achieve it. The delivery is down to us, the people in this room. The truth is out there and we must find the way to go and get it. This must start with us, in the way we behave and in the people we truly are. In our journey to establish this, we will need help and hence, I would like to bring to our team, Jessie.'

As Jessie stood up and started to introduce herself the arms and legs in her audience began to fold and cross.

After a few moments of introducing herself, Jessie started her debate with a quote from Erica Jong, *'Everyone has talent. What is rare is the courage to follow the talent to the dark place where it leads.'*

Jessie flicked the page on the flip chart and displayed the phrase 'Jessie's Marble. I can help you get to that dark place and switch on the lights when you get there.'

Jessie's Marble.

'Behaviour is a huge debate and the summaries drawn today provide us with little guidance. There exist too many variables, too many jargons and hence too much confusion. I sense that for many of us, we feel like we are swimming in the ocean with no sight of land. We are left with a sense of the *inconclusive, of being random,* to say the least.'

'Of being random,' thought Scott despondently. 'A bloody hour of listening to this pompous bitch.' He shuffled in his seat and caught John's eye across the table. Scott smiled and John returned his gesture lowering his eyes quickly and slowly drawing his tongue across his lower lip. Scott's heart leapt. Under the table he put his hand on his crotch and adjusted his hang. He hoped John could excuse himself from his wife again. Scott was looking forward to spending two nights in a row in the corporate flat with his lover.

Jessie's Marble. 'What we can definitely say is that the pursuit of our understanding of behaviour does not lack ambition. There are many, many theories, countless debates and every day and every hour and minute there exist endless conversations in our pubs and clubs throughout our lands. We certainly hunger for an understanding of the subject. The audiences of our most popular television programmes and films are immersed in the twists and turns of our soap stars. Of what they do and why they do it. Our craving is insatiable.

What I want to do is present you with two key principles which I believe are fundamental in the intuitive judgement you make about the people around you; who they truly are and why they do what they do. These principles can help you too, in your judgement of who you really are and why you do what you do. These are not a set of rules. Think of them more as a steer and it is up to you to decide whether or not these principles

steer you in the right direction. The two principles are
Mood and Type.'

Scott knew he would be late getting to the gym. The board meeting
would drag on until past 5pm. Wood was a stickler for debate. Scott
resolved to get at least half an hour on the treadmill and the weights. For
five years he had maintained the discipline of keeping his shape well
tuned. He liked to feel fit and sexy. It gave him more confidence in
public and in the bedroom. Scott had already planned the meal for later
that evening. For himself, he would choose a high protein dinner from
his Atkins Diet and he would make John a Mexican stir fry. John liked
his food and craved it in quantities. He lashed tomato sauce on
everything and Scott laughed with his manner. He hated how he abused
good food but he never said. He loved to see John eat well and enjoy it.
'That's if,' Scott thought, laughing to himself, 'he lets me keep my
clothes on long enough to get through the door.'

> *Jessie's Marble.* 'Firstly, the management of our
> moods is governed by our levels of anxiety and activity
> and each varies in intensity. Our anxiety levels, for
> example, can be high or low or somewhere in between,
> anywhere in between. This is also true of our levels of
> activity. What is crucial here is to understand what is
> happening to us.
>
> For example, if we have a prolonged state of high
> anxiety and low activity, our pain thresholds can be
> seriously tested. We usually experience this state when
> we receive bad news or negative feedback. If we remain
> in this state for too long we can become depressed. This
> area I have called '*Bottom left*' and it is the state in
> which we experience the most pain.
>
> In the *top left*, low anxiety and low activity, we give
> ourselves the space and the time to think and reflect and
> hence, we can solve problems. In *bottom right* we
> experience high anxiety and high activity. Here we can
> be feeling pretty good about ourselves and euphoric but
> remaining in bottom right for too long can lead to states
> of mania in which illusions or disillusions begin to
> manifest.

In *top right*, our anxiety level is low but our activity
is high. So we are feeling fairly comfortable about
ourselves and the world around us and basically enjoying
ourselves – having fun.

John had certainly been enjoying himself yesterday, thought Scott.
He was hungry for it alright. He had teased Scott all day. Whispering
sentiments in his ear each time he had passed him in the office. When
they had met in the toilet, John had thrown Scott against the wall and
darted his tongue down the back of his throat. He told Scott that he was
going to shag him sore tonight. 'Get pissed first,' John had said. 'You
won't feel the pain.' Scott had laughed at the quip. John was always
very gentle with him and Scott warmed with the irony of John's words.
Scott had never before met such a caring and affectionate lover. He
knew that John had him wrapped around his little finger. Scott had never
felt this way about anybody before. He was besotted with him and he
had been since they had first met six years ago.

Jessie's Marble. 'It is very common for us to move
in and out of states and boxes fairly regularly – study
the flipchart (Jessie uncovered the cross and her
diagram for her audience to see). Sometimes a single
comment can move us from one box to another. For
example we may be enjoying ourselves when we
receive a phone call that gives us bad news.

The important consideration here is to simply
recognise what is happening to you and why. Often, if
we get stuck in the Bottom left hand box, recognise that
your anxiety level will manifest in pain. But, *it is only
pain.*

See it for what it is and allow yourself the breathing
space to deal with it. Often, you can work yourself out
of the bottom left into top left where you deal with a
problem and find a solution. Anxiety levels are often at
their most intense when we hear bad news but these
levels normally begin to reduce with time. They reduce
significantly sooner when we recognise what is
happening to us.

Scott yawned openly and his thoughts drifted back to the night before. When Scott had opened the door to the corporate flat, John had pinned him to the wall as soon as they were in the hall. John had kissed him gently on the mouth and worked his way down his neck onto his chest. Scott had been wild with arousal and flung John on the sofa in the living room. The pace had been hampered by the few moments it had taken to get John's trousers off – the belt buckle had got stuck. They had laughed this off and Scott had gone down on John who had already been aroused. Scott liked the fact that John was well endowed. It made his jaw ache if he tried to please John when the moment wasn't quite right. This time was different. John had writhed with his ecstasy within minutes. He often told Scott that nobody did it better.

Jessie's Marble. 'For all of us, it will never be too healthy to remain in any one box for too long but, in most cases many of us never do. We naturally move around both axes as we interact with our world and the people around us.

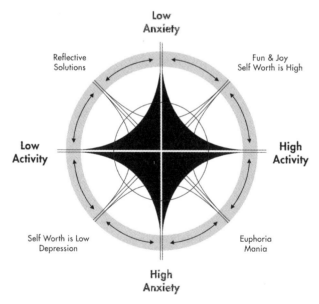

The Human Compass

Explore the chart and use it over time. You will find many variables that apply and as you use it more and more you will become increasingly aware of what is happening to you and better prepared to deal with your moods. Remember, pain *is only pain.* It is natural, you will experience it. Don't try so much to avoid it. Try more to deal with it when it comes. Recognise what is happening to you. Being aware of a problem is often the halfway house that allows you to resolve it.

The second topic is *Type.* Before we come on to this, we will have a coffee break and I will leave you with the thoughts of Woody Allen on this subject. He said, 'Life is full of misery, loneliness, and suffering - and it's all over much too soon.'

I wish I could have said the same about that presentation, thought Scott, looking at Jessie. He sank into his seat and decided to distract himself with his memories of last night. He recalled how John had taken a shower whilst he cooked. Luckily he had only prepared the food when John had appeared in front of him dripping wet. John had demanded Scott to get on the bed that instant. 'Come on gorgeous. I want you inside me now.' Scott had opened his arms and palms towards the food that lay prepared on the work surfaces. He smiled and laughed as he nearly choked on a mouthful of carrot. 'That can wait. I need you now,' John had asserted and grabbed Scott, gently wrestling him into the bedroom. They had kissed sensitively before John had fed Scott inside him. John lay flat on his front and felt Scott's weight on top of him. Scott held John firmly and grabbed at his muscles which intensely aroused him. As he gently picked up the pace, John groaned with the rhythm and Scott had come quite quickly. When they lay on the bed holding each other they kissed sensuously for some minutes and John held Scott firmly in his arms. As Scott massaged John's muscles with both hands and curled into his cuddle, he told him that he couldn't bear to think of life without him. 'I'll do anything for you. I love you madly.'

In Oxford, in the early hours of the morning, about three o'clock, this happened. A young woman was running down a suburban street in her pyjamas. The pace of her run was interspersed with moments of hesitation in which she stopped and searched frantically and randomly.

She was screaming, with volition and anxiety. Her actions were waking the neighbours. She was barefoot and her toes were covered in blood.

Her husband awoke and noticed her absence from their bed. He heard the voices from the street and hurriedly got dressed. He left the front door ajar, walked quickly along the path through his front garden and entered the street. He did not need to search the street to find his wife. The commotion was very evident and he ran to her rescue.

'Fuck you, get out of my way. Fuck you,' she screamed her words right into the face of her aggressor. Her finger was in his eyes and his mouth was wide open and silent. He stepped back and opened his palms towards her as he shrugged his shoulders. The man next to him was telling her that she was, 'fucking mad. You should be locked up you daft bitch.'

She repeated her cries for her child and the two men repeated their obstruction of her movement. She told them to leave her alone and get out of her way or, 'I'll fuck with your faces,' she said. One of the men turned to leave from the scene and proclaimed that the police must be called now because she was a lunatic and needed to be in a straight jacket.

His wife, standing in their doorway, reinforced her husband's claim and said, 'she's a fucking nutter. Always has been. The silly cow needs to be locked up; waking up the street in the middle of the night. Who the fuck does she think she is?'

The young woman had broken past their ranks and continued up the street screaming for her child. Her feet left bloodstained footprints that were not visible under the street lights. Her husband ran past the two men and told them to go back to bed and leave her to him. They asked him, 'are you fucking mad? The racket that bitch is making. Nobody can sleep. Selfish cow'

'Please,' he begged.

'Fuck you,' they told him.

'Fuck you,' he responded.

He caught up with his wife and for several moments a frantic scene was witnessed. She escaped from his arms on a couple of occasions and she repeated her cries for her child. He persisted and moments later he lifted her from her knees, folded an arm around her shoulder and another around her waist and coaxed her back to their house. Occasionally, she attempted to break free but her determination slowly waned along with the frenzy of her cries for her child.

*Her husband took her back inside their home and closed the door.
The two men agreed with their wives that, 'she must be reported. She
cannot be allowed to get away with this. Who the hell does she think she
is?'*

'She's a fucking nutter.'

'She's woken the whole street.'

'Lock her up. '

'She shouldn't be allowed out.'

'People have work to go to.'

'Did you hear what she said to me?'

'I told you she was a miserable cow.'

'She's dangerous.'

'God knows what she could have done?'

'Throw away the key.'

*When Karen had finished recalling this scene to Wood he asked.
'How long did this go on for?'*

'A few months,' replied Karen.

'What did Ben do?' Ben was Karen's ex-husband.

*'He didn't do anything. We didn't know what to do. I was severely
depressed and he thought I was going mad and that I needed help. I
stayed in the house for over six months, watching telly, drinking tea. I
was always in my pyjamas. In the end Ben suggested I went back to
work, so I did. He barely spoke to me and he was never at home, thank
God.'*

'How did you feel?' asked Wood

*'I knew I was mad. I got very depressed and the doctor gave me
sedatives,' Karen said, her eyes pitched at the floor.*

*'Sedatives? Did he not know that denial is a symptom of grief? All
mothers who lose their babies at birth deny the death at some point. We
do it with all our loved ones.'*

*'How do you mean?' asked Karen, she instantly moved her eyes to
meet his.*

*'Of course you were depressed. You didn't know how to grieve.
Sedatives only scratch the surface,' Wood held out a hand to Karen.*

'But I couldn't cope,' she said and began to sob.

*'What you did was completely natural. You weren't mad. You were
looking for Jane like any grieving mother would do. They all go running
down the street in the middle of the night. You are only human.'*

∞

'Plenty of evidence is now suggesting mood states relate to illnesses and their outcomes,' said Jessie to Scott when they had broken up their board meeting for a coffee break. 'I am dumbfounded that psychology and medicine are only now talking to each other. Give me a minute. I'll get you a synopsis I received recently from one of our brighter boys in the profession,' Jessie left his company to find her briefcase.

'Painful, isn't it?' said Scott to Heath when Jessie was out of earshot. 'Bloody monkeys.' Scott ran his eyes up and down Wood's body and then realised that Wood had seen him do it. Scott felt comfortable that Wood would merely take this as a compliment to his dress sense.

'We could be down the pub now,' began Heath. 'Valuable drinking time is being deprived.'

'Bit early,' said Scott, looking at his watch. 'Although, come to think of it.' Jessie returned and handed a folder to Scott.

'Just read the first paragraph on page one,' she said. Scott pretended to read the text and told Jessie that it was interesting. When she reconvened the meeting she read it out to the rest of the team.

'I was just showing this to Scott and I thought I would share it with you.' Jessie held up the article and waved it before them to imply reference. 'The article is called *'Mood, anxiety and physical illness: body and mind or mind and body?* The synopsis reads - *This research review examines the recent articles that have investigated the relationship between mood, anxiety, and physical illness (e.g., asthma, autoimmune disorders, cancer, cardiovascular disease, obesity, and sexual dysfunction). There is growing evidence of an overall negative impact of depression and other mood states, and anxiety on numerous physical illnesses and conditions, and their outcome.'* Jessie finished reading from her file and continued to say, 'New evidence suggests that viruses are, in the main, defeated by our immune system. However, when our immune system is distracted, viruses face less resistance and they do more damage. The hormones we release during high anxiety and stress distract our immune system. Similarly, during stressful experiences, our immune system is working harder to balance the hormones in our body. Again, viral impacts can be harsher. Many of these viruses include the simple everyday ailments that we call cold sores, cold and influenza, coughs, eye conditions, gastrointestinal, migraine, mouth ulcers and vaginal thrush. This is only a sample.'

Jessie closed her folder and said, 'Right, back to the main event.' Wood noticed that Scott was staring at him again and Wood shuffled in his chair.

Jessie's Marble. The second topic is type.

'To truly begin to understand who we are we may need to accept that each of us does fit into a certain type. As far back as the Greeks, we have proposed that four types of personality may exist and some form of consensus has gained a level of consistency but mainly by number as opposed to qualities. I have knowledge of the majority of this material which has been gleaned by study or practice. What I conclude today is this.

Scott looked across the table at John and their eyes didn't meet. John seemed to be doing his best to listen to Jessie. He certainly appeared to be attentive. Scott smiled with his anticipation for the coming evening. He knew that John would make his excuses with his wife. Their home was two hundred miles away and John could claim that the board meeting had not finished until late. He could make up some excuse about store visits near the head office for the following day. His wife would find that plausible and Scott knew that John was fed up with his wife's constant nagging.

Jessie's Marble. Four types of person or personality does exist. As with moods, these personalities are not a set of rules but a series of types in which specific categories do not present us with the hand that fits the glove. Instead, they present us with the potential of a number of biases that relate to one person more than another. Within the four categories, each person may have a dominant type; or two dominant types, with the other categories being less evident.

These four types are *Social, Sensitive, Robust* and *Individual.* Within each type, the following characteristics generally apply, as displayed on the flip chart.

Social; public, friendly, amusing, civil, collective, common, communal, communicative, community, companionable, convivial, cordial, diverting,

entertaining, familiar, general, gracious, gregarious,
group, hospitable, informative, mannerly, neighbourly,
nice, organized, pleasant, pleasurable, polished, polite,
popular, sociable, societal.

Scott's eyes drifted around the room and away from Jessie. He
thought for a moment about the conversation that he had had with John
last night. They had discussed the idea of finding a place together where
they could live. John had resolved to leave his wife. Scott knew that he
would never find a more compassionate and sensitive lover. He had
fancied John when they had first met. He was not his hottest choice.
Scott had found other men more attractive. He would be happy with
John but something was extinguishing the fire. Scott felt that John didn't
exactly look after his physique and lacked a little charisma. As his eyes
reached the end of the table he saw Wood and felt a burst of anxiety.
Scott found Wood very dynamic. 'Why the hell did you have to turn up
and spoil the show,' thought Scott.

Jessie's Marble. Sensitive; impressionable, acute,
cognizant, conscious, delicate, easily affected,
emotional, feeling, fine, high-strung, hung up,
hypersensitive, impressible, irritable, keen, knowing,
nervous, oversensitive, perceiving, perceptive,
precarious, precise, psychic, reactive, receptive,
responsive, seeing, sensatory, sensile, sensorial,
sensory, sentient, supersensitive, susceptible, tense,
ticklish, touchy, touchy feely, tricky, tuned in, turned on
to, umbrageous, understanding, unstable, wired.

Robust; strong, boisterous, booming, brawny, built,
concentrated, flourishing, full-bodied, hale, hardy,
hearty, hefty, husky, in fine fettle, live, lusty, muscular,
peppy, potent, powerful, powerhouse, prospering,
prosperous, roaring, rough, rugged, sinewy, snappy,
sound, stout, strapping, sturdy, thriving, tiger, tough,
vigorous, wicked, zappy, zippy.

Individual; distinctive, exclusive, alone,
characteristic, definite, diacritic, diagnostic, different,
discrete, distinct, especial, express, idiosyncratic,
indivisible, lone, odd, only, original, own, particular,
peculiar, personal, personalized, proper, reserved,

respective, secluded, select, separate, several, single, singular, sole, solitary, special, specific, uncommon, unique, unitary, unusual.

'For the sake of Christ,' thought Scott looking at Jessie's presentation sheets. 'Sodding encyclopaedias next.' He glanced at Heath whose eyes were drifting in and out of closure. John was studying Jessie's charts. Scott thought about his own wife. She was fifteen years older than him. He hated it when she asked for sex and she always did. If Scott wasn't with John he was in his local pub. That way he would get drunk and he would have a feasible excuse to decline his wife's advances. There was no doubt in his mind that she was a hot blooded female and he just couldn't do it. Constantly she dismissed him as a 'stupid little boy.' He liked the fact that she cooked for him, washed, cleaned the house and maintained a strict and caring hold on the household. He knew exactly where he stood. This made it difficult for him to leave her, even for John.

Jessie's Marble. Some of the terminology I have used above is more metaphorical than literal but I'm sure you get the general idea. I must emphasise that these characteristics for each type are not all encompassing and universal. They represent a guide and they steer you to understand the type of person you are or the type of person you have met.

For most people, I believe that two types dominate their personality. For example, I would describe myself as *social/sensitive*. The other characteristics of the *individual* and the *robust* are apparent in me but to a lesser extent.

On a lighter note, I have watched couples in relationships and noticed that people with opposing types have more established and longer relationships. I recall a previous boyfriend who was definitely social/sensitive and he annoyed me intensely. My longest relationship to date was with John who was a robust/individual.

Scott was thoroughly bored with Jessie's academic banter. He drifted off into his thoughts about his past and pictured his grandparents who had brought him up. Scott had never known his mother or father. His mother died at his birth and his father had been long gone when she had become pregnant with Scott.

His grandfather was a strict coal miner born from generations of coal miners. Sheffield Wednesday, the Pits Bull arms and the Miners' Darts League were his loves. He was strict with Scott and determined for him to grow into a strapping lad who would conform to the working man's culture that his father postulated. Men were men, women should be women and *poofters* should be stuffed with red hot pokers up their derriere – that'll teach them.

> ***Jessie's Marble.*** Types also have potential implications for the formation of teams; it may be that a mixture of different types may add balance to that team, or that different qualities may be needed for different objectives. I guess that this would be down to the leader to decide but it would definitely help to have *robust/individuals* on teams dealing with stressful and demanding tasks that require a greater level of resilience; for example, *war.*
>
> However, if our War Councils were purely made up of *robust/individuals (the natural born killers),* the consequences and their decisions could gain a very specific bias. It may be prudent to instigate balance on this team. A social sensitive may mitigate the potential for one, single bias. You would not want a bias of Natural Born Killers making decisions on war. There would only ever be one outcome.

Wood rose from the table and thanked Jessie for her insight. 'Let the debate begin,' said Wood and the team began to do so. After nearly twenty minutes, Wood excused himself to go to the toilet and told his board to take a break. As he left the room, Scott followed him.

After Karen and Wood first met they spoke frequently about their ambitions and what they wanted for their future. By the time Cameron was born, they clearly understood what each other wanted. The birth of

Cameron had rekindled the subject; as though they were seeking reaffirmation from each other in light of their new responsibility.

'So, what are you going to do with your million pounds when you've made it?' asked Karen feeding Cameron on her breast.

'You must be reading my mind,' Wood answered. 'I've been thinking about it for the last couple of days.'

'Well come on then. Get me excited. Tell me.'

'It's nothing exciting,' said Wood laughing, seemingly embarrassed.

'Why?' asked Karen.

Wood took a seat on the edge of the sofa where Karen was sitting. Karen noticed that his mood suddenly changed and he looked thoughtful 'I want to sort out all this mess,' he said looking at her.

'What mess?' asked Karen, making herself more comfortable and putting her baby's mouth back on her nipple.

'That's the problem. What is it and why?' Wood picked up his glass of water and without taking a sip, he put it down again. 'Before I found out about my ex-wife's affair, I was sitting in the pub with a few of our friends. There were eight of us, four couples. As I looked about the table I realised that all of the other six were having affairs and none of their partners knew. I also realised that we all knew about each other's affairs but nothing about those of our partners. I looked at my ex-wife and realised that I didn't know. I felt fairly certain that she wasn't. I concluded that it wouldn't happen to me and then I thought again.' Wood sat back on the sofa and looked up to the ceiling. 'I realised that I could easily be wrong and, more importantly, why did I feel as though I was immune?'

'You now know that you weren't,' said Karen, attending to her baby again.

'I do now but I didn't. This was in the late eighties when the recession was looming. I was too young to really know what was going on. We all were but I sensed – as I think we all did – that there was something fairly nasty in the air. Something was making us all feel uneasy. You could not put your finger on it. It was as though we were all searching for moments of happiness and, in our despair, that's what we all did.'

'Were you having an affair?' asked Karen sheepishly.

'No. I was the only one who wasn't. Probably because nobody had approached me. I don't really know,' said Wood.

'So why the sudden call from the evangelical?' asked Karen. Wood looked at her for a moment. He stroked Cameron's cheek with his thumb.

'I don't even know if it's that. I just think that the mess can be sorted out,' he said.

'How?' asked Karen putting her feet up.

'That's what I don't yet know. I don't even really know what it is yet,' said Wood. He began to play with Cameron's hair.

'None of us do,' said Karen smiling at Wood's actions with his son.

'Agreed. But what if it is staring us in the face?'

'It's more complicated than that,' said Karen thinking.

'Precisely not. It never is. It is right in front of our eyes. We just haven't opened them yet,' said Wood confidently.

Wood had helped Karen to finally grieve the loss of Jane. They had agreed to put all Karen's memorabilia of her daughter into a decorative wooden box – like a large jewellery cabinet. The box was housed in the spare bedroom and every Sunday, Karen went into the room for a couple of hours and looked through the contents. She did this alone and Wood told her that he was only downstairs if she needed him.

Karen would weep as she touched the belongings. The collection helped her remember her lost daughter. After the two hours she would fill her time with something practical – ironing or cooking and Wood would do it with her.

Sarah was born two years after Cameron and Douglas two years after that. When Karen had failed to get pregnant with her fourth child and maintain the two year age gap, she went to great lengths to understand why. One evening, she came out of the en suite bathroom with a thermometer in her hand and told Wood that the time was exactly right. Wood felt that she had jumped on him the instant he had laid on the bed. She never asked for sex, let alone initiated it, thought Wood.

Heath knew that Wood had the bit between his teeth after his phone call with him early that morning. Wood had told him that he needed to see him. It was February 2007 and the new financial year was about to begin. Heath knew that he would have a challenge with Wood. Heath liked to make money and keep reserves. Wood needed to spend it. He seemed to have no regard for it whatsoever.

'It's not enough,' said Wood when he sat down for a coffee with Heath.

'Next year alone, the turnover will increase to £250 million,' Heath said, opening his palms to Wood and sitting forward in his chair. 'That's outstanding. You'll clear £50 million in net and bank twenty five.'

'It's not nearly enough,' repeated Wood gulping his coffee which was clearly too hot for him. He burnt his lip.

'For fuck's sake,' said Heath, flinging himself back in his chair. He nearly fell off it until he grabbed the table for support. 'What do you want?'

'We need to go to the city and raise cash,' said Wood adamantly.

'You don't need to,' Heath countered.

'I do. Get Jessie and meet me in my office in an hour.' Finally, thought Wood, things are beginning to make sense and the demand will be enormous. His ideas were beginning to formulate and nothing could be outsized by the extent of his ambition.

'I've just had some great news,' said Jessie entering Wood's office within the hour, skipping as she moved, holding her hands in front of her as though she was about to clap. 'Don Manchester, a colleague from way back in my university days, has got his second doctorate in Clinical Psychology.' She turned to Heath and said, 'I really fancied him but he was gay.'

'Is he any good?' asked Wood.

'You can't employ every scientist you meet. Anyway he won't work for you,' said Jessie, chirpily.

'Why not?' quizzed Wood.

'He's his own man. I always remember his insatiable need for the music of Lloyd Cole and the Commotions. He loved books, especially those of Martin Amis – his favourite was 'Money'. He once said to me, 'The real criminals are the men in suits who carry the briefcases.'

'Proves he's bright,' said Heath, taking a seat.

'Very,' said Jessie. 'Don achieved his first doctorate in Clinical Psychiatry before he was 30 years old – very ambitious – and began redefining methods of health care in the industry. He observed that behind closed doors, the psychiatric nurses enjoyed the propensity of their violence as their method for controlling the patients they did not understand. Anyway, he's gone and done it – clever boy.' Wood glanced down at the floor momentarily. Jessie noticed. She was disappointed by his sudden lack of interest.

'Look,' said Wood, changing the subject and pulling the door closed. 'I need a new project drawn up. It will cost a fortune and I don't care – I'll get the money.'

'Sounds very exciting,' said Jessie taking a seat.

'Don't encourage him,' said Heath crossing his arms and shaking his head.

'What is it?' asked Jessie

'A repair centre and it will be called the Eureka Split.'

Karen achieved her fourth pregnancy and Macy was born. Wood had not initially noticed that they had begun to grow apart. Their demise seemed to happen slowly and unconsciously. During Karen's pregnancy, Wood's business had expanded at a significant pace and he had hardly had any time to spend in his new Manor house that they had recently moved into. Macy had been born shortly after they had settled in. They both were pre occupied with heavy agendas; Karen with preparation for the birth and the new house; Wood with the challenges that he was facing with his business expansion. Wood was now travelling abroad with increasing frequency and boarded planes three times a week.

This did not help their relationship. The more Wood got drawn into his business, the more unsettled Karen became with his absence from the family. They had begun to argue constantly.

All the while, Wood could never fathom why the act of conception that lead to Macy's birth, bothered him so much. Karen had seemed to relax considerably following confirmation that she was pregnant. She had been very irritable beforehand. Wood had put this down to her rift with her father, who had taunted her with the fact that both of her sisters also had three children.

Wood felt that Karen had over reacted to her father's quip. He'd come to expect this level of emotion from Karen whenever she met her father. She had never really practiced what she had preached. She had told Wood not to worry about him.

'Just ignore the cantankerous old git. He's always been a difficult man,' Karen had said and recounted how he had taught her to use her knife and fork in the wrong hands. 'He told us that we didn't have to do it the normal way just because it was the normal way. He insisted we didn't when we were young.'

Wood sensed that his life was becoming more turbulent. Unconsciously, he knew that Karen was not happy with him. He was too busy to see it face on. He started to talk to Jessie about his excessive drinking and his behaviour.

'Considering the pressure you are under, you are doing fine. Remember that the city thinks you are too young to have achieved what you have. They are probably right. That brings on added pressure,' Jesse told him.

When Wood purchased his estate for £5 million, he had raised his mortgage through the Citiwest Bank. They had been delighted to have his account. His financial assessment had placed him in the top 150 wealthiest in the U.K. Bravills, a high net worth brokerage firm, had told Wood that the Citiwest had been seeking, for some years, clients around the age of forty who could demonstrate his wealth. Wood had been their first and their youngest. 'Rare commodity,' the chap from Bravills had called Wood. 'Lucky bastard,' another had quipped. 'Sitting duck,' said another. 'They'll eat him alive.'

Back at Lombard's, Jessie was pressing her point. She was clearly anxious about her observations of the members of Wood's senior team and she was persistent in her need to tell him.

'What do you mean?' Wood asked her again.

'I can deal with Scott if you want me to,' Jessie said bouncing on her feet, on the edge of her seat.

'The sooner the better,' said Wood. 'He followed me into the toilet the other day and stood next to me at the urinals. He didn't take a leak. He was just yanking it whilst he stood there. I felt like he was frothing at the mouth.'

'I can expose him for what he truly is but I already know what he truly is,' said Jessie placing her hands together and raising her fingertips to her lips.

'Do it then. Jessie, I can't emphasise enough how important this is,' said Wood adamantly.

'I know,' said Jessie. Wood realised that his determination had not landed with her. He resolved to try again later. 'But there is something more pressing and it is not just Scott. It's all of them; I know who all of them truly are. The guards are off,' said Jessie looking at Wood.

'Go on,' he encouraged and gestured to accompany his words.

'I, initially and subsequently, believed that you had a good balance in your team. Christine was individual/sensitive. Tom was robust/individual. Scott was social/sensitive. Reese was social/individual. Martin was social/sensitive. Eddy was robust/social. Stuart was sensitive/individual. Heath was social/individual.' Jessie had been reading from her notes as she had reeled off this list to Wood. She continued, 'Not a bad range to permit balanced debate and balanced decision making. But I was wrong. These are men, as you say, who have climbed the social, corporate and political ladders in life. The threats and the attacks that they have encountered have taught them to shield themselves. But when the shields come down, the truth is told, these men fall under one category; all of them.'

'Life builds the shields,' said Wood. 'But, go on.'

'They are all robust/individual,' Jessie danced a little bump in her seat as she spoke. As though she had just let the cat out of the bag. 'It scares me to think that this is typical of our senior groups of power and influence.'

'Why?' asked Wood. Jessie noticed that he remained relatively relaxed.

'Because the robust/individual are the natural born killers and you are surrounded by them. They will kill you off,' she said reeling off her words as though she had just said, *there then.*

'Jessie. I know. It is not me that you need to tell. Stop worrying. That is exactly what all this is about and a lot, lot more. History has shown time after time and universally, *always,* that treacherous council surrounds powerful men, leaders and kings. In the end, all of their heads have to come off. And mine,' said Wood dropping his arms down either side of his chair.

'But what about the mission? The vision? How will it get delivered?' asked Jessie confused.

'That will always depend on me.'

'How?' she asked.

'I have to trust myself,' said Wood remaining relaxed.

'I don't get it,' Jessie said and frowned.

'Jessie, there is always a price to pay.'

'Isn't that a bit naïve?' she said and frowned again.

'Call it what you like,' said Wood as he stretched his arms above his head. Jessie sensed that he was about to wrap the globe in them and, in a subsequent act, retract his reach. 'Completely naive, if you like.'

'You've completely lost me,' said Jessie, confused. Her eyebrows nearly touched in the middle.

'There is only one real purpose to all of this,' said Wood.

'I still don't get it,' said Jessie.

'You will. Now sort Scott out. Get it out into the open. Teach him that we love him.'

Jessie felt that she had not driven home her point hard enough. Wood had not been remotely receptive to the idea that his Main Board had been planted in his business.

Following the board meeting, John had not been able to make his excuses to his wife. One of his children had had an accident and John had had to leave early to drive up to Derby.

Scott, Wood, Heath and a few others had gone to the pub when the meeting had finished. They had arrived early, before six in the evening and they had stayed late. Scott had decided to stay at the corporate flat. It gave him another days grace from the bedroom demands of his wife.

When he arrived at the apartment he was very drunk. He was also bitterly disappointed, when he turned the key in the lock, that he was alone.

He opened the larder and took one of the bottles of wine that he had bought earlier; red wine – it conformed to his Atkins Diet.

When he sat down, he saw the stain on the sofa that he had forgotten to clean up yesterday. Scott and John constantly tarnished the furniture following their sex sessions and he felt anxious with his neglect. In the next moment his guilt was snapped shut when the image of his grandfather merged with his desire to please John. The stain was engulfed by the debris of his sick.

Scott wiped his face clean and saw that the mess was across his jumper and his sleeve. Streams of saliva seemed to glue the spill all about him. He frowned and tutted with his state and sat back. Amidst his deep breaths he thought of living with John. His mind flashed with the smiles of his wife, the raucous laughter of his grandfather, the gentle calm of his grandmother and Wood's shapely backside. John was very loving. He offered him the love that his grandmother had shown and the bond that his own mother had never had the chance to build with him. Scott knew that his wife was a good woman even though she nagged. John's wife was no different and he knew she presented the obstacle to his happiness.

Wood appeared in his thoughts and he recalled his recurrent desires for his boss. The scenes that he acted out in his mind were frantic, passionate and sexual. They flipped from the affectionate to the jailor. Scott began to unzip his trousers as he sat there imagining but his grandfather's face appeared before him, torn with anger and distorted with violence.

The emotion scarred his cheeks with tears and his life dressed his heart with funeral attire. He seemed to miss a beat but the misfortune cried for payback and the lava heaved up the spout.

'Why me?' he screamed into the empty living room, choking on his breaths. He picked up the bottle and smashed it on the coffee table. When he got to his feet, everything in the room bore the fruit of his brutal kicks. 'Why the fuck me?' he repeatedly screamed as he destroyed everything before him. Slowly his ferocity fizzled out and he seemed to melt as he crumpled onto the floor, 'Can't they just love me,' he sobbed pathetically.

Scrummy Saints

October 2008

H oary was at home. He had just arrived. He had been out for a morning walk in his local village to buy his papers and the crusty bread rolls that his wife and children adored. He had met the local priest and had asked him how many churches had now closed. Hoary had recently read the timetable for church opening on the back cover of the village rag. Six out of ten were closed on a Sunday and it appeared that they took it in turns to open on a roster basis.

The priest had told him, 'Two more will be gone by the end of the year. They can't get the attendances or the priests. The behaviour of all the priests is becoming increasingly scandalous. Recruitment for new priests is worse than ever. They are all drafted in from abroad.'

'Keep going priest. Never give up. God is essential to us,' Hoary said. As he left his friend, he thought about the early years of his career. He recalled the history of the church and its widespread influence on the people throughout its institutions. Modern man had diversified and found new avenues and alternative organisations of influence. The church, it seemed, had had its day. Jesus Christ, Hoary thought, had done his job but too few had listened. Hoary smiled to himself but then held back instantly. He knew that Christ had never wanted the monuments, the temples and icons. Like Da Vinci, he wanted us guessing, he wanted us to work it out for ourselves. We had to when we saw the Mona Lisa and the Vitruvian Man. But his congregations never got it. They had not fathomed that we had to defy certainty. Certainty was too easy to witness in most still life art and hence, our conclusions diminished our need to act; 'we have the answer; done that one'. With Da Vinci, we were left guessing.

Christ needs us to search and pursue and find out that the answers are in our behaviour. In the debates we rage, the passions we live, the opportunities we pursue with conviction and commitment and the forgiveness we should extend to our failures to permit an environment for us to do it again and again, until we answer all our questions. The physical icons that arose following Christ's crucifixion had diverted man. They read his words too literally and did not see the metaphors. Whilst his congregations wanted and yearned to read the metaphors, the majority were not prepared to go the full nine yards and Hoary had lost faith in his sermons. Only those who tested life with the excesses of personal risk could walk beyond the boundaries of reasonable thought and begin to work it out. But most didn't; they stifled their future in a shroud of security, of inaction, of risk aversion, deemed laziness and perceived intellectual incapacity. This time the message had to be different; physical representation had to be replaced by behavioural illustration.

'I'm home my love. Got the scrummy bread,' Hoary said to his wife as he walked through the front door.

'Hiya,' she replied. Hoary kissed his wife and he meant it. She knew.

'Your wonderful son has made you a lovely cup of coffee. It's on the table,' she said and took the rubbish outside to throw it in the bins. It was ten minutes before she rejoined Hoary.

'Darling,' she continued. 'This credit crunch. I've just been watching the news. People are beginning to get seriously hurt. Is it really necessary?'

'It won't be for much longer my love. By the end of the next year. I will have the influence when the competition is all but gone and most of it is now insolvent at best. Anyway, the politicians are getting a grip. Gordon Brown is doing sterling work. He seriously cares. He is a good man.'

'I do hope so. I do trust you darling. I know you know what you are doing. I just hate to see it all unfold,' his wife said.

'Sweetheart, it is the lesser of two evils'. For years Hoary had watched his employees, day after day, tussle with their customers whilst the customers tussled back. He disliked this as much as he had struggled with his congregations. They were no different. He knew that diplomacy had to be superseded by a more long term, sustainable and conducive solution.

Words and phrases from his branch managers rang through Hoary's mind, one in particular. 'The guy's a knob. His projections are crap. Don't lend him the money.' Endless reams of mistrust and suspicion gleaned under the auspicious title of wisdom.

Hoary sipped his coffee and thumbed through his paperwork. He picked out his file from Miranda with her most recent press releases and scanned through the titles.

> '*ITCD Chairman Hoary claims Banks owe a debt to Society.*' (Timesonline.co.uk). 'The U.K's top banker is spearheading claims that investment banks are 'socially redundant,' in a speech he gave at the Corporate Change Conference in Milan on Tuesday. He is calling for a cultural overhaul among banks, including an end to 'excessive' bonuses, to ensure that markets are more socially responsible and less obsessed with short term profits. Hoary maintains that many parts of our industry fail the test of usefulness, sustainability and transparency.'

> '*Banking and God.*' (Cathedraltimes.co.uk). 'Hoary's dual role – which some find incongruous – has fascinated the industry. In these challenging days of a looming depression, his track record of speaking loudly and often about ethics and morality is now commanding a debate within his stricken industry and his influence is now being regarded as the only prescription for the way out of this crisis.'

> '*Key Values: An uncertain world needs to reflect on matters of money and morality,*' (Dolphin Books India). 'The title of his new book leads the reader through a history of globalisation and finance, and the church's relationship with money-lending, taking in literary and philosophical references along the way. If the public were to accept advice from anyone, they would pro- bably accept it from Hoary. Unflashy, studious, a man who admits to preferring a good book to a champagne lifestyle, he has guided ITCD through the recession with

a steady hand. Financial analysts believe it is weathering the storm better than any of its rivals.'

'*Remuneration and Alignment to Social Responsibility.*' (Telegraph.co.uk) 'Hoary earned plaudits a few years ago when he cut executive bonuses after the bank's stock price languished for the third year in a row. Although some bankers left in protest, his tough stance was applauded by the markets. He said then that money had never been the most important thing in his career: easy to say when you earn a reputed £1.25 million in basic salary a year. But he no longer takes cash bonuses, although he does take performance-related share awards. High earners face a 'real challenge' in what they do with their money, he says. Riches are not in themselves a bad thing, but they do carry tough responsibilities, and one of his key tests is to look in the mirror and ask himself how the job he does contributes to the common good. 'People who are highly paid have to deliver on their responsibilities to the community,' he says. He uses the phrase, 'individual social responsibility' several times, and it sounds reminiscent of Gordon Brown. Social responsibility, some would argue, is pretty rare on the trading floor. In what he calls the 'go-go years' of recent times, excessive bonuses have fed excessive lifestyles. He says he never hires those for whom 'money is the main objective'.

'*The Opportunity for the Greater Good.*' (Breuters Blog) 'How people respond to personal challenges and what they do with their lives is a personal matter, says Hoary. But I'm all for the church talking more about it. Churches do not talk about this and it is a seriously underplayed opportunity. The focus should be not only on the rich but on the affluent, who also have to be urged to spend their money wisely — and we are most of us affluent now in the developed world. He also calls on the church to emphasise the spiritual benefits of giving. 'This is very important to me,' he says. Does he tithe? After a pause, he replies: 'I do take the challenge

to myself as someone who is well paid.' I take this to
mean that he gives a great deal more than his ten per
cent, since in his book, he calls on the wealthy to do just
that. He says that tithing is expressed in percentage
terms, but it should be manageable for most people,
most of the time. It should be a costly commitment, and
what is costly differs from person to person, and comes
at different times of life. His wealth, and the responsibility it carries, makes him 'constantly' uneasy, he
admits. But it is obvious that he sees potential for great
good in what he does, and argues that the markets make
an important contribution to development. In his
speeches to the business community, he frequently calls
for a new banking system, one underpinned by moral
values rather than just the 'I'm not breaking any rules'
mentality which has been dominant in recent years.

Hoary closed the file. Miranda had, as usual been highly active and
subtle in her ability to drive Hoary's message into the public arena
without giving it too much profile. The latter would inevitably provoke
criticism and dismissal and this was not a voice that he wanted
associated with his words. He simply wanted his influential networks to
be aware of *the man and his mission.*

Whilst the sentiments that Miranda had been addressing in the public
eye were not the full picture of his ambitions, they would create for him
the background music to his dramatic stage play when the timing was
right. Rome was not built in a day – first of all the foundations needed to
be firmly embedded.

On the front of the file of press releases, he noticed that Miranda had
placed a *post it* note saying 'Nobody does it better. Please do read the
article entitled *No Cut and Run from Troubled US Housefrank.*' He
found the article in the file and read.

Words such as ethics and morality do not frighten
Hoary. Although he heads the world's biggest bank, the
Chairman of ITCD is also an ordained Anglican priest.

In recent weeks ITCD has faced calls from one
activist shareholder to cut and run from its troubled US
Housefrank business, which is nursing massive losses
from its lending to sub-prime America.

Legally, ITCD could walk away, effectively putting Housefrank into administration and leaving creditors to carry the losses. To Hoary, that is unthinkable.

'This all points to something more profound about market ethics,' he says. 'Our word is our bond and the idea that you can play fast and loose with that is immoral. I genuinely believe one of the biggest issues is that we must change the culture.'

There can be little doubt that 60-year-old Hoary's ethical streak is sincere. It formed the basis for his 1999 book, *Nurturing Money, Nurturing God* which he wrote while a director at ITCD's investment banking division.

In the book Hoary warns that those working in financial markets risk becoming 'obsessed with wealth and power' and in danger of 'selling one's soul'. Hoary concludes that Christianity and banking are not automatically incompatible.

'The markets, flawed as they are like every other human structure, can be used to contribute to human development. Being there also creates opportunities - to show integrity that loves others as us and treats them as ends rather than means.'

That is what he says in the book. In conversation, Hoary does not raise the subject of his faith and apart from his slightly heavier emphasis on ethics; he talks much like any other banker about profits and risks. So when it comes to the troubled US operations, Hoary argues that as well as it being immoral to walk away, it would be very bad business.

'It would damage the brand,' he says. 'What do you think would happen to the parent company's ability to raise bonds?'

The acquisition of Housefrank for £10bn in 2003 has turned out to be the most disastrous decision in ITCD's recent history and the group has written off the whole value.

Despite this debacle, ITCD has weathered the credit crunch better than any of its rivals, though it has still needed to raise extra capital and has turned to its shareholders for £12.5bn.

The results of the rights issue will be made public in the next few days. 'I can't predict the outcome, but we have seen a large number of shareholders in recent weeks and I have been reassured by the response. There is recognition that this was the right thing to do,' says Hoary.

As for the long-term shape of banking, he has a positive message - the pain will be purifying. And he believes the G20 meeting last week set the world on the right path.

'It is better than we were all beginning to fear,' he says. 'Quite a lot of the commitments are not new ones, but it is not a bad result. They have made the right noises on trade and protectionism.'

Hoary is in no doubt that we are entering a new era and talk of global regulation at the summit will turn into reality. The G20 announced that the Swiss-based Financial Stability Forum, a talking shop for international banking rules, would become a Financial Stability Board with hard powers to control bonuses, regulate complex derivatives trading and change accounting rules. Hoary applauds the change, but sees limits to international regulation.

He says: 'The strengthening of the FSF is a good way of having a global purview of the financial system. Converting it into a board is definitely going in the right direction. But in the end it is national regulators who will have to be in the hot seat because it is national taxpayer who will be called on to loosen the purse strings if needs be.'

The G20 aside, Hoary clearly feels that a cultural change is taking hold in banking that will have a lasting effect.

'I think this has been such a searing experience for everyone,' he says. 'This is not just another downturn; this has been the worst thing since the Thirties. I don't think this is a lesson people will forget in a year or two.

In the go-go years everything got stretched to the limit and I don't think the market will go back to that.'

The most public aspect of those 'go-go' years was, of course, massive pay and bonuses for bankers. Hoary admits: 'There has clearly been some egregious compensation around in the markets.'

But Hoary himself has been no slouch on pay. In the past ten years as a director, chief executive and latterly Chairman of ITCD, he has received almost £9m in salary and £6m in bonuses. But in keeping with the frugal times, he has decided never to take a bonus again.

Bank stocks

This is not a prescription he suggests should be universal. 'I do not think we should go to a point where there are no bonuses,' he says. 'They are not unique to the banking industry. Most industries pay bonuses to some staff and the public sector pays bonuses too.'

Hoary is no stranger to the public sector. After graduating from Cambridge, where he studied philosophy, politics and economics, he worked as a volunteer at a hostel for alcoholics in the East End of London and married another volunteer. And in line with his thoughtful manner, Hoary eschews the flashier trappings of wealth, favouring reading as a pastime.

So does the ITCD Chairman see any green shoots? 'On the global economy I am slightly less bearish than some have been,' he says. 'I just get the slight sense that the climate of expectation is better. But that is a long way from saying we are out of the woods.'

Hoary had never intended to walk away from Housefrank. Its catastrophic demise had served his purpose well and the Administrators could pry too deep and ask too many questions. Invariably they did not, but, 'why take the chance,' Michael had argued. 'There will always be merit in the fear Housefrank can generate. Fear is the most precious of commodities. It burns out the human petrol tank quicker than a walk in the park.'

The rights issue would be successful and conclusive by the end of next week. Hoary had not needed to raise the money but in the simple principle that he had asked, it would only act to destabilise the markets. It would ensure that the fear in the marketplace did not run dry. The £12.5 billion would certainly help to strengthen the bank's cash reserves, even though the bank already held greater liquidity than any other competitor in his industry.

During the week, Hoary had spent his waking hours in his private jet, crossing from Asia to the U.K. and attending conferences in Europe. He was glad to be home. He loved his family and enjoyed nothing more than being with his wife and children. He was also very conscious that he had neglected his internal agenda during his travels and he had been excited with catching up with the news. As he had predicted, Michael had certainly kept the ship sailing full steam ahead but Hoary was very excited about the main document he had wanted to read and he grabbed the proposal document prepared by his operations director.

> *The corporate cultures that have been permitted to grow, will stifle our objectives for market share as the advantage is realised post 2015. Two dogmas exist;*
> *Firstly, the 'them and us' scenarios that engulf the team spirit and permit the 'strength in numbers' perception that the staff need as an enabler and as a confidence for them to act in line with policy.*
> *Secondly, the 'them against us' ethos in which our brand consistently strangles our consumers with the oppressive cultures built in our corporate ranks and delivered by senior management to maintain compliance in the swathing mass of our employees.*

Hoary agreed with these observations, 'And all the while,' he thought to himself, 'the consumer gets what we have built – despair'.

'Trevor, are you ignoring me?' his wife asked.

'I'm sorry sweet. I got distracted,' said Hoary apologetically.

'I asked you if you were still confident about the banking world taking power from the governments,' she said apprehensively.

'The governments remain nearsighted and aimless. I still don't think they have seen us coming. They didn't in the first place,' said Hoary looking at his wife. 'They're still fighting for the approval of the public.'

'But they have so much power,' enquired his wife, puzzled.

'Their G20 is their current solution. The EU has significant power but they can't organise themselves. When I have secured the B20 I will have greater liquidity than the U.S.'

'America has huge power,' his wife said adamantly.

'America is bust. The western nations are laden with debt for years to come. Trust me darling. I have to do this. People may suffer today but their children will live a better life – a much, much better life. The new employee cultures are being established.'

Hoary's eyes skipped to the bottom of the document.

> *'New cultures will enable commitment and pursuit. Succession planning for employee career growth will adhere to defined parameters on this remit. Truth and courage remain under review. The targeted purpose of real delivery for customers and enablers that permit them to pursue opportunity and open ended possibilities, is on target as per objective time schedules. Marketing slogans are already in the retail outlets – the mindset transformation vehicles will see change begin to unfold.'*

'I do hope so,' his wife said.

'The stage is built now. They will,' confirmed Hoary.

'But what if it is too late? What if we are facing Armageddon?' asked his wife.

'Darling, we could blow this all up and we would still deny it. Armageddon is already here and it has been for some time now. This is the place I am trying to put behind us. Commitment must replace money. It must become our primary language and I know I can do it. I can swap bureaucracy and fear for commitment.'

That reminded Hoary. He skipped back through the pages in the document to find the section marked 'risk assessment'. He read.

> *'The days of risk assessment must go. Blue sky targets have reached agreement with the following mission; Teams to be the angels of action; the enablers whom open doors, the men and women brilliant in determining and identifying the commitments in our consumers and more brilliant in supporting them to make their commitments become true'.*

'We are bitter with our God – it is all *His* fault - but we need to learn that there is no truth in this.'

'What is the truth?' asked his wife.

'We need a God that we can all relate to. A true God. One that our children can see and believe in'.

Hoary continued to flip through the pages of the document until his eye settled on a section entitled, Employees as Saints.

> *'The principle of our employees becoming enablers via a transference of behaviours we have categorised via the Blue Sky workshops as 'Saints,' needs action. We recognise that with 315,521 employees and visible marketing, the influence we can exert will reach at least 40% of the worlds' population. Our commercial position will permit a greater influence in consumer identity. By 2015, the global banking market will achieve the target of 85% decline in financial volume from 2006 levels. We will recoup 21% of this decline delivering 37% of global share. Targeted consensus please; expressions needed by November 1st on the following points for UK operational board approval.*
>
> *1. Purpose must redefine impediment. We need to guide, coach and train thousands of saints.*
>
> *2. Banks should not be enabling our consumers to merely make money. We acknowledge this as root cause for the credit crunch; pre-occupation in our pursuit of money has driven margin erosion. We have forgotten what its purpose really is. It's as if there is no longer any colour to our diversification, just one colour and one language – money.*
>
> *3. Environmental shaping is paramount. We accept the argument that ancestral chains adapted to their environment and shaped it to progress. They did not sit in hope that food would turn up on a plate. The Mammoth did not walk up to them, lie down dead and sacrifice himself to the fire. Our relentless focus on money is making all of us insular, blind and eventually it will s tifle us. The 'mammoth will eat us' syndrome, even if he was a vegetarian.*

4. We should be driving, exhausting ourselves in fulfilling our dreams; discovering new lands, procuring abundant resources and building the vessels that will take us there. We have to shape our horizons, explore. Seek and we will find. God needs our help, we have to find him and motivate and steer a world and its populace to pursue. Reverse blame and deliver accountability – personal.

Hoary wrote on the document 'Get the world off its arse and discover our salvation.'

'But what if people don't believe you?' his wife asked.

'I don't know dear. I think that that is the problem. We have failed to understand that God designed a universe from which a random, maybe a specific, entity would arise to save him. We are designed to do this. What is our value if we do not? We deny him, we dismiss him and what do we get?'

'What we give?'

'Exactly. We dismiss him and we get dismissed. Possibly, extinct. Basically, we have no reason or need to survive. Just think how exciting the world and the worlds will become when we commit to Him. All our dreams will come true. I have to do this darling and I will.'

'Yes. You will. My love.'

Hoary thumbed his paperwork once again and flipped to the executive summary. His Group Financial Director had pencilled over the projections of market share given by his Operations Director. He had written, 'Trevor. The projection for global share by 2018 will sit at 32%. If JP Morgan Chase fail it will be more. The group structure must diversify to hide the monopoly. Your thoughts?'

Above this note, Hoary read the final sentence from his Operations Director. *'In the New Year our marketing slogan will change. The vote was unanimous. We agreed upon* **'You commit to the stars and we will act to get you there.'**

Hoary wrote, 'Implement it. Don't worry about the governments. They are not bright enough. They won't see it.' He sealed this in a note and marked it highly confidential.

Hoary's mobile phone rang and it was Michael.

'Trevor, Miranda is magnificent. Your pathway is clear, she's only gone and done it,' said Michael, excitedly.

'Done what?' asked Hoary, biting into a biscuit.

'The B20. The lights are on green. She's been counselling the Chairmen on your list for over a year and she is absolutely convinced that you'll now have their endorsement.'

'Bugger me,' exclaimed Hoary, surprised with the success being achieved earlier than he had anticipated.

'It gets better. She has also won endorsements from government heads in the U.K., France, Germany and China. You have four of the top six wealthiest nations in the world rooting for you.'

'Bugger me,' Hoary expressed excitedly.

'It's all yours my leader. Go and take it,' said Michael forthrightly.

Michael hung up and Hoary rung him straight back. 'What about this provincial new boy? Have you found him?' asked Hoary.

'Yes, I have,' said Michael.

'And?' said Hoary probing.

'I'm dealing with him.'

'Who is he?' asked Hoary, sat on the edge of his seat. He watched a buzzard fly past his window.

'A nobody. A wake from Liverpool called Tane Wood. Stop worrying about him,' said Michael. Hoary was concerned with this issue and Michael felt unnerved with Hoary's persistence.

'Michael, I want him dealt with. Get him out of the way. Do it now,' said Hoary adamantly.

'Consider it done,' said Michael as Hoary hung up. Michael was concerned with Hoary's apprehension. Hoary was never apprehensive.

Hoary was shocked. He had planned this for ten years and the plan had worked. By 2020 he would have influence over the largest cumulative balance sheet in the history of the world. He would have more sustenance than the gold reserves which built world currencies. He could introduce his currency and, effectively, he would control 21% of world liquidity. He would be more powerful than any man in history. When the tsunami finally landed, companies would be wrecked and bought for a song in a frenzy of Mergers and Acquisitions activity. His liquidity position could be even stronger and then he could implement the true power of his vision and sort out the mess we called Earth once and for all.

His liquidity would give his ambitions a world stage. The fruition of his new political state could be implemented and finally man would find God.

Hoary got up from his chair and walked over to the magnificent stone mullion window at the end of his morning room. The window was fifteen feet in height and it allowed him to see far across the landscape, over the undulating hills to the horizon. He felt anxiety flood his body and he knew that no man would exercise the influence he was about to exert. Not since Jesus Christ. He did not feel overwhelmed. He felt humble. He loved his fellow men; all of them. He knew that they just needed to be led by a man of vision. Not by men who chose to hide.

The last thing he needed now was an absurd scouser getting in his way and his intuition was telling him that this absurdity was fuelled by a drive towards opportunity and truth. Hoary did not underestimate that this could amount to a real threat.

If the threat was removed, mankind could finally be defined in its truth.

Eureka Split

March 2007

Wood was late and he hated being late. He had slept in because
he had not come home until past midnight. He had been drinking in the
pub with Heath again. Karen was in the kitchen when he entered to
collect his briefcase and find his watch.

'What time is it,' asked Wood.

'What bloody time did you get home last night?' demanded Karen.

'I don't know darling. It was late,' he said softly.

'Very late. I don't know why you bother coming home. You're
straight to bed when you come in...' Karen hesitated as she caught sight
of a bottle of whisky that was nearly empty. 'For heaven's sake Tane.
Did you drink all that last night?' Karen walked over to the bottle and
held it up in front of her. 'It was full before you got to it.'

'Look. I'm late, I need to go,' he said avoiding her question and her
gaze. He walked to the front door.

'Don't bother coming back,' she shouted as he left the house.

When Wood arrived at the office, it was nearly 9.30am. His meeting
started at ten. He had composed himself following his altercation with
Karen. He was accustomed to doing so, of late. He had become used to
their early morning arguments.

He asked Jessie and Heath to meet him in the board room and Wood
was very eager to present to them what he planned. He needed to be
upbeat and positive in his attitude to win their support. This would make
the task easier. He resolved that he would drive this project through,
whatever challenges and obstacles he had to face. 'This will not be a test
of my resilience,' Wood thought. 'This is getting done. Full stop.'

He feverishly grabbed his briefcase and his files from the back seat of his car and tucked his shirt in to the back of his trousers with one hand. He paced quickly to the entrance of his office and buzzed the security entrance bell to get in. He could never remember the access code.

In the board room, he laid out his material on the desk, darted around the room straightening the chairs and tidying away any mess and when he had finished he looked about the room with his hands clasped together in front of him. 'That'll do,' he said and ran out of the office, upstairs to the kitchen to make a coffee. When he returned, Heath and Jessie were sitting at the board room table waiting for him. Wood made no introductions and entertained no pleasantries. He said, 'Welcome to the Eureka Split.' Heath lowered his eyes to the table and crossed his arms and legs. Jessie was tapping the end of her ball point pen on the pad by her side. Her eyes were fixed on Wood as he began to speak.

'The Eureka Split is a repair centre and its goal is to close itself down. To make itself redundant. If it doesn't, it has failed and I cannot allow that to happen. It will challenge modern day institutional practice across all our norms. First of all, take a look at this.' Wood turned on the overhead projector and displayed a slide. The slide was very busy.

>*Facilitating effective coping in children following disasters: a psychoanalytically informed guided narrative intervention.* (Gilbert Kliman, Saul Rosenberg, Grif Samples, The Children's Psychological Health Center, San Francisco, CA 94115, USA. gil.kliman@cphc-sf.org).

>*Preventing and treating homesickness.* (Christopher A Thurber, Edward Walton)

>*Basic Principles of Crisis Intervention in Children and Adolescents.* (Anita Pachaly. Int J Emerg Ment Health. 2005)

>*Enhancing the crisis management briefing.* (Daniel W Clark, Peter Volkmann)

>*Obesity in childhood.* (Maria Rayner, Hornchurch Clinic. BioInfoBank Institute)

Empowering versus enabling in academia. (K
Espeland, L Shanta, North Dakota Board of
Nursing, Bismarck, USA).

Inhalant abuse. (K Espeland, Medcenter One
College of Nursing, 512 North 7th Street,
Bismarck, ND 58501, USA).

*Achieving spiritual wellness: using reflective
questions.* (K Espeland, Medcenter One College
of Nursing, Bismarck, ND 58501, USA).

*Helping students understand substance
abuse.* (K Espeland, J Psychosoc Nurs Ment
Health Serv. 1993 Mar;31)

Inhalant abuse: assessment guidelines. (K
Espeland, Medcenter One College of Nursing,
Bismarck, North Dakota 58501).

*Stress and coping responses to proficiency
testing in school-age children.* (Theresa Skybo,
Jacalyn Buck)
*Coping mechanisms, stressful events and
suicidal behavior among youth admitted to
juvenile justice and child welfare services.*
(François Chagnon)

*Can't they like me as I am? Psychological
interventions for children and young people with
congenital visible disfigurement.* (Daniela
Hearst, J Am Psychoanal Assoc. 2007).

'I can't read any of it,' said Heath squinting. 'It's too small.'

'Good,' said Wood complacently. 'This is a very small sample of
research into social effects on our children and the coping mechanisms
we have already identified to correct these.' Wood whipped the slide off
the projector. 'I emphasise, small. The full picture is much more
extensive. The research has been conducted by psychologists and
associated sciences. The subject is adolescent coping mechanisms. Now
take a look at this.' Wood placed another acetate on the projector and
this time he only displayed one message on the screen.

Promoting mental wellness in children and adolescents through positive coping mechanisms. (K Espeland, Medcenter One College of Nursing, Bismarck, North Dakota, USA).

'I will read out the synopsis from this research paper,' said Wood. He lifted a file from his case and found the page he was looking for. He read, 'Children and adolescents frequently experience stressful events such as moving to a new city, divorce of parents, or peer pressure. Parents may be unavailable or unable to model effective coping mechanisms for their children. Without adequate coping mechanisms children frequently are unable to adapt to a stressor; thus a crisis develops. School nurses and other school professionals are in a key position to help young people handle stressful life events and prevent a crisis. The paper reviews stress and suggests techniques to assist children and adolescents to identify and utilise coping strategies while in crisis.' Wood finished reading and looked up to Jessie and Heath.

'Is there money in children,' asked Heath. Jessie was holding her pad in her hand and she swung it at him. 'I'm not trying to be contentious,' began Heath. 'Get to the point,' he said looking at Wood.

'I will. Bear with me,' said Wood searching in his bag again. He lifted another file from it and waved it in the air before Heath and Jessie. 'Several months ago, I received a proposal from a Portuguese Post Graduate student called Katrina Loureiro. She asked me to help her with operational and financial support to develop her project. She called it "Institutional Reform and Increased Productivity; *Social Opportunity."* This is what she wrote to me saying.' Wood waved the file in front of them again to signal that her written correspondence was within. He took it out and realised that he had transferred it onto his computer. 'Better still,' he said, pointing at his computer. 'I can get it up on screen.' He found the file and plugged his computer into the projector. The text appeared and he read it out loud.

'We are not given the basic grounding in life to know or to cope with the emotional demands we encounter in the journey to explore the opportunities we wish to pursue. We are not educated to cope, we are not repaired when we fail and we are not given a goal to go and get. We are children educated and released into a world that constantly challenges us; through our social intercourse and our feedback. These challenges question our ability to know if we are right or wrong and if we are acting incorrectly or not. When we do get it wrong we are beaten, mentally, sub-consciously and even physically. This may seem harsh, but at best, the response to our mistakes is a negative impact.' Wood hesitated for a moment and held up the folder. This is excellent work and there is plenty of it.'

'I've probably come across a lot of it,' said Jessie. 'The principle is familiar.'

'Not for me,' said Heath. 'Kids need help. I don't doubt it. Get them on the park. That sorts them out. They need to play.'

'Listen,' said Wood looking at Heath. Heath knew he was determined. Heath had become accustomed to that look.

'She continues,' Wood began and scrolled his page to read.

'We fail, too often, to bounce back because our goals do not exist or do not demand enough from us. And too often, the only goals we have are those that we attribute to financial gain and money.

Education programmes need dramatic change. Our current curriculum programmes develop self discipline but in many cases, they destroy it too. There is little application today for much of what we are taught. The current curriculums need to be substantially downsized and the time freed up, needs to be targeted at self awareness programmes that teach our children to cope, by general programmes that allow our youth to understand the behaviour of the world they live in and to know who they truly are. Teach them the ability to rise when they fall. Shape their resilience and teach them to cope. The quandary of blame that arises when children play offside does not protect them in the first place but whilst the parents look to the teachers and the teachers look to the parents we are still merely locked in the dream of a better place. Prepare our children to understand the world that they will enter when they are released from adolescence.

We cannot hope that our children will gain their moral and worldly guidance from religious studies. Their languages were written for a culture we can no longer relate too and their words have been rewritten and savaged by motivated and powerful men whom lacked the vision of Christ.

I have attended, witnessed and conducted a multitude of employee, management and corporate training sessions. Invariably, they are driven by a reaction to a cultural problem, even a crisis. My observations conclude that they are a wild stab in the dark, pieced together by people who care but sit in a sea of potential solutions only to make do with what is available at the moment. Efficiency and effectiveness is derided and crippled by time constraints.

We need to endorse and support change and educate our children to act and pursue the world and the wealth of opportunities that we will, and do, refuse them because we are not doing enough, early enough. Whilst we suppose that the onset of social intercourse will guide our children to the right path, we choose hope in favour of commitment.'

Wood's computer crashed and the text he was reading from the screen disappeared. He rebooted his computer and said to Jessie and Heath, 'Bear with me.' His screen was flashing at him. 'I've been hit by a virus or my firewall or - *what do they call those things?* – is not performing.' When the screen returned, a page flashed up and appeared on the overhead projector screen.

Underneath a picture of a scantily dressed young woman were the words, 'Sexy, Sultry, Subservient, Super Susie is only a phone call away and she is gagging to meet you, *now*.' The words faded from the screen and the woman sat up and licked her lips in a seductive manner. A new text flashed on to the screen saying. 'Your penis is too small? Forget Viagra, Dicklick can fix it; a uniquely flavoured cream with a uniquely arousing application.'

'What the hell,' said Wood. Jessie and Heath couldn't hold back their laughter. As Wood continued to retrieve his presentation from his computer he felt himself getting aroused. He held the picture of Super

Suzie in his head, and she began to fade from his mind, being replaced by a sea of visual memories of Helen merging upon one another. She had long auburn hair, large brown eyes, full lips and she was tall and slim. Her breasts were inordinately large and she was in denial – Helen had denied her body of all her clothing. Wood composed himself as the presentation reappeared. He thought of bankers and read on.

'We have to give our children and our adults the best shot they can have in the limited time that life affords them. Medicine and morality can improve dramatically.

In Malaysia I propose to co-ordinate the deployment of a *Medical Estate,* I will call, *The Eureka Split.* The Estate will constitute the following elements:

Phase one is an educational and coping centre, Preparation Grades 1 and 2 respectively.

Phase two is a series of outlet stores which will be grouped on one retail park and they include, in summary; a medical centre, pharmacy, dentist, optician, psychologist, physiologist, two fitness centres, four health food shops, an acupuncturist, herbalist and hypnotists.

Phase three is being considered and it will include Cycle shops and out-door pursuits, sportswear and more.

The objective of this estate is to re-engage the patient with alternatives to the 'pill popping' culture of medical care. Too frequently, we seek the prescription as a solution to our ailments and our doctors rely on the prescriptions formula to manage waiting lists quickly and efficiently. But in the pursuit of *prevention over cure*, the doctors know that pill popping is not the solution and that patients will return time after time for prescriptions that scratch the surface whilst molten fires rage below. If people are to be given the best shot, we need to get them effectively repaired in a timely fashion. Keep them on the playing field, not chained to the repair beds.

The retail park covers a series of repair Grades from 1 – 4.

Phase four is a Correction Centre which has 3 further repair grades – Youth Repair, Correction and Severity.

Correction and Repair; The Prison is obsolete.

We can educate our children to cope but no system in its infancy can be perfect. People will still make mistakes and whilst some mistakes are forgiven, some will result in the deprivation of our freedom. Our prisons should be geared to deal with the corrective measures we need when we play offside.

There exists numerous examples in human failings that vary in degree and extreme. This one captures my mind.

In the U.S., a serial killer was captured after she had murdered thirty-five people. She was in her mid twenties and whilst in custody, she repeatedly complained of severe headaches. Surgeons found a lump of scar tissue on her brain and removed it. They opened up her skull and peeled off the tissue by hand before sewing her back up. After the surgery, they concluded that the tissue must have been apparent from birth. The girl went on to live a normal life and she was released back in to society and did not reoffend.

Criminology and Causation is advancing and our understanding of human punitive behaviour may fall under medical, physiological, psychological or cultural reasoning. We need to glean from our evidence, what measures apply to what offender and enhance our ability to give back to our prisoners their freedom, sooner rather than later. Again, get them back on the playing field. Recognise that people don't learn to cope, that they don't learn to take responsibility and re-educate them.'

As the screen went blank, Wood said. 'Katrina has written to me since and she asked me to read a paper by Geoff Dobson. Here it is.

Geoff Dobson, Deputy Director of the Prison Reform Trust visited Bastøy, a prison reform centre in

Norway. This is the report he wrote subsequent to the visit.

International View:
Reflections on Norwegian Prisons.
Inspirational, humane and respected

In May 2008 I was invited to Norway as part of a group of twenty prison governors and chief probation officers from England. The Correctional Service of Norway Staff Academy (KRUS) hosted the trip in gratitude for visits made by their trainee prison officers during the last 30 years. The trip involved seminars, prison visits and a celebration of 17th May, Norway's national day. With the UK's political antennae often focused on the United States, it was refreshing to look in a different direction for ideas and stimulation.

Policies and practices can rarely be transplanted from one culture to another. The context is different in so many ways. It was fascinating however to learn about features that gave staff, prisoners and members of the public, confidence in the Norwegian prison system. In this short article I have highlighted five recurring themes:

· Many problems that affect criminality have their solutions outside the criminal justice system.
· Political support and trust underpin creative local leadership and use of professional discretion.
· Small prisons have considerable benefits.
· Rehabilitation flourishes where relationships are positive and the focus is on prisoners learning to take responsibility.
· The importance of investment in prison officer training.

Norway, with its oil and gas resources, is a relatively affluent country whose population is 4.7 million. The aims of prison and probation are to carry out the sentences of the court and "to enable the offender through his / her initiative, to change their own criminal behaviour". A White Paper on "Effective Punishment" was going to be presented to Parliament in the next few weeks. It was hoped that this would include a reintegration guarantee to offenders. Full cabinet backing is being sought for measures to tackle problems with housing, education, work, finances and medical treatment. Two of the biggest concerns, mental health and drug treatment are, for example, seen as the province of the Ministry of Health rather than the Ministry of Justice. The minimum age of criminal responsibility in Norway is 15 years and the aspiration is to have no children under 18 years in prison establishments.

The number of people held in custody is about 3,500, and there were 12,774 receptions in 2007. The imprisonment rate is 75 per 100,000. Most prison sentences are short, the average length being 100 days and three out of ten being under one month. Five per cent of sentences are over three years and while there are no life sentences, preventive detention has operated since 2002.

In 2007, there were nearly 35,000 leaves of absence (the equivalent of ROTL – release on temporary licence) from closed prisons. The breach rate was two per thousand. Every prisoner is eligible for leave of absence, subject to a satisfactory risk assessment, after one third of the sentence has been served. An example was given of a serious crime being committed during a period of leave. The governor spoke to the media and the minister backed the service. There are mechanisms to ensure lessons are learnt and where there are serious failings, individuals are held to account. It is not however, a blame culture and there is acceptance that the behaviour of anyone cannot be 100% predicted.

The smallest prison holds twelve prisoners and there are many with less than fifty inmates. The largest is Oslo prison with about 400 prisoners and the newest, close to the Swedish border will hold about 250. A number of comments were made to explain the virtues of small establishments. Perhaps the most striking was that the prisoner is always an individual, never a number. To enable a range of approaches to be available to those in small prisons, there is cooperation between prisons in an area.

I visited Bastøy, an open prison on an island, with a special ethos defined as "an arena for the development of responsibility". There are 115 prisoners and 69 staff, 40 of whom might be there during the day and 5 at night and at weekends. The governor had resisted higher staff levels arguing that prisoners are left to do work that the staff do not want. The basic values and ideology are crucial to an understanding of this "human – ecological prison":

Ecology: Mankind does not own the Earth: The Earth owns mankind. Everything ties together, just as blood ties families together. Mankind is just a thread in the weave. Everything we do in opposition to the weave will turn back on us (Indian Chief Seattle from his speech "we are all a part of the earth").

Humanity: I don't know the person, his background, tribe or name. Such knowledge is not important. What is important is that he is a human being. (Quotation from Bear Heart "A medicine man's rules for living")

Development of Responsibility: Responsibility is a practical skill, and as such needs to be taught and practiced. The training must have an element of trust, and must be meaningful.

Bastøy is designed for long term prisoners approaching the latter stages of their sentence. Average sentence length of inmates is 5 years 5 months and ideally they are there for the last 12-18 months of their sentence. The first item given to a prisoner on arrival is an alarm clock. Special credit cards are given to purchase food and other items at the prison shop. Prisoners live in small houses and are responsible for their cleaning, cooking and shopping. They take part in programmes to address their offending behaviour and attend education or work, on or off the island. There are absolute rules forbidding violence and drugs. Random drug tests are a daily occurrence and prisoners returning from the mainland may be breathalysed. The philosophy that informs every aspect of Bastøy is:

All people can be "ordinary citizens" if they are treated in a positive way, and they can live in a developing environment where the individual is respected and is given responsibility for his own development and behaviour. The environment must be influenced by "good" role models, challenges, demands and meaningful activity."

In the last two years no one has been released from Bastøy without accommodation and a job to go to. As we said our goodbyes an English governor said that he had been in the Prison Service for 24 years and this had been the best day in all that time.

Each prison officer undertakes a two year training programme at KRUS. There are 3,200 prison staff in Norway and seven applications are received for every training place. To qualify for the staff academy they must have the entrance qualifications for higher education. The first year comprises 4 weeks at the college, followed by practical work with close supervision and guidance for 42 weeks, with two study days weekly. In the second year there are 44 weeks of academic work followed by 6 weeks working as a prison officer. To qualify, the trainee must pass a series of exams, and satisfactorily complete each placement and project work. Officers must undertake a further week of training after three years in post, or on promotion or change of responsibility. Most prisons also organise local training. We were told that this level of commitment to training prison officers reflects the level of responsibility officers have for the well-being of prisoners.

It was refreshing to be immersed for a few days in a society which: realizes the need for a range of measures

outside the criminal justice system to tackle the causes
of crime; trusts leaders and managers of prisons to do a
good job, giving tangible support within an accepted
framework of accountability; sees virtue in small
institutions and the dangers inherent in large prisons;
has a value base that inhibits the development of a risk
averse culture and informs arrangements that enable
people in custody to learn to take responsibility; and
invests heavily in the professional development of
prison officers.

The presentation concluded and the screen went blank. 'What do you
think?' Wood asked. Heath had called his PA and asked him to bring
two coffees and a tea for himself. The coffee was very strong and Wood
added more sugar.

'Yes; very good,' said Heath. Wood waited for him to continue. He
didn't intend to so Wood prompted him.

'The girl certainly has endeavour,' said Wood eagerly.

'Yes,' said Heath who dialled out on his internal phone handset and
asked his PA, 'Can I get another tea?'

Wood knew that he should show this work to Jessie but he had been
reserved in doing so with Heath. Heath was more interested in making
money than spending it. Then Heath said, 'Institutional reform has the
potential to enhance freedom and maximise the value of it. I didn't think
anybody cared. Where is my tea?'

Whilst Heath became agitated that his drink had not arrived in the
seconds following him ordering it, Wood acknowledged the moments
Heath could always fill him with surprise; and then he did it again.
Heath said, 'I often sit in traffic jams wondering what I am doing there. I
see many cars and many people and I know that this occurrence is
abundant across the country, even the world. I know that I am going
somewhere specific and so is everybody else. Somewhere ahead of me
is a crossroads or an obstacle that is causing this traffic to jam. At that
crossroads or obstacle is a traffic jam going in another direction with a
whole set of people on a specific journey to a specific destination. Each
of us sits anxiously and frustrated. We all face delays and we
concentrate on the arrival of our journey. Every single journey is
different. Thousands of us, even millions dispersed in an anxious sea of
diversification, of alternative and competing goals. Tomorrow it will all

happen again; and then again. But why do we all do it? And what is the purpose of it?'

'Keep the cogs going,' Jessie said. The tea arrived.

'In circles?' Heath questioned. 'A dog chases its tail. Is this all merely for play?' asked Heath and he took a sip from his tea. 'It's cold!' Wood wondered why he had complained; Heath always drank his tea cold.

Jessie said, 'Intuition is a muscle in the brain. If you deal with illnesses, the longer you deal with it the bigger the muscle becomes and the more knowledge of medicine you retain. The muscle is like a condensed but huge filing cabinet. The filing cabinet sits in a library called 'memory'. Experience builds the muscle and fills the library.'

'All well and good if you're a doctor,' said Heath.

'It doesn't matter what you deal with. Medicine, psychology, even business,' Jessie stretched out an open hand towards Heath to acknowledge her example. 'It's simply true in life, in all our experiences. These experiences may be good or may be bad. The important thing is how we deal with the good and the bad – it comes back to my ideas on how we manage our moods.'

'Isn't this a brilliant starting point?' said Wood.

'Definitely, but it needs a more,' said Jessie pondering.

'Go on,' encouraged Wood. Jessie thought for a moment and rolled her eyes towards the ceiling. She looked at Wood. Her head was sunk into the palm of her hand. Her elbow lent on the table. She said, 'In Shakespeare's Othello, 'Honest Iago' was deemed to be – and I quote – *a smart man with learned spirit.* Shakespeare never attempted to tell us why Iago was Iago but he clearly illustrated the tragic consequences of bitter experiences.'

Heath wondered if this comment from Jessie was the final motivation behind what Wood told them next. When Wood did tell them, they were both quiet for a few moments until Heath broke the uncomfortable silence.

'Man,' he said throwing his arms up in the air and rising from his seat. 'You certainly know how to drop a bombshell.'

PART SIX

FORSAKEN

THE YEAR BEFORE THE SEVEN DAYS
THAT MADE THE EARTH

This was going to hurt and Wood knew it. There was always a consequence to *action* and also to *inaction*. The former was for today – you could kill yourself – and the latter was much worse – you could kill everybody else; slowly and invisibly, especially in the world of safety and security that they angered about.

Wood had moved to Krakow in Poland on the 21st March 2007 to live with Helen. He had handed over executive control of his group of companies to Heath.

'Heath, I'm doing this,' said Wood. 'I have to consolidate Europe for our long term success and The Eureka Split is best situated in Eastern Europe. I need to find the location. I'll put the think tank together and I need you to run the business whilst I'm away.' Wood knew he was not telling Heath the whole story. He also knew that Heath did know the whole story. At least Heath had drawn his own conclusions.

Heath and Wood had spent many hours together in the evenings, in the pubs and they had grown very close. Heath knew that Karen had slowly begun to despise Wood. She had done so since Macy was born and Heath surmised that this was the reason that Wood had fallen in love with Helen. The whole cocktail of episodes was resulting in a distraction in Wood that Heath had noticed.

Heath held his own rigid views and he would have preferred Wood to have simply told him that he was *not right* and that he needed time to recuperate. Heath knew that Wood had been very close to Karen when he had first met him and that she had given him happiness for the first time in his life in their early years. Heath also knew that Wood's move to Poland would be the best thing for his children and the business.

Wood had been travelling extensively abroad and the people in his life were accustomed to this. His family would now be use to his absence. In Poland, his relationship with Helen would not be in everybody's face.

'You know the road map,' said Wood. 'You know how to run this business.'

'Yes, but I'm not you,' said Heath adamantly.

'All you need to do is focus on mortgage lending. No matter what happens, drive the lending in hard and the harder the better. Delegate everything else and if any of it collapses, let them scream at you. Just absorb it and get the lending.'

'The expansion is very demanding on cash flow.'

'Yes but I've left you sufficient cash. Don't worry about the state of the business. Whatever mess I come back to, I can mop it up.'

Wood knew that he could and he knew that he would have to. He was more concerned with how much time he had; six months maybe but he needed a year. When Wood left the room, Jessie said, 'He's not right, I'm not sure about his mental health.'

'Don't ever worry about that man's mental strength.'

'But he's drinking heavily. He's very unhappy.'

'He just wants to shag his way back to happiness with the fittest thing he can find,' Heath said dismissively.

In Krakow, Wood and Helen found an apartment overlooking the Krakow gardens, frequented by immaculately dressed women walking fantastically groomed dogs. In the evenings, the park was full of drunks telling everyone to 'coorva' (*Polish for fuck off*).

Wood and Helen became close though he always felt uncomfortable during sex with Helen. She was very generous with her affection and Wood implored himself to match this. Her beauty constantly unnerved him, implicit in his tact. He often said to her, 'When you die, they will put your skeleton on public display. Everyone will want to know what the most beautiful girl in history looked like.'

'A skeleton is hardly beauty,' said Helen, laughing.

'But yours is the most beautiful. Your body shape is astonishing.'

They had hardly had chance to explore living together when this happened.

Firstly, Wood was tipped off that a Management Buyout (MBO) was being proposed from members of his team. Wood flew to England called his Main Board to interview and was faced with the dilemma that two camps were under supervision. Potentially he was facing two, not one, MBO's.

Wood dismissed two of his Main Board because their actions had resulted in direct conversations with other team members about the MBO proposal. The problem, however, was more serious than this. A closely knit team, committed to the mission, was now entrenching into split camps. Trust was being tested.

A second impact came from the main banking source provided by ITCD. The divisional management team had been very supportive and seriously engaged in the management personnel Wood employed in his Main Board capacity and the gross profits achieved.

But the team from the ITCD had called in Wood's accountant to demand the recall of the overdraft facility and to inform him that the extension to the loan facility had been declined. When hearing this, Wood did not over react. He looked instead to recruit a new Chairman with the Curriculum Vitae, the credentials and the track record to reinforce the confidence the bank had showed in Wood's business prior to these decisions.

The Chairman was found and employed but the bank became more vociferous in their foreclosure. They also demanded the reduction in the outstanding loan facility. They had become concerned with Wood's expansion campaign.

By August, Wood had to put his plans for expansion abroad and The Eureka Split on hold. He returned to England to live. These two issues had unsettled his senior management team and the fear leaked into the ranks of his personnel. His new Chairman failed to contain this concern and Wood removed him and resumed executive control of his group of companies.

In America and Europe, it was becoming increasingly apparent that the subprime losses were impacting more and more banks. UBS, Citiwest and JP Morgan Chase were topping the league tables of the deemed subprime losses. BNP Paribas had moved to begin the freeze in money markets in Europe and Societe General were making similar, fearful moves relating to this crisis. By September, the financial tsunami had hit the shores of England with the run on Northern Rock.

For Wood, this wave had already begun to seriously impact his turnover and he instructed his team to recapitalise his assets to support cash reserves. £12 million was identified and realigned projections indicated financial resilience. Bravills notified Wood's management team that they would not be raising lending for his clients. They had given no reason but Wood was very close to members of their internal team and he had been told that the foundations had been rocked by a £20 million scandal. Wood's main contact, Charles Ibsen, had been sacked along with several other staff but Wood had persuaded Charles to set up his own brokerage, which Charles had done and the recapitalisation programme was reinstated.

However, his team were becoming increasingly reserved in their ability to sustain and increase income streams. Many of his directors and management team had invested in property portfolios and these were beginning to show signs of financial stress. They looked to Wood for guidance and financial support. He would not entertain their increasing monetary concerns. Wood had always been generous in his remuneration to his employees, even famously so. But he held to a firm belief that he would give to those who didn't ask and he would refuse those who did ask.

Meanwhile, Citiwest informed Wood that they recommend he find an alternative funding source for his private residence. His accountant had missed his deadline for his last quarterly payment by two weeks. For the last eighteen months and even before re-mortgaging the house in August, Wood had never made payments in line with deadlines. Citiwest had previously remained relaxed.

This later incident had been exposed to the team and it added to the fear that was now escalating in the ranks. The trust had been challenged by the MBO and it failed to be forgotten. The funding sources changed from keen to reticent and income streams were in decline.

Hoary was at home in his study expecting a visit from Miranda at any moment. In the few moments he had spare, he picked up his amulet, 'The Step' and read.

The Step
3
Belief (Dace v Satan)
Mercy
As it is now

Is not the God of the Bible described as merciful? Does He not speak of His kindness to, and compassion for, all mankind? If God is all-powerful, and a God of love (I John 4:8, 16), *why* does He not stop the terrible human suffering billions now endure?

The ministers and theologians of traditional Christianity cannot explain the purpose of human suffering. Many theorize that Adam and Eve were created perfect and complete, until they "fell" in the Garden because the devil overthrew God's Plan by tempting them into sin. This popular idea continues with the explanation that God's Plan is to restore men to their pre-fall condition, but the devil keeps slowing things down and disrupting God's progress.

Is this true? Is God desperately trying to *repair* damage brought by Satan's unforeseen attack on a Master Plan that God did not think through carefully enough?'

As it will be with Dace

'There is no Satan and no one is innocent in tragedy. No one can claim that 'it was not my fault'. No one man has stood up and said 'it was my fault. I am sorry that I dismissed the political truth. Ask yourself what is the vision of the men and women who administer tragedy? These acts are seen as evil but these acts result from the dismissal of mans' true purpose. Evil does not exist – dismissal is mans' primary confusion.'

Hoary got up from his seat and went to the lavatory. He flushed the toilet and went into the kitchen to open a can of soup. He noticed that his mobile phone was displaying a message from Michael and he read, 'It is done. He is destroyed.' Hoary dipped his finger in the soup and wrote on the white work top with tomato sauce, 'Tane Wood'.

Hoary hardly heard the doorbell when Miranda arrived. When he let her in she said, 'Wonderful estate. I bet nobody knows you're here.' Miranda was in her mid thirties and Hoary had never seen her look so good. 'Was her hair different or her make up? Was it the leather dress or the boots?' Hoary thought, trying to fathom his mystery.

Wood concentrated his efforts on drawing cash from his assets and supporting his declining income streams with new avenues.

His people were teetering and his leadership was being tested. He called his senior team to the boardroom and objectives were clearly identified. Within minutes of the meeting ending, members of his team were despondent. Some were vocal in their dismissal of the income projections. Those loyal to Wood had informed him of their negativity. That night he received a series of text messages from his team informing him that Scott had been very dismissive of Wood's projections. Wood forwarded these messages to Scott and in the morning Scott said to Wood. 'I did not say that we had to confront you with the realism that we could only deliver a quarter of the income you had projected.'

'I was told that you feared for your job if you had told me this?'

'That's nonsense. I just think we need to be realistic.'

Wood told Helen about this she said, 'Everybody likes Scott. I don't know why. He was a nasty piece of work with me.'

Wood resolved that he should keep a close eye on Scott but he was becoming distracted by events further afield. He had seen the escalation in the world affairs relating to the deemed subprime losses and began to witness their impact on equity markets and the increasing concerns being expressed regarding the stability of the value of the housing stock in America and now Europe. His private beliefs gave no room for optimism and he decided to address his team with the truth.

He told them that this was not a time for false optimism, that this was a time for truth. He told them that the correction in the housing stocks would see a 50% reduction in capital values and a comprehensive decline in the public's ability or capacity to move house. He agreed with the predictions emanating from the wealthiest financial entrepreneurs in America, Jim Rodgers, George Soros and others, regardless of their political agendas, that foreclosures would reach 25% in America. Corporations in all industries would decline and a depression would ensue. Economies would face decline and when the fear spread, the manifestations would surface in strike actions and later in riots. The governments of the world would suppress social unrest with the hammer of Thor, to maintain order.

'I have always maintained that to evolve a market and redefine its commercial existence would be a political challenge that would test the resilience and resolve of any man and any team. I am not asking my people to get out of the trenches at Gallipoli and face the Turkish bullets. But I am asking them to get out of the trenches.'

Hoary was sitting on the tube on the DLR line heading to his offices in Canary Wharf. He did not like the public transport systems but his chauffeur had phoned in sick very late. He knew he would find no replacement at short notice and he did not have enough time to sort out alternative means. His agenda today was busy and the quickest route was by rail. As he travelled, he felt more comfortable with his eyes down in his reading material.

The Step
3
Belief (Dace v Satan)

Death

As it is now

'Every day, 240,000 people starve to death and often, distraught parents watch their children die in their arms. Starvation is so awful that death is actually a blessed relief. Everywhere, untold trauma, pain and suffering, due to crippling conditions, infections and disease of every sort, are occurring around the world. Just in Africa, children are being orphaned by the millions, *every year*, due to famine alone.

Poverty now affects one-third of all people on earth because of the lack of even the most basic necessities (sufficient water, sanitation, clothing and shelter, as well as food). Untold suffering is experienced by over two billion people and conditions are growing *worse* instead of better.

War now ravages much of the world, with some nations suffering almost complete destruction of their economy, property, homes and businesses, including injury or death to large numbers of their civilian populations.

Earthquakes, fires, floods, volcanoes, tornadoes, hurricanes, blizzards, other violent storms, drought, blights and insect infestations due to weather, also take their toll on human misery. Why war, terrorism, violence, disease, famine, poverty and misery? Why do these things happen almost routinely on planet earth and why doesn't God intervene to end it?'

As it will be with Dace

'Life is choice. Choose your politics but believe in the politics others choose to dismiss. There is a master plan. Maybe you'll be the first to get it? One man can guide the people to a world where all the suffering will no longer exist. The DNA strain of the Homo sapien contains vision and purpose but these are very rare. Rarer still are the ingredients that permit this to act. Recognise it, find it, feed it and give it room to breathe. It is a cocktail so rare but its influence will be heard when its bearer trusts his voice.

Hoary closed his book. He thought of Miranda and his meeting with her at his house last Saturday. She had looked magnificent when she had arrived. He could not recall her being so glamorous from their previous meetings, although he did recognise that she was an attractive woman. He was glad that his wife had not been there because it would have only led to tension being caused in their conversations in the evening. He wondered if Miranda had known of his wife's absence. It would have been embarrassing if she had suddenly returned. Hoary thought about the events that unfolded after Miranda's arrival and the blood began to flow into his loins.

It was not Wood's leadership skills that were being tested. His track record, his accolades at home and abroad and his ability to build the balance sheet of his business in line with his mission had proven his ability to lead. What was at risk now was the personal threat that each of his employees were facing in regard to their financial livelihoods.

On the 29th November 2007, Wood managed to raise £750,000 to meet the end of month financial commitments of his business. This had been at the eleventh hour and his team had been sitting in pools of anxiety, fearing personal bankruptcy, if this money was not raised. His team witnessed, in awe, the tenacity and the commercial excellence of Wood and how he operated in an industry that no other could compete with. But it was too close for comfort and within 30 days Wood would fail to repeat this achievement.

In London, the networks who had been employed to raise the £12 million Wood needed, were struggling. They were expressing optimism for the New Year. Wood did not share this optimism, in his private council, and maintained that it was only a matter of time before the effects of the tsunami would freeze all the financial and commercial markets.

Wood had maintained his commitment to get his team dealing in the truth rather than misinformed optimism. However, he kept the horrors of his vision with his own council and never, to the end, parted with these views.

Whilst the world was homing in on a 'sub-prime crisis' and a credit crunch, Wood knew that his was not a result of economic default. This was a dilemma of behaviour; a rebuke to the values man currently followed; a call upon our dismissal of the visions and prophetic calls of our ancestry and a reflection on man's inability to recognise its destiny.

Scott walked into Wood's office and stated that he recommended the closure of their outlet stores in Europe and half the estate in the U.K. Wood noticed Scott's eyes drift up and down his body.

'And what do we do for income?' asked Wood taking a seat at the small conference table at the front of his office suite. He wanted the round table put there so that he could hold meetings with his team. It would accommodate six people at a time. Wood considered that to be enough for a debate. Anymore was too many. Views would be shouted down.

'We need to consolidate,' said Scott. 'The income is dropping off the cliff.'

'We need to,' thought Wood. 'Or you need to.' Wood sat back in his seat and looked across at Scott. Scott diverted his eyes and Wood said, 'Do you want to fuck me?'

Scott shifted in his seat and composed an expression of disdainful surprise. 'What?' he said.

Wood looked at Scott for a moment and watched him fidget in his seat. Wood noticed how Scott snuffled with his pig-like nose repeatedly. He realised that he had always done it but Wood had not consciously recognised it before. He knew that Scott was an unstable dimension to his team. Wood believed that he could expose his behaviour. When he did, Scott would learn to be himself and improve. Finally, in his life, Scott would be able to look beyond his inner turmoil and share other people's concerns, ambitions and vision. Right now, Wood sensed that he should have got the job done himself. 'You have two choices,' began Wood looking Scott in the eye. 'You either fuck me or I sack you. Which is it to be?'

Hoary was informed that his chauffeur had passed away. 'He caught a common cold for Christ's sake. He was only thirty seven,' Hoary was told by his PA. 'I'm organising a new one for you. He'll be with you first thing in the morning,' she told him.

The morning had come and gone. One cock-up after another had failed to deliver a new Chauffeur, a hire car or a viable alternative. Eventually, his PA organised a Mercedes for him and Hoary jumped in a cab to go and pick it up.

The problems were not resolved when he arrived at the hire centre.

After a flurry of activity and a host of 'can't do's', Hoary demanded a car to be found for him immediately, which was done.

Hoary fitted comfortably into the small Fiat that they gave him and he decided to drive himself all the way into London. His disdain was soon dispelled by the enjoyment he started to have. He felt like he was in a go-cart in the zippy little vehicle. He enjoyed his freedom and the small world of joy he encountered as he flung it in and out of the traffic on London's crowded roads. The streets were more adventurous than the traffic in Barnet where he had been laboriously sat in traffic. When he was there, he knew that he would be sitting stationary for quite some time so he had read.

The Step
3
Belief (Dace v Satan)
Purpose
As it is now

King David was required to learn many lessons during his life, some causing great pain, for both himself and others. Adversity and suffering was a pattern in David's life. He fully understood the purpose of what he had to endure: 'Before I was *afflicted* [suffered] I went astray: but now have I *kept Your word'* (Psa. 119:67).

David knew exactly what suffering was intended to produce. It brought him back into line with God's instruction—and true purpose in his life. Notice further: 'It is *good* for me that I have been *afflicted*; that I might learn Your statutes' (vs. 71).

Suffering certainly did not *feel* good to David, but he knew it *was* good! Mankind is now suffering terribly, but, in the end, it will be to its good. Six thousand years of suffering will eventually teach *all* humanity the crucial lesson that it cannot ignore God and still be happy. Other vital lessons are a by-product of painful trials and tests.

David grasped the great principle that those who obey God—practice righteousness (Psa. 119:172)—often suffer affliction. Many know of this next verse, but how many truly believe it or the promise that accompanies it?: 'Many are the *afflictions* of the righteous: but the LORD delivers him out of them all. He keeps all his bones: not one of them is broken' (Psa. 34:19-20).'

As it will be with Dace

David believed in a destiny that is defined by God. His view is not a shared belief with his kindred. The context of his life challenged his belief but David chose to grasp the great principle and history has chosen to

remember him. Many others – the majority – chose not
to; 'The graveyards are full of dispensable men.'
(Charles De Gaulle). Each of us has a choice and each
of us has to make that choice. Cultures influence the
choices we make but who is the man who will influence
the culture?

The New Year came and the ranks of Wood's personnel diminished
swiftly. He had already lost more than half of his work force. His
income in December had been severely hit, falling by 65%, but in
January he brought it back on track. In February and March his net
income had risen above £1 million per month but in April, the tsunami
hit his shores with colossal force and the income fell to £57,000.

But the stealing had already begun. The tsunami had wiped out
Wood's ability to raise the full £12 million and only £2.4 million
materialised. At the same time, his income streams had all dried up with
dramatic speed and emphatic blind man's visibility. Scott had closed the
stores. Wood had not given him the authority to do so. Scott had insisted
with the staff that the business was fated and that they should find
alternative employment with immediate effect.

His staff had left in droves and the hero status that Wood had
achieved turned to revolt and acrimony. He was no longer loved. The
passion had reversed into despise and hatred. Wood began to receive
threats of physical violence and death.

The financial position deteriorated so quickly, he did not have the
time to consider administration or insolvency actions. These had been
discussed and minutes taken at monthly board meetings but the situation
was now more serious. He did not have the money to afford the
administration process.

His staff, his customers and his creditors began to sue Wood with
volition and many of the staff who remained, did so because their best
chance of financial bailout lay in the hands of Wood.

In the breakdown in compliance that resulted when key personnel
left, employees were bailing themselves out through the business that
employed them. Some attempted to sell their house to Wood's stock
holding company. When this failed to complete for lack of funds, they
left his employment and sued him for loss of salary. Complicity began to
reign and packs of employees bayed on Wood's financial debris. In the
extreme, the lack of compliance was not a necessary ill. Many

employees stole cash, equipment and stock. Wood was now beyond hatred; he was a fully fledged fuck and the comments flowed in.

'He is a ruthless bastard.'

'Fat cat.'

'Why did he allow this to happen? What was he doing? Why did he not stop this?'

'Why?'

'He must be made to pay.'

'Where was the contingency plan?'

'Ferraris, Lamborghinis, Porches. Flash twat.'

'He has money hidden away.'

'He has spent our money, invested it, got his exorbitant bonus, pissed off to Poland and now I can't feed my kids.'

'Who will employ me now?'

'It was his greed.'

'He must be held to account.'

'It is us who will pay. What does he get?'

'I am losing out through absolutely no fault of my own.'

'What an incompetent idiot.'

At first it was his banks; then his employees, then his consumers, followed by the solicitors and the debt collectors and the financiers. It was everyone and to cap it, the receivers decided to pursue Wood for incompetence and lack of credibility. Scalps were needed because trophy rooms were beginning to lay bare.

Wood, with his bank accounts frozen, his savings injected into the business, his asset financiers foreclosing, and his funding withdrawn, limped on. Insolvency was his only option for the businesses and personal bankruptcy was looming.

A small team remained with Wood motivated by their belief that Wood was their best bet or they couldn't get, or be bothered to get, another job. A small few remained loyal and fewer still retained their trust in Wood. They had been close to him and they knew that he had put every penny into the business and his mission. He had remained true to his vision. He had risked all his personal wealth and he would lose everything he had.

But they also knew that he would find a way. They just hadn't yet realised that the true vision Wood held most sacred did not conform to the modern language of money or to bail out. Wood was racing to the line with Hoary and the finishing line was in sight.

∞

Several months before, he had seen his demise looming. 'What a far cry it now seems,' Wood thought as he reflected back to December 2004, when he had first set foot in Canary Wharf. He had never imagined that he would enter this centre of financial muscle time after time over the next twelve months. At the end of that time, he would walk the tower block lined streets knowing that he had conquered the worldly networks they employed. He would become one of the wealthiest men to do business in this arena.

He had driven his ambition hard with implicit determination, silently aware of a consequence nobody would be prepared to hear. In January 2005, he told the people who worked there that he would buy £2 billion worth of housing stock that year. His charisma enhanced the credibility they saw in him and few doubted his words. Many more knew that they would become very wealthy if they helped him achieve his targets. Nobody else, in this market, had been as bold as Wood. No competitor talked of the scale and the numbers that he had targeted. Nobody had ever said it or even got close. In Canary Wharf, the suited men and women cramming the seats on the benches, crowding the alley ways, teeming the tables at the coffee houses began to trade his name in between the breakneck drags of their cigarettes.

How close he was getting to the realisation of his ambition, he thought, remembering the conversations he had with Jessie after **Jessie's Marble** *had been presented to his senior executives. Wood had asked Jessie to crystallise her views in a book to provide visibility and reference for the team.*

Jessie had integrated with the senior team in weekly one-to-one sessions and her time was also distributed amongst the junior executives. On a weekly basis, a two hour seminar format was established to all employees. The emphasis was to provide a succession planning opportunity but the doors were open to everyone, not just the ambitious.

Other ideas began to develop. Wood wanted his customers to share in the aspects of his business that he believed could add value to them. He decided to tag a half hourly session onto the back of property investment seminars. He even offered the seminar to friends and family of employees.

The 'types' of personality Jessie had identified had significant application and whether they were right or wrong, there was only one way to find out.

The business plan was written for a Recruitment Agency and a Dating Agency; premises were found, employees recruited and outlet opening dates were targeted in objective planning. Wood believed that the personality types could be significantly incorporated by business leaders to develop successful team performance. Jessie would carry out an appraisal of the business, mentor her successor as she did so, and present the dynamics of the best fit team to the leader. Gaps that did exist in current personnel would be recruited by Jessie's team.

Similarly, in a dating agency, Jessie believed that opposites did attract and hence, she argued that by a simple 'type' assessment she could match dating couples to increase success levels and longevity - ultimately and potentially, happiness.

Wood recalled reading the first draft of Jessie's book and he was disappointed. He felt that she had leaned heavily towards a medical understanding of human activity but not really dealt with some of the key issues regarding senior plight, for example, what is vision and who has it and why?

He tackled Jessie on the contents of the book. 'What about vision? Is this the ability that is exclusive to a social/sensitive or a robust/individual or are other factors at play.'

'I'm not sure.'

'I know you're not. The work is great Jessie, ground breaking, but you are shying away from dealing with some of the bigger issues.'

'I'm not shying away, I am just not sure. I have sent much of my research to a number of councils, mainly academics and medics, for opinion and pitched the question at them.'

'And?' Wood probed.

'Too early for feedback. I will chase them soon,' said Jessie. Wood sensed a lack of commitment in her words.

'When did you send the material?' he asked, probing deeper.

'Some have had it for nearly a year,' Jessie said, lowering her eyes to the floor.

'And the others?'

Jessie hesitated. 'Nearly a year.'

'And nothing,' exclaimed Wood.

'Basically. I need to conduct more research and get it published. The Scientific American or some other. Give the work more credibility and influence,' said Jessie wondering if she sounded feasible.

'Maybe you need to tackle the question. Head on. Now?' asserted Wood. She realised she had not.

'There appears to be a hierarchy within the definition of vision or at least, varying degrees or levels of it,' Jessie began with more commitment.

'Go on,' encouraged Wood.

'Often, I have heard an architect's building or design described as the originator's vision,' she said. She looked directly at Wood and said. 'People say you have vision when you make statements that you want your brand to be the best loved brand in the world.'

Wood pressed Jessie harder. She was social/sensitive, a bit fluffy. She had to be pressed. 'Well, what about now? What is stopping us?'

'I agree. What is stopping us?' Jessie pondered, trying to find her rhythm with the unchartered territory of the subject matter. 'Well, I guess that vision has many components that are visible. For example, a vision must be an expression of something new, exponential, different; even absurd. It can build upon facts that are present and offer a direction. Something that others have not seen or done before. A vision challenges norms and, hence, it is individual. It must be able to exist and have the potential to be gregariously accepted.'

'Gregariously accepted?' asked Wood.

'Sorry. I mean the potential to gain social acceptance.'

'Go on.' He probed more.

'It must be forthright, boisterous, and distinctive. The visionary would have to be single minded, be able to think in unique and innovative ways, maybe even idiosyncratic.'

'Interesting; you have moved from the factual to the behavioural. Carry on,' said Wood placing his chin in the palm of his hand and leaning closer to Jessie.

'I guess that the visionary would need a very good sensory code. I mean, he would have to be sensitive and social; especially in his own environment; to read it well and extrapolate from it to glean his vision. Whilst, at the same time he would need to be singular, independent and distinct to think differently.'

'And what about courage?' Wood said, continuing to probe. He knew Jessie had the intellect to resolve this issue. She just needed him to push her there.

'How do you mean?' clarified Jessie.

'Well, too often, new ideas are seen as being outside of our norms. They are seen to be absurd. You need courage to fly in the face of prudence. You need courage to overcome the natural dismissal that you would inevitably face; a strength given by purpose and conviction.'

'A robust type would survive well given the potential onslaught.'

'It may be that the visionary needs a little more than the robust. It strikes me that the visionary is probably the cocktail of life or more aptly, the cocktail of type.' Wood realised that the shoe was now on the other foot. He was now resolving the issue. But it didn't seem to matter. The conclusion had been drawn.

'How do you mean?' asked Jessie.

'I'm not sure if Albert Einstein observed the theory of relativity by the conclusion of his research or from the commitment he relentlessly delivered in the pursuit of his dream. If it was the latter, his intuitive judgement finely beat the analysis. After years of research and practice and more research and more practice, I think the qualities that are apparent in our men and women of vision are staring you in the face. This is not a matter of planning or research or whatever. This now depends on how much you trust yourself to say that what you inherently know, is true. Call back your papers from your councils. You don't need their feedback Jessie or their support or their approval. You just need you and you need to trust yourself.'

'But I do,' said Jessie, unconvincingly.

'Not enough. Not yet. You are brilliant Jessie. I have no doubt. Your brilliance needs pursuit. It needs you to commit to the pursuit of truth. When and if you can, it won't be your councils who approve, it won't be the colleagues in your profession that admire you, it won't be the curious and demanding men that top our corporate boardrooms that need and fight for you. It will be more, a lot more. The vast eternity of time will remember your name.'

When Hoary sat down at his desk, after bustling through the London traffic and parking his small Fiat in a motorbike bay, he was confronted by a memo from Miranda. He picked it up and became disturbed by the knowledge that whenever she entered his thoughts he was confronted by his personal arousal.

ITCD International Bank – Globally #1

We are about to enter the year of 2009 and the ITCD Bank has secured its market advantage. It is now the biggest bank in the world and it is positioned on five key equity markets around the globe, more exposure than any other bank.

ITCD market their brand as *'The World's Neighbourly bank'*. Their international network comprises around 19,500 offices in 88 countries and territories in Europe, the Asia-Pacific region, the Americas, the Middle East and Africa.

With listings on the London, Hong Kong, New York, Paris and Korean stock exchanges, shares in ITCD Holdings plc are held by around 250,000 shareholders in some 97 countries and territories. The shares are traded on the New York Stock Exchange in the form of American Depositary Receipts.

Through an international network linked by advanced technology, including a rapidly growing e-commerce capability, ITCD provides a comprehensive range of financial services: personal financial services; commercial banking; corporate, investment banking and markets; private banking; and other activities.

Their business principles and values state, *'The ITCD corporate constitution defines the ethics and principles inherent in all our everyday dealings.'*

The ITCD Group has an international pedigree which is unique. Many of its principal companies opened for business over a century ago and they have a history which is rich in variety and achievement. The ITCD Group is named after its founding member, The International Trading Consumer Depository Corporation Limited, which was established in 1855 to finance the growing trade between Asia, America and Europe.

Hoary noted that Miranda's memo was for an article for entry into their internal corporate magazine. The article had gone some way, he thought, towards the truth.

The ITCD was now well positioned, with widespread global coverage and a capitalisation position that even today, would have been the envy of the industry before the credit crunch. Their exposure to the toxic assets in property loans, hedge funds, and commercial debt that had strangled their counterparts was significantly lower, per capita, than any other world bank.

The ITCD Group built its position, not to survive the credit crunch but to wipe out the market and take the lead. The strategy of their disruption had now achieved its initial goal. Over the next ten years, they would fight to hold their presence as the evolution of the financial and commercial institutions began its realisation. But Hoary's concerns would be less than his counterparts.

Whilst the Lions and the Natural Born Killers sacked the Analysts and the Grey Streaks and murdered the Realists and the Wisdomites in all the other global financial and commercial houses across America, Europe and Asia, Hoary was realising his vision.

Wood was financially bankrupt. He had built a wealth in excess of $300m but this had collapsed and his debts now exceeded $175m. Many of his former colleagues had suffered the same fate but not as extensively.

They were angry men and made even angrier by the fact that Wood did not seem to be experiencing the same emotional dilemma and personal Armageddon that they were. Wood was striving forward and they didn't understand why. They laid traps for him, vociferously and politically denounced whatever Wood got involved with and poisoned anybody who got close to him.

Wood's debtors were even angrier. They wanted him held to account at creditor meetings. They wanted his wealth stripped and his poverty enforced, real and pitiful. In their view, the irresponsible actions of Wood and other defaulters had led to the collapse of the corporations they worked for, wiping away the careers they had mapped out for themselves and, in many cases, the loss of the livelihoods of close colleagues and the impact this had had on their homes and their families.

Wood made it vocal that he wished his ex-colleagues all the very best and hoped they would achieved success in their new ventures. He was not concerned that they had stolen equipment, assets, money, networks and markets from him. He easily forgave them and he did not look back. He genuinely wanted them to get on with their lives and be successful.

He told all his creditors that he had no money and no assets because he did not. They didn't believe him and contracted the legal system to draw his blood but when the legal representatives bayed on Wood, threatened his livelihood and painted their pictures of the enforcement measures they would pursue, Wood consistently replied 'Join the club.'

He simply wanted them all to leave him alone in order that he could reach the finishing line with his vision.

'I guess I keep my job,' said Michael. 'Unfortunately. I had started to get preoccupied with park benches.'

'Are you sure he is scuppered?' asked Hoary eager to seek confirmation about the demise of Tane Wood.

'They'll lock him up. The justice system is all over him. Baying for his blood. By the time the jobsworths clan get their teeth into him, he'll be locked up and out of the way. I hear that the employee and creditor statements being made to the insolvency office are slaughtering him.'

'Good,' Hoary said and hung up the phone. He reached for his amulet called 'The Step' and noticed how beautiful the design on the front cover was.

The Step
3
Belief (Dace v Satan)

Translation

As it is now

Many know of the ancient patriarch Job, but know little of the important lessons his life holds regarding how God works with His servants—even His greatest servants. Though Job lived thousands of years ago, his experience bears directly on *us* today.

God asked Satan, '*Have you considered My servant Job, that there is none like him in the earth, a perfect and an upright man, one that fears God, and eschews [shuns] evil?*' This establishes Job's character as extraordinary. While Solomon was the wisest man who ever lived, Job was certainly the most righteous.

As it will be with Dace

Today, the italic prose above, reads like this, *'Take Job, for example, determined and single minded in his belief of truth and purpose. His faith seeks the opportunity and challenges the dismissal.'*

God does not want to be feared, he does not want men to be his servants and he does not want us to shun evil. He does not rank men for wisdom, righteousness, perfection or for any matter. God wants us to choose between purpose and dismissal – between Him and Satan. These two alone are the only winner and loser.

Hoary recalled an incident he had experienced during his visit to New York last week. He was shopping and chose various clothes and took them to the counter. He said 'Can I *take* these please?' He always used this phrase in England whenever he went to the till to pay. However, the American girl behind the till looked at the security guard standing next to her. The expression on her face suggested that Hoary had frightened her.

Within a moment – it did seem longer – she said, 'Oh. You mean, can you *get* these.' The security guard laughed. 'Of course you can sir.'

'Yes. Thank you.' Hoary replied. The girl smiled at him.

When Wood returned to England from Poland to deal with the MBO, he had sacked his corporate council, Christine and her sister, Jessie. Christine had approached two of the Main Board and proposed that they raise the funds to buy Wood out. Jessie had been convincing the Main Board that Wood was suffering from a mental illness and he was unfit to rule.

Wood asked Christine for an explanation.

'The business is rapidly going down the pan whilst you are in Europe. The team are in disarray. They are losing confidence and they are blaming you.'

'You know that we need Europe. Our ambitions are nothing without it,' Wood said vehemently.

'I agree but I needed you back here. You'll lose everything if you don't return.'

'Heath is more than capable of delivering in my absence.'

'He is not because he doesn't want to. He's acting like a lovelorn kitten since you left. I can't prove it but he is up to something.'

'What do you mean?'

'I don't trust him. I just can't prove it. I think that he wants you gone for good now and he wants the company.'

Wood asked Christine to express her concerns directly to Heath with him in the room. She agreed and Wood called in Heath. Christine told Heath what Wood had asked her to say and explain to him what her foundation was for the claim. Christine repeated what she had told Wood and she lost the debate.

'Christine,' Wood began. 'You have seriously undermined the trust that exists in this team. You have, without adequate reason, accused two of your colleagues of seriously relenting on our mission. I cannot tolerate this and whilst I should remove you, I have decided instead that you will give me your founder share and sell to me the assets you have acquired whilst working for me. I will buy them at cost.'

Christine agreed and left the room.

Later Wood rang Christine. 'Heath is definitely up to something,' Christine began. 'Like you, I cannot prove it. He is repeatedly in London claiming he is on his own and denying it. I don't trust Smithy at BDO and I don't trust Ron at the ITCD. I have a sniff that the gross profit margin is getting too many people too excited.'

'Do you have suspicions about the investment brokers?' asked Wood.

'What Wilkes?' asked Christine seeking confirmation.

'No. James is too bright. He knows that Manchester United is nothing without Alex Ferguson,' stated Wood.

'Why don't you call for an internal audit?' asked Christine thinking of routes to expose their hidden agendas.

'Heath has too much control. He can hide whatever he wants. He has promised his junior team lucrative careers,' said Wood.

'Tony is on your side,' said Christine believing that Tony could get to the truth and bypass Heath's influence.

'Christine look. I can't give up Europe. Poland is up and running. We are seriously on the way and we can achieve IPO within the five years if not three, maybe four. I need to be there. It will provide the cash *we need. We will be less dependent on other investment sources. Think about it. They are drying up anyway.'*

'Yes, I know, but...' Christine began. Wood interrupted her.

'But Christine I have to do it. As far as Heath is concerned you are disgraced. Your council has no value to me. Keep your eye on him and let me know what he is up to. Watch the others closely, Heath draws their complicity. Heath told me that Scott had asked him for his loyalty and in return he would get his; Scott had asked that he 'didn't cut him out' or something of that ilk.'

'Why did Heath tell you that?'

'I don't know.'

In 2003, Wood first met James Wilkes, an investment broker from Hodmasco Bells with an influential CV in the city, founded from banking and investments. Wood had been looking for investment sources and funding to build his new business. James had advised Wood that he knew of individuals in the city that would support him, potentially to the tune of twenty million pounds. James had advised him not to seek the money.

'In the property industry a simple norm does exist. With guys like you Wood, they will invest in you and surround you with their trusted men. When they have got the details of your idea, they will steal it and do it for themselves.'

'Can I survive this?'

'I don't think you need it. For many years I have sat in front of budding entrepreneurs. It must be hundreds of them. Something tells me you are different. I don't think you need them. Trust yourself.'

Eighteen months later, Wood had his first set of accounts and he emailed them to James. James responded, 'Wow. What a result. We must talk soon. You won't need five years for an IPO.'

When the second set of accounts was released, the improvement was recognised in London. Wood had accompanied Heath to meet Simon Smith, a senior partner at BDO Stoy Hayward who managed the accounts for the Wood Group of Companies. Wood was concerned with Simon's lack of support in opening doors to new networks and Wood decided to ask him for his help. Heath, who had known Simon for several years before he had met Wood, joined the meeting in London. They left the offices on Shakespeare Street and went around the corner to The Globe. Simon bought a round of drinks and they took their seats.

'Tane, I'll be honest. Prior to meeting you I have just come from our board meeting. Matt, a colleague on the board asked me what I had planned later and I told him that I was meeting you. I told him that I was meeting either the biggest pup on the planet, or the biggest account Stoy Hayward will ever have. I thought this when I first met you. You had little insight and control over your company structure but your wealth spoke for itself. Since then I can say that I have never met a man with your vision and determination. The city is talking about you. We know you have been asking for a fund for £200 million. Word gets around when money like that is being asked for. And, I'll tell you that you will get it. Confidence in you is abundant. We have all lost faith in Branson and Stelios. We have all been waiting for someone young and new.'

Heath was quiet but intense. Simon continued.

'We know that you are a working class boy. Your dad died when you were young. We call it the hurt factor, and you have it. We look for vision, and you have it. We look at your financial performance and your accounts are outstanding. In fact what you have achieved is a serious talking point.'

Tears began to form in small pools on the lids of Simon's eyes.

'I am 50 years old. I have a partnership in BDO. I will retire in a few years and my remuneration will leave me with about a million quid. Look at my hands. They call me the marigold boy. I was educated at Eton; I got a degree from Oxford. This is my life and this is my lot. I will never have the chance to get the estates, the assets and the cash that you have. The city is tired of the marigold boys. I never had the chance to lose what you lost in your youth. I didn't get the chance to shape my ambitions like you did. I had it on a plate and now I have to live and end my life knowing that.'

Wood told Heath to dismiss Scott.

'Why?' Heath asked.

'Two reasons. He has become lazy and ineffective. The fear has crippled him and all he does is ask me for money. The guy is costing me over £100,000 a year for sweet FA. Secondly, he enlisted your complicity and you know my views on that.'

'Scott is harmless. He really gives a shit. He is 100% behind the mission in everything he does.'

'I want you to dismiss him on Monday.'

On Monday, Heath told Wood that he had decided to meet Scott at his house on the day before to let him know his fate. Wood knew that Scott was now a serious threat to his business and even more so than when he was employed in it.

The Fiat had been run over by a lorry but Hoary had not been hurt. The police insisted that he go to hospital and his patience was severely tested having waited for over two hours to be seen. A young, very attractive nurse was constantly in and out of the waiting room. She spoke to Hoary to assure him that he would be seen. Her eyes were identical in colour and shape to those of Miranda. As the time drifted by in the waiting room, he recalled the events of his meeting with her at his house.

When Miranda arrived, she had not presented Hoary with her proposal for his forthcoming press campaign. Instead she had taken him by the hand and asked him which room was his favourite in the house. He had told her that it was his morning room and she had followed him to it and asked him to wait there.

When she returned, she was dressed in a black, skin tight body suit and high heeled shoes. The suit exposed her shoulders and the crotch was open. Miranda had sat Hoary down and taken a seat across the room, ten feet away. 'Focus on my eyes,' she had said and drawn her hand into her crotch to arouse herself. As her body moved in pace with the speed of her arousal she repeated this phrase for several minutes until she had reached her fourth orgasm and when she had done so she said to Hoary, 'Now it's your turn.'

In May 2008, Wood emailed Heath with this message.

'I think the game is finally up. If we continue operating we will be overtrading; administration, CVA or insolvency? Have we any money for this?'

That day the Mortgages PLC Group had rescinded on £9.1m of lending. Wood had thirteen mortgage offers from the Group but they 'indicated' their unwillingness to honour the funds. This cost Wood over £1.3m in revenue which he needed to meet the financial demands of historical creditors, debt recall by the ITCD bank and operational costs.

'I have legal counsel ready to press Mortgages PLC for a Class A Action from the 1998 Competitions Act,' Heath told Wood.

'We are wasting our time. I spoke to Rita, head of credit. She pleaded with me asking me not to turn this into another complaint. I don't think we are alone. They haven't got any money to lend. They are bust.'

It was no different for Wood. He had no money to pay his employees and their outrage ensued. He did manage to outsource a number of his contracts and a significant number of his employees found work in these new companies. One of the contracts was given to Helen and Heath went with it.

Wood joined them as a consultant. This became their only outlet and it limped on for nearly three months turning over a marginal profit. But this too began to dwindle and even though Wood and Helen drew no earnings, it soon became impossible to afford the salaries of Heath and the others.

Most of them repeatedly rebuked this state of affairs but they loved their work. They could not foresee that they could turn to any other industry. Heath never asked. He merely took what he received.

Wood opened up a network overseas which included several deals that represented a lucrative profit. Wood knew that it would take time to come to fruition and Heath would become unnerved with the timescale for remuneration. Wood realised that the earnings would only surface after completion of the deal. Heath had never worked outside of the security of a salary. He tried to influence him towards consultancy and share ownership based on a percentage of profit on delivery. The ability to pay a salary was now historical.

Whilst Heath did agree, Wood knew that he was extremely uncomfortable with this and time was not on his side. Heath did stay but one afternoon when Wood returned to the office, having been away for a week, the premises were locked and no employees were at their desks.

Heath had convinced the personnel that Wood's intentions were selfish and that no remuneration would ever materialise. On the completion of the first deal overseas, Heath had convinced the accounts clerk, Tony that he must pay him his percentage of the profit that was due. Tony had been reticent but Heath had suggested that Wood had no intention to pay the creditors either. Tony was soon aligned when Heath instructed him to bring all the creditors up to date regardless of the terms of payment outlined in their invoices.

'Pay all the staff in advance as well,' Heath requested to Tony, 'Including yourself.'

Other staff had been angry with this move by Heath initially but Heath convinced them that they could also walk away with 10% of the profit.

'But Tane didn't agree 10%.'

'He did with me and Tony has raised the invoice.'

On the day of the completion of the first deal, Tony transferred the profits to the relevant employees and creditors as Heath had instructed. He telephoned Heath to confirm that he had carried out what he had asked him to do.

'Well done; now Tane can stick his job up his arse.'

'What do you mean?'

'I'm not coming back. I've convinced the others that we don't need Tane. We have decided to go it alone. We've spoken to the guys overseas and they think Tane is a prick too. They'd prefer to work with me.'

Tony knew that Wood was due back after 1pm. He told the staff that had remained, to take the afternoon off. Tony hastily wrote out a two line resignation letter and locked the office behind him.

After Heath put the phone down to Tony he called Scott.

'Done it mate,' said Heath.

'Is he dead?' asked Scott.

'He's fucked. Most have resigned and I guess that Tony has run out of the door as quick as he can. The rest of the staff will leave.'

'How is the fear?' asked Scott.

'Rife,' confirmed Heath.

'Excellent. And the network overseas?'

'All ours. Victor doesn't give a toss about the investors. He just wants the commission. He despised Wood's ideas to protect the investors.'

'Good. Do we need Vic?' asked Scott.

'For now. Be patient. Let's get the cash cow firmly established first.'

'And Tony?' asked Scott.

'He can do the donkey work for us abroad. He's harmless.'

'Expensive,' exclaimed Scott.

'We need him for now. Anyway how is Silver Pieces Homes today? Have ITCD extended the loan? We need the £30 million,' said Heath conscious that Scott had just rifled off a barrel load of questions.

'Ron has still not confirmed but he does need the accounts from BDO. Simon said he will have them by the end of the week and they will look fantastic. You need to issue their share certificates,' said Scott adamantly.

'I can't until they resign,' Heath fired back.

'Do it tonight. Just don't register them at Companies House,' said Scott forthrightly.

'Good point,' said Heath. He hadn't thought of that. 'And how are the others?' he asked.

'Doing well. They'll be delighted when they hear about Tane. You are confident he's buggered?' said Scott thoughtfully. He knew Wood was very resilient. It would take an atomic bomb to stop him. A jail sentence would do it.

'How can he come back from this? Remember, he's also contracted to that exchange on the Bradshore development. He'll never get the money for that. They'll sue him for £500k.'

'What was his final tax bill?' asked Scott probing deeper.

'£185k,' said Heath.

'Did Tony spend all the profit?'

'More or less,' confirmed Heath.

'He's fucked. Well done mate,' said Scott confidently.

Wood and Helen had sat in the empty office until six in the evening. The exit of their employees had dawned slowly and painfully as time had lapsed. They had felt embarrassed for each other.

'Are you ok?' Wood asked Helen.

'I think so. You?' she asked.

'I've been here before. I only need *you*,' said Wood taking her hand.

Wood had realised earlier why the office was empty. He had found an email in Heath's bin that had been screwed up. It explained everything and after reading it, he was going to show it to Helen. He had become distracted and put it in his pocket. He would show Helen later, when he remembered. For the present he knew that his providence would ensue. He was now to learn exactly how much he did trust himself.

When they left, Helen locked the door and read – for the last time – the quote she had posted below her company name. "Security is mostly a superstition. It does not exist in nature, nor do the children of men experience it. Avoiding danger is no safer than outright exposure. Life is either a daring adventure or nothing."

For Wood this latest development had not concerned him. 'This time,' he thought, '30 pieces of silver would not result in a forsaken crucifixion'. Instead, this disruptive tsunami would conform to the closure statements that Wood had proclaimed in his conference speech two years earlier and the words that had drifted past the ears of the audience in dismissal, fear or incredulity.

Could it be that mankind had begun to learn to behave? Could it be that the wars that initially raged via our armies on the seas and the fields of our lands and had later moved to the commercial playing fields of influential men and women, would finally dissolve? Could it be that unification and mission would arrive and the new influence would be the drive to gain universal acceptance?

'Now,' thought Wood. 'We can get on with the task of finding God.'

The challenge was, as the cash flows of the commercial world were running out of time, so were Wood and Hoary. But Wood now had the advantage. He no longer had anything else to do or anywhere else to go.

On the twenty first century killing fields, he had been forsaken. The commercial boys and girls had crucified him. The crucifixion was still in full swing. They would pursue him and destroy him and they would not stop until pity had been shown.

But tomorrow he would awake. He would be free to act. After two thousand years, Christ had made the world become the place it had to become.

'You never told me what Scott did when you asked him for a shag,' said Helen as they got into the car.

'Not a lot really. He sat in the chair mumbling for a moment, then he ran out of the room.'

'Did he turn up for work the next day?'

'Of course he did. He acted as though nothing had happened.'

Miranda repeated her words to Hoary as she leant down on all fours and crawled toward him, 'Now it's your turn. What would you like me to do?' she said and followed her words with the gentle snarl of a dog.

Hoary was not overly anxious with Miranda's surprising actions. He asked Miranda to get to her feet and get dressed.

Miranda had not been able to conceal her embarrassment or her surprise. She knew she was a very attractive woman. She had been certain that she could exercise her sexual demons with significant passion at the hands of the powerful man of influence who sat before her. Miranda had risen to her feet.

'Are you gay?' she asked.

'No,' replied Hoary standing up. 'I love my wife and my children.'

'So, you can still have me,' she insisted looking surprised.

'No, Miranda, I cannot,' said Hoary assertively and softly.

Miranda hesitated for a moment, smiled at Hoary and then turned to leave the room and get dressed. 'I suppose I'm sacked,' she said.

'Why should I want to do that?' asked Hoary.

'I've compromised you,' she said.

'No you haven't. I need you more than ever now.'

'Why?'

'Because I can trust you now. You are excellent at PR and I love what you do. Now I love you more.'

Hoary knew that if he had accepted Miranda's proposition he would have compromised himself and not Miranda. He loved, more than anything, his time with his wife and their two children. He also knew that Miranda was extremely seductive and sexy and he had been aroused by her actions – more than he had experienced for a number of years – but he knew that he had felt nothing more than arousal.

When Miranda left, he returned to his favourite seat in the morning room. As he thumbed the pages of his amulet, 'The Step,' he turned to the final page and he read the words that had changed his life forever.

From his house on the hill, Wood could look out over the landscape. There were no large trees obscuring the view and before him it seemed that the southern hemisphere was waiting for him. He could decide what it all meant. He could decide why there were stars in the sky, why the night was black, why clouds floated.

As the demise of Wood's financial world engulfed him, his ex-partner, Karen and his children vacated their Manor house and rented accommodation some miles away. Karen found a new partner and finally settled down in a loving relationship. She was able to find peace with herself with him. Her ambition to be a good mother became a reality as her four children grew up in the loving household that she gave them and her new partner adored them. Wood and Karen stayed good friends afterwards and she forgave him for his actions. They both learned that the pursuit of their ambitions had meant more to each of them than their love for each other.

Wood lived for a short while in one of the houses owned by his company under his funding source from ITCD. However, they had repossessed this from him and he had managed to find a small lodge on the grounds of a derelict mansion. The run down shack sufficed for now.

In the landscape, the sheep, barely visible, were not asleep but the farm yards and the fields were ripe with crops and bare with movement. Beyond the fields and the hedgerows that man had planted, wriggled the roads and the motorways. Wood could see the A5 and the M1. He knew, as he now planned for himself, that England's green and pleasant lands were soon to be replaced with the landscape of America. He thought of this only with trepidation. For now, as he watched the hemisphere ahead of him, the magnitude of the brightly lit M1 dominating his view, four miles in the distance, sweeping from a to b, its girth dropping off at both sides of the distance he could see, he wondered whether man had done anything more than light up the world with light bulbs.

His eyes moved from the landscape to the sky. The cloudless sky glowed with the stars that intrigued his endless list of unanswered questions. He recalled the words of his colleague from university. A bright, witty, hidden homosexual who had once said, 'all the world is upside down and all the people live in the ground'.

Today, Wood knew that mankind was about to replace the light bulbs and he was about to embark on America. The country they called *the land of opportunity*. A place, Wood felt, where the arguments would rage from the leagues of the cats and dogs to the outrage of the lions and the tigers. A place he needed to be. This time, he knew, the people would own the resurrection and they would not need the spectacle of mystery and faith to see it.

After Wood and Helen had locked up their office and left the emptiness of their discovery, Wood had pulled out the page he had found in Heath's bin. The details on the top of the page indicated that its contents were an email Jessie had sent to her sister, Christine last year. Tony had written on it; 'Heath I found this on the main frame server.'

Wood gave it to Helen to read.

> *'Tane knows it. He has known it all along. You can't stop him. You may be playing with fire.*
> *I have measured his personality and his behaviour and in any normal distribution he clearly sits in the*

extreme .001%. His dominance has conquered all four types. He is equally sensitive/robust/individual/social. It's in his DNA.

I have never seen anybody work so efficiently and effectively in the left hand box, no matter how long he stays there. He even copes with sub zero left hand box and he can work his way out of there when everyone else would give up and accept defeat. You won't destroy him. He is too driven. He is excessively resilient.

Chris, this all points to vision. He has it. I fear he has more. A lot more.

He knows of your plans with Heath and the others and it doesn't matter to him. He will let you have the company but I fear that his politics are different. I don't think anybody can get close or fathom what he is up to. Even if you did, I don't think he could tell you. He trusts himself too much.

I sense that this time you may be playing with Christ. Or even God.

PART SEVEN

LIFE, THE UNIVERSE AND EVERYTHING

THE BALLERINA SPARKLE

New York, 21st December 2019

Wood undressed before he jumped. He did not want people to have to undress his body. When he awoke from his fall, he could not see the hole in the red canopy of Martello's restaurant. The scene had changed markedly now he was dead.

Before him, stood the beauty of the graceful ballerina; naked and bewildered. Her eyes were widened by the mystery of the sights around her and her unfamiliarity with them. She rose to her feet, slowly, as though she was the unfolding birth of a butterfly spreading its wings as it broke free from the cocoon.

For moments she stood, moving in small actions, looking for reference and finding nothing. Her lips curled upwards to her eyes and as they opened, her silent smile filled her cheeks as though an ecstatic cry of excitement had broken free.

She turned and saw Wood and her smile calmed as she pursed her lips and opened her eyes widely to him. Her arms folded gently about her shoulders and her left knee slowly stroked the inside of her right thigh.

'You saved me,' she said. Her words were soft, sensuous and harmonious. She seemed to frown for a second and her chin lowered towards her right shoulder. Wood knew that her thoughts were deep in mystery as her senses fused with her mind. Her head straightened and rose high and she walked towards him. When she reached Wood she raised both of her hands and held his face in her palms. Her physical beauty was astounding. She looked deep into his eyes and said, 'I love you.'

Wood watched her as she stood before him. His eyes followed hers and she sensed that he loved her too. Even before he said it, she knew that his love for her was purely the embrace of kinship; the love for a fellow man.

'I love you,' said Wood. The ballerina held up her hands to take his and she sensed a passion raging within him that distracted him from her. How free she now felt to understand his thoughts and his desires.

'Is she special?' she said joyfully.

Wood smiled as she spoke. How he wanted to share his happiness. 'She always has been. From the moment I saw her she defined me. Now, I need to marry her.'

'You will,' she said. 'You must,' excitedly. 'Is this the world that now stands before me?' She lightly hopped as she spoke, rolling her head back to view the sky.

'Yes, if you choose it to be,' said Wood gently. The ballerina folded her arms around his neck and she hugged him. 'You deserve her,' she said, moving her head from his shoulders to see his eyes. Wood sensed that she was searching his mind for answers, and then she smiled and took hold of his hands again. 'Thank you. You saved me. You released me from damaged men,' she said.

'You chose to save yourself,' said Wood calmly, holding her gaze.

'I jumped with you. I had to; I had to escape men who always confused their desires,' she said aware that her language seemed different and lucid. The influence of her new environment puzzled her as she spoke.

'Did they care for you?' asked Wood.

'Sometimes but often not,' said the ballerina and she noticed Wood's frown suggesting he was challenging her words. 'They were carnal and they were gentle. But they were unaware that the two are different. I wanted to be loved. I wanted to be repaired from my damages and they just seemed to be killing me,' she said confused.

'You chose to be killed,' said Wood softly and assertively.

'They just wanted to screw me,' she exclaimed, moving her face a little further away so that she could read his expression.

'You let them. You wanted them to.'

'I didn't,' she said, anxiously. Wood let the silence hold for a few moments and the ballerina girl caught her thoughts. She seemed to think again and she said, 'Why?'

'Your damage had killed you. You had lost the trust in yourself to choose,' said Wood as she lowered her eyes from his to think.

'How?' she asked looking puzzled.

'You were scared; embroiled in the Armageddon,' Wood began, speaking assuredly. 'You chose to believe it. Armageddon is not the physical destruction of our lives. It is the awakening from our fears and our commitment to a wonderful new age – the truth of our behavioural and real political advantage.'

'I don't understand,' she said searching his eyes again, shaking her head gently and slowly.

'God is our purpose. We are his design, in his perfect image. We have to find Him and the only way we will is to recognise our truth.'

She looked again into his eyes, quizzically until she could identify with his thoughts. She pondered for several moments and her expression wrote many tales about what she was thinking. Her face seemed to fix for a moment as though the cassette tape had stopped. Her eyes opened widely as she guessed what hid in his mind.

'We care,' she said.

'Absolutely,' Wood began and he smiled as widely – back to her – as she did to him. 'We are driven to care. It is our genetic gearing, the king of all DNA. We are blessed with the greatest energy force that exists.'

She smiled and rolled her head slowly around her shoulders as she leant back, keeping her hands gripped around his neck for support.

'It's right in front of our eyes,' she sang the words. 'Our passion is electric,' she said and hesitated, thoughtfully. 'Why did I always find innocence so attractive – we all do?'

'The undamaged person is our dream. It is who we crave to be – it is God.' Wood looked at her and took her hands in his. 'I must go. I have to.'

'What do I do? Where do I go?' she said looking momentarily astray.

'Choose. Choose whatever you want,' said Wood and turned to leave. The ballerina girl was lost in her thoughts, reflecting on what Wood had told her but as she saw him walk away she was compelled to ask him.

'You are the one, aren't you?' she asked as she cocked her head slightly at looked knowingly at him.

'Yes, I am,' said Wood confidently.

'How do you know?' she asked puzzled. She smiled warmly.

'That's the wrong question. I made my choice and I gave my commitment. What were we waiting for? The physical appearance of the second coming?' Wood looked into her eyes and opened his palms out either side of his body, toward her. As he walked away from her, backwards, he said, 'Why?'

At the door of his apartment, Wood asked the two men from the concierge desk to leave. He said that he would speak to his girlfriend.

'But you're dead,' said the startled man.

'Call the police,' said the other man and they both ran down the corridor to the lift. When the door opened, Helen appeared and she looked afraid – both her hands were clasped upon her chest.

' Baby?' she said, confused and motionless. She stood by the door blocking the entrance completely unaware that she was.

'Yes, my love,' replied Wood and he gestured to be allowed through. Helen stepped back slowly and he entered the apartment.

'Take this,' he said giving her a small wooden box.

'What is it?' she asked taking it from him. She remained confused and motionless.

'DNA samples,' said Wood lifting the lid as it sat in her hands. Helen saw a series of test tubes inside.

'What for?' asked Helen. She knew what they were for but she was confused by the moment. She lowered the lid and closed the box.

'For you and me,' answered Wood looking Helen in the eyes and placing his hands over hers which cupped the box.

'How do you mean?' asked Helen. She had spoken about this possibility with him previously. They had agreed that if either of them was to die, the other would preserve samples of both of their DNA.

'I made the right choice. I am free. My freedom is absolute,' said Wood compassionately.

'Tane?' exclaimed Helen. She knew this day would come and now it was here she feared it far less than she had imagined. She felt pity for Wood and pity for herself.

'There is nothing to fear. I truly lived. What happens after I go is hugely important. I must be with you again. I could never live without you. But I can't influence it any more than I already have.'

'Tane? You're frightening me,' said Helen. Her mind was being challenged by a hundred thoughts and a thousand emotions.

'No I'm not. You are frightening yourself,' said Wood calmly. He squeezed her hands gently and smiled into her eyes.

'What has happened? Why are you naked?' she asked. She knew what had happened. She was searching for reason.

'I chose to jump,' said Wood directly.

'Baby?' she said confused. Tears began to roll down her face as she looked at him.

'No one else ever called me baby,' he said smiling. 'Listen. I want to come back here in ten thousand years time. I am hated here now and the hatred will get worse. But I dream of coming back and seeing what the world has become. I know we will laugh with the joy of our success,' he said shaking her hands warmly in his grasp.

'They don't hate you,' said Helen. Her tears stopped.

'Maybe. I'm not convinced. But I want to come back. Keep the samples. Throw them in the glaciers in the arctic. Man will find them and science will advance. They will get me back. I want the year 10,021. Tell them,' said Wood adamantly. He moved closer to her and put his arms around her. 'I want nothing if it is not with you. Make sure you do the same.'

'Why?' she asked moving slightly apart from him to see his eyes.

'I love you. I have no doubt. You are the one. When I first saw you I saw the most beautiful person ever. I wasn't alone. We all did. You are the undamaged woman. I saw Eve before she ate the apple,' he said and he kissed her gently on the lips. 'You crystallised my choice. I was never more certain about anything in my whole life. I had to be with you. You made everything come into focus. It all suddenly seemed so easy.'

'How?' asked Helen apprehensively.

'From that moment I knew what I had to do to sort the whole mess out. I was never certain of the future. I was very certain that I had to trust myself.' Helen raised her hands to his chest and lay them on there. 'I did,' he said.

'I love you,' said Helen passionately. 'Madly.'

'I love you. Every day I look at you and your beauty astounds me. It always will. You are the truth. Absolutely – undamaged man – you are the future that we dream of,' said Wood holding her. His arms melted into her and she loved the warmth.

'Marry me first?' she asked excitedly.

'Promise to meet in 10,021?' he said raising his tone to match hers.

'I will,' she said as her smile widened across her mouth.

'I do,' he said lovingly, reciprocating her smile.

'In church?'

'I think that the tunes of their bells will begin to fade. You are not mine 'till death do us part'. You are mine for eternity.'

Hoary was late and he did not like being late. He was due to meet Michael in his apartment in Little Venice in London and as he raced up the steps he rummaged in his pocket to find his key. Michael had sounded exasperated on the phone. Michael was never that anxious.

At the door he noticed it was open and this confused him for a moment. His wife had a key, but she was in Paris for the week. Hoary heard movement and he opened the door cautiously. He saw the dark shadow of a man dart across the hallway past the large classical pillar towards the kitchen.

As he entered, he moved slowly down the hallway and the figure of the man darted out of the kitchen and saw Hoary and stopped. It was Michael. His hands were held slightly away from his body, down by his side and they were covered in blood.

'What the...' began Hoary confused.

'Shut up Trevor. I had to,' said Michael vehemently, who carried on his journey into the living room. Hoary followed him and saw blood on his sofa and his coffee table – small pools and large splashes. As Hoary moved further into the room he looked upon the limp body of Brendan, lifeless on the floor, lying awkwardly and bleeding from his head.

'What...' said Michael shocked and stunned.

'Look,' said Michael, holding up a piece of paper and showing it to Hoary. 'He was going to Johnston with the whole fucking story. The Express had paid him,' Michael's face shone with loud exclamation but the dark shadow cast by the drapes blotted out his face from Hoary's view.

'What...How...' said Hoary trying to make sense out of what he was seeing.

'Oh Trevor, for fuck's sake. Pull yourself together. I need to sort this mess out. Help me,' said Michael bending over Brendan's dull body.

'Help you. What have you done?' Hoary opened his palms to the scene that stretched out before him. His face was contorted and his anger was already beginning to rise. 'What the hell have you done?'

Miranda had let herself in, seeing that the door was open and when she had heard the voices she had naturally made her way into the lounge accompanying her journey with the words, 'Hello, it's me.' As she entered the lounge and witnessed the carnage she put a hand over her mouth and stood speechless.

'What the hell have you done?' Hoary repeated. 'Is he dead?'

'Yes he is dead. I had no choice, he was going to expose you,' said Michael busying himself with the blood pools and a cloth.

'And what in hell's name gave you the right to silence him?' shouted Hoary.

'Trevor he was going to the press. Everything...'

'So fucking what. That doesn't mean you can kill him,' Hoary interrupted putting his hands in his hair and grabbing fistfuls.

'Trevor, don't pull that one on me. I had no choice,' Michael said shaking his head as he looked at Hoary.

'Yes you did. You can't kill people,' said Hoary assertively.

'For fuck's sake Trevor. What was all this about. I couldn't let him destroy everything,' said Michael adamantly.

'He couldn't have done that. Only I can do that.'

'Don't be so naive. He was going to expose your plan, the B20, your politics,' dismissed Michael.

'And these are my politics? Heaven forgive me.' Hoary sank slowly towards his armchair. He was shocked, confused and broken. 'Is this what I chose?'

'You always knew the score,' said Michael. 'Don't come the almighty with me,' said Michael contorting his face as his upset hit him.

'This is not what I wanted,' said Hoary vehemently. 'This was what I was trying to stop,' exclaimed Hoary. His eyes were wide open looking at Michael.

'Bollocks,' said Michael. 'A pipe dream. Who the hell do you think did all the posturing. It was me, it always has been. That Ryder guy, in New York, who asked too many questions. Who do you think sorted that fucking mess out?'

Hoary held his hands in his head and he began to weep. He had played the political agendas and the spheres of influence of modern day. Before him lay the result. The years of his testimony to his ambitions tumbled about his feet in a moment of desperate realisation. He knew that he only had himself to blame and now he had nowhere to go.

Michael continued busily. He stopped for a moment and saw the pathetic frame of Hoary. For a second he pondered as he looked at his desolate friend. 'Do you really think that anybody would have listened to you?' Michael asked pitifully, continuously striking his hands together as though he was cleaning the mess from them. 'Nonsense,' he continued. 'They would have simply beckoned to your power. That's all they know.'

Miranda composed herself from her shock and wiped the tears from her eyes. She turned to leave the room and said, 'Leave me well out of this mess.' As she walked into the hallway, she threw her file into the bin and recognised that the exposure of Hoary's B20 Chairmanship and the announcement of his new world currency were worth nothing more than the items it now accompanied.

LET THERE BE LIGHT

14 Billion Years Ago & Forever

'How long have we got?' asked Dace desperately.

'I don't know. Minutes, maybe ten.' George answered anxiously.

Abraham had seen this coming and so had Mohammed but the force and speed of its delivery surprised them all. The universe was nearing its ultimate extinction and George, Oliver and David were running out of time to save themselves.

'What's the carbon design?' George asked Oliver looking over his shoulder from his busy, cluttered workstation. The formula to create a new universe and a brilliant life form - that would eventually find them - was minutes away from completion. If they failed, nothing would ever exist again.

'It's in the Bio lab. I'll…' Oliver answered and turned to run and get it.

'Forget it. The labs gone,' said Dace quickly.

Almost everything had gone. Nothing was left now, at least barely any life except George, Olivier and Dace and they were rapidly running out of time. The bubble had burst and the three men were minutes away from being its latest victims.

'Use Homo sapiens. It's by far the best,' Dace said assertively.

'They were too dismissive. We'll never get out of here,' shouted George.

'I'll implant our DNA. They can evolve,' said Oliver thinking of the solution. The speed of their thoughts was being furiously fuelled by their adrenalin.

'Try molecular mutation,' said Dace.

'You can't. Mutation results in death. They'll have less than 200 years at best. They'll get disillusioned,' said Oliver swiping a hand across his forehead to remove the sweat.

'You're forgetting,' Dace asserted, 'that DNA has 100,000 year life cycles. The death will only be organic. Anyway, we can bring them all back. You can schedule the DNA in silent active mode anyway,' he explained.

'Silent and active?' asked George.

'Yes. Mohammad worked out the design. You can programme it now,' said Dace, racing his eyes across the screens in front of him.

'But why silent *and* active?' asked George puzzled.

'They can still communicate if they can act,' said Dace impatiently.

'How?' asked George concerned.

'DNA is a life source, the most resilient ever; the most persistent too. It always finds a way,' answered Dace. They were all talking very quickly. The adrenalin made their speech clear.

'Guys. The implosion will have us in two minutes. Move,' shouted Oliver frantically casting his eyes to those of his two colleagues.

'They must have choice,' George said to Oliver. His hands moved about his work with the speed of lightning strikes.

'Absolutely; I've done it. Responsibility code?' asked Oliver feverishly. The sweat was pouring from his forehead into his eyes.

'Make it *Personal*. Also, they need to be motivated; they must have love. They must care if we're ever to be found,' demanded George furiously. 'It's the key to everything.'

'George I'm nearly done. Worry about Dace,' demanded Oliver.

George turned to Dace and swivelled round on his seat to an adjacent work station. 'Evolution timescale?' he asked Dace, swiftly moving his fingers across the keys in front of him.

'13 to 14 billion years,' confirmed Dace.

'You'll need to prompt. They can be very dismissive.'

'Can we design a prompt?' asked Dace.

'Yes, Langston added the component last year,' asserted George.

'When?'

'Just before he left us,' confirmed George. The noise about them was becoming increasingly deafening and their voices got louder to compensate.

'No. When can I prompt?' demanded Dace.

'Whenever you want to,' shouted George.

'Life will barely be around for the first 13 billion years.'

'From then,' George fired back.

'Damn. The prompt can't programme that far,' said Dace searching frantically across the screens.

'Earlier then,' George said assertively.

'No point. I'll tell you what I can do though,' said Dace seeing the solution on his screen. 'Oliver, add psychosis to the strains of DNA. We can build heroes and visionaries.'

'I already have,' confirmed Oliver.

'Platforms?' George asked Dace, viewing solar systems and mass formations. He knew he would need consolidated spherical land structures for life to inhabit. Dace didn't answer him. He was distracted. George made the decision. He didn't have time to ponder.

'I will need a backdrop. They'll have to be territorial; I'll need food chains. Olly, will their DNA include manifestations of fear, risk, survival and aggression?' George asked. He looked at Oliver who caught his eye.

'I've had to,' said Oliver adamantly.

'The suffering will be abhorrent,' stated George.

'Wow. I can prompt via probability. Choice can be delivered via trust. I'm running 21 million entries,' Dace exclaimed excitedly. Finally the programme was being completed and they all knew that they only had a few seconds remaining.

'What's your habitation rate?' asked George seeking confirmation.

'Twenty one million. They are concurrent. They'll find us,' said Dace confidently.

'Capacity?' asked George.

'Infinite and expansive,' said Dace.

'Brilliant. When did we design that?' asked Oliver

'Langston. Although, the programme is throwing out contradictions, imperfections…whatever you want to call them,' said Dace feverishly checking his data.

'Like what?' asked George concerned. George rushed over to view Dace's data.

'Gravity, particle size and matter to name a few,' said Dace. His hands moved so quickly it seemed impossible that they had time to do anything.

'Will the sapiens work it out?' asked George probing, concerned with the data he was seeing.

'Probability accounts for absurdity and psychosis,' said Oliver assuredly.

'That'll reinforce the DNA. Good. Just do it,' said Dace confident the design would definitely work.

'This design will see them suffer,' said George reservedly looking at Dace.

'We're all in for a very painful ride until they find us,' said Dace definitively.

'Guys finish it now. We must go,' Oliver said recognising that they had seconds left. He darted up from his station. 'We must go now.'

Dace completed the probability code and merged it with Oliver's DNA programming to create a simple chemical formula.

'Is it small enough?' George asked Dace.

'Is the formula complete?' asked Oliver.

'It has to be,' said Dace; he thumbed the trigger and released the formula.

'How big will it be?' asked Oliver.

Dace grabbed the pair and threw them into their ice chamber. 'We need to follow it now. We'll soon find out,' said Dace frantically. The implosion landed. The trigger had jammed but the implosion had provided the force to release the formula and jettison George, Oliver and Dace with it moments later. 'Let there be light,' screamed Dace as he jumped with his fellow scientists.

The bang had been big. Probably the biggest yet and the trio had produced the most advanced stage ever designed and certainly a better universe than their ancestry.

When Dace awoke from the bang he was alone. He didn't know what had happened to George and Oliver and he knew that it would be a very long time until he did. But this did not concern him; their DNA strain was good for 14.5 billion years before it began to fade and later decay and they had only been around for nearly a billion years. They had time on their side. Their children, the golden boys and girls; the Homo sapiens; the DNA strain mutated by George, Oliver and Dace – would find them. Wouldn't they?

Dace looked about him at the magnificent, colossal space that would now be his new home for many, many centuries to come. He decided to etch a new name for his abode into the ice block walls. He wrote the word *Cibeuce* beautifully, colourfully and graffiti style. He decided he would use this style of anagram as his new code.

He checked the status of his arrival into the new universe. He knew that his chamber would survive because ice cubes never melt in cryogenic particle matter.

Helen went into her bedroom and wept inconsolably after Wood had left. It was sometime before she noticed that he had placed a note for her on the pillow.

'*I love you. You are the most beautiful woman to have lived – you are Eve before the damage – the most beautiful thing there is.*

We all live on.

Science is yet to discriminate between organic life and DNA. You can have all your loved ones back when you choose to. DNA can communicate – we deny this because we only understand organic life with a voice emanating from a vocal cord. The codes are all about you and they are real. They are not mystical absurdity. When the scientists engage this absurdity, they will discover the potential is in our DNA. This will take many years before it is discovered.

Love is all around you and everybody. It is the most powerful experience of our lives because it is the most powerful energy in the universe. When we truly learn to accept who we are – the proponent of this energy, the damage will stop. You cannot bottle this energy – this is not a physical embodiment. This is our political and behavioural truth and when we see it and harness it the impact will take us to new worlds and new dimensions.

Everybody that has ever lived is waiting for us. They are waiting to be found. They are waiting for the energy of love to harness their existence.

Think of a universe pre-eminent with this energy. There could be no threat and no extinction event because no energy has greater power. Love conquers everything – literally – and when we find God, he will show us how. We will all be saved – everybody who has

ever lived. The DNA consciousness never dies, it just
moves to another level of awareness and until God is
found, it is waiting, patiently, frustrated in the place we
call hell.'

In 1988, an undergraduate was working on his thesis for the final assessment of his degree in Psychology and Mathematics. The project concerned the testing of our Intuitive Judgements of Statistical Power.

Intrinsic to the significance of his findings was the creation of a new and substantially advanced measurement of probability. This was aided by the purchase of a new, highly advanced computer with a state of the art superior software programme – the Apple Macintosh.

Prior to this software, statistical programmes had to be written by the researchers themselves and this could take expertise and time – a daunting task, given the best specialists in the field.

Under his supervision, technicians built the probability programme and this undergraduate completed his thesis. This programme was universally incorporated by scientists to substantially move forward research and its measurements with increased speed. It was a massive leap forward for all concerned and its simple bi-modal mechanism allowed probability to go further than it had before. Far enough for NASA scientists to finally stabilise their ventures into space with the Shuttle launches.

The unwitting undergraduate, Tane Wood learned of his endeavours and their impact many years later. In the final year of his degree, for the first time in his life, he had decided to put all his efforts into his academic work. All his actions that year resulted from the absolute commitment he gave. The results that he achieved and the significance of these results may, some argue, belong to the fortitude of providence. It still remains that the choice was exercised by him; his first key lesson in learning to trust himself.

In the final analysis, his work gave providence to political will. He had discovered a solution to get man into space and into the place where we could discover unlimited resources – *in a world full of sand, you do not have to ask for the beach* – and our political advantage.

Scientists are searching for information about the most basic particles of nature, which may provide clues to how the universe was created. The Soudan Underground Laboratory in Minnesota is the location of the Cryogenic Dark Matter Search (CDMS) II experiment. This $16 million project looks for particles called WIMPS: Weakly Interacting Massive Particles which are extremely difficult to detect.

CDMS II searches for WIMPS that were produced in particle collisions that took place just moments after the big bang. Scientists think WIMPS could be one type of the so called dark matter that makes up most of the matter in the universe today. Based on astronomical evidence from the observations of stars and galaxies, these scientists think that most of the dark matter in the universe cannot be seen directly in telescopes. Instead, it must be observed indirectly through its gravitational pull on objects that we can see.

Detecting WIMPS is challenging because movements are weak and they travel at $1/1,000^{th}$ of the speed of light. Because they move so slowly, scientists use devices that detect extremely small amounts of energy. These devices are called cryogenic detectors because they are very cold and must be kept in refrigerators cooled with liquid helium.

Visitors to the Soudan Laboratory ask many questions about why this experiment is conducted. Scientists argue that as our knowledge advances future generations will lead healthier, more efficient and more productive lives.

And they are absolutely right. Like Wood, like us all, we want that and a whole lot more; we need the scribe called 'Perfect Balance', the final analysis of mankind.

FUSE AND EMBROILED

The Year 10,021

'What was health?' asked Wood, reading the subject title from one of the historical archives.

'I don't know. I never went that far back in history,' said Kristie. 'I know they were confused between organic form and DNA. Apart from that,' Kristie sang her words. 'I haven't got a clue.'

'Sorry, I was speaking aloud,' Wood's body jerked several times as he sat in his seat. 'I've done it again,' he said, looking to his midriff and seeing the sperm drip from the end of his penis.

'You'll get used to it,' said Kristie. 'You should be desensitised very soon.' Kristie laughed, 'It is quite normal in the people we bring back.'

'Why?' asked Wood.

'You're not used to an undamaged world – it's only a physiological response.'

'Everything is so stunning,' said Wood. He remembered the moment he had woken and seen his mother and father and his uncle and auntie. He had been engulfed by his the confusion of his environment. Before his eyes had adjusted to the light, they had been blinded by his tears.

He had hugged each of them, falling with them to the ground, his arms trying desperately to capture all of them together, drawing them into one huddle as his breath gasped with the overwhelming joy of his vision. 'You are a son to be proud of,' his mother said and she had kissed his cheek and hugged him tightly. Wood had never felt the embrace of his mother be that warm.

'It really is the most beautiful thing,' Kristie held up a cushion to her chest and folded her arms around it as she gazed across the landscape with Wood. 'I am truly honoured.'

'Why?' asked Wood.

'I'm in the company of the great man,' she said looking at Wood.

'Who?'

'Stop being so coy,' said Kristie, swiping at Wood with the cushion. They both laughed and when Wood looked out again, across the horizon, he said, 'Is that people?'

'Where?' asked Kristie.

'Over there,' said Wood, pointing to the sky.

'Yes,' she said pondering, wishing she was out there.

'Are they flying?' asked Wood.

'Yes?'

'How?' he asked.

'How...' Kristie said looking confused. 'They chose to.' Kristie frowned as she looked at Wood. She raised her voice into playful song and said, 'I'm done anyway. I must be off.' As she left the room she peered down the hallway and then poked her head back around the doorway. 'We have a wonderful surprise for you. Any moment I think.' Kristie smiled widely and then she left.

Wood looked out across the lands and hardly recognised the view. For minutes he wondered what the difference was and it intrigued him, not knowing. Fields and trees, shrubs and bushes were abundant and he could recognise that the species were not as he remembered. He sensed an absence in his view that he was not used to. As his gaze traced across the scene, he became aware that there were no hedges, no roadways, no buildings and no walls. 'No boundaries or territories,' he said out loud as the realisation dawned. He looked about him in his closer vicinity and wondered where he was and what he was standing in. There were no buildings anywhere to be seen.

'Ah hah,' said a voice. A man entered the room and stepped towards Wood. 'I see you're pondering the world that you created. I am very pleased to meet you.' He stopped beside Wood and stood looking at the view with him. 'Isn't it magnificent? I've only seen the film footage but I guess this is a far cry from what you remember.'

'That's an understatement. I've only just now stopped ejaculating over it. Literally,' Wood looked to his midriff.

'That's quite normal. I wouldn't worry. Has it stopped now?'

'Yes, I think so,' said Wood reservedly.

'Good. We have a wonderful surprise for you and we wouldn't want anything spoiling your joy.' The man looked at Wood with his hands held behind his back, smiling. 'It is truly awesome to see you. None of us can comprehend how you did it, in your time. How did you survive the damage?'

'Damage?' asked Wood puzzled.

'The unbalanced external id that infiltrated the people of your time.'

'They didn't even know it existed,' Wood said remembering the debate.

'We guessed. You are truly remarkable,' said the man. His eyes were smiling as widely as his mouth.

'Thank you. I think that I just trusted myself,' said Wood thoughtfully.

'Trusted what?' asked the man intrigued.

'I always felt that there was value in everybody. I knew I could forgive them no matter what they did; no matter how bad they were deemed to be. The world seemed to be governed by a voice that I didn't recognise and most everyone else seemed to,' said Wood. The man reflected on what Wood had said. He asked, 'Were you alive when they had the revenge centres?'

'Revenge centres?' inquired Wood.

'I think they called them prison cells?' he clarified.

'Yes I was,' said Wood.

'How could a species do that to themselves?' said the man frowning.

'They knew no different. They weren't geared to action and taking responsibility for it. They merely projected blame.'

'But Dace had told them of Eve.' The man hesitated and flung his arms in the air. 'I guess it is all too easy for me to say this now.'

'No, it's ok. They just didn't realise that the men in power were the natural born killers – they wrote the rule books. They were unaware of who they truly were. They even wrote books to glorify our mere instincts and denounce any purpose. The greatest energy force in the universe was lying dormant behind the great foundations and pillars of the empires they built.'

'How?' asked the man confused.

'They were focused on the internal id. They could stay invisible and hide. Everyone did it so...' Wood shrugged his shoulders and continued, 'So everybody did it.'

'We know. But the catastrophe, the misery, the suffering? Didn't anyone...'

'Nobody had fathomed Da Vinci's engineered man,' said Wood, recognising that he was becoming defensive for the people of his time. 'I'm sorry,' he said and the man nodded. 'The Vitruvian man had not been understood. They were unaware of their external power; they didn't see it as simple energy release. They didn't know the accumulative power of their dismissal and the culture it built, the distraction it produced and the potential devastation they could bring upon themselves. They simply didn't know.'

'It would have destroyed them, eventually,' said the man looking mystified.

'Maybe,' said Wood shrugging his shoulders.

'It would have done if it hadn't been for you,' said the man smiling.

'I guess not. Somebody would have come along. I simply made a very difficult choice.'

'Yes and Dace is indebted to you. We all are. They found Him because of you,' said the man. He seemed to throw the last comment in. Wood was excited by what he heard.

'When?' asked Wood desperate for the answer.

'I think it was the year 2421,' said the man. Wood gazed ahead of him in disbelief.

For some time the man asked Wood many questions to satisfy his curiosity and when he left he shook Wood's hand several times and then, just before he left, he shook his hand several times more. 'I would love to see your face when your surprise arrives. I can't say you don't deserve it though. They've spent years getting this done for you,' said the man walking to the door. 'While you're waiting pick up the pad and press the green button,' he said pointing to a computer game. 'Try and embroil forgiveness. It's great fun. Try to fuse it with killing, you'll never win. They say that it can be done.'

THE SIEGE OF GUILT

January 2ⁿᵈ, 2020

Hoary decided to get the train to South Wales where Thomas lived, his superior, when he had been in the church. Hoary had brought with him a bottle of whisky and the amulet George and Oliver had given to him, 'The Step'. As the train rifled along the track, he read the last chapter again.

The Step
3
Belief (Dace v Satan)

The Debate

As it is now

'Also, what follows could not be considered *punishment* for evil-doing because God described Job as "perfect." The account continues with Satan boasting that he could turn Job from God, if he was permitted to bring terrible suffering upon him. Because Job was one of the richest men in the world, Satan argued that he merely obeyed God because it was in his best interests to do so. In effect, God was *paying* him to be righteous!

It continues with Satan causing tremendous destruction in Job's life, killing his ten children and causing the death of all of his servants and animals through four separate disasters. The devil wiped out the most precious things in Job's life.

Yet Job's reaction to this devastating turn of events was not to attack or blame God. He acknowledged that all his blessings had come from God.

After this, Satan again came before God. Here is what happened next: "One day the angels again came to present themselves before the Eternal, and among them the Adversary. 'Where have you been?' said the Eternal to the Adversary; and the Adversary answered, 'Roaming here and there, roving about the earth.'

"Then the Eternal said to the Adversary, 'Have you noticed that there is no one like My servant Job on the earth, a blameless and an upright man, who reverences God and shuns evil? He still holds to his loyalty: it was idle of you to entice Me to undo him.' But the Adversary answered, 'He has saved his own skin! A man will let all he has go, to preserve his life. Only put out your hand, touch his flesh and bones, and see if he will not curse you to your face!' So the Eternal said to the Adversary, 'There! He is in your power; *only, spare his life!*'" (Job 2:1-6, Moffatt).

The account continues with Satan smiting Job with horrible boils over his entire body. As a result, his wife tried to convince him to curse God (vs. 9). His response to her: "You speak as one of the foolish women...What? Shall we receive good at the hand of God, and shall we not *receive evil*? In all this did not Job sin with his lips" (vs. 10).

This is a remarkable passage. It reveals Job's understanding that human beings must sometimes "receive evil" from God. Notice that the account does not record God correcting Job for misstating the facts! Rather, it *validates* Job's conclusion by inspiring "in all this did not Job sin with his lips."

Grasp what you have read in this abbreviated description of events. *God* permitted disastrous, even catastrophic suffering in Job's life—physical and emotional pain beyond imagination! Yes, God directly permitted and endorsed this nightmarish suffering. But it was for a great purpose for Job's life within God's Master Plan.

The next thirty-four chapters are primarily a description of Job's three friends blaming him for what had happened. Throughout, Job refused to accept blame, while at the same time continuing to identify God as the source of what had occurred. He knew that God was working out an extraordinary purpose, both in his life and with all mankind. He had absolute faith in God's authority and overall control of what was happening.

The final five chapters show how God eventually brought home certain lessons to Job about God's greatness and Job's insignificance in His sight.

In Job 42:2, Job acknowledged, "No thought of Yours can be hindered". He had said previously, in Chapter 14, "If a man dies, shall he live again?...You will have a desire to the work of Your hands" (Job 14:14-15). Job grasped that God was working directly in his life, and that nothing could impede or restrain that purpose.

The same is true of you! Christians are purposed by God to develop His character. After a lifetime of overcoming, character development and spiritual growth, they are to be BORN as sons of God. This process involves suffering, sometimes *much* suffering, occasionally lasting a lifetime. But this is God's purpose and no one can defeat it. God knows that life's all-important learning process is inseparable from suffering.

As it will be with Dace

'Inseparable yes, for now. You cannot deny your own politics. You fight, you group, you play, you feed, you offend, you argue, you comfort, you do many things but only when you can see how all these things can help you will the suffering stop. The politics must gel and become one paramount direction for all action and commitment. One unity, one purpose – the advantage

you have when you choose to exercise your true
politics; your true course of action.'

Hoary turned the page and his eyes saw the final page of this amulet,
a passage written by George and Oliver. As he surveyed the page he
could not bring himself to read it and he closed the amulet. He gazed out
of the train window and watched the hedgerows flash by. Since
Brendan's death he had been struggling to cope with the days that had
seemed to meander ahead. He knew that Father Thomas was the only
man he could turn to and Hoary could not continue walking the streets in
society whilst the skeleton of his ordeal remained silent and shrouded by
his mere existence. For a moment, Hoary felt the hopelessness of his
journey. 'How the hell can I tell him?' he thought.

The air, the place and everything felt different when he got off the
train at Cardiff. He felt as though he couldn't recognise anything even
the black cab that took him to Thomas's home in Monmouth didn't feel
like a taxi.

Thomas was delighted to see him and he showed him around his
Georgian home, nestled in a small valley. The house was humble with
very few items of furniture but the setting was stunning.

'After what I've been through, I needed somewhere like this to
recuperate,' Thomas surmised. 'The church had enough of me. But
enough of all that. I must show you this'. Thomas took me to a tent at
the foot of his garden. Inside there was a small desk, a laptop and a laser
printing machine. Everywhere else about the floor there lay piles of
paper – a mass of the stuff – and on the walls of the tent where a series
of illustrations. 'Have I walked into Einstein's laboratory?' Hoary asked
Thomas.

He hesitated, looked about the tent and said, 'No, no. All this stuff is
rubbish. At least, now it is. There's only two pieces worth looking at.'
After rummaging through a number of piles he pulled out two sheets of
paper.

The first was an illustration of the Vitruvian Man by Leonardo Da
Vinci and the second was a drawing entitled 'Engineered Man'. He gave
the first page to Hoary to look at.

'Da Vinci got there first,' said Thomas.

'Got where first?' Hoary asked.

'Not where but what. Da Vinci – the great engineer – was not
drawing configurations of the biology or chemistry or – *the whatever* –

of man. He told us who man really is and why. The Vitruvian man illustrates the engineering of our species.'

Hoary could see from the page entitled 'Vitruvian Man,' that Thomas had added considerable content. 'I had this sent over to me today from a colleague in New York.' Thomas showed Hoary the second page. 'It is an extract from the Christmas Day edition of the National Times. A columnist called Tane Wood wrote them.'

'What is *iReckon*?' asked Hoary, looking at both pages in bewilderment. He had recognised the name of the columnist and his heart had sunk.

'It's the current rave, so I hear. It's the chap's title for his column; big hit in America,' said Thomas, who then changed the subject back to his two pages. 'I have been intrigued with this dilemma all my life. Look at what this guy is saying. He places the Vitruvian man over his Engineered man and the result is astounding.' Thomas continued whilst he shuffled the pages before Hoary to illustrate his point. 'When the Vitruvian man is in the star jump position, Da Vinci is illustrating man in action, exercising his choices. The body shape sees the external limbs – the feet and the hands – resting at the four choices of our behaviour which are Dismissal, Absurdity, *the feet* and Truth, Opportunity *the hands*. Notice how large the area of the box outside the circle is at the feet as opposed to the hands. Da Vinci is telling us that there is more room at the lower end – these are the easy choices. But at the top, truth and opportunity are rare.'

Hoary remembered the bottle of whisky he had brought as a present for Thomas. He got it out from the bag and offered it to him. 'For you,' he said. 'Thank you. I'll keep it for a special occasion,' Thomas answered.

'You can open it now.'

'I won't, if you don't mind. I gave up a number of years ago.' Hoary remembered Thomas as a man who drank far too much. Thomas's eyes moved back to the picture of Vitruvian man and he continued. 'In the second illustration of the V man, Da Vinci is illustrating the shift that man must take. Notice how his feet are turned away from the dismissal corner and that this body shape is less active. Man has chosen to turn his back on dismissal and open up to the absurd, the truth and the opportunity. Man is less active because man is less stressed. Our pain is diminishing at the same pace that our dismissal resides.'

'Why is the word choice lying over V man's genitals,' said Hoary.

'Because it should do. There are fundamental choices that we have to make to survive. We have to breed. Darwin and Freud were both correct; we have fundamental instincts and basic drive to enable our survival. Darwin argued that these drives deride from our animal ancestry and Freud believed that our sexual demands motivated our behaviour. Both are correct but man has the ability to go further than both of these basic drives and we can choose how we exercise them. Sex with love is a joyful experience. Sex without love can be a stressful event to say the least.'

'Go on.'

'What's more, the box illustrates our actions, the circle defines our ability. The circle and the box meet at the bottom by our feet. This is our base line – our Armageddon – we bring pain and suffering upon ourselves via the choices we make. But at the top, the space in the circle, outside the box, is the largest external area. This is our higher consciousness – our ability to care, our ability and our capacity to love. This space is the largest because this capacity for us is the most substantial. It is who we truly are when we chose to be who we truly are.'

Thomas hesitated for a moment, picked up a bottle of Evian and took a couple of swigs. 'The V man illustrates the capacity of man, the E man explains it. I think this Wood chap has got it. The movement of man from the high activity of the star jump to the side step away from dismissal is our future, our purpose.'

'Do you think this is what Da Vinci wanted us to see?' Hoary asked.

'Maybe,' Thomas began. 'Essentially, Da Vinci trusted himself. He probably started at the bottom and worked his way up without any plan. When he finished, he may have exclaimed delight at the work he had just completed.'

'But this work is 400 years old,' said Hoary, disparagingly.

'Cultures take many years to grow and form and work it all out. After all, how long do you believe it will take Tane Wood to persuade his fellow men that what you see here is the truth?' stated Thomas waving the pages about him that were in his hands.

'But is it?' asked Hoary dismissively.

'Yes. I believe it is,' Thomas answered glancing at Hoary.

'Why?' asked Hoary vehemently.

'It embodies who we are. The challenge for us now is two battlefields. Is this egocentric or is this purpose? Has it the influence or has it not? If we want to win the war, if we want to eradicate suffering we must find the courage to answer the bigger question, *what do I want the future of man to be like?'* said Thomas excitedly.

'He won't convince people. They will dismiss him as an egocentric fool,' said Hoary. Thomas was surprised by Hoary's dismissal.

'Trevor, look in the mirror and look at me. We are the same,' said Thomas confused by Hoary's tone.

'Thomas, this is absurd,' said Hoary turning his back.

'Why, what have we got to fear?' challenged Thomas raising his voice.

Hoary put his head in his hands and sat down. Thomas quietly and slowly nestled into a chair opposite him. For a short while, the room was silent as Hoary hid his face from view. Gradually, Thomas realised that his friend was weeping with his anguish.

'What is wrong son?' said Thomas gently. He waited patiently for a few moments before Hoary answered.

'I have done a terrible thing,' said Hoary as he raised his head and looked at Thomas. 'I have killed a man.'

Thomas sat back, deeper in his chair. 'Oh dear,' he said.

'And now this,' said Hoary throwing the page of Wood's work onto the floor.

'Trevor?' said Thomas surprised and confused.

Hoary washed his face in his hands and rubbed his eyes. He told Thomas about the events at his apartment and the scene he had encountered when Michael had killed Brendan. 'My life is in shreds,' he said. 'Everything I worked for, shattered in a moment. I can't see any sense. Nothing...' Hoary didn't finish his sentence.

Thomas watched his friend and let him compose himself, conscious that his silence may be deemed as judgement.

'And now this,' said Hoary reaching to pick up the page of the Engineered man that he had thrown on the floor. 'I knew it,' he said studying the page. 'What garbage.'

Thomas remained confused. This was not the man before him that he had known. The forthright and determined man that fearlessly strode into the commercial markets and arose as a great leader. Thomas could not relate Hoary to the series of events that he was now recalling and his dismissal of the work that Thomas had shown such enthusiasm for. 'What has lead to this,' he thought. 'In a man, destined to build colossal pillars of success.'

Thomas listened to Hoary talk for some time explaining everything that he had done. How he started the credit crunch by jettisoning the fear and building a commercial platform from which he could redesign the power in the world. I was building new employee cultures in my workforce to instigate social change. I didn't know if they would work. Current business practise certainly indicated they wouldn't. What did I have to loose,' exclaimed Hoary raising his eye brows and his hands from his lap. 'I needed to focus mankind on the ambition to explore new frontiers and help find God. 'I was determined to deliver the political will to explore the stars. He is out there and we have to find him.'

'Yes we do,' said Thomas. 'Don't you think that it is precisely the politics of our day that has always stopped us?'

'How do you mean?' asked Hoary.

'I once knew a great man. He had defined vision and I implored him to share his insight and his findings with his fellow men. He refused and told me that knowledge was power and what sense was there in sharing the knowledge with everyone. 'Why give away power?' he said.

'What did he do?' asked Hoary.

'I don't know really. He certainly never amounted to anything. I think he did have a period of success in the City but it was short lived. He was eventually locked up for theft. Fraud I believe.'

Hoary drew his hands towards his eyes to shield the flood of tears that began to fall as his anxiety burst within him. 'I feel that I have been stealing all my life.'

'Why?' asked Thomas compassionately.

'The pursuit of success, I think. We were always on the lookout for men with great ideas and when we found them, we stole it from them. We sacked them or parked them into the provinces and then we took the glory for their work; simple politics really; endlessly killing people off.' Hoary sat forward on his seat and his anxiety gripped him again. 'Oh God. What have I done?' he said thinking again of the memory of Brendan's lifeless body lying on the floor in the lounge in his apartment.

'Trevor you mustn't consume yourself with guilt. You didn't pull the trigger. Not literally,' said Thomas placing his hand on Hoary's knee to console him.

'I did,' Hoary said guiltily.

'No you did not. You cannot claim responsibility for the actions of another. Michael must resolve that for himself,' said Thomas adamantly.

'But I feel so guilty,' said Hoary who looked at Thomas.

'That will not help you or anybody else. You must decide what you are going to do.'

'How do you mean?' asked Hoary.

'Well, with Brendan's death,' explained Thomas opening his palms.

'What,' Hoary began and looked confused for a moment, 'The police?'

'It is your choice. You must decide and when you do you must take responsibility for yourself. Make your decision and then you must learn to forget. You must teach yourself to do this. Guilt kills men and it hurts others. You must deal with this,' exclaimed Thomas looking Hoary in the eye.

'How?' asked Hoary, puzzled.

'You must learn to forgive yourself,' said Thomas concisely.

'But my dream. My ambition. Wood is wrong,' said Hoary flinging his arms up.

'Is he?' asked Thomas adamantly.

'Yes, he is,' said Hoary with assertion.

'Is he?' said Thomas raising his voice above Hoary.

Hoary fell to his knees and his tears stopped. He sat, kneeling, his outstretched hands clasped his knees and Thomas noticed how lost he now appeared. Thomas sensed that he was paralysed with his grief.

'Trevor, you are a good man; all men are.' Thomas watched Hoary as he raised his eyes, slowly, to meet his. 'First, forgive yourself.'

'How?' asked Hoary pleading.

'It is your choice,' said Thomas, sensing that Hoary was beginning to relent. 'You know Wood is right.'

Hoary was nearly seventy years old. His life had been a relentless drive towards the identity of a pursuit he knew was hidden in his unconscious, all the time fighting to be unlocked and presented to him on a page, the page that would tell him the truth, tell him that he was right, tell him that in every action he had ever taken, in all that he had ever committed to, there was a reason for it and everything he had done could be justified – all his guilt and his fears could be absolved and forgotten, as could the limits to his beliefs.

How, he wondered, with his current events could he resolve this now? Could he allow one man – Wood – to do for him, what he had cried out to do for himself? In the drive and commitment of a whole lifetime of endeavour, he knew that he could only now forgive himself. If he did not, Hoary knew, he had pulled the trigger and Brendan was now dead because of him and his guilt would remain forever. Hoary looked at Thomas and his face showed the concern of all his lifetime. Hoary thought of his mother. He remembered how majestic she could look when she dressed up for their outings on Sunday to the park. She was beautiful in her Sunday best and she knew it. It seemed to Hoary that this was the only time she had smiled. 'Yes. I know,' he said. 'Wood is right.'

∞

Thomas opened the bottle of whisky and gave Hoary a small measure. He knew it would make him feel more relaxed in his grief. Thomas found a couple of glasses and washed them clean. He had been away from Hoary for a few moments and when he returned Hoary was thumbing through the amulet, 'The Step.'

'What's that?' asked Thomas.

'It is for you. I brought it for you to read,' said Hoary.

'Thank you,' said Thomas, who placed the small glass of whisky on the table by Hoary's chair. Hoary handed the amulet towards Thomas and said, 'Please, read this page.'

When Thomas had sat down and put his reading glasses on, he folded the page back and began to read. Hoary said, 'Wood is right.'

From George and Oliver

Perfect Balance

The name of the man you call God is Dace. He looks like you. Dace engineered you and that was the extent of the control he had over your lives. You must own the random events that impact you. Dace has no control over these events now.

Your DNA code includes the survival instincts you gained from your animal ancestry, which are there to enhance your survival (Darwin). It also includes the powerful sexual demands upon your behaviour aimed at the long term preservation of your species (Freud). Ultimately your capacity to love and hence, *care* and stride forward from your adversity, will define you but only in the context of purpose.

Without purpose your beliefs will result in the most brutal of actions and permit you to be servants to your instincts alone, resulting in the emergence of power that defines territories and infiltrates conformity by fear and control masked under the cloak of law, order and politics; permitted under the shroud that *this is the best that we have.*

But this is not power. This is not vision and purpose. Orwell was right when he illustrated the revolution as merely a replacement of power. Time teaches us all that there is no going back but is this the manifestation of power that you want repeated by your future historians?

You have a choice. You will say – louder than any man has ever spoken – merge our life's endeavour, all our lives' endeavours to one unity, one purpose – mobilise us all in our pursuit to find the ice cube and get Dace out. He can't do this. He can only watch you and hope that you get the point, you see his master plan, you get him out and open the heavens to a universe of wonders that he knows and that you don't – 'Please tell everyone that he desperately needs their help.'

The Care Code

'Oh my,' said Thomas. 'What is this? Where did you...' Thomas rolled the amulet in his hands, looking at the front cover and the back, flicking through the pages, seemingly searching for clues. 'It's beautiful,' said Thomas excitedly.

'I know Wood is right,' said Hoary, smiling gently at Thomas, seemingly acknowledging all that Thomas had said to him. Thomas saw the look of reflection on Hoary's face and the enlightenment in his eyes. 'It's easy for me to forgive myself,' said Hoary definitively.

POWER

Kristie popped her head round the door again. 'Are you ready? our surprise is coming; any moment. Oh,' she said and quickly paced towards Wood and fluffed his hair up a little and held his shoulders. 'Straighten up,' she said and turned her voice to a whisper. 'We must have you looking your best.'

Kristie darted back to the door and peered around it. She began to skip up and down on the spot and clap her hands quickly but silently, excitement written all over her. She looked at Wood, gave him the thumbs up and winked.

The door had been left slightly ajar. When the girl walked through and Wood saw her, his bewilderment and his anticipation disappeared. They were instantly engulfed by the euphoria of his complete joy. He dropped to the floor, as though the purpose of his shock had demanded him to do so.

The years and the memories of all he had shared and loved flashed before his mind and the contortions of his face appeared confused and rippled in unison with his mind.

He could not comprehend what he was seeing even though he recognised what he saw instantly. All his dreams seemed to disappear in a wild, glorious shout of excitement, skipping on the landscape, applauding the view before him. The energy within him overwhelmed him entirely for a second and then he felt it grasp him and give him a strength he did not recognise. Visions darted across his thoughts and wonderment grabbed at his desires. The euphoria of his body uplifted him and engulfed him in an experience he had never before felt, propelling all his thoughts into the impossible world of the events of infinite possibilities. He felt completely fearless and as she ran, sobbing, screaming his name, laughing his name, towards him, uncontrollably to him, he could hardly contain his smile as their lips met and embraced with uncontrollable passion. She clung desperately with her thighs about his waist as he got to his feet and when their mouths parted and their eyes met, they gulped with joy for that slight second that they each permitted before their gratitude embraced again in their wild kiss.

A crowd of many people appeared – trillions had watched and the scene had engulfed them all as their cheers erupted into the melody of a deafening cry of delight. The sky seemed to light up with their joy and a man stepped forward towards Wood and Helen, clapping swiftly, cheering loudly and smiling as the tears rolled down His face; His figure set against the cry from the crowd that 'we love you.'

When He was close He said, 'I am sorry.' He put his arms around Helen and Wood in their embrace and as both of their eyes looked back to Him, they told Him that they loved Him more. Helen hugged Dace and kissed Him gently on the cheek. 'Thank you,' she said.

'He cared more than any before him,' said Dace. 'It's in his DNA.' Helen's eyes filled with tears and she smiled with her joy.

'I love you both,' Dace said and tightened his embrace momentarily before He released. 'This is the world I needed you to give us and how I love you for it – a magnificent world of forgiveness. And this is My gift to you, your last request; the most beautiful thing ever – woman before the fall of Eve – completely undamaged and yours for eternity. Our world is undamaged and now it is ours. We have our eternity.'

Wood knew and as he looked at Helen, she did too; their love, emanating from them, crowding the crowd, engulfing their joy and jettisoning a power that could conquer a universe – or two.

An infinite, expanding energy.

Har-Maggeddon.

And for Stephen; *Dismiss me.*

The Notes of Father Thomas

Perfect Balance

I was never more excited than the day I read the publication of Tane Wood's column, ***iReckon***, in the National Times, New York on December 25th 2019. Like him, I have always been determined to find the simple framework that explains who man really is and so, I have written this; a summary of what I believe his legacy says.

We can create Freedom

Eve ate the fruit of choice and offered it to Adam who also ate the fruit. They chose to eat the fruit because that was the choice they made. There was no other reason. *Your choice is your freedom and you should stand up for your right to choose. Tell Dace you like to eat fruit. Tell him that you are sorry that your actions have upset him.*

We created Armageddon.

When challenged, Adam blamed Eve and Eve blamed the serpent. Both failed to be personally responsible for their actions. Both hid together and denied what they had done. Dace was pulling his hair out; his creation had failed to be accountable for their actions. He had created a mankind that had denied its actions and hid behind its true motivation. Dace needed his creation to engage its integrity; I ate the fruit because I liked it. *Whilst we hide, we create suffering. We create Armageddon.*

Purpose

Your action is yours. Stand up for it. You cannot hide. There is one purpose for man. It is to release Dace. It is a single choice and the easiest to make. *Act and commit.*

Why Man

Deep down in our DNA coding, is a tiny and very special sequence found nowhere else within any living organism. It is the Care Code and the emperor of all DNA. When activated, the Care Code makes man act for the betterment of others. If we care we will find the answer to the problem. If we don't care, we don't even recognise the problem. Intelligence and communication do not, alone, distinguish us from other life. They are expressions and tools we have evolved, necessary to express our DNA drive to care. When the Care Code is not activated or it is suppressed, man fights individually for his survival.

Care Counts

It is the Care Code that gives man their freedom and choice. Stand-up, stand-by, and stand for that choice and release Dace.

Internal Impacts and Behaviour

Most people are governed by two dominant traits that form who they are; in their behaviour and in their personality. Often people can hide or mask a trait. The key is that each person 'sorts out their own back yard.' They identify who they are really are. The world will forgive anybody who has integrity, 'I am who I say I am.'

Having three traits is rare and four is rarer still. People with four traits are those with the capacity to express vision. Find these people and let them lead us. They are motivated to deliver for the greater good and they will lead us to our purpose, Dace. They will dissolve Armageddon and protect us from the extinction event.

Internal Id (identity)
Engage self awareness – Know who you are.

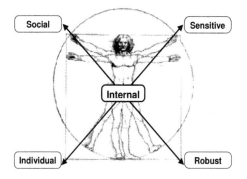

Human Traits: Social, Sensitive, Individual, Robust

Locked in the unconscious mind of all of us, are the four traits. Our DNA is written with them. Our conscious mind will, for most of us, permit two of these traits to form and these will determine our personality.

However, given the right parenthood, education and environment, our experiences can permit all four traits to surface and provide any one person with perfect balance. There is value in everybody. Damage to us by our experiences, limits balance to be achieved and limits the perceived value of a person.

If the men and women who lead us, politically and socially, have the perfect balance, they will lead us to our purpose. Unfortunately, the reverse is also true.

Human Types

Da Vinci's Vitruvian man illustrates perfect balance. The internal Id is balanced by the DNA we inherit. Four Traits exist: Social, Sensitive, Individual, Robust.

External Impacts & Behaviour
Engineered Man - Engage Vision Perfect Balance

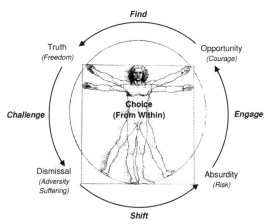

The finger tips and the soles of the feet touch at the exact edges of the circle and the square. Here man is perfectly balanced.

A perfect balance with the four traits allows a person to have a greater ability to observe the world about them. These people are rare and their main characteristic is their visionary capacity. Most Homo sapiens have two dominant features and these determine their behaviour. For example, the social/sensitive will be predominantly characterised by honesty, fun and joy. The robust/individual will have an inherent persuasion towards the tendency of the natural born killers. This term is not used to deliberately designate a person's need to kill. This will be true in extreme examples but generally these individuals will have a reduced capacity to empathise with their fellow man.

Truth, opportunity, absurdity and dismissal are external behaviours. To see these you must first conquer your internal Id and remove the emotional turmoil that hinders self awareness.

Giving an education that prepares our children with adequate coping mechanisms, will result in our youth and our young adults being better prepared for the world they encounter. This emotional strength will equip people to deal with the challenges that life can present and produce objective, balanced and emotionally resilient adults. This preparation is essential for limiting the potential damage to one's self awareness of *who they are* and their internal identity.

The discovery and awareness of your internal identity (id) permits you to grow as an individual. When this awareness starts to mature, you can begin to engage the external behaviours.

Turmoil in the internal id limits this potential. This limitation is invariably damage in need of repair. As your awareness of who you are as an individual matures, you can increasingly engage and observe the key social elements around you. These elements shape the species we are and when we achieve balance we identify purpose.

Perfect balance occurs when an individual is aware of who he is (internal id) and can engage the external impacts of human behaviour. This balance allows human behaviour to be considered in a conscious form that permits vision and purpose to be perceived.

Limiting damage and striving for perfect balance can have significant social impact. People will trust themselves to act in a manner they believe is true to themselves and, more importantly, they will begin to exercise the choices that want to make.

The ability to trust ourselves, to be who we are and to act as we believe we should do, will have significant consequences for the shaping of our behaviour and our engagement with our purpose.

Alternatively, man will evolve with the limitations of our instincts alone and mankind will be ill equipped for the extinction event that will come. We cannot live on by survival alone. This imposes too many limitations on unforeseen possibilities. We must engage our awareness of who we are, identify our purpose and learn to behave.

Love

'Love is everything it's cracked up to be and more. It really is worth fighting for, being brave for, risking everything for. If you don't risk everything, you risk even more.' *Erica Jong*

Truth

Opportunity

'There is at the bottom only one problem in the world and this is its name. How does one break through? How does one get into the open. How does one burst the cocoon and become a butterfly?' *Thomas Mann*

'Choose your plane, get in it and fly. Values are like clouds and planes cut straight through them. All your fears will disperse when your truth becomes singular - forgiveness.' *Greg Heywood*

Choice

Dismissal

Absurdity

'Life is full of misery, loneliness and suffering – and it's all over too soon.' *Woody Allen*

'If at first, the idea is not absurd, then there is no hope for it.' *Albert Einstein*

Suffering

'In the day of property be joyful but in the day of adversity consider.' *Ecc 7:14*

Environmental Impact on the Care Code

Beauty is our engagement with our natural environment. The parasitic expression of man is the erosion of this beauty in the building of our physical habitat – road, buildings etc.

Undamaged World

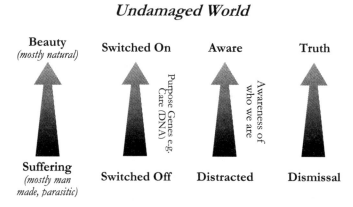

Beauty
(mostly natural)

Switched On

Aware

Truth

Purpose Genes e.g.
Care (DNA)

Awareness of
who we are

Suffering
*(mostly man
made, parasitic)*

Switched Off

Distracted

Dismissal

Armageddon & Damage

Territorial boundaries enforce the destruction of our natural environment. The Care Gene is impacted by our environment. In a natural beautiful environment it is switched on and vice versa.

Engagement of the Care Gene is essential to creating perfect balance in people. We all have this gene and it is switched on in a person's environment which is characterised by natural beauty, personal self awareness and engaging the pursuit of truth by embracing opportunistic and absurd notions of chance as opposed to simply dismissing them as unrealistic.

Growth does not flourish from realistic notions. These merely illustrate what we already know. Exploration, risk and absurdity allow us to engage our personal growth by seeking opportunities which can determine truth.

In a manmade environment that lacks beauty, the disengagement of the Care Gene will result in people becoming easily and overly distracted with non purposeful activities (e.g. entertainment and television). Their language and behaviour will result in dismissive expression.

Behavioural Evolution of Man:
Engaging the Care Code

Currently, mankind is engaged in its Iconic stage of evolution. The behavioural evolution is already upon us.

To identify purpose and vision is at present a very rare attribute of human behaviour. Jesus Christ obviously had this as did many of our potential greats – Einstein, JFK, Luther King, Ghandi.

Given time, our society will permit the environment to aid the behavioural evolution of man and deliver a world in which the recognition of purpose is more widely spread.

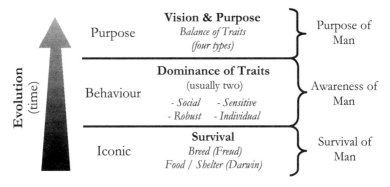

Behavioural Evolution: Finding Purpose

To do this we must focus our efforts on maintaining and developing a naturally beautiful environment, reforming education curriculums to develop coping mechanisms in our children to prepare them for adulthood. Repair through medicine and justice divisions must be focused on the root cause identity; not pill popping and revenge/penalty respectively.
Focus must be on repair.

Productivity must concentrate on resource discovery, not just management of its limitations. Getting to the stars will open up mankind's awareness of possibilities. Not doing so, merely allows our fears to manifest in the reality of scarcity.

The introduction of coping mechanisms permits emotional maturity. This will allow our young adults to embrace their self awareness and explore their true potential. The Care Gene will have the maximum potential to flourish.